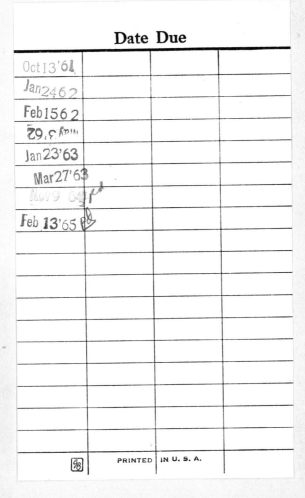

Date Due

Oct 13 '61			
Jan 24 62			
Feb 15 62			
May 3 '62			
Jan 23 '63			
Mar 27 '63			
Nov 9 64			
Feb 13 '65			
	PRINTED IN U. S. A.		

The High Calling

THE
High Calling

JAMES STREET

Garden City, New York

DOUBLEDAY & COMPANY, INC.

The characters, the location, and the incidents in this book
are entirely the product of the author's imagination and have
no relation to any person or event in real life.

For Lucy and Ann

The High Calling

Chapter 1

London Wingo was going back to Linden, Missouri, to resume his ministry where he had begun it more than twenty years before.

This time, however, he was traveling in a club car of the Wabash Railroad instead of a day coach that had delivered him to his first pastorate, and the traces of gray around his temples, the thread lines around his eyes gave him an appearance of eminence and confidence that he did not feel at all.

It wasn't the return that troubled him, nor the fact that he, in his middle years, voluntarily was giving up a wealthy Kansas City congregation for the hard work of organizing a Baptist church in a mill village. That was part of his commission for good works and it bothered him none at all, no more than his hay fever which returned every fall or the slight astigmatism that compelled him to wear glasses when he read, no more than the status of his bank account, which was better than most preachers' but not sufficient for long if his mission to Linden failed. He gave those problems no thought.

His daughter Paige was his only concern on that muggy spring day as his train rolled across Missouri, taking him forever from the rich fields and mahogany pews back to the poor furrows and the pulpits of golden oak, from the lush vineyard to the stony ground of tares. To himself he put it bluntly: he, the Reverend London

Wingo, Doctor of Divinity, an honor he had earned, and Doctor of Letters, an honor he had not earned, was leaving the big leagues for the minors. Or, subscribing to the vernacular of his calling, he was forsaking the good lands of Carmel, of Sharon, for the bitter valley of Achor.

He wished Paige were making the train trip with him instead of bringing the car down from Kansas City. But she didn't like trains. On a train, another person ran things; in a car, she did. That was the difference and it disturbed London, for his daughter was his pride and his calling was his humility, and how often they clashed. Only a man who has reared a daughter without a mother knows how close a daughter can be and yet how far away. Paige, in her early twenties, didn't remember her mother and London had never forgotten her.

Although he would not admit it to himself, his daughter really was the reason he had accepted a call to organize a church on the outskirts of Linden where a settlement called Plymouth sprawled around a shoe factory. There were other explanations, of course. He and Kathie had gone to Linden soon after they were married. There they had built a church and there she had died and then London moved to Kansas City, sharing his time between his God and his daughter, who was about a year old when Kathie left them. London felt he never had finished his work in Linden.

Also, a smaller congregation should give him a chance to write a biography of Roger Williams, a project he had decided upon years before and had never got around to doing. Yes, there were many reasons for London Wingo to go back to Linden, but Paige was the important one.

He belonged to a generation that believed farms and small towns had mystic properties for character building; that village folks were gentler than city people; that they were closer to God, the land, the brotherhood, the covenant—all the things he preached about and sometimes didn't understand himself.

A year or more in Linden should round out Paige's character, molded as it was by circumstances that had not seemed detrimental to London until his daughter was grown. These included a childhood without counsel or discipline of a mother, the formative years spent in the reflected glory of a father who preached to thousands about God until, in the child's mind, he assumed the personality of God; His strength, His mercy, His refuge.

The congregation made much to-do about her, adoration one day because she was adorable, and criticism the next because she was as mischievous as the other children, a prerogative often denied a preacher's child. She was fifteen when she slipped her first cigarette, and straightway a deacon's wife reported to her pastor, "Dr. Wingo, remember the words of Solomon, 'Spare the rod and spoil the child.'"

London was indignant. "Madam, you know less about children than you do about God's word. Solomon said nothing of the sort. Samuel Butler said it and Ralph Venning said it, but not Solomon. It's not even in the Bible."

He called a meeting of his deacons and through them informed the congregation to silence their forked tongues, to bear no witness against a child, and to keep their mouths shut about his daughter. Most of the church agreed with him, but Paige, her defense sharpened by many trials, convinced him the other girls were making life miserable because she was a preacher's daughter.

It was mostly exaggeration. However, he believed her, as he usually did, and sent her away to a preparatory school, to Stuart Hall down in Virginia. When she came home all the ties were broken with the other girls and her father was her only companion, except the boys who drove by their house and blew their automobile horns and sometimes took her to dances and the movies. She called them "clods," a word she picked up at school.

For two years at the University of Missouri she did well, but in her third year she buried herself in the teachings of Francis of Assisi, in the writings of T. S. Eliot, and the mysticism of Emanuel Swedenborg, seeking something she had missed along the way. She quarreled with her teachers and constantly was defending the Baptist ministry against all skeptics, the just and the unjust. Any criticism of any preacher, even the charlatans, the rabble-rousers, the money-changers, she took as a backhanded slap at her father and once, in an outburst of anger at an imagined censure of the clergy, told her professor of ethics, "My father is the only man I know who is more than forty and still has the faith of a child of three, the courage of a boy of twenty, and the sense of a man of thirty."

The professor was goaded to exasperation. "Miss Wingo, is your father a mortal? If so, he must be an exceptional man."

"Which, sir," the girl replied, "is more than I can say for you."

London knew none of that. He knew only that his daughter didn't quite fit anywhere, and it was the only personal worry he had in the world. He was a man of prayer and he prayed that she find herself, and his hope soared when she left the university and took a job on a Southern newspaper as a church reporter. They called her a religious reporter instead of a reporter of religion, and London teased her about it. He wrote her every week.

The job lasted a year, until she called her editor a lecherous heel and wired her father for money to fly home. London's only comment was, "Well, maybe you were a religious reporter."

A month later he accepted the call to Linden.

The journey back was almost over and nobody had spoken to him all the way down from Kansas City. Club cars are not as friendly as day coaches. A copy of *The Irrepressible Democrat*, a life story of Roger Williams, was in the chair beside him. He had read a few chapters, noted a few paragraphs, and then put the book aside. He wanted to talk to somebody about the land out there, the farms and towns; the weather, anything. He was lonesome.

The man across the aisle was reading *Newsweek*. He had boarded the train at Moberly and glanced casually at London, then sharply. For a second London thought he was going to speak, but he walked to the front of the car and picked up three leather-bound magazines and returned to his seat. *Nation's Business* he had finished. He read *Look* through two cigarettes and opened *Newsweek,* scanning most items but carefully reading of business affairs.

London noticed that he skipped the news of religion. Science and books, too. London himself was critical of news magazines' coverage of churches and matters spiritual, although secretly he wished to be in *Time's* Religion.

They passed the town of Mexico and still nothing to break the monotony of the trip. Perhaps he should have driven down with Paige. She had asked him, but she wanted to go by Columbia and see a few friends at the university, the few friends she had at the university. London reasoned he would be in the way, that she really didn't want him along.

He knew less about his daughter than she knew about him.

Nothing would have pleased Paige Wingo as much as to take her father by the university and show him off, his shoulders squared on an Oklahoma farm and never rounded by the burdens of his work, his blue eyes crinkling at the corners, his humor and tolerance as generous as his six-foot frame.

She had assumed he wanted to ride the train because he loved trains and often talked about them, particularly the time he butched on the Katy back in Oklahoma. He had earned enough that summer to finish high school and got through Baylor University and the Southwestern Baptist Seminary by punching cattle, bucking wheat, selling tinted photographs door to door, and preaching on the side. She had heard the stories so often.

And now they were going separate ways to their new home, she in the DeSoto and he on a train that was boring him into drowsiness.

London picked up *The Irrepressible Democrat* again. So few books had been written about Roger Williams. Someday he would be discovered as Thomas Paine had been discovered. London ran his fingers through his thick black hair, so black that his few white hairs were a striking contrast. Paine and Williams. Iconoclast and believer. Still they had much in common. Godfathers to liberty. Stepchildren in history.

He carried his horn-rimmed glasses in his coat pocket and slipped them on, checked a few marked paragraphs, and began writing notes on a sheet of paper clipped to the end pages of the book:

"R. W. befriended the Indian Uncas. (Avoid temptation to mention Fenimore Cooper.)

"R. W. sired freedom of religion in America? Too strong. Helped sire it. Nourished it. Held for liberty without license. Good sermon subject.

"R. W. a Baptist (in orthodox sense) for few months only. This will shock some of the brethren. Left Baptist group and became a Seeker. Religious freethinker. Spiritual anarchist? Dangerous ground."

London took off his glasses and rubbed his eyes and stared out the window, at the land green and plow-turned. Lots of apple trees in Missouri. And birds on telephone wires. He wondered why Missourians call their state "Mi-zoor-a" while so many outsiders call it "Mi-zoor-ee."

"Excuse me." He turned his head quickly and the conductor was standing there examining a ticket. "You're traveling on a clergy permit, aren't you?"

"That's right," London said. "Anything wrong?"

"Just checking. I got a couple more preachers up in the day coach and my record's balled up. May I see your permit, please?"

London produced a little book of vouchers that entitled him to make professional trips at reduced rates. The trainman checked the number on the book against his record. "Thanks, Reverend. I had two club tickets and just one coach ticket on permits. Straight now."

"Then you are not going to throw me off?"

"Not this trip. And hold onto that permit. You reverends about the only ones who get breaks like that these days. Pretty soft."

"I'll trade jobs with you." London slipped his permit in his inside coat pocket next to his wallet. The conductor grinned and moved on.

The man across the aisle put aside the magazine and ground out a cigarette. He was wearing two-toned shoes and a light suit although it was rather early spring for such apparel. He stood up, shoving his hands in his coat pockets. "Aren't you Dr. Wingo?"

"Yes." It was flattering to be recognized by a stranger.

"Knew I'd seen you before." He extended his hand. "My name is Benton Andrews. Heard you preach once."

"Still willing to shake hands?" London grasped his hand firmly, a preacher handshake, then moved *The Irrepressible Democrat*, making room in the chair beside him.

"Custom with many people. Habit with me." The tone was not exactly brusque, but it certainly wasn't friendly. There was nothing particularly friendly about Benton Andrews. Or unfriendly either, for that matter. He was not as tall as London and his hair was brown. His mustache tapered to the corners of his lips and was neatly trimmed, a few white hairs sprinkling the brown ones.

He sat down and crossed his legs and offered London a cigarette. The man was a chain smoker and London declined the token, explaining that he smoked cigars on occasions and a pipe every now and then.

"I've heard a lot about you." Andrews tapped a cigarette against the back of his hand but didn't light it. "I live in Linden. Run the radio station there."

London tested his memory quickly. Andrews. Benton Andrews. No, he didn't know him. "You came to Linden after I left." He was sure of his ground. A name and a face were things he seldom forgot.

"About ten years ago. I'm a friend of Cliff Carter's."

A smile of deep good feeling spread over London's face at the mention of Cliff Carter's name. He was about the only one left of the old crowd London had known in Linden during his ministry there. Cliff had headed the pulpit committee that presumed to call Dr. London Wingo from Kansas City's big Immanuel Baptist Church to Linden's little Plymouth Baptist Church, and Cliff was the one person who was not surprised when London accepted. "How is he, Mr. Andrews? The last time I saw him he looked worn."

"Cliff's wiry, but he should slow down." Andrews tugged at his trouser leg, adjusting the crease. "He's lonesome. Children all grown and gone. Cliff ought to marry again, but he can't forget Florine."

London turned to the window and watched the countryside, the hills spreading down into little valleys that fed into the Missouri River. The locomotive's whistle rumbled a warning, a harsh, cold signal so different from the friendly steam engines of other years. A crossing flashed by, then a hamlet. Florine had been dead for six years. Or was it eight? So many of them were dead; all the old crowd dead or moved away, or so rich they might as well be dead or so poor they probably wished they were. "He's still working hard, I suppose."

"Every day. Besides his undertaking business he owns a cemetery and a flock of real estate. You know Cliff."

"Yes, I know. Overcharging the rich and undercharging the poor, and everlastingly accusing the poor of laziness."

"His pet project now is this new church you are going to. Cliff lives and breathes the Baptist church. I am not a Baptist myself." There was a touch of defiance in the declaration and London interpreted it for what it was—an invitation to an argument.

"I knew you were not a Baptist." London felt in his pocket for his pipe, then remembered it was in his brief case.

A quick frown of annoyance passed over Andrews' face. "Are you serious?"

"Quite." He had dealt often with men like this who delighted in baiting preachers. "Had you been a Baptist you would have said so. My experience has been that Baptist brothers usually identify themselves to Baptist preachers." He was smiling. There was no pique or resentment. This was routine with a preacher as experienced as London and he long since had learned not to be provoked easily.

Benton Andrews rolled his cigarette between his fingers and looked down at the nicotine stains on his hand. "Smoke too much. Sworn off a dozen times and then forget." He rested his arms on the back of the chair and relaxed his shoulders. "See your point, Dr. Wingo. I didn't mean to step on your toes."

"You didn't," London said quickly. "My toes are sensitive. I am pretty tough around my shins, but if my toes get stepped on I jump."

"So do I. So if I was out of line forget it. I'm not a church man."

"Custom with many. Habit with some." London was looking up at the light fixtures on the car.

That quick frown again, and then Andrews grinned. "I set up that recoil, didn't I? I've heard Cliff say you're a man who'll take a lot of pushing but no crowding."

London wanted the subject changed. He probably would have

dealings with this man in Linden. Benton Andrews obviously was a person of importance. Be that as it might, however, London simply preferred friends to opponents. He would have enough opposition without courting it. "Where did you hear me preach, Mr. Andrews? You say you are not a church man."

"Up at William Jewell College." Andrews instinctively reached for his cigarettes, then shoved them back in his pocket. He was a nervous man, fidgeting with his coat lapels, the buttons on his sleeves.

"Oh yes. That was three years ago. The baccalaureate sermon. You a William Jewell man?"

"No. My son is." There was a second's hesitation and London sensed tension. "You've probably heard of the boy. Ministerial student. His mother was a dyed-in-the-wool Baptist."

It came to London then and it explained everything. "Are you Vance Andrews' father?" He asked it gently, never prying.

"That's right."

London debated with himself whether to continue the subject or deliberately avoid it. At such times silence often is more embarrassing than discussion, and inasmuch as Andrews himself had opened the matter it was evident that he wanted to talk about his son. It was part of London's work to hear the problems of others, so he said, "I thought Vance Andrews lived in St. Louis. I never connected him with you."

"He still calls St. Louis home, but he's in Linden with me."

"Now?"

"Yes. He's been up North to a seminary."

"I heard he had gone to Rochester." London was sure it was Rochester, although it might have been Union. Northern seminaries were more liberal than their Southern sisters, more apt to understand a student like Vance Andrews.

The father lit a cigarette then and broke the match between his fingers. "He's home now. Working with me. But he plans to go back to the seminary this fall. He thinks you're a great man."

London knew the boy's story well although he never had met him. His mother had been a Locke, one of the most influential Baptist families in the country, and she married an advertising man in St. Louis. That would be Benton Andrews.

The marriage ended in a nasty scandal and the court awarded the son to his father. That was twelve years ago or more. Maybe fifteen. London wasn't positive. The mother went to France. Or was it Italy? Anyway, she married again and died in a private nursing home.

Newspapers revived the story in World War II when Vance Andrews announced he planned to study for the Baptist ministry and pleaded conscientious objection to combat military duty. Several preachers denounced him as a coward and some radicals threatened to withdraw Baptist fellowship from him. London scorned the hysteria of the day and defended him in an open letter to the brethren, pointing out that Baptist principle holds a man's conscience inviolate. He whiplashed them with the words of Jesus, of Paul, of John Huss and Roger Williams until they withered and were silent.

Vance wrote his defender a note of gratitude and served out the war on a hospital ship. His father was too old for combat duty and yet he managed somehow to get into a combat unit and collapsed a few months later from sheer nervous tension. Then came the final ironical twist; the son was cited for bravery and the father was discharged as physically and emotionally unfit for duty.

And so this situation was facing London in his new field even before he reached Linden. However, he wasn't thinking of that, but of a coincidence. This man was Cliff Carter's friend and Cliff was London's friend, and all three were widowers.

"The boy has been helping out with the church you are going to." Benton was almost calm and much of the strain was gone from his face. "You'll be seeing a lot of him, I suppose."

London reached under the chair for his brief case and took out his pipe. He puffed several times, then examined the ash in the bowl and tapped it with his finger. "Mr. Andrews." He said it slowly, deliberately. "You don't want your son to be a preacher, do you?"

"He's all mixed up."

"What makes you think so?"

Benton scowled and stared past London and out the window. He glanced at his wrist watch and wound it a couple of times. "The next stop is ours. So let's get to bedrock. I don't think my son is cut out to be a minister."

"He's a grown man, isn't he?" London was patient, although his impulse was to warn this man to leave his son's soul alone.

"But he's all mixed up. He had a brutal childhood, Wingo. I'm afraid this thing might be the result of a guilt feeling. Shame, perhaps. Or some sort of a rebound. Understand?"

"No. Wasn't Vance Andrews a ballplayer in high school? Football or baseball or something?"

"Baseball. Pretty good, too."

"Didn't he write a college treatise on Aquinas, Wycliffe, and Huss?"

"Uh-huh. It was published in a religious magazine."

"And isn't your son the fellow who went through a blazing passage to save some patients on a hospital ship?"

"Yes, all that's true." Andrews was proud but impatient nevertheless. "What are you getting at?"

London rubbed his hand across the back of his neck and stared up at the light fixtures again. "Only that I don't think he is mixed up. You are."

"I know damn well I am." A wry grin twisted the corner of Benton Andrews' mouth. "I don't want my son to be like I am. The ministry might mess him up. You haven't got a son, have you?"

"A daughter."

"That's different."

"What's different about it?"

"It's just different, that's all."

London picked up *The Irrepressible Democrat* and put it in his brief case. Then he put away his pipe. "You could be right. However, I wouldn't worry too much about that boy. The ministry has a way of weeding out the unfits. You know, my friend, it's always open season on preachers. We call it an occupational hazard."

"I have no quarrel with the ministry, Dr. Wingo."

"Of course not." The sarcasm crept in despite London's effort to avoid it. "But there are some rascals in the ministry. There are only three hundred thousand clergymen in this country, and I know some who should be in jail. However, I have a feeling that, as far as brotherly love and good citizenship are concerned, preachers compare favorably with lawyers and doctors and congressmen. Even with radio men——"

"You miss my point," Benton Andrews interrupted. "Yours is a general outlook. Mine is a personal problem. I've heard Cliff Carter say you are always ready to help a man who is in trouble. Well, I am asking you not to encourage my son in this ministry idea."

That was the wrong thing to say to London Wingo. A red flush spread over his brown face and a frown bridged his eyebrows. He put his hand on Andrews' arm and spoke slowly. "One moment, brother. I won't interrupt you. And you won't interrupt me again."

"I'm sorry." Benton Andrews meant it.

"We will get a few things straight." London's voice still was low and deliberate. "I am a Baptist preacher. I happen to be one of those naïve Christians who believe the ministry is a calling. Therefore, so far as your son is concerned, I will pursue one course. That is prayer that God's will be done. Your wishes will not be considered."

Andrews' face reddened and he was apologetic again. "I've stated my case badly."

London nodded his agreement. "Very badly for an advertising man."

"Then let me put it this way. You have a daughter."

"That's correct." London sat up straight. Paige must not be discussed between him and a stranger.

"Let's assume you were worried about her emotional stability." Andrews adjusted himself more comfortably in the chair and leaned back. "And she had chosen a job that you thought didn't fit her make-up. A night-club hostess, for instance. What would you do?"

The time had come to end the discussion. London simply did not care to continue it. "Mr. Andrews." His good humor returned and his eyes were merry. "I have been in night clubs. If my daughter could do as well as some of the hostesses in those places, I would retire and write a book I have been fussing with for years."

They both laughed and the release changed Benton completely. His belligerence and contention passed and London knew then that they merely were an armor for his shyness. "You win." Benton planted his feet firmly on the floor and stood and stretched. "Let me know if I can be of help to you. My radio station is at your disposal."

"Thanks." London stretched too. "And let me make one more observation. Should I warn your son that the ministry means trials and tribulations, he would probably ask to be ordained tomorrow. I don't know if you believe in God or not."

"Neither do I." Benton said it frankly and without braggadocio.

"It's your business. But I caution you. Don't push your boy. And don't pull him."

"You could be right, Dr. Wingo. We'll be in Linden in a few minutes. So if you will excuse me, I'll be getting my things together."

He walked to the front of the car and returned the magazines. The train was slowing down, easing by section houses and clicking across culverts and crossings. London put his arm on the back of the chair and looked out.

Boxcars and gondolas crowded the sidings and warehouses flanked the tracks. Linden had grown. How it had grown. Factory stacks poked up in the distance, and he wondered if one of them was the shoe plant out in Plymouth Community. He started to ask Benton Andrews, who had returned to his chair, but the train slowed to a crawl and Benton headed for the rear of the car, the exit.

London put on his brown felt hat, shaping the brim in a quick sweep of his hand. Then he stood and brushed his shoes across the back of his trouser legs, a gesture he had acquired as a young man and one that always brought protests from Paige.

He picked up his brief case and stooped, watching the station as they pulled in, and stepped off the car almost directly behind Benton Andrews.

Cliff Carter squirmed through the crowd, slapping half a dozen people on their backs, waving first at Benton and then grasping London's hand.

"I've been beating his ears down," Benton said. "Happened to catch this train in Moberly and there he was."

"You make your living beating ears down," Cliff said, and looked around, then back at London. "Where's Paige?"

"Bringing the car down. She'll be here tomorrow. You all right, Cliff?"

"I'm always all right." His false teeth clicked when he talked and he was bald except for a fringe of thin sandy hair.

"You got your car?" Benton rested his foot on his traveling bag and lit a cigarette.

"Uh-huh. Give you a lift?"

"No, thanks. You look after Dr. Wingo. I'll bet he's tired."

"Not at all," London said. "In fact, I'd like to drive out by the church if we've got time before dark."

Cliff reached for his pastor's bag. "Want to go by your apartment first? The ladies been working on it, but it's sort of makeshift until you get settled."

"I know about what it looks like and it will do until we get our things down from Kansas City. I'd rather see the church first. Think I remember it. It was out in the country in those days——"

"That's right," Cliff said.

"A stone church. But abandoned and run down, as I remember."

"We been working on it, but don't expect too much." Cliff scratched the top of his head and his nails left marks on his thin dry skin. "It's an old Congregational church, you know. They sort of petered out around here and we rented it."

"They left us a good name, though." London stuck his brief case under his arm and tugged at his coat lapels. "Congregationalists often named their churches after old Plymouth Colony."

Cliff glanced over at Benton and grinned, then tapped his preacher's chest with his bony forefinger. "Look, brother. This Plymouth ain't got nothing to do with old Plymouth Colony. There used to be a chicken farm out there. Plymouth Rocks. That's where the settlement got its name."

London tilted his head and laughed. "I preached in a church once named Sheep Hollow Baptist Church. And one named Nag's Head Baptist Church. But this is the first one I ever heard of that was named for a chicken."

Chapter 2

Cliff stepped around to the trunk of his mud-splattered Buick to put away the luggage, and London used the minute to peep into the undertaker's glove compartment, hoping to find evidence that the years had not changed his friend too much. It was there all right; Cliff's black bow tie with the frayed rubber band.

The minister rested back in the seat and knew he was home again. Cliff usually wore loud four-in-hand ties but always kept a black bow handy just in case a funeral caught him without time to dress appropriately.

A low rumble from the locomotive and the train pulled out, and Cliff slid under the wheel. He did not start the engine, however, giving London a chance to look around.

Green busses hogged the main thoroughfare of the town and parking meters lined the curbs. London recognized the old Emporium, although the building had been renovated and the name changed to Thrift Mart. There was one office building of ten stories and several of six and eight, their windows lettered with the proper announcements that doctors, dentists, and lawyers worked within, by appointment. Many, many lawyers, several dentists, and many, many, many doctors, and they had the best offices. A Manhattan Café advertised K.C. steaks and a Missouri Café advertised N.Y. steaks.

"She's grown, ain't she?" Cliff started his car and began threading through traffic, waving to friends and constantly blowing his horn, although signs on the street said politely, "No Horns, Please."

"Quite a city," London said. "But all the old crowd's gone, huh?"

"Just about. The ones still around are mostly in the First Church. How did you and Benton hit it off?"

"All right."

"Brought up his boy, I suppose."

"He mentioned him." London never discussed one man's affairs with another.

Cliff steered with one hand and reached in his pocket for a package of gum and stuck a stick in his mouth. His teeth clicked sharply. "Benton don't want that boy to preach. Benton's an atheist."

"Or agnostic?" London asked.

"What's the dif? They both don't believe in God." He cut out of traffic and over to a quieter street of lawns and comfortable houses. "I keep telling old Bent that any man who don't believe in God is a dope. Ain't going to call him a fool because the Bible says don't call your brother a fool, but I have my own opinion about that. Look at them trees and that sky. A man's bound to believe in God."

The preacher shrugged and smiled. "Look, Brother Carter." London put his hand on his deacon's shoulder and patted it. "Let's not be disturbed about that now. I know some men out of the Church who are better Christians than some men in the Church. Andrews' convictions are personal matters."

Cliff was not ready to drop the subject, so confident of his own faith, so contented within the high walls of his orthodoxy that he wanted only to share his simple world with all mankind. And yet Cliff could have dragged the fagots to the heretics' feet, prayed for them and wept for them, then given them a thousand-dollar funeral for three hundred dollars, the bedrock cost of his best casket. "Bent don't aim for his boy to preach, all right. But that ain't all that's eating him. Did he say anything about Mary Upjohn?"

"No." London was looking at the big houses along the way, all conventional and cousins in design and purpose. The owners probably were Episcopalians. Perhaps some of them had once been

Baptists, but prestige and ambitious wives and children had led many Baptists to Canterbury, where they struggled to sing the words of "Panis Angelicus" to the music of "The Old-Time Religion."

"You remember her, don't you? You married Mary's mother and daddy."

"Great day, Cliff! The woods were full of Upjohns. I remember old Newt Upjohn." He smiled at the recollection of the Upjohn clan, the poor, shiftless collection that combed a living from a few rented farms thereabouts.

"Newt's dead." Cliff stopped at an intersection, peered both ways, and was off again. "Mary is his granddaughter. Her daddy is time-keeper at the shoe factory."

"She will be one of my members then." Any mention of a father and daughter reminded him of Paige.

"Uh-huh. Mighty fine girl. Good Christian. Vance Andrews would marry her before nightfall if she'd say the word. That's what's eating on Bent. His son loving an Upjohn."

Oh, good heavens! London took off his hat and ran his fingers through his hair and over his eyes. Biology was responsible for more church squabbles than choirs and committees, almost as many as the budget. "Don't load me with problems before I get my feet on the ground." London realized he was a bit tired from the long trip. A good hot bath and supper would revive him. He would eat at his apartment because he didn't feel up to a meal with a member. The apartment would be drab and lonely, but he'd make out until Paige arrived and brightened things up.

Cliff slowed down again. "Just wanted you to know the score. Recognize where you are?"

London glanced around quickly, and down the street, on the next corner, was the church he and Kathie had built. It had been en-larged and the steeple was gone. A squat belfry was in its place. However, not even Baptist functionalism had erased entirely the graceful lines of the church. A neon sign proclaimed:

FIRST BAPTIST CHURCH
THE FRIENDLY CHURCH

Gone was the linden tree that had shaded the door and the fountain by the tree. In its place was a bulletin board:

FIRST BAPTIST CHURCH
H. HARRINGTON WARD, PASTOR
Sunday School 10:00
Church Services 11:00

Cliff pulled his car over to the curb and both men were silent for a few seconds, staring at the church. "Want to go in?" Cliff asked.

"No."

"You know Dr. Ward?"

"Uh-huh. Not well, but I know him."

"What's the 'H.' for? You happen to know?" Cliff put his arm on the back of the seat and was sad as he looked at the church he had helped build.

"Harding."

Cliff laughed and smacked his gum. "I often wondered what that 'H.' was for. He likes to be called 'Harry.' He's head of the ministerial council in town." The car moved away.

London looked back at the church, remembering so much. "Why did you pull out? Or do you care to tell me?"

"I couldn't take Harding Harrington Ward."

"A church is bigger than any pastor."

"Not that pastor," Cliff snorted. "He's one of those up-and-at-'em glad-handers. You know the type."

That wasn't sufficient. Knowing Cliff Carter as he did, the minister knew it would take something serious to cause him to leave the church of his youth and help organize a new one. However, he dropped the subject, confident his friend would tell him all he needed to know, and more, in due time.

They reached the outskirts of town, and the pavement ended and the houses of the shoe-factory workers lined a broad road. A bulldozer was chewing up the road and a scraper was smoothing it in preparation for asphalt. The houses mostly were bungalows, not shacks at all, and there were several brick and stucco buildings around.

Cliff started down the road, then changed his mind and backed out, detouring around the block to avoid the machinery. "Harding Harrington Ward has done all right for himself."

The truth was coming sooner than London had expected. "Let's call him 'Harry,'" he suggested. "If a man wants to be called 'Harry,' let's oblige him."

"You are right." Cliff cut his wheel sharply to miss a tricycle in the street. "Harry's in real estate on the side. Started building houses after the war. Cleaned up."

London knew several ministers who had done such things and took issue with them in conventions and councils, but never publicly criticized them. His calling was to oppose evil, and although he preached that the love of money and power was evil, nevertheless the stewardship of honest wealth was a matter for man to decide with his God. He cut his eyes over at Cliff and his eyes twinkled. "What's the difference in a preacher making money by sheltering people and a deacon making money by burying them?"

"There's a durn heap of dif, buddy. And you know it." Cliff stuck another stick of gum in his mouth, folded it with his tongue, and chewed vigorously. "But I could take my pastor getting rich on houses. I just couldn't take him grabbing dollars and forgetting folks."

The minister was listening while giving the appearance of not being interested at all, and looking at the community that was to be his field. There was a park that needed attention, but the baseball field was in excellent condition. A Kroger store occupied a corner and a super-market advertised fresh asparagus. Now that was something—asparagus for a factory village. London was pleased. Asparagus and a park and children on tricycles indicated a progressive company and perhaps absence of labor trouble in the factory, hence absence of a labor issue in his church.

"Harry's insurance agent told me all about it." Cliff turned down another street where the trees had been spared and most of the yards were neat. "Ever' time Harry started a house he went first to his insurance agent to be sure he was protected. Never once did he worry about a man getting hurt, only if he was protected if a man got hurt.

Then one day a fellow fell and broke his back. Harry hot-footed to his agent and paid off, but he never did go see the fellow or nothing. Just paid him." Cliff shook his head slowly. "That did it for me. I pulled out of his church and moved my letter out here."

London nodded his understanding. "It's done and let's quit talking about it. We won't have much fellowship with the churches in town. Our church is across the railroad tracks." He took off his hat and enjoyed the breeze in his hair and against his face. "Looks like the shoe factory is a good company."

"One of the best." Cliff cut his speed to twenty-five miles an hour in conformity with signs along the way that warned motorists of the law and urged them to protect the children.

"Union plant, I suppose."

"Uh-huh. But no trouble out here since before the war. Both sides learned the hard way. You won't have any labor blowups in your church. We call it the Missouri way."

"What's that?" London never had heard the expression over in the western part of the state around Kansas City.

"Live and let live. We're doing O.K. here in Missouri." Cliff bobbed his head emphatically, then cocked it to one side to stress his words. "We got a President and generals and a little bit of ever'-thing. Folks who cuss Truman and Vaughan forget that Bradley is a Missourian."

"We've got a good battleship too." London could not fail the opportunity. "Best in the world until she hits a mudbank."

The deacon nudged his pastor and laughed. "That's us, all right. Best in the world as long as we steer a true course. Live and let live. Trust in the Lord and do good."

A policeman, wearing a wide white belt and no pistol, held up traffic while a group of children crossed the street. They waved at Cliff. So did the policeman. The factory was at the end of the way. It was a conventional plant of six stories, and a thin wisp of smoke curled out of its stack. Cliff signaled properly (the policeman still was in sight) and turned down a gravel road, past a filling station and a Woodmen of the World hall.

He eased his car out of gear. "We're going to pave this one next."

The Buick drifted over to the curb and to a stop, and the deacon was watching the preacher's face.

"Is that it?" London stared at the little building.

"That's it, brother." Cliff said it proudly and hopefully.

For a second or so London Wingo was silent, just looking at the church and taking in every outside detail.

"You ain't let down too much, are you?" Cliff was on edge. "Told you not to expect too much."

Again London reached over and put his hand on his friend's shoulder, still looking at the church. "It's beautiful. Much more than I expected."

So it was. It was a stone church, the stones turned gray and ivy clinging to the crevices at the rear of the little edifice and drooping at the roof. London's heart beat a rapid echo to the fullness of his soul and he blinked quickly, his face turned from Cliff. "I remember it, now that I see it. You've done wonders with it."

Cliff was relieved and his happiness lighted his face. "Don't know where they got them stones. This church was built before the Civil War, when New England folks were coming this way heading West." He opened the car door and stood there, looking from his pastor to the Plymouth Baptist Church. "Ain't that ivy pretty? Looks like a picture in *Life* magazine."

London Wingo had no words for the minute, only gratitude, and he expressed it in silence and prayer. He had expected nothing and here was so much; a community of tricycles and a park where he thought shacks would be. Cool, green asparagus instead of greasy fat meat. A strong sanctuary where he had expected broken windows and rotten planks, a temple instead of a tabernacle. He wished for Paige that she might share this experience.

His name had been in large letters near the door of the Kansas City church. Here it could be in small letters, on a bulletin board over there near the corner where the lilac was green. It must be a simple board and hide none of the lines of the church or the jonquils that bloomed along the path.

"Take a gander at that ivy." Cliff stepped around the car and opened the door for the minister. "Look how it's all bunched at the back and none around the front. Some folks say it's a matter of sunlight, but me and Mary Upjohn figure the Lord grew it that way a-purpose. The way open, and once you get inside ever'thing calm and close and sheltered."

London left his hat in the automobile. "Have you got the key?"

"There ain't no key, Preacher. I hope there won't be no key."

Again London was grateful, for all this and a friend. "We will never lock it."

"The church is the key, ain't it?" Cliff led the way up the path. "Now don't expect too much inside." He spat out his gum and took off his hat. "We got to have a new heating plant. But it's clean. Mary Upjohn and Vance Andrews been working ever' day. Scrubbing and fixing. Look at that door."

It was an oaken door of six panels and a heavy wrought-iron ring, rubbed smooth. London grasped the ring and swung open the door, and a good smell of old wood and green ivy and mossy stones greeted him. The pulpit was in shadows, but behind the pulpit twilight drifted through two stained-glass windows.

He walked down the aisle, feeling the floor as he walked. It didn't creak and he thanked the Lord for that. A creaking floor was an abomination. He went up to the pulpit and felt it, and it was walnut and not golden oak at all. The pews were oak and expertly he judged the seating capacity at four hundred. There was no baptistry. Well, he could baptize in the river or the creek.

"It has a good solid floor." He spoke softly to his deacon, almost a whisper. A low voice fitted these walls, the shadowed pulpit, and the light coming through so softly.

"Good oak." Cliff pressed the floor. "But it ain't the floor that counts in a church. It's the foundation. Don't know about them colored windows, though."

"What's wrong with them?" London turned and studied the windows. No imagery at all, only stained glass, and leaded.

Cliff scratched his fringe of hair and sat down in the front pew, looking from the preacher to the pulpit to the windows. "Some of the folks think they are Catholic like."

"Well, we won't worry about that now." London sat beside him, leaning back in the pew. It was a hard seat and not too comfortable. The curve at his back was too sharp. Oh well, that was a minor detail. A rug runner down the aisle would soften footsteps. He wanted it dark red, but the Building Committee would have to decide and they were sure to insist on a mustard-brown rug. They always did. Brown wouldn't show footprints as badly as red.

The deacon crossed his legs and tugged at his shoestring, tightening it. "You halfway satisfied, London?"

The preacher nodded.

"I like them windows, don't you?"

Again London nodded.

"I wish us Baptists had more pretty things in our churches." Cliff rested his arms on the back of the pew and relaxed. "I take *Life* magazine, and you don't see many Baptist churches in *Life* magazine. Catholics and 'Piscopalians got us beat when it comes to pretty things in their churches, and pretty names. Even Methodists and Campbellites got us beat. How come we don't have pretty names for our churches?"

London was thinking of a dozen other things and answered casually. "The early Baptists were the Plain People. They wanted everything plain. A church house was a meeting place and nothing more. We are supposed to believe in salvation through faith and in good works as evidence of faith. Cathedrals and spires and bells had no place in the lives of the Plain People."

"We got a bell now." Cliff tapped him on the knee. "We got the prettiest bell in Linden. No kidding."

London turned his head and looked back up the aisle. "I saw the rope."

"The 'Piscopalians are mighty proud of their bell. Presbyterians got a good one too. But we got the best bell of the whole bunch."

"Congregationalists usually have beautiful bells," London explained.

The deacon crossed in front of the preacher and started up the aisle. "Come on. I'll show it. It rings just as clear. You can hear it clean down to the river and up that slope on the other side. Just as clear."

They walked together back to the vestibule and the bell rope was hanging over a peg. Cliff fingered it, peering at his friend and then up the rope to the bell tower, a mischievous twinkle in his eyes. "Let's ring it, brother."

It was all good, all peaceful, standing in the vestibule with Cliff Carter, who wanted to ring a bell because it was so clear. Again London wished for Paige and smiled his contentment, his anticipation of joy in things to come. A little church, a walnut pulpit, and the light coming through. "I don't know of any law against ringing a church bell, but this is Monday, you know."

"What's the dif?" Cliff was a bit annoyed at his friend's caution. "That's the trouble with us Christians. We spend half our time preaching eternity and the other half watching a clock. What's Monday got to do with it?"

"Go ahead and ring it," London said. "Peal out the tidings."

Cliff hesitated. "You ring it. You're the preacher."

"Oh no. You are the deacon. You ring it."

"Let's both ring it." Cliff reached for the rope. "You grab hold and I'll grab hold and we'll pull together. Get it? Pull together."

London grasped the rope, his hand close to Cliff's, and they pulled, staring up at the tower as though expecting a miracle or a calamity. The bell tapped a halfhearted note, a downright puny note, but on the swing back the clapper bonged into the bell, pealing its call clearly. Cliff grinned like a child who had reached for jam and found jam.

"I hope it confuses nobody." London was grinning too. "A church bell on Monday is rather out of the ordinary."

"Now there you go again," Cliff said. "Nobody is going to pay it any mind. Right now down at Kroger's somebody is saying, 'Wasn't that the Baptist bell?' And somebody else is saying, 'Nope. Can't be. It's Monday. Must be a train bell. Gimme a bottle of ketchup.' Man and God get together on schedule these days. You know that as good as me."

London glanced around for his hat and remembered it was in the car. "Let's go. When an undertaker turns philosopher, it's time to go."

Cliff closed the door. "Want to see the Sunday-school annex? It's right behind the church. Your study too."

The annex was a two-storied frame building, much newer than the church, and they walked down the hollow corridors and peeped into a few of the classrooms. The pastor's study was a small room in the rear of the church and was empty of furniture. A worn rug was on the floor. One of the windows had curtains and the other window was bare.

"Ain't been used in a long time," Cliff said. "But we'll fix it up for you."

"I have my own desk and books," London said. "Paige and I will fix it up."

They walked to the front path again and Cliff said, "You'll eat supper with me."

"No, thanks." The spring afternoon was turning cool and London's coat felt good. "Drop me off at my apartment, please."

"Ain't nobody there," Cliff protested. "Don't want you lonesome the first night. And eating hamburgers."

"I'll manage. I'll rustle a sandwich or something and pile in bed early. I'm tired."

Back down the gravel road to the pavement, thence into Linden, and both men silent as Cliff maneuvered his car through traffic. They came to Elm Street, about five blocks from the business district. London remembered the street. It was the edge of town when he left Linden.

"That's your apartment house down yonder on the corner." Cliff pointed, then felt in his pocket for a stick of gum. "Ain't the best in town, but it's respectable and homey."

"Paige and I are Apartment No. 4, aren't we? Second-floor front." The spring insects were rasping in the trees and people were on their lawns and porches.

"That's right." Cliff pulled over to the curb. "If you need anything, let me know."

London got his brief case and luggage, declining Cliff's help. "Do you eat at home these days? You are worrying about me, but what about yourself?"

"I'm always all right," Cliff boasted. "I'll drop by my place and see if there's a call. Then I'll grab a hamburger or bowl of chili and hit the hay. Sort of tired, myself."

The Buick rolled away and London watched it disappear, then walked into the apartment house. His name already was on the mailbox. Some of the church ladies must have done that. His name was printed in ink: Dr. London Wingo. Apt. 4.

He wished his congregation would call him "brother," a Southern tradition, instead of the Midwestern "Reverend" or "Doctor." He never had got used to "Dr. Wingo." Sounded like a chiropractor. He even had been called "Rev" and "Doc" and in Kansas City had preached a sermon, quoting Webster instead of the Bible, that "reverend" was a colloquialism when referring to a clergyman and offensive to some ministers. After services several members had told him, "We certainly enjoyed your sermon, Reverend Wingo."

The apartment house smelled like an apartment house, Clorox in the washing machines and chemicals on the hall floor. There was no elevator and a black rubber runner protected the stairs. The second floor was gloomy and London put on his glasses and found Apartment 4.

A chilling thought assailed him as he reached for the doorknob. Suppose some of the church ladies still were there, cooking his supper or cleaning up. Well, he would plead a headache and go join Cliff for a hamburger or chili. He rapped quickly and firmly from dint of habit and entered his own home.

Paige was standing in the living room, a dust rag in her hand and her face contorted in preparation for a sneeze.

"What in the world?" he demanded, and was frightened. "Anything wrong?"

She sneezed, then hurried to him and kissed his cheek. "Come right in, Reverend. But like all preachers, you call at the wrong time."

"What's wrong, Paige? What are you doing here?" He put down his luggage and consternation clouded his face.

"Nothing's wrong, Dad." She sat on the edge of a chair and smiled at him. "I didn't go by Columbia. I got to thinking about it and decided I didn't want you here by yourself. So I drove straight through."

"You must have burned the wind," he admonished. However, he was pleased, very pleased, and the apartment was cheerful simply because she was there, her dark brown eyes dancing with the fun of the surprise and her light brown hair cut short and extreme, so light it was almost blond.

Had anyone asked London Wingo to describe his daughter, he would have said, "Oh, she comes to about here on me, about to my shoulders. She needs a little more meat on her bones and her lipstick and fingernails are always the same color."

Actually, she was five and a half feet tall and often shunned potatoes and bread to keep her weight at one hundred and twenty-five.

She took charge of her father and the conversation, asking first about the church.

"Beautiful," he said. "New Englandish." Then on second thought, "Pretty as a picture in *Life* magazine."

She hung the dust rag over the arm of the chair and got up, slipping off her navy-blue suède shoes and walking in her stocking feet. She was wearing a blue spring suit, the skirt with a kick pleat and the blouse with long sleeves and French cuffs. "Come on. I'll show you around. We'll have supper in a minute. The church ladies brought enough for an army. The place was swarming with them."

"Cold potato salad, I presume." London followed his daughter over to a window and looked out on the lawn and down Elm Street.

"With onions."

He grimaced. "And hard-boiled eggs and deviled eggs. Ham. Two kinds of cake and a pie."

"And a loaf of homemade bread." Paige turned from the window and nodded toward the french doors to the dining room. "They'll have to come down."

"Homemade bread?" London looked beyond the doors into the dining room, the walnut table, the heavy cupboard. "You got any butter?" He loved good bread and sweet butter.

She nodded and kicked up the edge of the rug, peeping under, and was surprised that it was clean. "The same lady brought butter. Her name is Mrs. Elizabeth Ramsey. Friends call her Lizzie, no less. She giggles. Soprano. And I'll have you know her father was a Somebody in Kentucky or Tennessee or somewhere."

"Now, Paige." He sampled two or three of the chairs, bouncing in the largest and finding it comfortable.

"Sister Lizzie is trouble." She went to a wall and took down a picture and stood there, undecided whether to hang it elsewhere or store it; a Grant Wood reproduction that was too light for the room. "Her people are all Presbyterians and she joined us Baptists because Brother Ramsey is such a good man and such a good Baptist and husband and wife should be in the same church, don't you think so?"

London was chuckling. In many ways Paige was like her mother, lighthearted and merry, and gifted with a frightening intuition. "But is the bread any good?" He reached out for the picture and tried it on a wall by a window. They both looked at it and shook their heads.

"Naturally it's good bread, Dad. Sister Lizzie got the recipe from her sister. Old family secret. Her sister is the wife of a rubber big shot in Akron. Episcopalians. High Church and snooty and Sister Lizzie doesn't know why because everybody knows an Episcopalian is nothing but a Catholic too lazy to learn Latin."

"No, Paige." He put his head in his hand and laughed. "Not that one."

"It's the truth. That's what she said. Now, come on. I'll show you your room."

A hall joined the living room, and the bath was at the end of the hall. "Shelf for you and a shelf for me." Paige nodded toward the bath. "Tub clean. Faucets don't drip. No shower. *And*, Reverend Wingo, there's a place for your washrag. I'll put a red mark by it so you'll remember. That's your bedroom in there."

The door was open and London walked in and looked around. A closet, a bureau, a warm rug. "Bed clean?" He glanced over his shoulder at his daughter.

"Bed clean." She propped against the door and watched him.

"Bureau drawers stick?"

"Drawers stick."

"Windows work?"

"Roger."

"What about your room?"

"Over there." She nodded toward a door in the hallway. "It will do until our own things arrive and we get our ducks in line."

London sat on his bed, testing it. He had a phobia about his bed and, during his ministry, had spent so many sleepless nights on uncomfortable beds. He liked a hard bed. Someday he was going to own a horsehair mattress.

There was a runner on the bureau and pictures on the wall. Jesus in the temple at the age of twelve, a New England landscape complete with red barn, and a lithograph of a Missouri River steamboat appropriately named *Sam'l L. Clemens*. "We will remove Brother Clemens. I like him in books, not on boats. And what's that on my bureau?"

He crossed the room and picked up a new razor in a plastic case, a tube of shaving cream, and a lotion called Bridle and Saddle.

"Sister Bledsoe brought those." Paige opened the lotion and sniffed it. "Gift from her husband. She brought the potato salad."

"All right. Report on her." London looked at the picture of Jesus in the temple and shuddered. That was the spot for his Po River landscape, the one he bought in Florence on a return trip from the Holy Land.

Paige removed *Sam'l L. Clemens* and Jesus in the temple and laid them face down on the bed. "Mrs. Bledsoe is tight-faced. First name Margaret. Her friends *don't* call her Maggie. She sings soprano too. Apparently there is a surplus of sopranos for the choir fight."

"Uh-oh-h-h." London grimaced. "Well, let's have some bread and butter, honey. Then maybe things will look brighter."

She stood on her tiptoes and kissed his forehead and went to the kitchen.

London followed her and got a quart of milk from the refrigerator and put it on the table. She got the bread and placed it before him and handed him a knife. He broke the bread with his fingers and buttered it lavishly. It was good bread and he buttered a choice crust and handed it to her. "I can forgive a woman anything if she can bake good bread. Now, the other church ladies. Who else was here?"

Paige drank several swallows of milk and wiped her lips. Her dark eyes were dancing again. "A girl named Mary Upjohn."

"I've heard of her."

"Tasteless meringue, Dad. Very sanctimonious. Pretty, though. She looked hurt when she saw me smoking. Not angry or critical. Just hurt."

London put the bread in the refrigerator, a custom he learned from Kathie when they first started keeping house. Refrigeration prevented mold and he wanted the rest of the loaf for his breakfast. He drank the last swallow of milk and put the bottle in the sink, filled it with warm water, and set it aside. "Have you a good report on anybody?"

"On Mary Upjohn, yes." Paige tapped a cigarette against her red fingernail. "You can count on her. Her name should have been Ruth or Naomi."

"Not Esther?" The father looked at her sharply.

"Never Esther." She felt for a match and, finding none, held out her hand and London handed her one. "Esther was a schemer and a vengeful woman. This girl is Ruth. Ready to follow." She took two or three draws at the cigarette and flipped the ashes in a saucer. "Then there was Forrest Roberts."

"Let's have it."

"Oh, she's darling."

"What!" Here was a fillip. "You met one you liked?"

"Yes, sir." Paige brushed the crumbs into the saucer and stepped over to the sink. "Forrest, like the Confederate general. Not the tree kind of forest. Schoolteacher."

"And she was not found wanting on your scales?"

"She's darling. Helped me shoo out the others before you arrived. Thinks Roger Williams was greater than Paine and in Jefferson's class."

London tilted the milk bottle, emptying it, and then stood it on its top to drain. He wiped his hands on a towel by the sink and led the way back to the living room, switching on the light in a lamp by the big chair.

A good feeling of weariness came over him and he relaxed in the chair, his hands folded behind his head. He was back in harness again, back in the field heavy for the harvest, the vineyard of strong vines and weak vines, of good grapes and little foxes and tares. This was where he belonged; this was his covenant and his calling.

But he did wish they would call him "brother" instead of "reverend."

Chapter 3

London spent the next morning in the apartment preparing his agenda while Paige went shopping at the five-and-ten for curtain rods, a towel rack, and other things the church ladies had forgotten to furnish. Their own household goods should arrive by van within two weeks at the latest, and meanwhile they could make out. Like most preachers, London was accustomed to makeshift arrangements and, like most preachers' daughters, so was Paige.

He watched her back the car out of the garage, whipping it around expertly and threading into traffic. Then he pulled a chair to the dining-room table and opened his brief case. It was bulging with notes, clippings, and books, mostly Haldeman-Julius Blue Books on everything from astronomy to a biography of Joseph Stalin. A spare toothbrush and a razor also were in the case, as was a twenty-dollar bill folded in an envelope marked "emergency" and clipped inside of Browning's *Complete Works*.

First he sharpened two Mikado pencils, using the Keen Kutter penknife Kathie had given him during their seminary days. He grinned as he shaved the lead to a fine point, knowing that if Paige were there she would tease him, for this was another habit that always brought a joke from his daughter. He owned two or three pen-and-pencil sets, gifts from members and admirers, and yet he always used Mikado pencils and always sharpened them, deliberately and smoothly, with the little knife. He wiped the blade on a piece of paper and put the knife back in his pocket.

Let's see. This was Tuesday. Tomorrow he would be busy with the church, arranging to meet the membership that night. Day after tomorrow he must transfer his bank account to Linden. This he rather hated to do, for in small towns a preacher's bank business was subject for discussion, and his finances were in better shape than most clergymen's. His salary in Kansas City had been six thousand dollars a year, plus his apartment and car expenses, and he had managed to save several thousands in cash in addition to investments that brought him a side income of seventy-six dollars a month.

His salary in Linden was to be two thousand dollars a year, plus forty dollars a month apartment rent. That was all right. If his church grew, his salary would grow and, in the meantime, if he had to tap his reserve, so be it. Paige would find a job and take care of herself, and his own needs were slight. Money was not a thing that bothered London Wingo, although he insisted that churches pay all they could afford. It infuriated him for members to expect their pastors to live on dimes while they squandered dollars.

Next week he must begin visiting. First the sick, then the aged. He long since had learned that a church is built on pastoral visits, that more work is done in the home than in the pulpit; sympathy for the ailing, compliments for the wives, and encouragement for the husbands, including agreement, if possible, on politics, Communism, the errors of other churches, and women's styles.

He searched through a sheaf of papers until he found a list of the deacons of Plymouth Baptist Church and adjusted his glasses as he studied it. The deacons constituted his cabinet. Cliff Carter headed the list. Well, he could count on Cliff. Then there was Leonardo Ramsey (where in the world could he have got that name?) and Champ Clark Upjohn. He would be Mary's father, probably. There were only seven names on the list, and that was good. It meant the board could be enlarged if necessary, and the Board of Deacons was an honorable place to retire a troublemaker, if he could be outvoted by friendly deacons, and always a reward for good workers.

London checked each name carefully. Experience, bitter experience, had taught him never to prejudge a deacon. However, if things ran true to form, Brother Leonardo Ramsey should be a mild fellow inasmuch as his wife apparently was a fireball. Two forceful personalities in one family were unlikely. Therefore, the chances were that Leonardo would serve as deacon in his wife's name.

Then there was Sisler Mason. London wondered if he were named for George Sisler, the first baseman of the St. Louis Browns back in the twenties. He hoped so. He liked baseball, which he seldom saw, better than he liked golf, which he played occasionally.

He put a sheet of paper in front of him and pushed everything else aside and began drafting a church covenant to be presented to the membership the next night. Spadework for the new church already had been done by Cliff and the other deacons, but the finishing touches to the organization must be applied and these included a covenant, the selection of the Finance Committee, the budget, and the choir. Oh lord! The choir. London took off his glasses and rubbed his eyes. Paige could help him with that problem. She was a diplomat with choirs. Mary Upjohn probably could be of service, too, and Vance Andrews always was available.

Well, the choir, like judgment, was a bitter morsel to be tasted later. He wrote "Our Covenant" at the top of the page and underlined it. Then he closed his eyes and prayed. A covenant between brothers was a privilege to be approached prayerfully, and London asked for guidance.

Slowly he wrote the first paragraph.

"Having been, as we trust, brought by divine grace to embrace the Lord Jesus as our personal Savior, we do now solemnly and joyfully covenant with one another, to walk together with Him in brotherly love, to His glory as our common Lord. We do, therefore, in His strength engage:

"That we will exercise a Christian care and watchfulness over one another, and faithfully warn, exhort, and admonish one another as occasion may require:

"That we will not forsake the assembling of ourselves together, but will uphold the public worship of God, and the ordinances of his house:

"That we will not omit religion at home or neglect the duty of training our children religiously, and those under our care, for the service of Christ and the enjoyment of heaven . . ."

On and on he wrote, and the words were comforting, not because he wrote them. Oh, never. But because they touched his brothers and his Master.

The draft was finished and he pushed back his chair and closed his eyes, thankful for his privileges as a servant of his Master. What a glorious heritage was his, the right to covenant with his brothers. To himself he whispered his favorite Scripture, a portion of Paul's letter to the Romans. "For I am persuaded, that neither death, nor life, nor angels, nor principalities, nor powers, nor things present, nor things to come, nor height, nor depth, nor any other creature, shall be able to separate us from the love of God, which is in Christ Jesus our Lord."

He had no idea of time and was outlining his sermon for the following Sunday, when Paige returned. She brushed a kiss against his cheek and tossed her bundles on a chair. "It's too hot to cook lunch," she said. "I hope you like cheeseburgers."

He wasn't sure exactly what cheeseburgers were and followed her to the kitchen, where she opened a sack of the sandwiches. "Huh," he said. "Dolled-up hamburgers." He stepped to the refrigerator for mustard and put it on the kitchen table.

"You don't mind them?" Paige turned on the gas stove and began heating water for coffee.

He said, "Not a bit." And he meant it. A veteran in the vineyards, a campaigner at dinners-on-the-ground and all-day sings, he had a preacher's digestion and could eat anything. A strong stomach and good feet were prerequisites of his calling.

She went to her room and changed to blue slacks and halter, and the coffee had dripped when she returned. London said grace and bit into his cheeseburger. The mustard was too tame. He liked English mustard, hot and authoritative. Paige wiped her fingers on a paper napkin. "It's quite a town," she said. "Larger than I thought. Whole lot larger."

"And still growing," London said.

"There are two newspapers." She spread cottage cheese on a cracker and ate it. "Owned by the same corporation, but supposedly separate."

"Which one carries Li'l Abner?"

"The afternoon paper."

"Dick Tracy?" He peered over at her.

"Same one." She was smiling at him, her eyes sparkling. "But you'll have to take both papers. The morning paper carries Steve Canyon and the Sunday morning paper carries Gasoline Alley and Prince Valiant. You are hooked."

He finished a cheeseburger and looked at the peanut butter, the cottage cheese and other spreads, and reached for the peanut butter. "We'll start this afternoon. I missed Li'l Abner and Brother Richard yesterday. Can't get behind."

Paige ate lightly. She was vigilant of her weight and shunned sweets and starches until temptation, or hunger, overcame her will power and then she stuffed on them but was ever ready to assure herself that this time was an exception and to alibi that, after all, she seldom gave in to the lure of fattening foods. The cottage cheese was filling, although not filling enough, and she wanted some jam or jelly. However, she put the urge behind her and glanced over at her father. "Do you remember the doings up at William Jewell about a student named Vance Andrews? A conscientious objector. He lives here."

London nodded and kept nodding slowly until he swallowed. He had not told her about meeting Benton Andrews on the train because so many other things had come up. However, he told her the story and added, "Mr. Andrews is antagonistic to the ministry. Can't say that I blame him. I wouldn't be too happy if my only son chose the ministry; that is, unless he were called."

"Maybe Vance Andrews was called." Paige touched her finger to the mustard and licked it.

"Maybe."

Paige pushed back her chair and crossed her leg over her knee. "Mr. Andrews owns the best radio station in town. There are three in all. His is pretty good. The others are weak sisters."

"You've been here only a few hours, but you already know more about Linden than I do." He drained his coffee cup. "Now, what's on your mind?"

"A job."

"Good."

"Wait a minute." She held up her hand and laughed. "Don't say it that way. Sounds like you want to get rid of me."

"If idleness is the devil's workshop"—he peered at her and affected a stern look—"then an idle woman is the straw boss."

"No sermons, Reverend." Her laughter was spontaneous and infectious. "I dropped by the newspaper office. Nothing doing there. But I heard that Mr. Andrews needs a smart girl."

"Doing what?" It came quickly.

She began clearing the table. "Oh, selling ads to local merchants and plugging them on the air. A little music. Lots of talk and clever repartee. You know. Sort of a small-town Mary Margaret McBride."

"Sounds interesting," he said. "But can you do it?"

"There's only one way to find out."

Her confidence comforted him and yet it worried him. She was so sure of herself in all she did. "You've never been on the radio, honey."

"He won't know that. Unless you tell him."

London was cautious. The idea of his daughter failing or even being frightened terrified him. Just the thought of her being hurt brought a hard lump to his stomach.

She sensed his mood and rubbed her fingers in his hair, tousling it, then smoothing it down. "I haven't got the job yet."

He rolled the paper napkins into a ball and tossed it to her and put the butter away. "When will you see him?"

"In a day or so. I don't want him to think I am too anxious for the job. That's not the way to do it."

He almost commented on how hard jobs were to get when he was a boy and how anxious young people were to work in those days. However, he knew she would laugh and point out the difference in then and now, so he said nothing until they were in the living room, where he examined the purchases she had made. "What else did you do this morning?" He glanced from the curtain rods to the windows and grimaced. It seemed he had spent half his life putting up curtain rods and it was a task he hated.

"Nothing much. Just looked around."

"I thought perhaps you went out to see the church." He said it hopefully.

Paige picked up one of the rods and pulled a chair over to a window, then stood on the chair and measured the rod. She nodded approval of the fit and got down and crossed the room to her father. "I was waiting for you to take me out to see the church, Dad. I wanted to see it first with you."

At that minute, in that place, there was nothing she could have said to please him more. A catch came to his heart and a warm glow drove it away. "We will go out right now," he said.

She gathered the bundles and hurried toward her room. "Just a minute. I'll be dressed in just a minute."

That also pleased him, that she would not enter her Lord's house wearing slacks. He watched her door close and reached for his pipe, filling it slowly and tapping the tobacco with the end of his pencil. Had she said those things only to make him feel good? He wondered. There had seemed a trace of rebuke in her voice because he had not offered to drive her out to the church. Or was that her feminacy, a woman's way of outwitting a male—any male: father, son, brother, or husband? Kathie had worked that way so often, he remembered. Making him feel guilty of something he had not done at all. So had his mother, his aunts.

His pipe was tasting just right when Paige came out of her room, raking a comb through her hair. She put the comb on a bookcase and looked in her compact mirror and brushed a few loose hairs off the shoulders of her dress. "I'm ready when you are." Her dress was brown, a deeper brown than her eyes.

London knocked the ashes out of his pipe and scattered them in an ash tray and reached for his hat.

"Must you wear a hat, Dad?"

"Huh?" He glanced down at his hat, a Stetson given him by a friend in Kansas City, and over at her. "Of course I'll wear my hat.

I'm no fancy Dan around here. Lounge lizard. Jelly bean." He called up the slang expressions of his youth. "I might meet Sister Ramsey." He adjusted his hat and looked at himself in the hall mirror. "Why shouldn't I wear a hat?"

"Oh, I don't know." She stood behind him, peeping around him and into the mirror, fluffing her hair. "You look better without a hat. Younger, too. Lots of men your age don't wear hats."

Up until that second London had loved the Stetson. It was soft and easy on his head, a fit that time had perfected. It was almost a part of him, like his bedroom slippers, his Keen Kutter knife, and his Mikado pencils. However, he took it off and stood there snapping the brim. "Well, now. It's pretty warm outside. And they tell me a bareheaded man never is a bald-headed man."

He laid the Stetson on the bookcase by her comb and they walked out together. London felt partly undressed without his hat and then she took his arm as they descended the stairs and he forgot about the Stetson. It didn't matter any more. If that was the way she wanted it to be, that was the way it would be. Every man has a vulnerable spot and London Wingo's was his daughter. So it is with most fathers. A wife is a mate, a comfort, and ofttimes a martinet whose own ambitions fruit in a husband's achievements. A son is an image in whom a father yearns to see his own reflected glory. But a daughter is a mystery.

There were hairpins and Kleenex on the front seat of the car and London brushed them off as Paige slid under the wheel. Quickly she was in traffic and quickly she was out of it, bearing north from Linden toward Plymouth.

She commented on the things they passed, the houses and the streets, and then changed the conversation abruptly. "I may see Mr. Andrews tomorrow. How do you think 'A Page with Paige' would be as the name of my program? If I get the job."

Her father stared at her. "Are you serious?"

"No."

"Thank goodness." He shook his head and laughed. "'A Page with Paige.' Oh, brother."

"What about 'Customers' Compass'?" She whipped the DeSoto around a corner. "You know, a sort of a guide for buyers."

Again he shook his head. "That's terrible too." He glanced at the speedometer to be sure she was within the speed limit. "Now, if I were doing it I'd get my name in it. Paige Wingo. What's wrong with calling it just plain 'Paige Wingo'?"

She cut her eyes quickly at him and smiled approvingly. "You are a showman, Dad."

"Preachers sometimes have to be." He was pressing the floor board as though the brake were there. "But I am thinking about the rabbit stew. You know the first thing to do to make a rabbit stew?"

"I will get the job all right." That confidence again, that frightening surety. "I dropped a few hints around the newspaper office about what a bang-up radio girl I am. Newspapermen are better gossips than the Women's Missionary Union."

London sighed and ran his fingers through his hair. "I hope you know what you are doing. You've never been on the radio in your life."

She reached over and patted his shoulder. "Columbus had never crossed the Atlantic either, but he made a successful round trip. Now, which way to the church?" She stopped the car and he looked around for his bearings.

There was the factory and the Kroger store. He pointed left. "Turn at that corner. And take it easy, honey. I don't believe in hell-fire or pearly gates, but I am not anxious to prove myself wrong just yet."

The sun moved behind a bank of clouds and it quickly was chilly as a north breeze came in, and Paige was thankful for her light spring jacket and her father wished for his hat. He touched her arm and nodded down the street toward the church. The breeze was teasing the ivy and Paige slowed the car and looked, saying nothing, and then eased the car to a stop.

Together they went up the walk and London swung back the heavy doors and they stood there, the gloom of the afternoon shadows slowly lifting in the soft rays through the stained-glass windows. Still Paige did not speak and London was glad, knowing silence often is a sincere tribute while words are hollow praise.

She took his hand, holding it tight as a child in a strange place and perhaps afraid, and they walked down to the pulpit and on to the windows and looked up. "That light is like a prayer," she said slowly, and they were her first words.

"An evening prayer," he said.

She turned from him and walked back and sat on the first pew, watching the light, and he sat beside her and his eyes were closed. "You know something, Dad?" She did not look at him, still watching the light.

He said, "Sitting here, I realize how little I know."

"Colors remind me of God. Is that sacrilegious?"

He opened his eyes slowly and looked from her to the window and his cup was filled. Her words brought back her childhood. Her very tone pushed back the years and there was her childhood of questions and miracles and abiding faith. God in colors. She had always talked that way—smearing red crayons on the wall and brushing green water color on her books. "It is not sacrilegious," he said. "If we can worship God in song, we can worship Him in colors."

"The green is His justice," she whispered. "The blue is His mercy and the red is His anger. Or maybe His sacrifice."

"It is a beautiful church, isn't it?" He tiptoed to the pulpit and straightened the heavy green cloth.

"It is more than that." She waited until he was beside her again and, her eyes on the window to the right of the pulpit, spoke softly. "God is here. Right here. And this is where you belong. Up there in the pulpit with the colors streaming through."

He was puzzled by her words and glanced at her sharply and up at the pulpit and the windows, and frowned. "If we see God in colors, honey, then the pulpit is bare——"

"Not if my father is in the pulpit."

He wondered if she were teasing him or baiting him. "Now wait a minute." The frown deepened and he shook his head in that slow motion that indicated complete disagreement. "The pulpit is simply a platform for the messenger. It is not an altar. There is no altar in our church and the pulpit is consecrated only in proportion to the messenger's faith. Never forget, young lady, that when your father is in the pulpit he, too, is a repentant sinner saved only by the grace of God, the Father."

She smiled at him, her eyes away from the window and on his face and a mischievous twinkle in them. "There are a lot of fathers in this procedure. Our heavenly Father and an earthly father, and if the earthly father goes to heaven, he is a father in heaven. No wonder kids get confused."

"And adults go crazy." He got up and moved a step or two up the aisle. "You about ready to go home?"

"Yes, sir." She looked again at the windows and the smile left her face and she was serious. "When I was about six or eight I always thought of the Kansas City church as belonging to you. God was out there somewhere, way over on the other side of the river, but you were it. I don't feel that way about this one. I feel that God is here."

"You are growing up." He moved up the aisle. There were other things to do and he was impatient to be about them.

His daughter touched his arm, checking him, and she smiled again. "I've been grown a long time, Dad. But age does not dissipate the images of childhood. Uh-oh!" She clapped her hands over her ears and rocked her head. "That sounded learned, didn't it?"

"A page from Paige, perhaps."

They both laughed, and their laughter was not out of place at all in that quiet temple where God was.

The sky was deeply overcast and the wind was raw as they hurried to the car. Paige started the motor and cut on the heater. "These Missouri springs are tricky." She shuddered and rubbed her hands briskly.

"I will build a fire when we get home." He was anxious to try the fireplace in the living room. Like most men reared in the outdoors, a fire was more than simply a flame to him. It was a friend, a confidant, and a confessor. If he did not worship God, he easily might worship fire and sun. He had never seen God in colors, but had seen Him often in the warmth of fire.

Paige eased the car into gear, glanced behind her, and was off. "A fire will be nice. And I'd like to fix supper early. I'm going out tonight if you don't mind."

He hoped his disappointment wasn't apparent. He had looked forward to an evening with his daughter; a good supper, a fire, and talk. "Is it all right if I presume to ask where you are going? Or isn't it any of my business?" Yes, his disappointment was apparent.

"I won't be out long, Dad. I heard about a little study group that meets monthly. They are discussing T. S. Eliot tonight. You know my weakness." The windshield was clouding and she cut off the heater and turned on the wiper.

"Of course I want you to go." He was piqued at himself for letting his feelings betray him. "Let's stop up at Kroger's and do a little buying. If I am going to preach out here, we should trade out here."

She came to a full stop at an intersection while a dog ambled into the street, turned scornfully and looked at the car, and ambled on without haste or obvious destination. There were many dogs in Plymouth Community, almost as many dogs as children. Paige crept around the corner, remarking that the tall hedges obstructed the view, and drove down to Kroger's store.

They went in together. Most of the vegetables had been picked over and the fruit was skimpy. London gave scant heed to the vegetables, however, and looked around at the people and headed for the meat counter. The butcher glanced up, smiling mechanically. He was a slight, harassed man in a large apron. London offered his hand. "I am London Wingo. The new Baptist preacher out here."

It was more of an announcement than an introduction and he spoke it in a tone louder than was his usual custom. Several people heard him and smiled at him and moved toward him. Paige also heard him and was embarrassed. It wasn't like her father to announce himself in a public place. It wasn't like him at all, and she pretended not to hear him and began fingering a bunch of carrots, one of the few vegetables that were plentiful and fresh.

The butcher came from behind his counter, rubbing his hands

on his apron. His store smile was gone and a genuine smile was in its place. "Well, now, I do know," he said. "I'm Estes Oliphant. Glad to make your acquaintance, Brother Wingo."

He called him "brother." Paige heard it and was glad, although she wanted no participation in the little ceremony over by the meat counter, the handshaking and back slapping. She hoped her father would not call her over there.

"Want you to meet some of the folks," Estes Oliphant was saying, beaming his delight in his minutes of importance. "Brother Wingo" —he put his hand on the preacher's arm and his drawl was evidence of his deep South heritage—"this is Mrs. Ross. Bluestocking Presbyterian and mighty good folks. Shake hands with my pastor, Mrs. Ross." He saw the introduction well done and addressed another woman. "Mrs. Lindsey, meet Brother Wingo. Mrs. Lindsey is Methodist. Her husband used to be Baptist until he switched to his wife's religion. Now his membership is in her name, huh, Mrs. Lindsey?"

He knew everybody in the store and took London by the arm and showed him off, and London loved it. There were four or five women around him, nodding and smiling, and two or three men, when he looked around for Paige. "Want you all to meet my daughter," he said proudly, and called her.

Paige cringed deep within herself. However, she fixed a smile and walked over to the crowd. Estes Oliphant took over, bowing politely to Paige and wringing her hand. "Well, now. So this is your little girl, huh, Preacher? Raising your own missionary, huh?"

London cut his eyes quickly to her and she swallowed the retort that was burning to be spoken. The women looked her over carefully, her nylon stockings, the casual cut of her jacket, and her confident bearing. She shook hands with all of them, speaking polite nothings and returning the looks of the women, giving no ground before the assault of their stares.

Mrs. Lindsey drooled her words. "I suppose, Miss Wingo, you will be leading the choir in your father's church."

"I don't know one note from a hole in the ground," said Paige diplomatically.

"Oh, I'm sure you are only being modest," said Mrs. Ross. "A congregation expects big things of a pastor's daughter."

Again Paige swallowed a retort and even bit her lip to be sure of her silence. However, London took it up. "My daughter," he said, "expects much of the congregation. So do I."

Mrs. Lindsey and Mrs. Ross exchanged glances and excused themselves. Paige purchased a pound of bacon from Estes Oliphant and nodded to her father that she was ready to go.

She waited until they were in the car and she had pressed the starter hard, almost violently. "Dad!" Her resentment and embarrassment boiled over. "I am surprised. You acted like a camp-meeting preacher. Back slapping and loud talk. You never did such things in Kansas City."

London shoved his hands in his coat pockets and leaned back, debating with himself whether to rebuke his daughter for her presumption. He seldom had raised his voice to discipline her and always had given her the right to speak out, encouraging her to express her opinions and assuming that absolute freedom would teach her the difference between liberty and license. She had been reared a free soul. It was his responsibility, often his burden and sometimes his pleasure. Therefore, he could not rebuke her for the result of a cause that he himself had advocated. The child had been spared the rod. Pray God the woman was not spoiled.

He smiled slightly and closed his eyes, determined upon a soft answer. "Honey," he said, "this is not Kansas City. I was under wraps there and now I am back home and free. I am a camp-meeting preacher. A brush-arbor preacher. Besides, I knew Brother Oliphant was a Baptist. I could tell by his looks."

Paige was ashamed of her outburst but did not apologize. She did not know how to apologize or retreat, only how to shift her course. "Oh, wait a minute now." The resentment was concealed instinctively and her tone was pleasant again. "You can tell a Baptist simply by looking at a man?"

"Sometimes." He slouched deeper in the seat and adjusted himself more comfortably. "Brother Oliphant had that sort of tight look around his mouth. An offensive-defensive look. It is pretty common among people who have been pushed around."

She turned the heater on to the first notch and lowered her window an inch or so. "I never thought of Baptists as being pushed around. There are too many of us. I have known us to do a little pushing."

"Baptists are not persecuted in this country," he said, looking straight ahead and seeing nothing because his mind was upon his words. "But we are ridiculed. It is partly our fault. We are aggressive one minute and defensive the next."

"I don't follow you." She did, however. She had heard him talk this way many times, but was leading him on, smoothly adopting her role of sounding board for her father's ideas and sermons. She drove slowly. Nothing must distract him. It was his work to think on problems about his people, and her work to help him. Out of these talks came his sermons.

He did not speak directly to her, but aloud and mostly to himself, a slow monologue as he measured his words and weighed them. "We are the Plain People. A peculiar people. Baptists, of all people, should understand the evils of anti-Semitism, for in many ways we are like the Jews."

"Many Baptists won't like that," she suggested. "Or many Jews."

He locked his hands behind his head and closed his eyes. It didn't matter to London Wingo what people liked. He was concerned only with truth. "We scorn the ancient Jewish idea of God's chosen people and contend we are Christ's chosen people." Slowly he shook his head. "We practice spiritual exclusiveness and demand social inclusiveness. Yes, we of all people should understand the Jews."

"What has this to do with the tight lines around Mr. Oliphant's mouth?" She was still leading him.

"Like most of us, Brother Oliphant is in a spiritual turmoil without knowing why. He believes in a brotherhood through Christ, but on Baptist terms. It is the tragedy of Christianity. Be it Catholic, Baptist, Methodist. It is still a tragedy. The army of Christ in scattered camps. Separation is third only to power and ignorance as a breeding place for intolerance and evil."

She turned into Elm Street and slowed the car to about twenty miles an hour. "I have never seen any medals on us Baptists for tolerance. Especially us Southern Baptists."

London sat up straight and glanced around. They were almost home and he was glad. He wanted to build a fire. "You are wrong, Paige. That's why I want to write a book on Roger Williams. To show the greatness of our Baptist heritage. Our faith grew out of one of the most liberal and democratic movements of all Christendom. We have abused it. I often am ashamed of Baptist practices, but never of Baptist principles."

"It will make a good sermon," she said, and stepped up her speed.

"And don't think for one minute, young lady, that Southern Baptists have a patent on intolerance. You will find bigotry where you find power, be it in Catholic Boston, Baptist North Carolina, or Israel."

She cut into the driveway of their apartment house and checked her instruments at a glance. She must have the oil changed tomorrow. "I suppose all that is what put offensive-defensive lines around Mr. Oliphant's mouth." She began smiling. "I suppose he is tormenting his soul over spiritual exclusiveness and social inclusiveness." Her smile grew into a laugh. "Let's face it, Dad. Mr. Oliphant's only concern probably is how he will meet his bills." She wheeled the car around and backed it into the garage.

London put his hand on the door. "Right now his main concern is Mary Upjohn. He's kin to her by marriage, or somehow."

"And what's wrong with Mary?"

"Oh, the Andrews' again. You probably heard that Vance Andrews is trying to marry her."

"And what's wrong with that?" Paige pulled her jacket close around her neck and cracked open her door.

"Nothing that I know of. But Benton Andrews is against his son marrying an Upjohn. The Upjohns are against it because they think Vance Andrews is flighty."

Paige got out of the car and inhaled deeply of the sharp spring air. "The church is full of trouble. I sense it, Dad."

London came around the car and stood beside her and looked

up at the threatening clouds. "Don't worry about it. Baptists and trouble and deep water go together. The real problems here will be the same old things. How to practice charity in a world of greed. How to turn the cheek in a world at war. And how to love your neighbor when your impulse is to slap him down. Now you go get supper started. I'll join you in a minute."

She ran into the house and he went into the garage, seeking splinters for kindling. He wanted fat pine splinters, if he could find them, and three good logs for his fire.

Chapter 4

Paige was in the kitchen fixing supper and humming "My Foolish Heart" when London came into the living room and laid the wood on the hearth, then brushed the sleeves of his coat and hung it on the back of a chair. She didn't hear him. The cold water was running on the fresh asparagus she was preparing and the warm water on a package of frozen lima beans. She stopped humming and began singing the words.

It was her favorite popular melody (his was "The Third Man Theme") and she sang it passing well. As a child she had taken piano and voice, but, hating the practice lessons, had convinced her father she had no talent for music and he had allowed her to drop it. Since then he often had criticized himself for not persuading her to continue. That he should have compelled her to do so never occurred to him.

She heard him moving in the living room and called out that supper would be ready in a few minutes, meaning at least thirty minutes, and he went to the wastebasket and fished out several sheets of soiled paper. These he twisted into tapers and laid them in the fireplace, just so. On top of these he distributed the kindling and carefully adjusted the logs into a pyramid, a piece of good dry oak on top of two logs. He stepped back and examined the result and moved the top log a fraction to the left. It was a ritual with him.

Even Kathie used to laugh at him about it; going to all that trouble for a fire that soon would be ashes. However, to have the logs just so delighted him and satisfied something within him. A yearning for orderliness, perhaps.

London lit the tapers and watched them twist into yellow flame and the kindling into red flame that licked the logs and curled the bark until the fire was its own master. A puny beginning, then triumph, a warm, useful thing that he had helped create.

For several minutes he stood with his back to his fire, rocking on the balls of his feet, and then turned and poked the fire, although it did not need poking, and lined the logs up again. His face was red from the heat and he loved it.

Reluctantly he left his friend and went to the telephone in the hall and tested it. It was working and he called the newspapers and ordered morning, afternoon, and Sunday editions. His hat was on the bookcase by the telephone and he glanced at it and grinned and went in the bathroom and washed his face and hands, rolling his shirt sleeves high and soaping his arms to his elbows. He dampened and combed his hair and parted it on the side and brushed it smooth.

The asparagus and lima beans were in the pressure cooker and Paige was arranging cold sliced ham on a platter when he joined her in the kitchen. He got the remnant of the home-baked loaf from the refrigerator and sliced it. Paige always bought sliced bread. It was simpler that way.

She was no cook at all. There was no reason why she should be; no mother to teach her and a father who made no demands. Green salads were her only culinary achievements, and never in her life had she baked pastry or roasted meat. In Kansas City they always had eaten Sunday dinners with members and went out four or five times during the week to the homes of friends or to restaurants. London assumed cooking was an art that came naturally to women, but somehow he never had expected his own daughter really to cook pies and cakes and roasts, and she didn't.

Paige turned off the pressure cooker and pronounced the vegetables done. They were light green and tender, undoubtedly full of vitamins, but with no flavor. She put butter on them, commenting that oleo was cheaper and that she would buy some tomorrow, and set them before her father. He said grace over them and reached for the ham and mustard.

Geographically, London Wingo was a Southwesterner, but his heritage was Southern and he liked vegetables cooked well and seasoned with pork and pepper sauce. Paige moved the asparagus close to his plate, a hint that he should help himself. "It's good for you," she said in the everlasting way of her sex.

He spread butter thick on his bread and nodded agreement. "I am sure it is. Man discovered fire for the purpose of enjoying raw vegetables."

"Now, Dad——"

"Besides, a man can worry himself to death about his health." The mischievous little lines were playing around his eyes. "I will give up my hat for the sake of health and youth, but I will not eat raw asparagus, parsnips, or spinach."

"Then try some of the lima beans."

"We called them butter beans when I was a boy." He put some on his plate, also a little asparagus, and enjoyed them simply because she had fixed them. However, he admitted nothing, but fixed a stare on her and said, "I suppose when you get your radio program you will tell the ladies how to cook, and all that."

"Naturally." She assumed a pose, beaming a tooth-paste smile as she pretended her glass was a mike. "Now, ladies—you girls." Her tone became persuasive and dulcet, and her expression angelic.

They laughed and finished their supper in banter and merriment. It took only a few minutes to straighten the kitchen, and they went to the living room and he hung curtains and rearranged the furniture under her direction, moving chairs from one place to another and then back where they were at first.

The car drove up alongside the apartment house and Paige peeped around the curtains. "It's Mr. Carter," she said in a stage whisper, although there was no one to hear her except London. "He has a man with him."

London peeped around the curtains, too, and identified the other man as Benton Andrews. Paige touched her hair, feeling it. "Oh lord," she lamented. "I wanted an overhaul job before I met him. Hair. Nails. Everything." She hurried to her room and left her father to meet the guests.

Cliff came in rubbing his hands and bustling. Benton greeted London amiably and respectfully and walked toward the fire, holding his hands to the blaze and then reaching for the poker. He hesitated and glanced over his shoulder at London, the poker poised above the logs. "Dr. Wingo," he said seriously, "how long is a man supposed to know another man before he takes the liberty of poking his fire?"

London stroked his chin and looked up at the ceiling. "The code says eleven years. However, there are special dispensations."

"Then I have your permission to poke?" An expression of youthful eagerness was on Benton's face and the tight, hard lines were gone.

London held up his hands as though in benediction and intoned, "Poke, brother."

Cliff stepped closer, offering suggestions on the proper way to poke a fire, and stood on the hearth to see that the ceremony was performed correctly. Benton squatted before the fire and raked the ashes a bit, loosening them. Cliff and London exchanged deliberate glances and nodded solemnly. Benton accepted their approval and began poking the logs, the back one first, and lined them again and stepped back.

"Um-m-m." Cliff pursed his lips and passed judgment. "The brother qualifies."

"He's in the lodge all right." London bowed his congratulations. "Of course a master always raps his poker twice against the top log. Once to dislodge the soot and ashes and once for luck."

They pulled chairs close to the hearth and stretched their feet to the blaze, as is the wont of men. Benton lit a cigarette and Cliff put a stick of gum in his mouth. London slid low in his chair and locked his hands behind his head. "I'm glad you gentlemen dropped by. A visit, or is there something I can do for you?"

A pause, and in that interval Paige came out of her room and, voicing her pleasure, hurried to Cliff and greeted him with genuine affection. He put his hands on her shoulders and looked at her. "My, my." And again he said it, "My, my."

London presented Benton Andrews to his daughter. There was a handshake and a bow and Benton offered her his chair and pulled another into the circle for himself. Casually he spoke to Paige about the cool spring weather and then turned to her father, by no means ignoring her and yet by no means directing any particular attention to her. "Cliff suggested we drop by." He glanced around for an ash tray and London handed him one.

"Uh-huh." Cliff smacked his gum in enjoyment and his teeth clicked. "Bent and I figured we'd drop by to see how you are making out."

"We are making out fine." Paige took up the conversation and noticed that Benton Andrews was giving their living room the once-over, his eyes lingering on the frayed rug, the crack in the mantel, and the dingy corners. That she resented.

London got up and stood on the hearth, warming his hands. It was too warm there and he returned to his chair. "I don't know about you, Mr. Andrews. But I know Cliff. He's got something on his mind." He still was too warm and pushed his chair back a few feet.

The fire was crackling a blue flame and giving off more heat than was needed. Cliff pushed back his chair and ran his hand over his bald head, where beads of sweat had oozed out. He wiped his hand on his trousers. "You explain to him, Bent," Cliff said. The pronoun was singular and Paige looked quickly at her father, and away. There was no deliberate slight of her. Cliff had known her since her babyhood and to him she still was a child.

Benton also addressed his remarks to London. "It's about an apartment." And then it occurred to him that Paige should be considered and he turned his face toward her, including her. "There is a much better apartment house in town than this one."

"Whole lot better," said Cliff. "And I want my preacher to have the best. It's on out Elm Street a way. It's called Elmscourt."

"What's the difference in rent?" Paige asked immediately and before her father could speak, laying the practical aspects of the matter before them. She demanded attention and she got it, and even Cliff was impressed by her authoritative manner.

For the first time Benton addressed her directly. "The apartments run from eighty to one hundred dollars. About double the rent here."

London arose slowly and his deliberate movements gave notice that he had something to say and expected to be heard. He crossed the room to a table and got his pipe and blew into it hard. It was clogged and he stuck it in his pocket and returned to his chair. "Who owns the apartment house?" he asked innocently, and began shaving a kitchen match with his penknife.

"I am one of the owners," Benton said frankly and quickly. "Harry Ward also is a part owner. He is pastor of the First Baptist Church."

"Yes, I know Brother Ward." London jabbed the match into the pipe bowl and blew into the stem again. It was clean. "Is Elmscourt the best apartment house in town?"

Benton nodded. "Far and away. But, as I said before, it is pretty expensive——"

"We don't think eighty dollars is exorbitant," Paige volunteered. "Not in these days." She turned to her father as though no one else were present. "I think I passed it today. It's right nice outside. A little ornate."

If her purpose was to attract Benton's attention, she succeeded. He looked closely at her, then over at Cliff and back at her, really seeing her for the first time. She was about the age of his own son, but Vance Andrews never would have expressed himself so confidently in a council of his elders. "Elmscourt is modern, Miss Wingo. I am not trying to rent an apartment. This was Mr. Carter's idea."

Cliff was disturbed, almost distraught, at the turn the conversation was taking. "Uh-huh, I asked Bent to come by." He was speaking to London. "He knows the setup between the church and you and rent. It's no secret, is it?"

The tension in the room—and there was a bit—evaporated when London smiled. "Brother, nothing a preacher does is a secret. So let's get down to business. If Elmscourt is the best in town, we definitely are interested."

"As I understand it," said Benton politely and in good will, "the church pays forty dollars a month for your rent."

"That is correct," London said, glancing a warning to Paige that she should be silent.

"The two-bedroom apartments at Elmscourt are eighty dollars a month," Benton explained. "However, I am sure I can arrange concessions."

Paige closed her eyes and compressed her lips. This was the kind of talk that infuriated her. Concessions to preachers. Largess from the rich. A crumb from the mighty. London read her mind and his look spoke his gratitude for her silence. He packed his pipe slowly and lit it. "Mr. Andrews, my daughter and I will look at the apartments. If one suits us, we will rent it. The only necessary concession is that you accept our check on the first of each month."

Benton Andrews flushed and turned to Cliff as though for an explanation. "Now, wait a minute," said Cliff, always honest and aboveboard. "Bent is taking my blame. This whole idea was mine. I figured to save you a little money and do you a favor. It ain't a question of you taking favors from nobody. I was just trying to help out."

A soft answer was on London's lips, but Paige spoke first, smiling at her guests and dissipating the strain immediately. "May I fix you gentlemen some coffee?" She got up and stood by the door to the dining room.

"Now that's an idea," London said, rubbing his hands briskly.

"Sounds good," said Cliff. "It keeps me awake, but I'm game."

"How about a little bourbon and branch water?" Benton suggested in an attempt at joviality. "That's the only thing I have in common with our fellow Missourian—Mr. Harry S-for-nothing Truman. We both like a little bourbon and branch water. And him a good Baptist."

Now that was the wrong thing to say, definitely the wrong course to take; not the mention of Mr. Truman's church affiliation, but the assumption that reference to whisky in a preacher's home was witty. Similar remarks were common to many men in their awkward efforts at good-fellowship in the presence of ministers. London understood such remarks for what they were—attempts by laymen to span the imaginary barriers between themselves and the clergy. He long since had reconciled himself to the lonesomeness of his calling, to the fact that he, as a preacher, would never be wholly accepted into the camaraderie of other men simply as a human being, a man of virtues and faults.

Nevertheless, he cringed at Benton's *faux pas*, knowing Paige's blind resentment of any hint or suggestion that her home life was different from any other girl's (although it was) or that her father was a sanctimonious long-face. Quickly he prayed that she would not let her resentment command her tongue. He held his breath, expecting her to pounce on Benton Andrews, to say, perhaps, "You and Mr. Truman have another thing in common, sir. You both are presidents. You of a jerk-water radio station and he of the United States." It sounded like her and he could almost hear her saying it, and dared not look at her.

Her laughter brought him up short and quickened his heart. She was leaning against the dining-room door and her merriment and friendliness were genuine. "I am sorry, Mr. Andrews, but we haven't had time to stock our cellar. Ordinarily the church includes beverages with the rent."

She turned and went to the kitchen and London puckered his brows. She really must want a job with Benton Andrews, he thought. Never before had he seen her control herself with such admirable restraint. He was proud of her and his face beamed his pride. The fire was dying down and he reached for the poker and then, on second thought, handed it to Benton. "Want to poke?"

"Thanks." Benton jabbed the logs several times and rapped the top log twice. Carefully he propped the poker in its stand and faced London. "Dr. Wingo, I got off on the wrong foot with you coming down on the train. I don't want it that way."

"Then it won't be that way." He leaned over and patted Cliff's shoulder, but still was speaking to Benton. "And we are grateful about the apartment."

"Now we are getting somewhere," said Cliff, and tears came to his eyes. He was an emotional man, and any evidence of good will made him so happy that he always filled up. "Of course Harding Harrington Ward takes every concession he can get. He takes cuts on his groceries, gasoline——"

"That is his affair," London said firmly.

Cliff chewed his gum vigorously and nudged Benton. "Didn't I tell you he'd say that? Didn't I tell you?"

Benton braced his hands against the small of his back and stretched. "I assume it won't matter that Harry Ward lives in Elmscourt——"

"Rent-free," interrupted Cliff. "He rents out the parsonage and lives rent-free in Elmscourt as one of the owners. Even deducts his living room from income taxes. Calls it a real estate office."

London was vexed. He didn't choose to share an apartment house with another Baptist preacher, with any preacher, for that matter. They should have told him sooner that Ward lived out there, and yet, on the other hand, there was no reason they should have told him, and there had been no opportunity. Ward had three children, as he remembered. That was several years ago. Maybe he had more by now. London remembered Mrs. Ward very well; and fondly. She had been a friend of Kathie's.

The room seemed stuffy to him, the fire burning bright again, and with his guests' permission he raised a window a few inches and came back to the circle of chairs and sat on the arm of one of them. "If Brother Ward prefers an apartment to a parsonage, then that, too, is his affair." He slid into the chair and crossed his legs. "As I said before, my daughter and I will look at the apartments, and if one suits us, we will take it." His voice had the quiet authority of his personality, a notice of finality, although Benton Andrews detected a trace of annoyance in his tone.

Cliff threw his gum into the fire and London was glad Paige didn't see him, because the gum stuck to the back of the fireplace and melted into an unsightly blob. Cliff patted his pockets, feeling for fresh gum, and then pounded his pockets almost frantically.

"Out of ammunition?" Benton laughed and London laughed

with him, partly at Cliff but mostly in the knowledge that Benton Andrews was a man who really enjoyed laughter once a basis for understanding was established between him and his fellow man.

Cliff began pulling papers out of his pockets and piling them on a chair, and London noticed that most of the papers were circulars from *Life* magazine. There were two or three subscription cards from the publication, and London picked up one. "You save these things?"

"Uh-huh," said Cliff irritably, still feeling for a stick of gum. "Hobby with me."

"He is not kidding." Benton smoothed his mustache and, in so doing, hid his smile. "He has a feud on with *Life*."

It was an excellent chance for a pun, and London liked puns but passed up the opportunity. He was enjoying the banter and grinned broadly at his deacon. "Is it a secret?"

Cliff found a stick of gum in his inside coat pocket and ripped off the paper and tossed it toward the fire. It fell on the hearth. "I ain't sent *Life* a dime in two years, but they keep sending me the magazine and all this junk." He began stuffing the papers back in his pockets. "Ever pay any mind to one of these things?" He held up a subscription card, turning it slowly. "Look." He feigned amazement. "Just holes. Little square holes."

"Ingenuity," suggested Benton, and London knew by the way he said it that he was responsible for Cliff's subscription to *Life*.

"Ingenuity, my hind foot." Cliff was scornful. "They put my name on their subscription machine years ago when I paid up, and they ain't got around to taking it off. Look at this card." He passed it to London. "Got a machine up there that changes those holes to words. They run your card through that machine and it tells 'em how much you owe and all about you." He scratched the fringe of hair around his head. "I been trying to figure it out for years."

Benton dragged his chair closer to the window. He heard Paige moving in the kitchen, and the aroma of fresh coffee delighted him. "Mr. Wingo——" He began with the air of a man about to reveal a secret and called London "Mr. Wingo." It sounded friendlier than "Dr. Wingo." He pointed a finger at Cliff. "Your deacon over there has two ambitions. The first is to get to heaven. A Baptist heaven. And the second is to harass *Life* to distraction."

"What have you got against *Life*, Cliff?" London pulled his chair nearer the window, and the air was fresh and cool.

Cliff stayed close to the fire. He was older than the other men and the heat was good to his tight, brittle skin, so tight on his face that his cheekbones stood out. "Well, now, I'll tell you." He chewed his gum vigorously. "You remember years ago when they had that crazy radio program about men coming down from Mars? H. G. Wells, or somebody——"

"Orson Welles," said Benton solemnly.

"Anyhow," Cliff continued, "*Life* magazine carried pictures about it and showed a picture of a man in New Jersey with a gun. All set to jump them men from Mars. *Life* magazine said his gun was a rifle. It was a shotgun——"

"A 12-gauge Stevens," suggested Benton.

"A 12-gauge Stevens!" London suppressed his mirth. "Any fool in New York ought to know the difference between a 12-gauge Stevens and a rifle."

"That's what I told 'em," Cliff said. "In my third letter. I tried to be polite. Just wrote 'em to straighten 'em out, and they didn't pay me no mind." He propped his hand against the mantel. "Then they carried a picture of some American general riding a horse in Greece. Wasn't a horse a-tall. Blame mule. I wrote 'em nice and polite again."

London scowled his exasperation. "And they've never published one of your letters?"

"Not a one," Benton said. "Cliff has been writing *Life* an average of six letters a year, pointing out errors. I think he has the right of complaint."

Cliff eyed Benton closely. He never was sure when his friend was jesting. "It ain't that I want my name in print." He still was looking at Benton. "I just don't like to be ignored. So I quit taking *Life* magazine, but it keeps coming. I get a letter every month and one of those cards full of holes every three months."

"Why not throw them away?" London was as solemn as Benton. The deacon scratched his bald head, his nails making a rasping sound on his dry scalp. "Well, now, I'll be honest with you. At first I was scared to. Figured the letters might be important. And those cards got my curiosity up; trying to figure out them holes. But they kept pouring in and I got mad and started saving 'em. Got a stack as high as my knee. Know what I aim to do?" he asked triumphantly.

"There is no telling," said London. "Charge them storage, perhaps."

Cliff's eyes shone in anticipated pleasure. "One of these days I'm going to bale those circulars and send 'em back to *Life* magazine with a nice polite letter telling 'em what they can do with 'em."

Benton jerked up his coat sleeve and looked at his watch, then tapped a cigarette against the back of his hand. "Cliff's real peeve is that he thinks Harry Truman is the greatest man since Champ Clark, and *Life* doesn't agree with him. Neither do facts."

"That ain't so," Cliff said vehemently. "All I ask is an even break for Harry. I know his cousin."

The levity might have continued, but Paige came in from the kitchen with a tray of cups in her hands. Benton moved to help her and, at her direction, put a card table before the fire. She put down the tray and Benton helped her pour coffee.

"None for me," she said. "I must go fix up a bit. I am going downtown for a while." She glanced at her father and said slowly, "You said something about wanting the car tonight, I believe. Well, I'll be back early."

He caught the signal of her look and words. "Well, now——" He wasn't sure exactly what she wanted him to say and was playing for another cue.

"May I be of help?" Benton asked. "Cliff and I came in my car and I can drop you off in town."

"If you don't mind." Paige passed the cream and opened a box of cookies. "I am going to Lyceum Hall——"

"Oh-h-h," Benton said. "The T. S. Eliot group. You an Eliot addict?"

"Not an addict, Mr. Andrews," she replied rather testily. "An admirer."

Benton seemed pleased that she was going there. "I'll be happy to take you by the Lyceum, Miss Wingo. My son will be there. He's more than an admirer of Eliot's. He's an addict."

"Now there's another good old Missouri boy." Cliff jerked his head to one side and nodded enthusiastically to emphasize his words. "That Eliot fellow. Born in St. Louis."

London was surprised that his deacon was interested in T. S. Eliot, and Paige was astonished. "Do you read Eliot, Mr. Carter?" There was a hint of incongruity in her tone.

"No, ma'am." Cliff was emphatic. "Too deep for me." Then his eyes brightened and his pride was evident. "But I've read *The Robe* twice. Now there's a book for you. Ever read it, Miss Wingo?"

Her father dreaded her reply, fearing her critical opinion might hurt Cliff's feelings. However, she nodded her agreement to his judgment and smiled at him. "Yes, I've read it."

"Good book, ain't it?" He was so happy that she agreed with him, that he had something in common with his friend's daughter. His head bobbed up and down and he clicked his teeth and then looked over at Benton as though daring him to take issue on the merits of *The Robe*.

"I enjoyed it very much," said Paige, and started toward her room.

Bless her heart, London was thinking. Bless her kind heart.

"If it's no trouble"—she was speaking to Benton—"I'll take you up on that ride to town."

"No trouble at all," he said.

She closed the door to her room and they heard her singing. "My Foolish Heart" again. Benton listened, staring into the fire, and Cliff was listening, too, and thinking of the church choir. London was thinking what an actress his daughter was. She had impressed Benton Andrews. That was obvious. His thoughts were broken by Cliff's words. "I always said *The Robe* was a great book. And there is *another* Missourian—Lloyd Douglas. Born up in Maryville——"

"Careful now," Benton warned. "That's Homer Croy. Douglas was born in Indiana." He turned to London, closing the subject of *The Robe*. "You have a talented daughter, Mr. Wingo. She is about the age of my son."

"I helped raise her," said Cliff, determined to be a part of the conversation and anxious to steer away from Lloyd Douglas now that his error had been exposed. "She's a lot like her mother."

London thanked them and poured more coffee, and the refreshments were about gone when Paige rejoined them. She was dressed plainly and smartly in a spring suit, and her light coat was unbuttoned. London went to the door with them and invited Benton to drop by any time. He watched them down the steps and returned to the fire that was dying to embers and ashes. Cliff aroused the embers, poking noisily. They heard the car start and sat down facing each other, and London put his leg over the arm of his chair and relaxed.

For a minute they were silent and then Cliff said, "I am glad you and ol' Bent were hitting it off better. He's a mighty good man. In his way."

"He's lonesome," said London.

"Who ain't?" Cliff peered into one of the coffee cups and pushed the cup to the center of the card table. "I know Bent is the one who subscribed to *Life* magazine for me. But I don't want him to know I know it. He gets so much fun out of it."

A feeling of compassion came to London Wingo, compassion and a cleansing emotion of humility. What a noble thing is friendship. He had an urge to embrace Cliff and cling to him as an unsteady child clings to a banister while descending a stairway.

"Tell you something else," Cliff said softly.

"What's that, brother?"

"Bent's the one who catches those errors in *Life* magazine. He tells me about them. I ain't got that much sense."

London leaned far out of his chair and touched his friend on the knee. "Now I'll tell you something. Benton Andrews would trade all of his sense for one ounce of your faith."

Cliff filled up and his eyes brimmed tears. He was proud of his pastor's words and yet he was embarrassed. "It's easy to fool folks," he mumbled. "But you can't fool the Lord. I've done a lot of mean things in my life. I've got a lot to make up for. Now, tell me——" He changed the subject abruptly. "You all set for the meeting tomorrow night?"

"I think so." London cleaned his pipe again and put it in his mouth but did not light it. "I have drawn a draft of our covenant. Its adoption will be our first business."

Cliff Carter immediately was disturbed and ran his hand over his head, scratching the fringe of hair. "Now, London"—he looked closely at his pastor—"you don't jump flat-footed into the nigger question in that covenant, I hope. And labor and world peace and all them things——"

"No." The minister smiled at his deacon's agitation. "I have learned never to throw dynamite into a bed of ashes. The covenant holds for brotherhood and justice. It is a Christian's duty to decide, through prayer, the meaning of the Word of God, and then stand fast." He got up slowly and stretched and walked to the far end of the room for his brief case, and handed the draft of the covenant to Cliff.

The deacon read it, holding it close to a floor lamp, and began nodding as he read. "Nothing in there to cause a fight." He laid the document on the card table. "Nobody can disagree with that. Not even Leo Ramsey or Estes Oliphant."

Uh-oh, London thought. So they were the troublemakers, the dissenters. Oliphant, being a Southerner, would be touchy about the Negro question, an issue that plagued so many churches that stood for brotherhood and practiced segregation. Well, he had handled Oliphants and Ramseys before. The left cheek was the best way; a soft answer, and prayer. "So you call him Leo?" The pastor wanted to shift his deacon's thoughts from any possible issues. "I was wondering about Leonardo."

"Ain't that a mouthful?" Cliff said. "Good old Missouri boy, though." He began laughing, and the tiny curves around his mouth spread like ripples to his cheek. "His mother tied that onto him. She went to the Jamestown Exposition and saw a picture by Leonardo Whatever-His-Name-Is——"

"Da Vinci," said London.

"Yeah, that's right. So she tied that name on him and old Leo has had a time living it down."

That was something to remember, and London made a mental note of it. Be sure to call Brother Ramsey "Leo" and never "Leonardo." He picked up the covenant and returned it to his brief case, then lit his pipe. "We'll need somebody to read the covenant to the church. What about Brother Oliphant?"

Cliff shook his head. "Won't do. Estes would stall around and trip over the words and then make a speech about what good Baptists his folks have always been."

"What about Brother Ramsey?"

Again Cliff shook his head. "Clark Upjohn and Leo don't see eye to eye, and if Leo read it, Clark would find fault with it just on general principles."

"Well, it's not wise for the pastor to submit it. And I don't want you to read it. I'll bet they already are saying you run the church."

Cliff agreed and mulled the problem in his mind. "Sisler Mason won't do, either."

"What's the trouble?"

"Can't read much. But don't let him know you know it."

"Then what about Vance Andrews?"

Cliff threw up his hands at the suggestion. "Good lord, no! Some folks think he's a nut. Mind you, I'm on his side, but if you want to split the church before we get going, just play ball with Vance Andrews."

"Wait a minute, Cliff." London was impatient, almost exasperated. "We are organizing a Christian church, not running a political campaign or popularity contest. We will use our best reader to present the covenant to the congregation. Who is the best reader?"

"Forrest Roberts." There was no hesitation. "She's the best in town. Schoolteacher."

"We will use her." London's voice had that quiet tone of authority again.

The deacon still was skeptical and frowned his uncertainty. "But she's a woman. Ain't so sure about a woman presenting the covenant."

London went over and pulled down the window. The fire was out and the room was comfortably warm. "She is the one," he said, returning to his chair. "You take it up with her."

"Maybe we ought to go see her."

"That's a good idea," London said. "It's still early. Has she got a phone?"

"Uh-huh." Cliff walked toward the hall where the telephone was. "I'll see if she's there. She might be at the Eliot to-do. Or P.T.A., or something. She stays busy."

London heard him dial and, by his conversation, knew that Forrest Roberts was at home. He picked up the coffee cups and took them to the kitchen, and when he got back to the living room Cliff had on his hat and had pulled the wire screen in front of the fireplace. "She said give her a few minutes," Cliff said, "and then for us to come right on over."

He began checking details in the room to be sure it was straight and that the fire was safe. London folded the draft of the covenant and stuck it in his inside coat pocket and turned out the floor lamp. "We'll leave the light on in the hall in case Paige gets home before we do."

They walked into the hall and instinctively London reached for his hat and then, smiling to himself, put it back on the bookcase.

"Don't you wear a hat?" Cliff asked.

"Not any more," said London Wingo.

Chapter 5

The apartment house where Forrest Roberts lived was on Taney Avenue, five blocks from Elm Street, and a yellow light was burning in the vestibule to discourage insects. It was a two-story dwelling and its respectability was evident by its location, and its comfort by the budding maples that shadowed its weathered stucco walls.

Her apartment was on the first floor and Cliff led the way and pressed the doorbell repeatedly, each time holding it longer than London thought was necessary. The bell still was buzzing when Miss Roberts opened the door, inviting them in and at the same time acknowledging Cliff's introduction of her pastor. The hallway was dim and lighted only by a floor lamp in the adjoining living room, where a radiator grumbled notice that the furnace heat was coming on.

She showed them into the living room and indicated that London was to take the chair by the lamp. He turned to thank her and the light was full on her face, and her lids were puffy and her eyes streamed water. Cliff saw it, too, and was the first to speak. "Anything wrong, Forrest? You in trouble?"

"Only my vanity," she said, and smiled at him and then at London. "You must excuse me, Mr. Wingo."

London flung up both hands in a quick gesture of comprehension and helplessness and shook his head slowly. "No explanation is necessary. Ever try benadryl?"

"You too?" she asked, and put her handkerchief to her face and sneezed. Cliff looked from one to the other.

"Only in the fall," said London, and sat in the chair and rested his hands on the arms. "Goldenrod and ragweed."

"Mine is the spring variety." She went to the divan over by the radiator where a box of Kleenex was on the window sill. "In the spring my fancy turns to pyribenzamine. Benadryl is too strong."

It came to Cliff then what they were talking about and he grinned his triumph of deduction. "Oh-h-h. Hay fever. I had an aunt up in Moberly who had it——"

"That past tense doesn't make me happy," London interrupted. "What about you, Miss Roberts?"

"A little disconcerting." She caught his glance of understanding and smiled her appreciation. The light touched her eyes and they were gray behind the tears. She wiped the tears away and sneezed again, and sighed the pleasure of a cleared nasal passage.

"Oh, she didn't pass away with hay fever." Cliff spoke of death with the casualness of one who lived with death. "She just punied up and passed away, but her hay fever was a fret." He crossed the room and sat by Miss Roberts, his hands folded over his knee. "They figured she was allergic to cats. You got a cat, Forrest?"

"Why, Cliff!" She rebuked him in arched-brow pretense. "I haven't been a schoolteacher *that* long."

"Sleep on a feather pillow? They asked her that too."

Forrest Roberts picked up an inhaler of Benzedrex and put it to her nostrils and breathed deeply. "If you are really interested——" She tossed the inhaler to London. "Try it. New kind." Then back to Cliff: "If you're really interested, I sleep on a foam pillow. And a plastic pillow slip that crackles when I turn over."

London read the fine print on the inhaler and unscrewed the cap and sniffed. Cliff was not to be sidetracked. "This aunt—Millie Malone was her maiden name and we called her Aunt Millie; us Carter boys. She swore by Vicks salve. Ever try Vicks, Forrest?"

It was time to go to her rescue, and London got up and handed the inhaler to her and stood at the end of the divan, smiling down at his deacon. "Cliff, the Lord spared Job two tribulations. Hay fever and friends who talked about hay fever. I suggest we see Miss Roberts later——"

"Oh, by no means," Forrest protested. "It'll go away in a little while. May I fix some coffee?"

"How 'bout some bourbon and branch water?" said Cliff, imitating Benton Andrews. "Me and Harry Truman are Missouri Baptists who like a little snifter ever' now and then."

Forrest got up from the divan and turned the radiator knob until it was opened as far as it would go. "I have some sherry. Some very good sherry." The radiator had quit growling, and she put her hand on the pipes and jerked it away quickly.

"I would enjoy some sherry," London said. "They tell me a little sherry in the spring is good for hay fever in the fall."

"I'm game too." Cliff slapped his knee. "I'm as game as the next one."

Forrest started for the kitchen and at the door she paused and looked back at her guests and began laughing, the tears splashing down her cheeks as she laughed. "This is a fine beginning for the Plymouth Baptist Church. Serving sherry to my pastor and my deacon."

Cliff jumped up to help her. "They served wine when Jesus organized the First Baptist Church of Jerusalem. And what was good enough for them is good enough for Cliff Carter." He followed her into the kitchen, still talking. "Ain't had a drink of wine in five—good lord—eight, nine years. Since the day I put ol' Newt Upjohn away. Had four funerals that day and had to squeeze ol' Newt between Hanley Overton and Sister Honeycutt. I was so wore out I was almost ready to crawl in there with ol' Newt and hit the glory road. Me and him."

London glanced around the room while they were gone and was conscious of the faint scent of perfume. Lavender or Chanel No. 5, he supposed. To him all perfumes were lavender or Chanel No. 5. Actually, the perfume was Arden's Blue Grass Flower Mist.

Her books were stacked carelessly but usefully in a walnut case and her eyeglasses (he assumed they were hers) were on the top of the case. There was a bowl of maple buds and they were arranged so simply and beautifully that he looked at them a second time. He loved flowers and often wished he dared sport a blossom in his lapel. For that matter, he wished he dared carry a cane, and one of his secret desires was to own a gay cummerbund and a cape with a red silk lining.

The radiator started growling again and he struck it with the heel of his palm.

"Kick it," Forrest called from the kitchen. "It reacts obediently to abuse."

Her voice was cheerful, and London, sensitive to tones and smells, instinctively catalogued her voice as compatible. However, if at that minute somebody had asked him to describe Forrest Roberts, he would have pondered the question and replied, "Oh, I don't know. Not quite as tall as I am. Little taller than my daughter."

He was standing by the radiator when she brought in a plate of Lady Baltimore cake and dates stuffed with pecans. Cliff followed her, bringing three crystal glasses on a tray and the sherry in an old decanter. Forrest poured and the two men commented on the bouquet, although neither knew the difference among sherry, port, or elderberry. London had taken possibly a dozen sips of wine since his ordination because Baptists never use fermented spirits in observing the Lord's Supper, which always is called the ordinance of the Lord's Supper and never the sacrament of communion. It is observed, never celebrated and never holy, only in remembrance of the Last Supper and not commemorated, a testimony and not a memorial.

However, the preacher and his deacon were authorities on cakes and enjoyed the food much more than the wine. London accepted a second piece without any urging. "This is mighty good cake," he said. "Where did you buy it, Miss Roberts? I'd like to tell my daughter so she can get some."

"I baked it——"

"Don't you know the difference in homemade and store-bought cake?" Cliff demanded. "This here is a Lady Baltimore."

London was slightly flustered. "I knew it was homemade. But you can buy homemade cakes. Paige often does."

"Mr. Wingo is right." Forrest saw his embarrassment and came to his aid. "I happened to bake this one myself, though, and I'll be glad to give Paige the recipe." She picked up a crumb of the icing and tasted it. "And, by the way, she and Benton were by here earlier. She wanted me to go to the Eliot reading with her."

"I sort of figured you'd be there since you go in so heavy for that sort of stuff." Cliff's mouth was full of Lady Baltimore and he sipped his wine daintily, his little finger extended like a D.A.R. drinking tea.

Her sniffles were gone and her eyes were clearing. She fished in the plate for a crumb of the filling and was satisfied with its flavor. She had been afraid her Lady Baltimore might have been a little stale. "As a matter of fact," she said, pushing the plate nearer to Cliff, "I seldom attend such things. I have learned that the younger generation doesn't appreciate my generation when it comes to T. S. Eliot."

"Do you think it is a fad?" London was interested immediately, very interested.

"Eliot a fad?" She was puzzled and looked at him frankly, frowning slightly. "Never. Henry Miller, perhaps. But not Eliot."

"I didn't mean Eliot himself as a fad." London was quick to explain his question. "I meant is the attraction he has for young people a fad. He is almost an idol to them."

"A pattern, I'd say, rather than a fad." She smiled and touched the lobe of her right ear, fingering it thoughtfully. "And I must add, Mr. Wingo, that as an idol for youth he is an improvement over the idols of our generation. Mencken and *Cap'n Billy's Whizz Bang*. I never discount youth's feel for expression. Eliot or bebop."

London Wingo looked at her closely and was impressed. He moved his chair a few inches closer to her divan and leaned forward intently. "Do you think it is significant? Is Eliot a prophet for youth?"

She shrugged her shoulders. "Who can say? Was Mencken a prophet for us?" She opened her hands in a wide gesture. "We rallied to Mencken in rebellion against the narrow, dreary orthodoxy of our parents and wound up in skepticism. A spiritual mess.

Young people today are demanding a simple spiritual diet. None of the raw meat that was stuffed down our throats, but none of the fluff that we thought was sweet and found bitter." She was speaking rapidly and with animation and then she stopped abruptly. "Oh, dear. I'm talking like a schoolteacher."

"You do think it is significant. I can tell the way you talk." London led her on.

"Yes, I do, Mr. Wingo." She crossed her legs and smoothed her dress. "I teach high school seniors and I dare think that young people are demanding the return of Christendom to Christianity. It is significant that a deeply religious man like Eliot is their modern prophet while their old prophets are Swedenborg and St. Francis——"

"Now, wait a minute, Forrest." There had been no avenue by which Cliff could enter the conversation, but now he had found a detour and he took it. "You know that us Baptists don't saint nobody."

Forrest's laughter was as relaxed as her bearing and as gay as the printed design on her spring dress. She patted Cliff's arm in obvious affection. "I know, I know. But I can't help sainting St. Francis."

"Neither can I," said London. "Matthew. Paul. All the Apostles I never saint. But Francis is different."

The cake was gone and she offered them more wine, and when they declined she put the stopper in the decanter and pushed the tray aside. "Cliff said on the telephone that you wanted to talk to me about the church."

"Oh yes." London felt for the copy of the covenant and took it from his coat pocket. "I'd like for you to read the covenant to the church at the meeting tomorrow night."

She accepted the paper and began reading it without her glasses, and Cliff jumped up and got them from the bookcase and handed them to her. "I don't need them. Thanks." She held the paper closer to the floor lamp. "I never use them except when I do a lot of reading." It took her only a minute or so to scan the covenant and then she returned it to her pastor. "I will be glad to read it, Mr. Wingo. And vote for it too."

Now here was the kind of member he liked. Ready without palaver or guile to give her talents to her church. "The covenant will be our first business," he said, and got up, thus indicating to Cliff that they should be on their way.

Forrest arose too. "Paige tells me you are writing a book on Roger Williams."

"Trying to. Not getting very far, very fast."

She walked toward the door with them, slipping her right foot tighter into her shoe. "I did my master's thesis on him. You are welcome to my notes."

"I will probably take you up on that," he said, and visibly was pleased. It was good to find someone with whom he could share his idol and again he looked at her closely. No, she was not as tall as he even in those high-heeled shoes. "Could it be that Roger Williams is your prophet?"

"One of them. Along with St. Francis and Voltaire and Jefferson and Paine——"

"Great day," he broke in. "How do you reconcile all that conglomeration?" They had reached the hallway.

She fingered the lobe of her ear again and met his look. "Mr. Wingo. Women don't think; they feel. Didn't you know that?"

"I used to know it," he said. "But I had forgotten."

She picked up Cliff's hat from the hall table and glanced around for London's, then asked, "Didn't you wear a hat?"

Cliff snorted, pulling his hat tight on his head. "He don't wear one. Trying to get young again." He held open the door for London and shook hands with Forrest, bidding her good night. "And you better get rid of that wool rug in yonder. That's what they told Aunt Millie. Don't you get sick or nothing now, Forrest. If you do, let me know."

She was standing in the doorway, smiling at them. "If I get sick, you are the one person I don't want to see—professionally."

"Don't talk that way," Cliff said emphatically, scolding her. "It ain't funny when you talk that way."

She patted his hand and nodded obedience to his orders. "All right. And good night, Cliff. Good night to you, Mr. Wingo."

"Good night, Miss Roberts," said London Wingo. "And thanks."

He missed the warmth of his hat as they walked under the maples to the curb and his automobile and, being the host, he opened the door for his friend. Cliff felt in his pockets, seeking gum, and then asked London to drop him off at the undertaking establishment. There might be a call and, besides, Cliff was out of gum. "Ain't she a cutter?" he said, jerking his head back toward Forrest's apartment house.

London manipulated the car slowly and not nearly as expertly as Paige. "I'll bet she is a good teacher."

"The best." Cliff struck his knee with his fist. "Best in town. Take the next right, London. She came over from around Sedalia. Watch it along here. Sort of rough. I met her the first time she came to church, and that was the first Sunday she was in town. Right off the bat folks got to wondering why she never got married. Now, take the next left——"

He kept rattling on and London listened, missing not a word.

"Ain't no mystery to it." Cliff pressed the floor board as London swung around a corner. "Her daddy left 'em young. Flu. She went in debt to finish school and then she had a sick mother to take care of. By the time she got ever'thing squared away and her ducks in a row she'd turned thirty and was aiming her sights too high. Ol' Bent sort of shined up to her a few years back, but it didn't come to nothing. Now keep right on straight. My place is right down yonder."

London knew where it was. The old lawn trees were gone and the building with its white columns extended to the sidewalk. A blue neon sign proclaimed Carter's. Cliff was so well known that no further identification was necessary. London let him out and backed into the driveway and under the portico (called porte-cochere in Linden), then out again. It still was early and he drove leisurely through town, seeking landmarks that he and Kathie had known. Only a few were left.

He cut across the Wabash Railroad tracks and circled Linden

and came into Plymouth from another direction, driving slowly by
the church. On an impulse he stopped his car and walked back to
the church and swung open the heavy door, standing there a few
seconds in the gloom of evening. Then he stepped to the back pew
and sat down and stared toward the pulpit and the windows behind it.

London Wingo was lonely. There in his church with his God
he was lonely. After more than twenty years he still missed Kathie.
He lowered his head, resting it on his hands, and his hands on the
back of the pew in front of him, and he prayed; for guidance and
for his daughter, for his church, his brethren, and his country, then
for all mankind. "Grant us peace and brotherhood, and forgive
our sins."

He walked out and was lonely no more, and drove across to Elm
Street and down the thoroughfare slowly, looking at the houses
and the lights within, and the lawns of hedges and junipers. He
was almost past the big apartment house on the left and turned
quickly and looked back. He bet that was Elmscourt. He cut around
and drove by again and his lights caught the sign in the driveway.
Yes, it was Elmscourt. The sign announced it in proper square
letters. Under the sign was a smaller sign, just as proper:

HARRY WARD
Realtor

It was a nicer sign, a friendlier sign than the neon blaze at the
First Baptist Church and the bold announcement that H. Harrington Ward was its pastor. London smiled to himself and remembered something else about Harry Ward. He had led a campaign
in the Southern Baptist Convention against Baptist participation
in the Federal Council of Churches and had vigorously supported
a resolution to have the President of the United States recall his
personal observer from the Vatican. London had held that such
matters were for each church to decide as democratic cells within
the convention and had been roundly criticized. They had smirked
that he was a Landmark Baptist, branding him a reactionary in one
breath, a radical in the next.

He recalled it all, driving home down Elm Street. He must see the Wards soon. He must see Harry because they were fellow preachers, and he wanted to see Mrs. Ward for old times' sake. She had been Shelby Beaumont when he and Kathie knew her in Baylor University and then the seminary. She used to laugh a lot and play the piano, entertaining them with "The Sheik" and "Hindustan" when the professors and long-faces were not around.

His watch showed nine-twenty when he put the car in the garage. There was no light in their apartment and he had expected none. It was too early for Paige to be home. He went upstairs and switched on the hall light quickly because he hated the dark. The living-room radiator was hissing warmth, but the fireplace blaze was out and the dead ashes were gray and ugly. For an instant he debated whether to build another fire and have things cheerful and cozy for Paige when she got back. However, she would be tired and probably go straight to bed, and he was tired too.

He went to the kitchen and poured a glass of milk and looked around for some cake or cookies. He found some graham crackers and was standing at the kitchen table munching them when Paige opened the door to the hallway. The young man with her was Vance Andrews. London sensed it and then knew it. The boy had his father's restless eyes and straight, proud nose, but none of his father's confident bearing.

Paige introduced them and, tossing her coat on the back of a chair, went directly to her room and left them alone for a few minutes. London motioned toward a chair by the radiator, but Vance declined politely, explaining that he would stay only a minute or so. His hair was cut short and he wore a green shirt with no tie and a sports jacket. He looked to London like any of a thousand boys of his generation, and yet there was a suggestion of oppression in the thin lines of his lips and a haunting look in his eyes, the eyes of youth eternally seeking and never finding.

Vance rested his hands on the back of the chair where Paige's coat was. "I want to thank you personally, sir, for the stand you took for me years ago." His voice was as soft as a child's and his shyness was as evident as his loneliness.

"It was a matter of conscience," said London. "Your church stands for freedom of conscience." His voice, too, was soft, much softer than usual. There were many things he wanted to tell the boy then and there: hold up your chin, don't let them push you around.

"And I want you to know, Dr. Wingo——"

London stopped him. "Brother Wingo, Vance."

"Yes, sir." The lines of his mouth curved into a quick smile. "And I want you to know, Brother Wingo, that we are honored to have you as pastor of our church." He slipped his hands in his coat pockets, automatically squaring his shoulders, and they were broad, much broader than they had appeared at first. "If you need me, let me know."

"We'll need you," London said, and felt for his pipe and beat the bowl against the palm of his hand. "How are your studies coming along?"

Vance sat on the arm of the chair and dangled one foot and was relaxed, the little lines gone from around his mouth. "I am going back to seminary in September. I found Greek pretty rugged."

"Who doesn't? What about Hebrew?"

"I do pretty well with Hebrew."

"And Latin?"

"You think I should study Latin?"

"By all means," London said, and stepped to the table for his tobacco. "There are more religious works in Latin than any other language. You should study them. Not necessarily believe them, but know them. Of course"—his eyes twinkled at remembrance of his own youth—"the wiseacres will want to know if you are studying to be a priest or have been called to be a preacher. You know the answer to that one, don't you?" He filled his pipe bowl too full and some of the tobacco spilled on his trousers and he brushed it off.

Vance was smiling, already a different boy from the one who had entered only a few minutes before, a slight measure of difference, to be sure, but a measure, nevertheless. "I think I know the answer; that there are more good priests than good preachers because there are more priests."

"More bad ones by the same token." London struck a kitchen

match on the sole of his shoe and puffed away. "And remember one thing. Jesus wasn't out of character when he took that whip into the temple and established justice." Instinctively he was instructing the boy, charging him with the commission of his calling.

Vance nodded and stood up and was close to London Wingo. There are times when a man must stand, when a man must be close to his brother. This was a time, and Vance said, "Sometime this summer, if I am worthy, I want my church to license me to preach."

He was referring to the first ecclesiastical step toward his ordination into the Baptist ministry, for a Baptist church, a spiritual and political unity within itself, reserves the right to launch any candidate toward the highest office within reach of the Church, any neophyte toward his high commission, simply by voting it so; and ultimately to ordain him by the laying on of hands.

London touched the boy's arm, then gripped it. "We will present this matter to your church."

"And"—Vance said it slowly and distinctly—"if the brethren satisfy themselves that I have been called of God, will you participate in my ordination?"

"I will," said London Wingo.

It was a covenant between an older brother and a younger brother, a union between the younger brother and his God. Let Benton Andrews dare put it asunder.

Paige joined them, and Vance, after a few casual remarks about the unseasonable weather, bade them good night, shaking hands with London and bowing to his daughter.

"Thank you for bringing me home," she said, and accompanied him to the door.

London walked back into the kitchen to finish his milk, and Paige joined him after hanging up her coat and kicking off her shoes. She shook her head when he offered her milk. "Vance and I stopped for a chocolate malt. What do you think of him?"

"Perhaps you are a better judge of young men than I am. What is your verdict?"

She broke one of the graham crackers in half and nibbled it. "He's a Brain, Dad. A shy fellow. Afraid of his own father."

London changed the conversation deliberately. "Did you get the radio job?"

"Not yet." She ate the rest of the cracker and loosened the collar of her blouse. "It didn't come up. Mr. Andrews let me out at the Lyceum and I met Vance. He has his own car. Chevrolet convertible."

"How was the meeting?" He finished his milk and rinsed the glass and wiped his hands on the towel by the sink.

"All right. Better than I expected."

They walked into the living room and he poked the ashes in the fireplace, hoping for a spark, but there was none. "Was Mary Upjohn there?"

Paige laughed and stretched, holding the back of her hand over her mouth as she yawned. "Not Mary Upjohn, Dad. She wouldn't know the difference between T. S. Eliot and George Eliot. She'd think *Murder in the Cathedral* was a mystery." She didn't intend for that to sound as sarcastic as it did, as superior. Often she spoke phrases simply for the fun of turning smooth phrases, giving no thought to the meaning and to the possibility that her words might bruise the sensibilities of others.

Her father tilted his chin and undid his four-in-hand tie, slipping it from under his collar and tossing it across his shoulder. "Isn't it?" he asked innocently. "Isn't *Murder in the Cathedral* a mystery?"

"Why, no!" she protested. "It is a deeply religious story."

London put his pipe on the mantel and stood with his back to the fireplace and stretched, bending low and extending his arms up and out. "I see. Of course there are fools among men who think religion is a mystery; that *Murder on Golgotha* is a mystery story. Who was responsible, and why?"

His reproof, gentle and sly, was not lost on her, and she flushed quickly but did not continue the discussion. This was ground on which she dared not tread, knowing her father could be pushed so far and no farther. However, instead of renouncing or denying the satirical witness she had borne against Mary Upjohn, she changed her course nimbly. "Now what did you do after I left? Front and center, Reverend, and report."

"Cliff and I went by to see Miss Roberts. We got there right after you left."

"Isn't she a darling? Didn't I tell you?" Paige picked up her shoes and scooted them across the floor toward her room.

"She's a good church worker." It seemed a lame thing to say.

"And pretty, too," said Paige. "Didn't you think so?"

London raised the shades in the living room so the morning sun could get in. "Uh-huh. She's a nice-looking lady."

His daughter laughed at him. "I'll bet you didn't notice. What color are her eyes?"

"Oh-h-h, about like yours."

"Dad! My eyes are brown. Hers are gray."

"Well, she had hay fever and her eyes were kind of red and puffy. You know how mine get——"

"What color is her hair?" She challenged him again.

"I don't know, honey. Sort of like yours. Little longer."

Again she laughed at him. "Fine thing, I'll say. Fine thing. My hair is brown. Hers is deep red, almost auburn." She crossed the room in her stocking feet and kissed his cheek. "Good night, Dad. You may be a John the Baptist preaching in the wilderness, but you are no Powers' talent scout."

She turned from him and started for her room and he took a deep breath. "Cologne, huh?" All perfume was cologne to him. "Smells good."

"It's Blue Grass. Forrest Roberts gave me a squirt or two while I was there. Nice, but a little old for me."

She went into her room and then he heard her singing "My Foolish Heart." The faint scent of the perfume remained in the room and he turned out the lights and went to his own room, and was humming "The Third Man Theme."

Chapter 6

A small crowd was inside the church and a smaller crowd was waiting around the door when London and Paige drove up and parked about half a block away, directly behind Cliff's muddy Buick. It was almost eight o'clock, the hour for the meeting.

Vance Andrews took Mary Upjohn's arm and, unmindful of the stares, they walked away from the group at the door and out to meet the newcomers. Proudly Vance presented Mary to the minister and turned to Paige and welcomed her to Plymouth Baptist Church.

London had imagined how Mary Upjohn would look and that's the way she looked: an elfish face under a plain brown hat, a touch of powder on her smooth, pallid cheeks, and no lipstick or rouge. She held to her pastor's hand like a lost sailor to his tiller, a tender vine to an oak. "Call on me if I can be of service." Her words were precise and rehearsed, and she glanced from him to Paige, at the sheer nylon stockings, the trim pink coat, and on up to the perky little hat.

"I understand you play the piano." London walked beside her, and Vance and Paige preceded them.

"I'm not very good at it, Brother Wingo, but I'll do my best." She fell in step with him, and his stride was not as long as usual and hers was a bit longer. "It's not a good piano. Sister Ramsey lent it to us. Been in her basement for years. I dusted it and waxed it——"

"We will have to do the best we can." He was looking at the group on the church steps and saw Cliff and Forrest go inside, leaving Estes Oliphant and eight or ten others around the door to the vestibule and all of them staring at Paige as she and Vance walked along together, laughing.

"Someday we'll have an organ, won't we?" Mary's voice was so low and so mild that London had to strain to hear her.

He wanted to tell her to speak up, that if she intended to marry Vance Andrews and be a preacher's wife she had better get some iron in her backbone and learn to talk louder and not so much. She wasn't at all like her grandfather. Old Newt was hickory bark until the day he died, but Mary was like all the Upjohn women—calm without and burning within, and strong as coarse cotton thread woven into a pattern of obedience and subjugation.

"We'll have an organ someday," he assured her, and turned onto the walk to the church.

Vance stepped forth to meet him and to introduce him to the group, but Estes Oliphant took over. "Waiting for you," Estes said, and put his hand on London's shoulder. "Want you to meet some of the folks. Sister Ramsey, this is Brother Wingo."

London dared not look at his daughter, but accepted Sister Ramsey's hand and bowed. Lizzie Ramsey, he said to himself. She was a plump woman, almost squat, and her face was round and pleasant. Her lobes were pierced and she wore two exquisite jewels in her ears, and London was fascinated by the jewels. An expert, after long practice, of analyzing church members, he instinctively catalogued Lizzie Ramsey. Here was strength—and trouble, a strong ally and a stronger opponent.

"And this is Sister Bledsoe." Estes was enjoying himself. "Mighty fine folks. Baptists from 'way back."

Margaret Bledsoe, London remembered. And don't call her Maggie. Her neck was scrawny and her chin was pointed. She also wore earrings, but her lobes were not pierced and she imitated Mrs. Ramsey in offering her hand, extending it warmly, like a salesman greeting a customer.

The minister catalogued her as an echo to Mrs. Ramsey and said to them, "Paige told me about you. And that was mighty good food you sent us."

Leo Ramsey was not as London had supposed him to be. Not at all. London had assumed he would be a meek man inasmuch as his wife was a reservoir of strength. That was the way it usually went; strong woman, weak man. However, Mr. Ramsey was a man he could not put his finger on immediately. His handshake was warm enough and his voice was pleasant. He was about London's age, perhaps a few years older, and he carried himself with pride and dignity. "I am glad to know you, Dr. Wingo," he said. "We are honored to have you as our pastor."

At that instant Mary Upjohn stepped to the back of the crowd and took the hand of the man there and presented him. He was Champ Clark Upjohn and she introduced him proudly. "This is my father, Brother Wingo."

London would have known him anywhere. He looked like old Newt, just as tall and just as gaunt, his hands blunt and strong. Clark Upjohn grasped his pastor's hand. "Papa sure thought a lot of you," he said. "I remember you good. You married me and my wife."

"I remember," said London, and he did.

"If you need me, whistle." Clark Upjohn melted to the back of the group, and Estes introduced Sisler Mason.

No, he wasn't named for the great baseball player. He was too old. His hands were splotched and he was a rangy, stooped man, somber in his blue serge suit and heavy black shoes. His left eye was glazed by a cataract, but his right eye was lively and bright. "What Clark says goes for me double." Sisler Mason's handshake was limp. "If you need me, whistle."

Mr. Bledsoe introduced himself, not waiting for Estes to do the honors and thereby depriving him of a second of his minute of importance. "Just call me Buck," said Mr. Bledsoe in a booming voice, grasping the minister's hand and arm at the same time. "Buck Bledsoe. I'm in automobiles. See you drive a DeSoto. Pretty good car. But if you want a trade, look me up. Been a Baptist all my life. Deep water and bass voice. That's me, Preacher. Buck Bledsoe."

London liked him. This man he understood. Clark Upjohn and Sisler Mason too. Only Leo Ramsey baffled him, and he turned to Mr. Ramsey and probed for a cue. "What kind of business are you in?" he asked in a tone that suggested only casual interest.

"Barber."

"But he doesn't cut hair," Mrs. Ramsey broke in. "He owns two shops."

"Cut hair if business justifies it," said Mr. Ramsey loftily. He turned and took his wife's arm. "I think it's time we got started. Eight o'clock means eight o'clock."

He and Mrs. Ramsey led the group into the church and Paige dropped back and walked with her father. Vance and Mary went in together and sat together, the only ones in their pew. Paige went straight to the pew where Forrest Roberts was sitting and nodded for her to move down. Forrest slid along the pew and Paige sat beside her, and London beside his daughter. Forrest's hay fever had cleared up and she leaned over and greeted him in a whisper. She was not one to talk above a whisper in church.

London's eyes swept the church and expertly he estimated the crowd at fifty-five or sixty and, quickly and unnoticed, he nodded to Cliff that the meeting should be under way. The chairman of the Board of Deacons stepped to the fore, directly under the pulpit, and faced the members. He must act as moderator until a permanent organization was voted and he was a happy man in this chore, his eyes brimming tears that he kept wiping away with the back of his hand.

"We'll open the meeting with prayer," he said. "Ever'body stand and repeat the Lord's Prayer."

Some of the voices were clear. Others were whispers and others were mumbles. Some said "forgive us our debts" and others said "forgive us our trespasses," but the meaning was the same. A feeling of serenity, of spiritual peace, came to London in this, the first step in an organization for fellowship between God and man. It was so simple and quiet, the Plain People together and asking direction of the Holy Spirit.

Cliff rubbed his hands and was slightly nervous. "Now we'll open the door of the church for any new members," he said. That was proper. London Wingo had been elected pastor of Plymouth Church, but he could not be a member until he was voted into full fellowship. "If anyone here desires to unite with us in full fellowship"—Cliff did not look at London—"then let him or her come forward and thus testify to his intent."

London touched Paige's arm and they walked together down to the front of the church and shook Cliff's hand and stepped back and sat in the first pew. Cliff raised his voice. "There comes to us by letter from the Immanuel Baptist Church of Kansas City Brother London Wingo and Sister Paige Wingo. All in favor of receiving them into full fellowship of this church let it be known by holding up the right hand."

The vote was unanimous. Nevertheless, Cliff said, "All opposed by the same sign." He waited a second, then shook hands again with the new members. "Brother and Sister Wingo"—he was speaking for the church—"we welcome you."

London and Paige returned to their seats beside Forrest Roberts, and the business meeting really got under way with Cliff explaining the purpose of the gathering. This was the people's business, not the pastor's, and in this hour London Wingo was only one vote and one voice.

"First order of business," Cliff said, "is election of permanent moderator. Any nominations?"

There was the inevitable silence, and London leaned back and watched the proceedings, intent (but not visibly so) on how the factions would shape up. He knew there would be factions. There always were, and usually in three groups: the liberals, the conservatives, and the independents, although they often were called the modernists, the fundamentalists, and the wishy-washers.

This was the interval for church politics, the polite or bitter skirmishes, the jockeying and the compromises. It used to bother London, but he had learned that organizational politics was a part of church progress from Rome to Salt Lake City, by way of Mecca. The word politics no longer shocked him, only the connotation of the word.

Cliff Carter gave the impression of a novice in this field, and for a minute London was worried, fearing the opposition—and there was always opposition—might take control here and now and set up its own committees and dominate procedure. If Cliff were wise, he would never allow himself to be elected permanent moderator and thereby remove his voice from the floor and the probable debates. If he were bold or highhanded, he would maneuver the speaker for the opposition into the chair and thus tie his hands.

However, if he were skilled in the ways of Baptists, he had his own organization and through it would seat an independent and thus give everybody an opportunity for expression. That was exactly what happened, much to London's relief and gratitude.

Clark Upjohn, clumsy and embarrassed, nominated Sisler Mason for permanent moderator. London made a quick mental note of it and Paige nudged him, for she, too, understood the maneuver and its meaning; that Upjohn was a Carter supporter (and therefore a Wingo man) and that Mason was a neutral.

Forrest Roberts was on her feet immediately, seconding the nomination. Other seconds came rapidly from several members and almost simultaneously from Vance Andrews and Mary Upjohn.

But Mr. and Mrs. Ramsey and Mrs. Bledsoe did not second. They noticeably were silent, and London read the signal correctly. Well, there was the opposition leadership, and again Paige nudged her father. However, Estes Oliphant also was silent, and that puzzled London.

The motion to close the nominations brought a quick rap from Cliff, and they were closed. Mason was elected unanimously, but, nevertheless, the seconds to his nomination had given testimony to the division within the church; Cliff Carter on one side, Leo Ramsey on the other, and Sisler Mason in between. London wondered about the opposition. Was it against Cliff or him? Or was Ramsey simply a recalcitrant? And where did Estes Oliphant fit in? Perhaps Vance Andrews was the key, or his romance with Mary, a relative of Estes'. His opposition to the match was well known, and yet the colors of the picture did not blend, for Mary's father and Vance had voted together. London ran his fingers through his hair and turned it all over in his mind. His church was full of eddies. Well, the Lord willing, he must not allow the eddies to work together into a dangerous channel.

Sisler Mason, all dignity and reserve, stepped to the front and cocked his lively eye at the people. "The next order of business," he said peremptorily, "is the adoption of our covenant. Sister Roberts will read a draft of a covenant. Then anybody who wants to can have a say-so. Sister Roberts."

Paige crossed her legs and squeezed them against the pew and London stood up to let Forrest pass. She walked down and stood by the moderator, who shook her hand and then took a seat in the front pew alongside Cliff.

She slipped on her harlequin glasses, the supports through her hair and over her ears. London noticed then that her hair was auburn and that the glasses did not make her look any older. He wondered how old she was and had no idea because he was a poor judge of ages, particularly the ages of women. To him all mankind fell into three age groups: young people (such as Paige), then people of his own group, and then old people. Forrest Roberts belonged in his group. He guessed her age as thirty-two and was five years off. She was thirty-seven.

Quickly she unfolded the paper and raised her eyes to the people, commanding their attention before she began reading:

" 'Having been, as we trust, brought by divine grace to embrace the Lord Jesus as our personal Savior, we do now solemnly and joyfully covenant with one another . . .' "

Her voice had a teacherish quality of modulation, pauses for commas and long pauses for periods. Each word was well rounded and spoken distinctly. Paige smiled at her father, indicating her approval, and London relaxed and was confident the covenant was in capable hands. Leo Ramsey was staring up at the ceiling but taking in every word, and Estes Oliphant was leaning forward, weighing every word. Cliff was nodding his head slowly. The words seemed so beautiful to him.

" 'That, as we are the light of the world, and the salt of the earth, we will seek divine aid to enable us to deny ungodliness, and every worldly lust, and to walk circumspectly in the world, that we may win the souls of men:

" 'That we will cheerfully contribute of our property, according as God has prospered us, for the maintenance of a faithful and evangelical ministry among us, for the support of the poor, and to spread the gospel over the earth:

" 'That we will, in all conditions, even until death, strive to live to the glory of Him Who hath called us out of darkness into His marvelous light.

" 'Amen.' "

Cliff echoed the "Amen" and wiped his eyes. Mary Upjohn murmured, "Amen," and London whispered it.

Forrest removed her glasses and put them and the paper on the rostrum at the base of the pulpit and addressed first the moderator and then the congregation. "I desire," she said, "to speak for the covenant." She held her hands behind her back and smiled, inspiring confidence. "This is a general covenant and I think that is wise. It was written by our pastor, and he has had much experience in such matters." She bowed slightly to London. "I think as a tribute to his wisdom and experience we should adopt it as the broad basis for our work. Therefore, I move the adoption of the covenant."

She apparently expected no opposition. Neither did Cliff. There was nothing in the covenant that was controversial. London, however, had learned by bitter experience never to take anything for granted in a Baptist church. He felt a tingle of suspicion. Something was in the air, something brooding.

Leo Ramsey, of all persons, seconded Forrest's motion, and Paige stared at him and then glanced quickly at her father. The maneuver was apparent to London. Leo Ramsey wanted to get to the discussion, and the discussion was called for.

London's intuition warned him that if dispute were coming it would come soon, and then he saw it, saw it instantly because he was somehow expecting it: a quick exchange of glances between Estes Oliphant and Leo Ramsey, and then Estes was on his feet and was recognized.

"Brethren, let's take a look at this covenant." He spoke in a slow, disarming drawl, but London Wingo was not deceived. So there was the skirmisher, the sharpshooter. So Estes Oliphant was the scout for Leo Ramsey's forces. London touched Paige's arm and smiled. Her face, however, was taut. She, too, grasped the situation, and although the covenant was of no great importance to her, this was an affront to her father. And that was important. That man was daring to question something her father had done. Estes had spoken only a few words, including "brethren," and Paige was ready to spring on him.

"It's a beautiful covenant," Estes said, smiling at all of them. Here—here in his church—this man was no chain-store butcher. This man was adroit, and London was disturbed. More than that, he was worried. Cliff could not match persuasion with Estes Oliphant and Cliff was the logical spokesman for the covenant. London himself had hoped to avoid participation in any debate, but if he must speak, he would. This was the time and this was the place to drop the gauntlet or to pick it up, to settle forever whether he would lead or follow.

"Yes, sir, it's a beautiful covenant." Estes raised his hand as though blessing his words. "But, begging my pastor's pardon, it don't say much. Just pretty words. It don't go far enough." He took a deep breath and sighed as though he regretted the duty he must perform.

An expression of bewilderment was on Cliff's face, and Forrest was visibly confused, glancing quickly from Cliff to Clark Upjohn. They had not anticipated an attack on the covenant from this quarter and in this manner.

Estes realized their consternation and beamed at the congregation. "Now, ever'body who has been around here for long knows where I stand. I'm a Southern Baptist. Deep water and missionary. And this is a Southern Baptist church. I think our covenant should show where we stand."

Mrs. Ramsey and Mrs. Bledsoe nodded approval. Buck Bledsoe was looking straight ahead and scowling. He felt trouble coming, and Buck Bledsoe wasn't interested in covenants, only contracts. He didn't give a continental hooray about all this rigmarole but wanted only to live in peace in a world devoid of taxes and Democrats, and wives—perhaps.

Estes stepped to the rostrum and picked up the covenant and glanced at it. "It goes without saying——" He folded the paper and tapped it against his hand. "It goes without saying that Baptist doctrine holds for close communion. It ought to be in our covenant."

London Wingo was startled and baffled, then appalled. Estes was reaching back into antiquity to bring forth one of the oldest issues of Christendom, back to the ages of Anabaptist and the Particular Baptists, who, in some ways, were spiritual kinsmen but never brothers. And London wondered why. He had not heard the controversy of close communion or closed communion raised in a Baptist church since his boyhood.

"I hold with the old ways," Estes said. "Baptist doctrine is that Baptists don't participate in the Lord's Supper with any other denomination." He smiled the surety of his position. "That's pretty good close communion, but it still ain't bedrock. It goes without saying that bedrock Baptist doctrine is that one Baptist church does not participate in the Lord's Supper and fellowship even with another Baptist church." He stressed the point by pounding his right fist into his left hand. "Each church to itself. Each church its own master. That's close communion as I was raised on it. And it ought to be in our covenant."

London pressed his lips to hold back his protest, and Paige's chin trembled her indignation. Was this the reward for her father's leaving the security of his Kansas City pulpit? Good lord above! Close communion an issue in the middle of the twentieth century? Why not go back to the stake, the fagots—to infant baptism and Arianism and Socinianism and all the other doctrines that had plagued Christians for almost two centuries? They were baiting a trap for her father and she, too, wondered the purpose. Why didn't Cliff Carter speak out? Or Forrest Roberts? Where were her father's defenders?

"A point of order, Brother Moderator." It was Vance Andrews, his hand raised for recognition and the people craning their necks to see him.

Estes frowned at the interruption, but Sisler Mason nodded permission for the young man to make his point of order. Vance looked around the church slowly, right and then left, and his eyes lingered on Cliff and Forrest. London's perception penetrated the tactic instantly and he was impressed, then fascinated. Vance was holding the line to give Cliff's forces a chance to organize. H-m-m, London mused. "Wise as serpents, and harmless as doves." A prerequisite for preachers. Well, now—the young man showed promise.

"The subject before us," said Vance in an unhurried voice, "is adoption of a covenant and not Baptist doctrine. I point out to the brother that if all these things go without saying, then why say them? I also point out that close communion is not Baptist doctrine. It is Baptist tradition. We have many traditions." His tone was quiet and not especially forceful, but he was at ease on his feet, and his sincerity shone in his face. London watched him closely, his delivery, his inflections. Vance was serious, although an impish gleam came to his eyes. "One of our traditions was the silence of women in our churches——"

Mrs. Ramsey tossed her head and glared at him and then Mrs. Bledsoe tossed her head and glared also. Buck Bledsoe grinned and Leo Ramsey ran his tongue around the inside of his cheek.

"Another tradition was to pay the preacher in whisky. Or horses. A good team of horses and a barrel of rum could get a year's worth of preaching." There was a titter in the church, and Vance rested his hands on the pew in front of him and cut his eyes at Paige, a gesture that told her all was well.

So here was the champion of her father's cause. Here was the defender of the covenant. There suddenly was a warm glow within her, the joy of finding an ally where no ally was expected, the comfort of finding a friend among strangers.

"Perhaps we should include *those* traditions," said Vance, and sat down, and his hand touched Mary Upjohn's hand as though by accident, although it was intentional, and slowly she moved her hand and blushed. The blush could not hide the pride on her face.

Some of the confidence was out of Estes and he pounded his fist in his palm again. "All right. If Mr. Andrews wants to split hairs—

close communion is tradition and not doctrine. But I, for one, want it in the covenant."

Leo Ramsey cleared his throat and got slowly to his feet as though reluctant to say what must be said. "I'd like to hear from our pastor on the subject."

"So would I," said Mrs. Ramsey. "I must agree with my husband. I've heard Dr. Wingo preach several times. I'd like to hear his views now that he is pastor of *our* church."

Cliff and Vance leaped to their feet and so did Forrest Roberts. The Carter faction had united and now was rallying and shifting to the attack. There was no signal and yet they worked as a team—Cliff the leader, Forrest the lieutenant, and Vance the field captain.

The men deferred to Forrest, and her cheeks were flushed in indication of her exasperation, and her gray eyes were snapping. "The voice is the voice of Jacob"—she faced Estes Oliphant as she said it—"but the hand is the hand of Esau." She turned to the Ramseys. "What camel now is in the tent of Israel, what lamp under the bushel? Let us uncover the lamp and let the light be burning. Is it a Christian light? A Baptist light?" She lashed the questions at them. Her schoolroom demeanor was gone and she was tense, even agitated, and her eyes swept the group, seeking her opponents and indicting them.

Her behavior delighted Paige, but London was concerned. Forrest was a firebrand, and a firebrand often fans flames that otherwise would die out in due course. He still was probing all of his experience for an explanation to this turn of events.

Forrest stepped closer to the front pew and arched her arm in a wide gesture. "When this church—when a majority of this church voted to call Mr. Wingo as our pastor, we knew he was a man of liberal views."

She was offering him background to the dispute, informing him that his call had not been unanimous. He listened to every intonation of her words, hoping for a cue. His concern was gone and he felt the same warmth that Paige had felt, comfort in the knowledge that friends were near, that an honest man is never alone. However, he still was baffled by the subterfuge. He was ready to state his views on the issue: that he personally did not partake of the Lord's Supper with other denominations, although he would not deny the ordinance to any Christian. The idea that all Baptists should not share the blessing together was preposterous to him.

He was debating with himself whether to take the floor and rip aside the subterfuge and probe for the canker that well might afflict his ministry in Linden. He knew where to probe, but not which sore to seek. There might be a dozen, or any one of the countless problems that beset little churches. He must be sure. He must not probe for greed if the trouble was jealousy.

Forrest still was speaking, measuring each word and looking from one member to the next until her eyes met London's, and she held his attention and said, "I commend to all of us the words of Jesus in Mark 3:25: 'If a house be divided against itself, that house cannot stand.' " She waited a second, then added, "Jesus said it of the Kingdom of God. Lincoln said it of our nation. I, therefore, presume to say it of this church."

Instantly London caught it. And instantly he was annoyed at himself for not having caught it sooner.

Too long had he trod the pavement of Jerusalem. Too long had he been away from the ditches of Samaria. He had sought the answer in the lofty atmosphere of Baptist intellectualism while it lay at his feet in Baptist primitivism. His mind had moved from one high-level issue to another—Baptist participation of the Federal Council of Churches, the union of Northern and Southern Baptists, the educational and missionary programs. His eyes were on the clouds and he had overlooked the largest of the boulders along the path the Plymouth church must move.

"With all this in mind," Forrest was concluding her remarks, "I, too, will be pleased to hear from our pastor." She had flashed the warning and raised the guard rails, and now it was for him to proceed with caution.

She went back to her pew and sat beside Paige, and London felt all eyes turn upon him. He massaged his forehead like a man in deep thought, then slowly stood up as though uncertain whether to speak where he was or go to the rostrum and face the people. Paige knew he would take his stand in the fore of the church. She knew every gesture of his repertoire and every mood that every gesture indicated, and she glanced from Vance to Forrest, thus telling them to fear nothing, that her father was now in command.

A moment of hesitation, and London stepped from his pew and resolutely down the aisle to the rostrum. And there he faced them and was silent, knowing the power of silence. He rocked forward on the balls of his feet and back to his heels, just looking at them, the light touching the gray of his temples and his eyes compassionate, then burning and then soft again.

The effect was instantaneous. Estes Oliphant licked his lips and Leo Ramsey looked away. Mrs. Ramsey and Mrs. Bledsoe stared at their hands and Vance Andrews touched Mary's arm and leaned forward, watching a master and learning.

"It is good to be back home," London began. His voice was easy and rippling, life water over shallow rocks, but moving steadily toward deeper rocks and deeper water. He looked directly at Mr. and Mrs. Ramsey until they were compelled to return his gaze and then he said, "It is always a happy occasion to see husband and wife in agreement." His smile took some of the edge off his words.

Cliff was beaming, nodding approval to every word as he, too, looked at the people as though reminding them, "Told you so—told you never to crowd London Wingo—now fish or cut bait."

Estes Oliphant shifted uneasily and London moved nearer to him. "This is the first time since my boyhood that I've heard Baptists argue over close communion." He stepped directly in front of Estes, there in the first pew, and leaned over and put his hand on his opponent's shoulder. "Deep water and bass voice." It was the gesture of a camp-meeting preacher, and he was a world away from the striped trousers and black tie of his Kansas City pulpit. "Baptist from 'way back." His tone was intimate, for he must separate Estes from the Ramseys, he must feed the grapes and honey of Canaan to the scout and return him to the enemy's camp; a foe into a brother.

"My grandmother was a close-communion Baptist." He backed to the rostrum and propped his hands on the platform. "She moved from Tennessee to Indian territory. In an ox wagon. Baptist from 'way back." Again he rocked slowly and his eyes were dancing. "She wore a linsey-woolsey dress and a brown bonnet and believed the world was coming to an end in 1893. That's the year Grover Cleveland was inaugurated for the second time and the Democrats took over. So maybe she was right." He cut his eyes over at Buck Bledsoe and hid his smile behind his hand, rubbing his hand over his mouth. Bledsoe must be brought into camp too. But that should be easy.

London paced a few steps as though contemplating his next words. Actually he was giving the congregation an opportunity to shift on the hard pews and scrape their feet and get as comfortable as possible. He waited until they were still and swept them with a glance, and his eyes darkened. "Those of you"—the words flicked—"those of you who really are interested in your pastor's views can find them in his record." Then he lowered his tone and dropped his challenge to them. "Or hear them in his sermons."

The room was so quiet he heard Sisler Mason's heavy breathing and the wind rustling the ivy against the windows. "And now, being a man in darkness"—his voice was gentle again and soothing—"I must ask some light on this problem. Has someone been intruding upon Baptist privacy to share the Lord's Supper with his Christian brethren? Has some heathen defiled our ark, the disbelievers our temple? Or have some of our Methodist friends, or Presbyterians, or Adventists sought a crumb at our feast? I doubt it. They have their own bounty."

He was smiling and disarming them all, even Paige, who knew him so well. "Could it be"—an expression of incongruity came to his face—"could it be that our Catholic neighbors have partaken of our grape juice and unleavened bread in remembrance of their Lord's Last Supper?" He was chiding them as he set his stage. "A Catholic Christian in brotherly fellowship with a Baptist Christian? A miracle in Linden? For how far are scattered the tents of the hosts of our Lord? So what now threatens the sanctity of our tribe, our barricades on holy Jordan?"

He looked from one face to the next as though expecting someone to answer, but knowing full well that none would. He shrugged his shoulders and held out his hands. "Then I am in darkness, and a man in darkness must ask the way. Brother Upjohn!" he called to his deacon. "How many Negroes do you work in the shoe factory?"

A gasp swept the congregation, and Clark Upjohn answered in a clear voice. "About three hundred, Preacher. Moved up during the war."

"And do they have a church?"

"Yes, sir. Tabernacle Baptist Church. About twelve blocks from here."

Again the room was very still and London was silent, staring at them. This boulder must be removed from the path and buried so no jagged edge would remain to trip any who came this way. Slowly he turned to Estes. "And so, Brother Oliphant, the sons of Shem are threatened by the sons of Ham? The whites by the blacks?"

"Yeah." Estes was so agitated he forgot his manners. "I don't share supper with niggers in my home and I won't share the Lord's Supper with them in my church." He spat out the words as though relieved to be free of them, and then looked to the Ramseys for aid, but they were silent.

The servant had revealed the designs of the master and now he was alone in the camp of the enemy. Mrs. Ramsey's face was flushed, but she was composed. Leo Ramsey was erect and unruffled, apparently not concerned with the whole sorry spectacle.

Cliff expected his preacher's wrath to descend upon them like the hordes of Sennacherib and he shuddered at the possible consequences. One bitter word, one bolt from Jeremiah might sunder the little church and bring all of Cliff's dreams crumbling at his feet. He mumbled a prayer that his friend would not scourge the Philistines or cleanse the temple with his whip of fury. "Make him turn the other cheek, Lord," he prayed. "Make him walk the second mile with them."

With the tip of his right shoe London Wingo traced a meaningless design on the floor while brooding silence spread over the church and hung heavy. Then the pastor raised his eyes to them, and there was no rancor in his voice. "The Negro again." He shook his head sadly. "The same old problem that is harassing Southern Baptists from Maryland to California. There are fifteen million Baptists in the United States and we are divided into tribes that will not march together—Northerners and Southerners, black and white——" He began smiling. "Freewill Baptists and Primitive Baptists, Duck River Baptists, General Six Principle Baptists, and Two-Seed-in-the-Spirit Predestination Baptists. Lord have mercy on us."

His levity eased the tension and again he moved closer to Estes Oliphant. "The race problem has threatened Christendom from the beginning. It touched Peter when he drew back from the Gentiles, but the Holy Spirit prevailed and he went forth and built upon a rock. It touched the Romans, and they drew back from the barbarians. The conquistadors and Puritans from the Indians. But once more the Holy Spirit triumphed. Today only the children of Ham remain in exile." He leaned over, and Estes drew back instinctively because he was expecting a rebuke, but instead London put his hand on the man's shoulder, comforting him and giving testimony to good will. "And now, Brother Oliphant, let's settle this issue in our church once and for all. I am glad you brought it to our attention."

Paige's surprise showed on her face. She had anticipated her father's wrath, only to witness his mercy. Cliff's mouth drooped in amazement. Was this his friend of no compromise, his champion who asked and gave no quarter? Was this London Wingo who had fought racism in a dozen Baptist conventions and a hundred Baptist associations? Yes, it was the same man—older, surely; wiser, perhaps.

He unfolded the covenant but did not look at it immediately. "Close communion is not the answer." A snap of authority was in his tone. "That would be like denying dessert to a dinner guest. The only way to prevent fellowship with a Negro or an Eskimo in this temple of brotherhood is to bar him from the door. Never let him in. It can be done in our covenant."

All the color drained from Forrest Robert's face, and Vance Andrews writhed inside of himself. Even Clark Upjohn was appalled, and Sisler Mason was staring at his pastor. A covenant with God that barred a soul? What mockery was this?

London tapped the covenant with his finger. "It can be done right here," he said. "Let us declare ourselves right at the beginning, let us tell our Lord where we stand." And slowly he read:

" 'Having been, as we trust, brought by divine grace to embrace the Lord Jesus Christ, and to give ourselves wholly to Him, we do now solemnly and joyfully covenant with each other——' "

He raised his eyes and fixed them on his people, and then on Estes Oliphant. " '—white man unto white man, to walk together in Him with brotherly love . . .' "

The words trailed off and again he looked at them and saw the horror on their faces as the echo of the pronouncement reverberated in the conscience of a church bounden to a Master of sacrifice and beholden to a God of brotherhood.

" '—white man unto white man . . .' "

London repeated it, tolling each word, and continued:

" 'That we will uphold the public worship of God for our white brethren. That we will seek divine aid to win white souls. That we will spread the gospel over the earth to white men——' " He hesitated only long enough for the effect to accumulate, then asked, "Will that meet your requirements, Brother Oliphant?"

Estes' jaw trembled and he looked around frantically for support, and none came; and he looked to his pastor for comfort, and there was none. "It don't sound right, Preacher," he mumbled, and his face twitched his misery.

"You mean it don't sound righteous!" Clark Upjohn spoke out.

London lifted his hand for silence and presented the covenant to Estes. "Then perhaps you can figure out a way." He turned his back to the man and walked to the foot of the pulpit and addressed the people. "We will sing."

The Broadman hymnal was on top of the pulpit and London could not reach it from the floor, so he stepped onto the rostrum and to the pulpit, and instantly the room was hushed. The pulpit was his fortress and there were his weapons, the Bible and the hymnal, and he lifted the hymnal.

"Number 269," he announced. "We will stand and sing Number 269. 'Higher Ground.' " He nodded to Mary Upjohn, and she slipped from her pew and went to the piano, and London said, "Sister Ramsey will lead us."

The woman's hands trembled as she gripped the hymnal and she breathed deeply to steady herself.

> "I'm pressing on the upward way,
> New heights I'm gaining every day——"

She tried to sing and she could not. The words choked her and the song floundered, and then, from a quiet corner where none had noticed him, came the clear, strong voice of Sisler Mason as he gathered up the faltering words and, keeping time with his arm, led them on, rejoicing.

> "Still praying as I onward bound,
> Lord, plant my feet on higher ground."

London's heart swelled with the music and was overflowing with gratitude, for there stood his choir leader, that stalwart old man whose arm swung above his head like a painter splashing colors on the ceiling of heaven, who lifted up the people for the chorus and sang it out:

> "Lord, lift me up and let me stand,
> By faith, on heaven's table land,
> A higher plane than I have found;
> Lord, plant my feet on higher ground."

The voices filled the room in a melody of hope and triumph, and all the verses were sung, even the third verse, which usually was neglected. Sisler Mason lowered his hands and spread them out like an umpire signaling a runner safe at home, and then led them into the closing notes as Cliff Carter called out, "Amen."

A new light was shining in the eyes of Estes Oliphant and he sat very still, holding tight to the covenant. Slowly he spoke, and clearly: "There ain't no way to do it, is there, Preacher? There ain't no way to duck around it."

"Not that I know of, Brother Oliphant."

Estes got to his feet and held the covenant high for all to see and handed it to his pastor. "It's as plain as day to me now, Preacher. Just as plain as day. It ain't like in my house a-tall because this is the Lord's house, ain't it, Preacher?"

"That depends on you, Brother Oliphant," said London Wingo, and stepped from the rostrum and walked up the aisle to his pew.

Mary Upjohn was weeping. Vance's head was bowed and Sisler Mason took out his handkerchief and wiped his good eye, and the mist went away and his eye was lively again.

The vote was called for and the covenant was adopted without dissent. The Ramseys dared not protest, and Mrs. Bledsoe had moved an inch away from Mrs. Ramsey and an inch nearer her husband.

Paige slipped her hand against her father's and pressed it, and then, forgetting for a moment where she was and who she was, Forrest Roberts leaned in front of the daughter and touched the preacher's arm. It was an impulsive gesture intended to express gratitude, but it also bespoke admiration.

Chapter 7

The Plymouth Baptist Church was organized that night without further dissension, and London formally accepted the commission as pastor and then, quickly and surely, arrayed his forces apparently without regard to cliques or his own feelings.

Sisler Mason was put in charge of the choir, which always was a latent incubator of trouble, particularly if dominated by women. Therefore, Mason was an excellent selection for three reasons: the choir leader was not a woman, he was not connected with any faction, and he could sing. The pastor thanked the Lord for such a break. Most preachers were not so lucky with choir leaders.

Leo Ramsey was made treasurer and Cliff Carter was elected financial secretary. Only Forrest, Paige, and Vance realized immediately the wisdom of London's maneuver. The treasurer didn't matter. Leo contributed one hundred and two dollars a year to the church, and Cliff's pledge was for twenty-six hundred dollars a year. Hence there was no question as to who would run the finances.

Casually, and for no obvious reason, the pastor pointed out that when the Women's Missionary Society got going and needed a leader Mrs. Elizabeth Ramsey would make a good one. And Mary Upjohn was the ideal member to head the young people's program. Lizzie Ramsey could not say she was slighted. However, the chances of one woman dominating the missionary society were remote indeed because women, as a rule, will not tolerate dictators. The missionary ladies inevitably would divide into factions or circles, each competing against the others, and that would help the church. London knew that competition, under the guise of progress, usually did more good than harm.

His forces were in command and the pastor pushed his selections rapidly. Clark Upjohn as chairman of the Executive Committee. Buck Bledsoe as chief usher—a job that fitted him perfectly, as it gave him a chance to meet the folks at the door and back-slap and be seen by all.

Then London asked for a Census Committee and appointed Leo Ramsey as moderator pro tem and took the floor himself to speak as a member and not as pastor.

"We should take a religious census as soon as possible," he said. "The woods around here"—the twinkle came to his eyes—"the woods around here are full of Baptists, and we ought to flush 'em."

It was a brush-arbor humor, and Buck Bledsoe chuckled and the others smiled. But not Paige. Such levity, such broad humor did not become her father and was beneath his dignity. Her cheeks tingled her own embarrassment and London saw it and quickly changed.

"Seriously," he said, "every Baptist in this community should be invited personally to our church. And I presume to suggest that Brother Oliphant is the logical man to head the Census Committee." He was opening the door for Estes to work with his pastor and at the same time was separating him from the Ramsey-Bledsoe axis.

"Brother Oliphant will need a lady to help him." London shoved his hands in his coat pockets and rocked. "Now as far as the pulpit is concerned, I think Sister Bledsoe is the member for this task. Of course Sister Ramsey would fit mighty well too. But she has the missionary society on her hands and I think it is unfair to put too much work on any one member just because she is willing. Therefore, I nominate Brother Oliphant and Sister Bledsoe as co-chairmen of our Census Committee."

The nominations were carried without discussion, and the alliance between the Ramseys and the Bledsoes was scuttled. There was a time in his youthful ministry when such tactics would have appalled London Wingo; a pastor maneuvering like a ward-heel politician. But he was older now and battle-scarred, and more realistic about his work. His calling was to advance the Kingdom of God, and the smoldering embers in his church must be scattered before they had a chance to be fanned into flames of rebellion and thus hamper the advance. If he must divide to conquer, then so be it. He had no personal feelings about the matter one way or another, neither joy nor regret. The road block must be stormed or outflanked, and he outflanked it.

Two more general officers remained to be chosen, the church clerk and the superintendent of Sunday school, and only two more active members were available for the posts—Vance Andrews and Forrest Roberts. London had planned it that way. He preferred Vance as clerk, an officer who, next to the chairman of the Board of Deacons, worked closest to the pastor. He wanted Vance by his side, to groom him and train him.

The young man was the most controversial figure in the congregation, and the office of clerk was the most uncontroversial position in the church. Hence it was logical to assume that the membership would retire the boy into the clerkship and thus, by compromise, avoid a crisis and at the same time not offend a brother by refusing him any office at all. And with Vance as clerk, the Sunday-school superintendency automatically would go to Forrest Roberts, although traditionally Baptist churches seldom favor women as general officers.

London Wingo was not concerned with precedent or tradition because he had work to do and would not be shackled by the past. His fences were mended and strengthened and he was ready to wind up the routine of organization and be about the harvest for his Master. Vance for clerk. Forrest for superintendent. It was all cut and dried in his mind as he resumed the post of moderator and called for nominations for clerk, looking straight at Cliff.

Paige was on her feet instantly, and London gasped his surprise. Never before had she spoken out in a general meeting, for the pastor's daughter should always be seen in church but seldom heard.

"Brother Moderator." Her words were clear and unhurried and

they all turned and looked at her, Vance Andrews looking steadily at her and Cliff Carter with trepidation.

"The moderator recognizes Sister——" London quickly was full inside of himself and his voice faltered. Sister Wingo? Sister Wingo, indeed. It was silly and formal. She was his daughter, the one person he loved above all others, and he smiled at her as though they were the only ones present. "What is it, Paige?"

"I nominate Miss Roberts for church clerk." She said it slowly, almost casually, and sat down, apparently oblivious that she had grated a gear in her father's program.

London was flustered for a second and wondered what she had in mind. Surely she was smart enough to know that some members would think he had coached her. Already he could hear the titters in the missionary society, the gossip at the Ramseys' dinner table. The preacher wanted Forrest Roberts as clerk. Well, now, I do know. She's pretty, ain't she? He's a widower, ain't he? Well, now, I do declare.

And the nomination meant more than that; it meant that only Vance Andrews was available for superintendent of the Sunday school, and any move to elect him to that position surely would precipitate a wrangle and thereby not only reunite the Ramseys and the Bledsoes, but would bring Estes Oliphant and the Upjohns over to their camp. Paige had acted most unwisely. That was as strong as London put it to himself, and he was annoyed at her. She must be reprimanded when they got home—well, lectured, anyway.

He glanced at Forrest and she was staring at the floor, and he wondered if she were embarrassed. The nomination into her pastor's coterie, into his confidence, and by his own daughter, had put her in an awkward position. Already she, too, could hear the titters. She's after him. He is her last chance.

There was nothing anybody could or would do about the predicament. Even Cliff dared not object, for an objection might be construed as a slap at Forrest. It was a delicate situation, calling for discretion and silence, and silence assured acceptance of Paige's proposal. She seemingly was not concerned by the dilemma, but looked over at Mary Upjohn and smiled.

The vote was taken and Forrest Roberts was church clerk and, without fuss or flurry, she walked to the front of the church, and Cliff handed her the notes he had been keeping and saw the faint blush high on her cheeks.

London saw it also and was almost angry at Paige, and debated with himself whether to postpone election of a superintendent until he could rally his cohorts and decide on a compromise candidate. However, a delay would be too obvious, an admission of indecision and weakness. So there was nothing to do but push on and hope for the best. His own daughter certainly had played the mischief with his plans. His lecture to her must be the sternest of her life. She had abused her prerogatives. He felt her watching him and his gaze wandered over the congregation, but he saw only her and the impish twinkle in her eyes, a twinkle that was part of her inheritance from him.

His eyes, he was thinking, but her mother's heart and mind. How like Kathie she was. He said it to himself as he announced to the assembly: "Nominations are in order for the office of superintendent of our Sunday school."

Again Paige was the first to her feet, and this time her father's ire was evident in his frown and in his tone as he recognized her.

"Brother Moderator." Her words still were calm and unhurried. "I nominate Vance Andrews."

Leo Ramsey's jaw clamped shut and Cliff writhed his premonition of trouble, and all the older people were shocked by her audacity. Vance Andrews to lead the Sunday school? A conscientious objector as a general officer of the church? Hold on, now. The son of the town's agnostic? A son of scandal, the rich boy who was turning Mary Upjohn against her own folks? The rich against the poor? They looked from one to the other, and at Vance scornfully and a long time at Clark Upjohn.

Suddenly, though, London Wingo was proud. That was his daughter out there in the forum of her elders, challenging for her ideas, arising to be counted. She was her mother all right, and yet he knew in this minute that she was more like him, for there he was in his rebellious youth, one hand ever out to the oppressed and a gauntlet in the other.

Paige held the floor, standing there until the whispers subsided, and she smiled assurance to Mary Upjohn and then Mary arose and Paige yielded to her.

"I second the nomination." Mary's voice came clear, but her chin was trembling and her hands were trembling. "And I want to speak to the church."

London was exalted as he motioned for her to come to the fore and face the people. This was youth serving notice, youth marching past the weary veterans in the army of the Lord, the recruits so long scorned by their canting elders as decadent and soft and shallow of faith.

Mary Upjohn was nervous and looked to Paige for comfort and Paige nodded encouragement, and then Mary glanced at Vance and moistened her lips and looked up at her pastor and over at Cliff and Forrest, but did not look at her father.

"The Sunday school belongs to us—to the young people." She fidgeted her hands and then put them behind her and was calmed by her own voice. "And we want a young leader." She wet her lips again.

"Besides"—her chin came up and it was trembling no longer— "Vance wants to be a preacher and we've got to help him. This is the church that's going to send him out into the fields wherever they are. He is one of ours."

London's heart was singing his joy. It was his own youth speaking and youth never changes, never skirts the barricades, but storms them in the righteous boldness of no compromise on Calvary, no expediency at Golgotha, no doubts at Gethsemane. Let the fearful be heard and let the faithless whine their doubts. If there was to be a fight on this issue, then let it come, for London Wingo, graying at the temples, knew where he stood; over there by Vance Andrews and with youth.

He held up both hands, commanding silence and attention. "Is there another nomination?" There was a dare in his tone, the old gauntlet at their feet again.

All the faces turned to Clark Upjohn and slowly he arose and Mary put her hands over her face and Vance's lips were white. Only Paige was smiling and, seeing her, London smiled too. "Yes, Brother Upjohn. Have you a nomination?"

"No, sir," said Clark Upjohn. "I just aim to second the nomination of Brother Andrews."

He stood alone and apart from the others, a gaunt figure with bent shoulders, and he looked at his pastor and at the stained-glass windows behind the pulpit. "And I move that the nominations be closed."

It was his simple message of a forgotten truth, that there must be no discord in man's chorus to his God, no friction in the house of the Lord. This was the brotherhood, this the unwritten covenant.

A tear dropped from the eyes of Forrest Roberts and onto the paper where she was recording the first chapter in the history of Plymouth Baptist Church. Mary Upjohn lowered her hands from her face and her eyes were red but wondrous-filled. Cliff called it out. "Amen," he called it out, and London echoed it—"Amen."

The "ayes" of affirmation came loud and clear from Buck Bledsoe and Estes Oliphant. Leo Ramsey mumbled his vote and his wife was silent, but Margaret Bledsoe was heard distinctly.

London held out his hands and the babble subsided and he said, "God bless you. And now let us sing 'Blest Be the Tie That Binds.' "

They stood and sang it, Sisler Mason waving his arm in cadence as he led them into the symphony of the Plain People, of the believers. Some of the faces were uplifted and some were bowed, and there were many tears as they sang it.

> "Blest be the tie that binds
> Our hearts in Christian love . . ."

And then it was over and Forrest Roberts wrote down that the first meeting of Plymouth Baptist Church was closed with a prayer by the pastor—Dr. London Wingo. And then she looked at what she had written and marked out the word "Dr." and wrote it "Brother London Wingo." The paper—it was cheap paper—had crinkled slightly where her tears had dried.

The people, wiping their eyes and blowing their noses, walked to the rear of the church and congregated there in little groups, and in the vestibule, congratulating one another and feeling very good and noble and Christian-like. London joined them and they shook his hand; Estes Oliphant gripping his hand and even the Ramseys overflowing with fellowship and good will.

Paige tugged her father's sleeve and they stepped away from the babble and she said, "I am going downtown with Vance and Mary. For a soda or hamburger or something. All right?"

"Go ahead," he said. "But, young lady, don't you ever get me out on a limb again." He was not annoyed any more, only proud of her.

"You were not on a limb, Dad."

"How did I know you had lined up your dominoes?" He frowned slightly, indicating displeasure that he had not been consulted about it all.

"I hadn't lined up anything." She was wholly frank and guileless with him. "I saw a chance to get you a good clerk and a good superintendent and I took it."

He patted her shoulder and watched Cliff and Forrest and Estes in conference over by the door, and Buck Bledsoe and Vance Andrews laughing and talking together. "Well, don't worry about it. But if Brother Upjohn had balked we might have had some trouble."

"Don't *you* worry about it," she said, her eyes twinkling again. "Mary had to second my nomination. She couldn't let me champion Vance by myself. And Mr. Upjohn wouldn't go back on his own daughter. Would you?"

"No, I suppose not," he said, and although he was impressed by her perception and finesse, he was not as proud as he had been a few minutes before.

They joined the nearest group and the folks exchanged a few more pleasantries and then the crowd began thinning out. Cliff turned off the lights and London closed the door and they bade each other good night and London drove off alone.

The trees along the road home were bud-bursting and he drove slowly, smelling the spring and thinking of Kathie and if she ap-

proved of the way he was rearing their daughter. There was a parking place in front of the apartment and he took it and went in and
quickly turned on the lights.

He hated a dark house and empty rooms, and any room was empty
unless people were in it. He enjoyed solitude in the woods and on a
river, but rooms should have people. He was a bit hungry and
opened the refrigerator, but nothing tempted him and he closed it
and smiled to himself, wondering as men often do if the light in the
refrigerator really went off.

Two dirty glasses were in the sink and three plates, and he
washed them and rubbed them until they shone and put them away.
Then he decided to drive the car into the garage. It might rain
and goodness knew when he could afford a new one.

He had backed the DeSoto into the garage, almost scraping a
fender, and was walking to the front of the apartment house when
another automobile turned into the driveway and Benton Andrews
called to him.

London stepped over to the car and Benton greeted him and said,
"Saw your lights on. It's a little late to be visiting."

"Just got in from the church." London propped his arms on the
car door. "Won't you come in?"

"No, thanks. I was riding around and saw your lights still on."
He switched off the dashboard lights and sat in the darkness, his
cigarette glowing red. "Took in a movie and dropped by the Elks
Club and was just riding around."

The man was lonesome. London knew it. Well, he was lonesome
too. He walked around the car and opened the door and slid in beside Benton. "I can rustle a cup of coffee in a few minutes. How
about it?"

"No, thanks. You by yourself? Paige home?"

London felt for his pipe and remembered it was in the house, so
he accepted a cigarette from Bent and a light. "Paige is downtown
with Vance and Mary Upjohn. They left church together."

"Everything go all right at your meeting?"

"Uh-huh. Pretty good." London took the cigarette from his
mouth and examined it. One end was wet and the other was burn-

ing unevenly, but he put it back between his lips and puffed as a pipe smoker will. "We got organized. Had to finagle a little bit."

"Preachers have to finagle, too, huh?" Bent flipped his cigarette away and it burned a second on the grass and then was out, for the dew was heavy.

London began chuckling. "Finagle? Great day, Benton." The first name came easy. "That reminds me of an old friend. Dead now. Page Musselwhite——"

"So that's where Paige got her name——"

"That's right." London tried to flip his cigarette away as Bent had done, but it fell on the concrete drive only a few feet from the car. "Page Musselwhite was a great preacher. Never made a splash. Great man, though. And back when I started my ministry he told me something that shocked me; that a pastor needs the skill of a ward-heel politician and an old-world diplomat."

Benton laughed quickly and mirthlessly and slouched back in the seat. "Most preachers won't admit that."

"Not to the public, perhaps," London said, and stretched his feet against the floor board and was relaxed. "There can be no compromise on Christian principles, but we often have to compromise on procedure. That means maneuvering. Finagling."

Benton's hands slid around the wheel of the car and then dropped into his lap and he looked away, the trees dark and a few automobiles moving along Elm Street. "Have you told my son that?"

"Not yet, but I will. He was elected superintendent of Sunday school tonight."

"Is that good?"

"I think so. Naturally. It shows the church is behind him and it's mighty fine training for the ministry." He hesitated, debating the wisdom of his next statement, and then said it. "He has asked me to participate in his ordination service."

Benton jerked out of his slouch and looked closely at London, his face quickly flushing. "That's a sort of swearing in for preachers, isn't it?" A twinge of sarcasm was in his tone. "Taking the oath of office and all that."

"Not exactly," said London pleasantly.

His civility soothed Benton's raw nerves and the man was ashamed of his sarcasm. "Then what is it?" His interest was sincere and he was relaxed again. "My boy never discusses these things with me any more."

London raised the window a bit, as the night air was damp and penetrating. "It is a service in which Vance will be ordained into a full-fledged preacher. We will get a Big Name to preach his ordination sermon and we will charge him on the duties of his calling."

"What's this charge routine?" Benton grinned at his own question.

"You know," said London, opening his hands and holding them in front of him. "Like you charge a jury. Duties. Obligations. I will charge him in the public service after I have counseled him in a private meeting."

Again Benton grinned. "Secret? Password? The grip?"

"In a way." London raised his hands high above his head, stretching good. "I will counsel him on some very important matters——"

"Theology and all that, huh?" Benton said in good humor. "Nicene and Worms, I suppose. And a few spiritual and biological miracles."

"No. Oh no. Nothing as lofty as that. Just some good advice for any young preacher." London used his right thumb and the fingers of his left hand to count off the injunctions. "Watch the women. And money. Pay your debts and don't borrow. Never tell a smutty joke and never laugh at one. Bathe and shave every day. Don't try to be a good fellow or a back-slapper. And watch the women——"

"You said that twice."

"Uh-huh."

They laughed together and then Benton was serious, his gaze full on the minister as he asked, "Do you think Mary Upjohn will make a good wife for a preacher?"

"I don't know." London shook his head slowly. "A preacher's wife has a tougher job than a preacher."

They both were silent, Benton peering straight ahead and

London looking down at his hands and remembering Kathie. A minute dragged by and Benton Andrews said, "It looks like it's out of my hands."

"It looks that way," said London softly.

"Then do something for me, Mr. Wingo. If the boy is going to be a preacher, help him to be a good one."

London Wingo raised his head and looked over at the man, sharing with him the bonds of fatherhood and wishing to share the bonds of brotherhood. There was nothing to say and so he said nothing, but put his hand on Benton's arm, saying with a friendly touch and blessed silence what words could never say.

Then he accepted another cigarette and the cigarette lighter glowed red on their faces as Benton held it for him. "I thought Paige would be home by now," said London, fanning the smoke out the window.

"There's a smart girl." Benton lit his own cigarette and shoved the lighter back into the panel board. "I hear she is interested in radio."

It was an invitation to discuss his daughter as they had discussed Benton's son and London immediately was cautious, for that was Vance and this was Paige and he did not propose to reveal any of Paige's hopes or plans. "Oh, I don't know," he said casually. "I've heard her mention radio once or twice. She used to be a newspaper reporter."

"Yes, I know." Benton was as casual as London. "Some of the newspaper fellows downtown told me the radio bug has bitten her. That's one reason I drove by tonight. I'd like to talk to her."

"She'll be home pretty soon." London still was on guard. He always was on guard where Paige was concerned.

"You wouldn't mind her working for me, would you?"

The question surprised London and he turned quickly to Benton and peered at him. "Of course not. Besides, it's up to her. She's grown."

"My station has a fifteen-minute, six-day-a-week spot. Locally sponsored. Variety. Music. Interviews. She may be exactly what I'm looking for." He was enthusiastic and held the steering wheel and pulled himself upright. "You make my son into a good preacher and I'll make your daughter a radio personality. Fair swap, huh—London?" The first name did not come easy.

The preacher's laugh was quick and deep. "I will owe you boot. There's a lot of difference between singing 'My Foolish Heart' and worrying about foolish souls." His laughter broke out and his eyes twinkled. "You radio folks won't admit it, but there's quite a difference in soap, cigarettes, and salvation."

"Hucksters and hustlings—that's the difference." It was a low pun, but there was no sarcasm in it and Benton grinned as he said it. "Ask her to get in touch with me."

London rubbed his hand across his chin and shook his head. "I'd rather not. It would take some of the fun and surprise out of it."

"You're right." Benton nodded agreement and switched on the lights of his car. "I'm going to St. Louis tomorrow, but I'll contact her the day I get back. Saturday. Maybe Friday."

"I thought she'd be back by now." London opened the door and rested one foot on the driveway.

Benton turned on his panel lights and the clock glowed. It was eleven-twenty. "You know how time flies when you are young. They're probably discussing Swedenborg or T. S."

"I'll bet Paige is on her second hamburger," said London, and stepped out of the car. "Playing a juke box, too. Swedenborg is all right, but not if a juke box is around. I hope Vance has got plenty of nickels."

"He sort of likes Wayne King. How about Paige?"

"Too sweet for her. Me too."

"How about T. Dorsey?" Benton was grinning.

"Now you're eating penders, pard. Johnny Mercer is sharper, but I'm strictly a Crosby man myself."

"So am I." Benton flipped on the ignition and started his motor. "'Mexicali Rose' and 'Star Dust.'" He leaned across the seat and shook hands with London. "I enjoyed the talk."

"Same here." London stepped back from the curb and held up his hand, bidding Benton good night, and then turned and walked into the apartment house.

The hall light downstairs was dim and stingy and he hurried up the steps and into his own apartment where the lights were brighter. His hat was still on the table in the hallway and he picked it up and looked at it and then opened a closet door and put it back on a shelf, away back on the shelf and out of sight.

He left the hall lamp burning for Paige and went to his own room and undressed slowly and lined his shoes neatly beside his bed. He put on his pajamas, loud striped ones, and picked up a Bible from the lampstand and sat on his bed as he flipped the pages to the Psalms and read the first one that caught his eye:

"God is our refuge and strength, a very present help in trouble. Therefore will not we fear, though the earth be removed, and though the mountains be carried into the midst of the sea."

He read it all, exalting in the words and believing them, doubting nothing and asking not why or how. "He maketh wars to cease unto the end of the earth; He breaketh the bow, and cutteth the spear in sunder; he burneth the chariot in the fire.

"Be still, and know that I am God."

The Book was closed and put away and he turned out the light and slipped to his knees and buried his face in his hands. "Please, Lord. Help me to be worthy of Thy blessings. Grant us peace and brotherhood. And guide and guard her, please, Father. Watch over her. Please, Lord. Please."

He got into his bed and closed his eyes and there was no fear in London Wingo. "Be still——" He whispered it. "Be still and know that He is God."

Chapter 8

The apartment in Elmscourt was exactly what they wanted. London knew it at first glance and Paige knew it the minute she saw the two bathrooms, the deep closets, and the airy breakfast nook.

She was as gay as a chickadee as she flitted through the rooms, her imagination rampant with plans for curtains and drapes, and often she looked over her shoulder at her father to catch his nod of approval. She was wearing a gray skirt and a yellow cashmere sweater and her eyes danced the excitement of the occasion.

"You'll take the front bedroom, Dad." She put her hands on her hips and estimated the living room at twenty by sixteen. Just right for their rug. "It's the best room for you. Three windows. And your own bath. Good morning, Mr. Astorbilt. Hiya, Brother Rockefeller."

"Why don't you take the front bedroom?" London suggested. "You keep a lot of doodads and frills in your room and you need space."

She put her hand over his mouth and then mussed his hair. "No arguments, Rev. I am the woman of this house. Front bedroom for you. And the glassed-in sun parlor is perfect for your study."

London shook his head emphatically. "Oh-h no, sister. No sir-e-e bobtail! I'll fix up that study at the church. I won't have folks tromping through my home every time they want to see me about a wedding or a funeral. Or some brother crying in his beer that his wife doesn't understand him, that his boss is a fool and his creditors all crooks. Or some sister whining that her husband is a rascal and running around while she works her fingers to the bone, and all that self-pity bunk. Oh no! This is for us, honey. My study will be in the church."

"O.K.—O.K., Mr. Anthony." Paige shrugged and laughed. "Needn't preach a sermon about it. We'll make it into a little sitting room. Come on, I'll show you." She led the way to the front of the apartment and the sun room. "Pretty curtains at all the windows." She gesticulated and curved the motions to indicate curtains. "A potted plant right over there."

"Snake plant, I presume," said London, who hated the things.

"No. Begonias. Or a Christmas cactus. Or geraniums."

"They go in the kitchen. Your mother always had geraniums in the kitchen."

"Then it will be geraniums in the kitchen, Dad." She crossed the room and measured the windows with her hands and stepped back and surveyed it again. "The television set over there when we get a television set. We'll call this the music room. We'll put the radio in that corner."

London ran his fingers through his hair and smoothed it. "You don't get much music on radio any more. Just lectures on the medicinal advantages of tobacco."

"There will be music on my program," she said. "I am going to play 'The Third Man Theme' every day; just for you."

"Going to slight 'My Foolish Heart'?" London assumed a moonstruck expression and held out his hands and crooned:

> "The night is like a lovely tune,
> Beware, my foolish heart . . .'"

His daughter swayed, accentuating her motions, and put her hand on his shoulder like an old-fashioned photograph, and fluttered her eyes and lifted her face.

> "How white the ever constant moon,
> Beware, my foolish heart."

She clasped her hands over her heart as she sang and then her laughter choked the words. "Oh, I'll probably play it a lot on my program. But I'll need a theme song that's different. Something sweet that everybody will remember."

London rubbed his chin and looked down at her. "You seem pretty confident that you'll get that job." He was revealing nothing.

"I'll get a chance at it." She followed him into the living room. "You wait and see. I mentioned it to Vance last night."

"Oh-h-h?" London arched his eyebrows.

"He'll mention it to Mr. Andrews. He even suggested a name for the program. 'Paige Wingo's Scrapbook.' And a theme song. 'A garland of old-fashioned roses . . .'" She sang it and waltzed around the room as she sang. "'Sweetheart I bring to you.'"

Her father watched her, his eyes suddenly filling, and when she drifted by him he took out his handkerchief and flicked some of the dust from the window and it fell on the bare floor, new and highly polished.

"Remember that song, Dad?" She came close to him and curtsied. "Ever hear it before?"

"Uh-huh. That's one everybody will remember." He did not tell her it was one of Kathie's favorite songs.

But she knew it. By the look on his face she knew it and quickly she diverted the conversation back to the apartment. "Now you go right down and sign the lease," she instructed. "And wire them to hurry up our furniture."

"Looks like we've made a deal," he said. "I'll see about gas, lights, telephone, newspapers. Anything else?"

"Can't think of anything." She slid across the floor and was careful that her high heels did not mar it. "Smooth as glass," she said, and glanced around quickly. "I am ready to go when you are."

London hesitated a second and Paige knew something was on his mind and then he said, "I think we should call on the Wards while we are here. They live right around the hall. First apartment near the door."

Paige was not enthusiastic at all but tried not to betray her feelings. She had already pictured the Wards in her mind and didn't feel up to a session with them. Brother Ward would probably greet her with, "Well, well. So this is London's little girl. Looks just like her mother. Well, well." And Mrs. Ward probably would sermonize or whine or mouth platitudes and serve weak coffee. "Shouldn't they call on us first?" she asked.

"Maybe so, honey. But I won't stand on conventions with them." He grasped the knob to the hall door and was glad it was good brass and not dressy glass. "Your mother and I knew Shelby Ward in seminary. She was Shelby Beaumont then."

" 'Southwestern Baptist Theological Seminary of Seminary Hill, Fort Worth, Texas, Where the West Begins,' " quoted Paige, and smiled.

London, however, did not smile. As he grew older he was becoming sensitive about his school and its memories.

Paige quickly sensed his mood and knew his mind was made up, and knew not to cross him. "Of course we'll call on them, Dad. I just don't want them to think we are running after them."

"Shelby is not that kind, as I remember her. They probably were waiting for us to get settled before they called."

"Were she and Mother good friends?"

"Not specially." London opened the hall door. It opened easily and noiselessly and that pleased him. "They have three or four children."

"Four." Paige took one more look at the hallway closet and the full-length mirror on the door. "The oldest boy is in Wake Forest College in North Carolina. Mary Upjohn told me about him."

London's brow wrinkled a bit and he stroked his forehead. "That old, huh? I didn't realize they had one that old. But come to think of it, they've been married quite a while. Good lord. Twenty years. At least twenty years."

"She is older than he is. A lot older." She said it as though it were a common fact, beyond dispute and not news any more.

It didn't sound like Paige and a tiny frown of disapproval formed across the ridge of her father's nose. "Mary Upjohn tell you that too?"

THE HIGH CALLING 119

"Why, no." She was surprised at his annoyance. He *was* getting sensitive. "It's obvious. His first name is Harding and I assume he was named for President Harding. That was around 1920. You and Mother were in the seminary with Mrs. Ward in the early twenties. I didn't intend to be gossipy, Dad. I simply was making an observation."

"Your deductions are silly," he insisted, and still was irked by the level of the conversation and was determined to close it. "If Harry Ward was born while Harding was President he is scarcely thirty years old. His elder son must be eighteen or nineteen. Brother Ward is much older than that."

"Oh well, it's their business." She stepped from the apartment and into the corridor. "I don't think age has anything to do with love. It doesn't matter if she is old enough to be his mother—if they love each other."

London closed the door and they walked down the main hall of Elmscourt. "Shelby Beaumont was the prettiest girl in Baylor and in the seminary until your mother came along." He squared his shoulders and glanced in a mirror by the elevator and smoothed his hair.

It seemed farfetched to Paige that he should refer to Mrs. Ward as a girl. Anyone older than forty was old, except her father. They turned the corner of the corridor and into the lobby, which was ornamented with mirrors and modernistic lamps and an artificial fireplace. At Apartment No. 1 by the main entrance London pressed the bell and stepped back and rubbed his shoes across his trouser legs.

Shelby Ward answered the bell and Paige's eyes widened in surprise. There was nothing old or tacky about this preacher's wife. Her hair was snow white, but alive and still bluish-tinted from the morning's visit to a hairdresser. Her skin was smooth and the color was fresh on her cheeks.

For a second she looked at them and her face brightened and she held out her hand. "London! London Wingo!" She held out both hands and he took them and they stood there laughing.

"This is my daughter Paige," he said proudly. He was proud of Paige and proud for her to see a woman who had known Kathie and had known him in his youth.

Shelby Ward nodded graciously yet gave scant attention to the girl, but stood there beaming her delight and joy at seeing an old friend. "Come in. Do come in." She held the door wide. "I heard you were coming to look at an apartment and I would have been hurt if you hadn't dropped by. Harry went up to Moberly this morning. He will be sorry he missed you."

She led the way into the living room and motioned for London to take the big easy chair over by the piano. To Paige she said, "Now make yourself at home. And if we bore you with reminiscences, I'm sorry."

"You won't bore me," said Paige, and was more subdued than her father had seen her in a long time. She sat on the divan next to Shelby Ward and watched her without any indication that she was watching her at all.

London relaxed in the big chair and was grinning. "You and Harry wouldn't come by to see us, so we came to see you——"

"Stop it." Shelby held up her hand and interrupted him. "Come down off that high horse, London Wingo. You've been preaching too long to stand on such formalities." She doubled one leg under her and buttoned the bottom button of a long row down the front of her dress. "We knew you were busy and were waiting for things to quiet down."

"We are moving into Elmscourt as soon as our stuff arrives." He felt for his pipe and lit it and sank back in the chair.

Shelby put a pillow behind her back and relaxed too. "So Forrest Roberts told me. I saw her at the beauty parlor this morning. She says you got your church organized all right."

"Uh-huh. I'm just about set."

"How do they look?"

"Average."

"Estes Oliphant is wishy-washy." She tugged the collar of her dress a bit higher. "Buck Bledsoe is all right, but his wife is a pain in the neck. The Ramseys are lethal. Sisler Mason is a sweetheart.

And you know Cliff. The Upjohns are pure gold." It was preacher family talk.

"Most of them are poor in money and rich in spirit," said London. "How's Harry?"

"Fine. Be back tonight. He says you two have crossed paths but don't know each other very well."

"That's about it. But we're teamed here and I expect him to do most of the pulling until I get used to my harness. Now tell me about yourself and your children."

"Plenty of time for that." She crossed the room and pushed an ottoman near London's feet and turned to Paige really for the first time. "Coffee? Coke? Or Pepsi-Cola? You know, 'more bounce to the ounce.' Or, as my children say, 'more burps for the jerks.' "

Paige reached into her pocketbook for her cigarettes. It was a deliberate gesture to show her independence. However, she had no matches and Shelby handed her a package of matches from a table and put an ash tray beside her. "I'm a preacher's daughter too," she said.

"Do you smoke?" Paige asked.

"No. But when I was your age I rolled my stockings and that was almost as daring." She turned her face toward London and laughed. "Called it jelly roll. You remember?"

London held his pipe in his hand and his shoulders shook his mirth and his eyes twinkled. "Sure."

Shelby tossed her head and her laughter was merry and carefree. "There were two kinds of jelly rolls, Paige. Below the knee and above the knee. Now what'll you have to drink?"

"I'll split a Pepsi with you," said Paige, and she had thawed completely and was enjoying herself.

"Make mine a Coke," said London.

"Coming up," Shelby said. "Remember when we used to call it 'dope'?"

"Uh-huh. And nice girls didn't drink 'em."

"What did nice girls do?" Paige asked.

"Same thing they do today," Shelby said. "Wished they dared be bad girls."

She went into the dining room and thence through a swinging door and into the kitchen, and when she was beyond hearing Paige ground out her cigarette and looked across at her father. "Why, Dad, she's stunning."

"Same Shelby. She used to be what we called a ball of fire." A faraway stare came to his face and he looked out the window at the shrubbery spring-green and the traffic heavy on Elm Street. "She studied gospel music with your mother."

"Did Mother jelly-roll her stockings?"

"Uh-huh."

"Above or below the knee?"

"Sometimes one. Sometimes another. And she was the first girl in seminary who dared bob her hair."

"Did you know Mrs. Ward before you knew Mother, or afterwards?"

"Before. As a matter of fact, I think Shelby introduced me to your mother. That was in Baylor, before we transferred to the seminary."

"I never heard you mention her. I've heard many seminary stories, but I never heard you mention her."

London knocked the ashes out of his pipe and was amused by her questions. "Paige, I hadn't thought of Shelby Beaumont in twenty or twenty-five years until I happened to remember that she married Harry Ward."

Shelby came back into the room and passed around the drinks and took her seat on the divan. "Harry will be sorry he missed you," she repeated.

The ice in London's glass got in the way of his nose and he tinkled the ice with his finger to melt it. "Was Harry named for President Harding——"

"You too!" Shelby exclaimed, and her face flushed. "You should know better than that. Harry was named for his mother's people. He was in his teens by the time Warren Harding was President."

"I knew that." London was defending his question. "I figured he might have tacked the Harding on later. Good preacher name— Harding Harrington Ward."

She put her glass down on the floor by the edge of the divan and crossed her legs and leaned back, smiling at him. "You figured nothing of the kind, London Wingo. You've heard some of the idle gossip in this vicious little town; that I am a whole lot older than my husband."

Paige's face reddened high on her cheeks and she lowered her eyes, glancing over at her father and then down at her hands. London was sorry he had put her in such an embarrassing position. Not that Shelby knew, but that he had embarrassed her in his own eyes. It was a good lesson for her. However, he didn't like lessons taught in such a manner and it hurt him deeply to see Paige embarrassed.

"Some people in this town"—Shelby still was talking—"some of our own members use President Harding's time to reckon our ages. They figure and check back. Like they do when a bride gets pregnant." She was indignant and her eyes flashed her temper. "If the fools would ask me I would tell them the truth. I am four years older than my husband. And two years younger than you are, London Wingo."

London held his hands high in token of surrender. "Draw in your claws, Shelby. I am your ally."

"No man is a woman's ally when it comes to age. Isn't that so, Paige?"

"I don't know, Mrs. Ward." Her voice was low and much of the animation was gone.

"You'll learn."

Paige drained her glass and held it in her hands. "I don't think age makes much difference. It might be a good idea to catch them young and bring them up right." It was a silly thing to say, but she wanted the conversation back to levity and laughter.

Shelby Ward leaned over and put her hand on Paige's arm and smiled at her. There was nothing motherly in the smile, only friendly. "It makes a lot of difference, honey. Don't kid yourself. And I didn't marry Harry Ward to bring him up. I married him because he asked me, and I loved him. Just in case you hear some of our good Christian sisters wondering about it."

"Let's forget it," London suggested. "Makes me feel old. Shelby, you remember the time we cut classes and went to the fair in Dallas and saw a hootchy-kootchy show and got caught because one of our teachers was there?"

"Do I!" Shelby put her face in her hands and rocked in laughter. "The classes we cut were Christian ethics, pastoral behavior, and Old Testament logic. You spent all your money and Kathie had to lend you carfare home."

Paige looked up at the ceiling and tapped her fingers on the divan. "Did the hootchies wear their jelly rolls above or below their knees?"

"It wasn't stockings those girls were rolling," Shelby said in mock horror. "Fine thing for a young preacher to be doing." She clucked her tongue and shook her head at London.

They talked for thirty or forty minutes more, laughing and scraping their memories, and then it was time to go. It was almost noon and the Wards' younger children soon would be storming home from school. Shelby wanted them to have lunch and meet the children, but London declined. He knew she wasn't prepared for company. It made no difference about him, but Paige was another matter. So London bade his old friend good-by, shaking hands in the inevitable Baptist tradition.

Shelby saw them to the door and rested her hand on his arm as she glanced around for his hat. "Don't you wear a hat?"

"Not on pretty days like this. Now you and Harry drop around any time."

"We'll do that. And do you think your daughter would mind if I kissed you?"

"I think not," London said, and his eyes filled and there was a tug at his heart, for he was remembering Kathie again.

She kissed him on the cheek and held his hand tight. "I am glad you came back to Linden. I feel better because you are here. You are a good preacher, London Wingo. All that Kathie knew you would be." Then she slipped her arm around his daughter. "And you come by to see me often, Paige. Remember, I am a preacher's daughter and a preacher's wife. Don't let them suppress you around here just because you are who you are. A preacher's daughter has a right to laugh and live."

Paige thanked her and walked with her father out of Elmscourt and down the street to their car. They were almost to their car before either spoke, and Paige spoke first. "She doesn't act like a preacher's wife. She tries hard not to act like a preacher's wife."

"You don't know much about preachers' wives," London said. "Most folks don't. They are a special breed. They have to be."

They reached the DeSoto and he opened the door for her and she slipped into the driver's seat but didn't start the motor, only sitting there with her hands resting on the steering wheel. "Was Mother like her at all?"

"Not much. Your mother was never smart-alecky or brittle." He closed the door and rubbed his eyes. The sun glare made them smart. "I had a feeling that Shelby is a little bit bitter. Your mother never was." He turned that over in his mind, then added, "Well, not much, anyhow. She married a preacher. It was her life and she never complained."

"Some preachers' wives complain, though. I've heard them. Usually about money. And restrictions."

"I have an idea that bankers' wives complain about the same things. Now where do we eat lunch? Home?"

"There's a tearoom down the street. The Cuckoo Clock Tearoom."

"I don't like tearooms. You know that."

"This is a nice one." She started the motor and the car eased away.

"All right. I'm not very hungry, anyway."

The tearoom was crowded with chattering women and London felt out of place. He looked at the doilies on the table and fingered the thin paper napkins. Paige began reading the salad menu and London said, "Think I'll have a chop and some vegetables. Pork chop or veal."

"Now, Dad. You don't order chops in a tearoom."

"What do you order? Tea?"

"Get a salad. Chicken. Shrimp. Tuna fish." She was glancing around at the women, at their clothes particularly.

He grumbled and straightened the doily and smoothed the napkin in his lap. "All right. Tuna fish."

Paige was the only person in the world who could make him eat tuna fish. And on dainty plates on dainty doilies. He remembered all the chicken and dumplings and roasts and steaks he had refused at camp meetings and revivals, and he grunted.

The waitress recognized him and called him by name and that made him feel important and lightened his spirit. She had seen his picture in the paper before he arrived in Linden. "Well, now," he said. "I'll have some tuna fish. And sweet milk." He was expansive and pleasant, for recognition can perform wonders even with preachers. "No, make it coffee. I'll have some coffee. You ought to have good coffee in a tearoom."

The waitress smiled politely (she had heard it a thousand times) and hurried to the kitchen for their food. London watched her, then said, "Now there's a pretty little girl. Baptist girl, I'll bet——"

"No, Dad," Paige protested almost frantically. "Don't ask her. Not here."

"All right. All right. I won't disgrace you." He turned in his chair and surveyed the place and all the women looked alike to him; hats and pocketbooks and moving jaws and jabber. "Where's the cuckoo clock?"

Paige laid her pocketbook on the table so the women could see it. It was a beautiful pocketbook from Kansas City's most exclusive store and she wished they could see the label on the inside flap. "There is no cuckoo clock. That I know of."

"It's the Cuckoo Clock Tearoom," London insisted, and continued his survey and pushed his chair back a bit to get a better view.

Paige opened her pocketbook and looked in the little mirror. Now they could see the label. Her gestures were deliberate and graceful and she bit her lips to redden them and moved her head from side to side and touched up her hair with her fingers. "That doesn't mean anything." She closed the pocketbook and smiled at him. "They don't play polo in the Polo Grounds. There are no storks in the Stork Club."

"That's right," London said. "I never thought of that." He pulled his chair closer to the table when their food arrived and looked at the salad and up at the waitress. "You go to school?"

Paige began cringing inside and kept her eyes on her plate.

"Night school," the waitress said, and poured the coffee and rearranged the bowl of flowers on the table. "I'm taking a business course."

"What about Sunday school? Go to Sunday school?" London asked, and Paige felt a flush creeping over her face.

"No, sir." The waitress refilled their water glasses and moved the mayonnaise closer to Paige. "I work hard on Saturdays. Sunday is my sleeping day."

Paige looked up at her father, her eyes quickly twinkling, and London looked down at his food. "Oh, I see," he said, and began eating, and the tuna fish tasted exactly like tuna fish.

The conversation thereafter was meager and pointless and they finished their lunch and London tarried at the cashier's counter, waiting for the proprietor, while Paige went on out to the car. The proprietor apologized for the delay and snapped the five-dollar bill London gave him and rang up the sale.

"Thought you'd have a cuckoo clock in here," London said.

"Used to have," the man said, and propped on the counter. Few men came into the tearoom and he always was glad to see one. "Used to have one right over yonder on that wall. But it busted and can't nobody around here fix a cuckoo clock. Telling my wife just the other day that we ought to send it to St. Louis."

"I wouldn't worry about it." London put his change in his pocket and wished he dared ask for a toothpick but knew Paige would have a fit. "They don't play polo at the Polo Grounds."

The proprietor scratched behind his ear. "Say, that's right, ain't it? Names don't mean much any more. You know something——" He rang up another sale and watched the two women walk out. "I used to live down in Memphis. Worked for the Frisco Railroad. St. Louis-San Francisco Railroad. But it don't go nowhere around California. Winds up in Florida. No, sir. Names don't mean anything any more." He shook his head sadly, as though there was tragedy in it somewhere, and eyed London closely. "Haven't I seen you around?"

"I don't know. My name is Wingo. London Wingo."

"Oh, sure. Sure. You're preaching out at that new Baptist church. Out at the factory. My name's Everett, Brother Wingo. And I'm mighty glad to know you."

London took his hand in a grasp of manly friendship. "Be happy to have you come out and worship with us, Brother Everett."

"Well, now, I'll do that. I'm a Baptist. Letter still in Memphis, but I was telling my wife just the other day that we ought to send for it and get lined up again. Come back to see us, Brother Wingo. Bring the family."

London assured him he would and walked out, feeling much better. Paige was smiling when he joined her in the car and she started the motor and began working out of the parallel position. "You didn't go back in the kitchen and try to change that girl's Sunday sleeping, did you?"

"Of course not." He put his head out the window and looked back to be sure she didn't crush a fender. "But I met the fellow who runs it. Baptist."

"Dad!"

"Uh-huh. Name's Brother Everett. From Memphis and is going to send for his letter. Used to be a railroad man."

"I give up." She wheeled the car out and cut it straight. "A Baptist running a tearoom. A hamburger joint or a truckers' diner would make sense, but you find one in a tearoom." She stepped on the gas. "Let me get you home before you start beating the bushes for more Baptists."

"It's a nice place to eat." London leaned back and rubbed his hands together. "We'll have to eat there often. Handy, too."

The traffic on Elm Street was heavy with people returning to work from lunch and Paige drove cautiously, saying nothing as she gave all of her attention to the road and the car. There was a tight parking space in front of the apartment and she whipped into it and London got out and stood looking at the apartment, waiting for her to come around from the other side of the automobile.

"Pretty dreary place, isn't it?" he said when she joined him. "The trees are nice, though."

"I'll be glad to get out of it," she said.

They walked into the vestibule and he opened the little black mailbox and took out a handful of letters, mostly circulars, and sorted them. The one from Radio Station WLMO caught his eye and he held it up and looked at it. It was postmarked 9 A.M. of that day and was addressed to Paige. He passed it to her and she was surprised, even puzzled, but quickly she ripped it open and he saw her face light up.

Without comment she handed it to him and was beaming triumphantly.

It was from Benton Andrews, correctly typed on expensive engraved paper which proclaimed in sedate black script that WLMO was the Voice of Linden. It said:

DEAR PAIGE:
Vance told me this morning that you are interested in radio. I heard the same report from some of my newspaper friends.

I am leaving in a few minutes for St. Louis, but will return this week end. Therefore, if you will drop by my office Monday morning we will discuss this matter.

Sincerely,
BENTON ANDREWS

London folded the letter and gave it back to her and was smiling broadly, partly in pride, yet mostly because she was so pleased. "Well——" He tapped the other letters against his hand. "It looks like you were right. You're on your way."

"You don't seem too surprised," she said, and a trace of disappointment was in her tone.

"I'm tickled to death, honey, but not particularly surprised. Some of your confidence had rubbed off on me."

"I am going to call Vance right now. He'll want to know." She dashed up the stairs and her eyes were sparkling.

London glanced at the other letters and threw most of them away and followed her upstairs. She was on the telephone when he entered the apartment and he walked on into his own room and took off his tie and turned back his collar and rolled up his sleeves, then went into the bathroom and washed his face and hands, glubbling and snorting as he buried his face in water.

He was drying himself, rubbing his face briskly, and heard Paige come into his room and stepped in there to meet her, the towel over his shoulder and his hair moist and curly.

"I'm going downtown to meet Vance," she said. "O.K.?"

"Sure. Was he surprised?" London used the end of the towel to dry inside of his ears.

She shrugged her shoulders. "Not very." Then she kicked off her shoes and hugged him. "We want to have a sort of format ready when I talk to Mr. Andrews. Open with our theme song and fade into 'Missouri Waltz'——"

"No!" he said immediately.

"That's what Vance said. No 'Missouri Waltz.'" She walked the floor a few paces. "And I guess he's right. But I want some shopping news early in the program. Just chitchat. Then a five-minute interview. For example, Dad—Mr. Carter to talk about Linden in the old days. The city hall janitor. The oldest bootblack in town. You know, the little people."

He tossed the towel over the back of his bed and buttoned his shirt. "Better duck the little people," he advised. "If they really are little they are pretty drab. Besides, the term has been done to death. I've been dealing with American people a long time. You'd better stick to the old formula: music, chitchat, and interesting interviews. Mary Margaret McBride has the right formula."

"I want to be more like Faye Emerson," she said.

"Clothes and all?" He arched his eyebrows and grinned.

Paige slipped off her sweater and dropped it on his bed and looked down at her blouse. It was wrinkled. "Clothes are her trademark. They are what make women look at her and envy her and criticize her. I am going to work toward television, and the Emerson format is the one I like."

She went into her own room and closed the door and London rolled down his sleeves and buttoned his cuffs and was combing his hair when she came back in. She had changed quickly into a fresh blouse and a gray jacket to match her skirt and had on her gray suède pumps.

"You know," she said, and took over his mirror and worked his comb around the edges of her hair, fluffing it, "Vance could be a big wheel in radio. He's good. Do you need the car?" She had forgotten about the chores he must do—the apartment lease and lights and all those things.

"No. You take it, honey."

So she kissed him good-by and hurried out and he waited until he heard the front door close and then he picked up his comb and picked off the brown hairs and rolled them into a little ball and dropped it into his wastebasket. He picked up her sweater and shoes and took them to her room and then put on his tie and coat and went to a window and looked down at the street. The car was gone.

He walked out of the apartment house and along Elm Street toward town, walking slowly and enjoying the spring day, and he spoke to most of the people he passed although he did not know them. First he went to the realty company and signed a lease for the Elmscourt apartment. Then he sent a telegram to the transfer company requesting them to deliver his furniture as soon as possible. The lights and telephone were arranged for, and when it all was done he dropped by Cliff's place for a few pleasant words with his old friend, but Cliff was out on a funeral—a Methodist funeral.

Well, maybe he'd take in a movie. There were five theaters in Linden and he looked at the billboards on each of them and none was interesting. He was particular about movies and saw only six or eight a year, usually good Westerns. He wondered if *Winchester 73* had been to town. He'd heard that was a good one; almost as good as *Stagecoach*.

He wandered around town and stopped and got a shine. The shine boy was a Seventh-Day Adventist and the man next to him was a Lutheran.

A haberdasher's window of hats drew his attention and he paused to look at them. There were green ones and brown ones and some had gay little feathers in their bands, and he was just standing there, his hands in his pockets, when Forrest Roberts tapped him on the shoulder. "You thinking of taking up hats again?" she asked.

"Ma'am?" He was startled and then he smiled. "Oh, hello. Hello, Miss Roberts." He looked from her to the hats. "I like that brown one over yonder. The one with the leather buttons on the band."

She shook her head in protest. "That dark green one is the prettiest. The one with the little feather."

"That's a woodcock feather," London explained. "You don't see many of them any more. Used to be a lot of them when I was a boy, but you don't see many of them any more. How's your hay fever?"

"Clearing up. That's the only thing I have against spring. Hay fever."

They walked away together and down the street and he was careful to be on the outside, and they talked about the church, but not much, and about the lovely spring weather. Missouri has beautiful springs. Summers too hot. But beautiful springs. That's what Forrest said.

"What about a Coke or a dish of cream?" London suggested.

"I'd love it."

They went into a drugstore and he held open the door for her and she passed close to him and there was that faint scent of Blue Grass again. He tried to recall what kind of perfume Kathie had used, but could not remember. It was one of the few things about her that he had forgotten.

Chapter 9

It was Sunday morning in Linden and the church bells rang at regular intervals, first the Roman Catholics' for early Mass and then the Lutherans' and Episcopalians' for early communion. The nine-forty-five bell was the Assembly of God, over across the tracks, and at ten o'clock a concordat of bells pealed their invitations to Sunday school—the Methodists', the Baptists', the Christians', the Presbyterians', and the Latter-Day Saints'.

London Wingo was in his study, which was partly furnished in a makeshift arrangement, including a few chairs and a table. He saw and heard the children pass his study and go into the Sunday-school annex and he sat at the table and studied the notes for his sermon. It was a sunny, mild Sabbath, a blessed day for his first sermon in his new charge.

However, he wasn't satisfied with the subject he had chosen and the notes he had prepared. He had a score of sermons in reserve and really was not troubled, only annoyed at himself that at the last hour he hadn't made up his mind. He divided all of his sermons (and never called them messages) into four basic categories. First were the Think Sermons: theology, dogma, and other weighty subjects. These he sprinkled liberally with anecdotes to lighten them. Next were the Joys-and-Hopes: sweet, gentle sermons that he called the Fulton Oursler Specials, but only to himself and never in sarcasm, for Mr. Oursler's prestige was enormous among the Plain People and he had taken O. O. McIntyre's long-vacant pedestal as Oracle of the East.

Then came the Gloom-and-Doom category in which man's inherent evil was mirrored, particularly the cardinal sins of greed, gluttony, hate, and vanity. The last group were controversial sermons, ranging from Stalinism to statism and including racism, creeds, and all the problems that mankind scorns in public and practices in private. He called these the Volga Boatmen and for no reason at all except he called them the Volga Boatmen.

He had prepared a Volga Boatman for today and now he didn't like it at all. The sun was shining and the spring birds were singing, and his digestion was good and the breakfast eggs had been just right; so he didn't feel like dropping a rope over his shoulder and hauling a Volga Boat into the Plymouth Baptist Church, where the Missouri River was the only river that counted, anyway.

One paragraph in his notes caught his eye:

"Christian must not deny his brother the right of success, but never must he deny him the right of failure."

Maybe he could twist that a bit and dress it up and make something of it. Not today, though.

Another paragraph attracted him:

"A snob usually is the person who screams loudest that he is not a snob. Snobbery is the fraternity for failures."

Platitudes. Brittle platitudes. All bone and no meat. Well, something would come to him. Always had.

He was sitting at the table, fingering through his notebook, when Cliff came in, his face beaming the excitement of the morning and his four-in-hand tie neatly clasped to his shirt by a little golden arrow. "All set for your sermon?" Cliff rubbed his hands together briskly. "It's filling up out there. Folks pouring in."

London got up from the chair and sat on the edge of the table and dangled his leg. "As a matter of fact," he said, "I'm not sure of my sermon. Don't like the one I'd prepared."

"You ain't all set? And the folks pouring in?" Cliff Carter was alarmed. Everything must go all right. This was his church and this was his friend and everything must go all right. "The factory big shots will be out there. And Doc Wentworth. Dr. Blythe Wentworth."

"Who's he?"

"Baptist, but he ain't been to church in years, and if we work it right he'll line up with us. Doctor, too." Cliff yanked a chair close to the table and sat down and leaned forward. "Of course he's just a one-Cadillac doctor. But we need a doctor in our church."

London nodded his head slowly. "A doctor will give us some tone. Some class, huh?"

"You know what I mean." There was no diplomacy in Cliff, only truth as he understood the truth. "This is a mill church, and a town leader like Doc Wentworth would make us look mighty good. The Wentworths are upper-crust folks and he's got his whole family with him. Wife's name is Myra. She was a Leggett. I don't know the names of their two little girls, but his son's name is Sloan. Sloan Wentworth. Medical student and aims to throw in with his old man and practice right here in Linden."

London continued to nod his head, and his eyes were crinkling at the corners. "I won't preach on Christ, the Great Physician, if that's bothering you."

Cliff rested his hands on the table and looked imploringly at his pastor, and the lines high on his forehead indicated trepidation. "And for Lord's sake, don't get on your high horse and gallop off in all directions. And for Lord's sake, don't get on how we treat niggers. Or all the poor, hungry folks in the world. We know all that, but we are hungry too. Starving for a little sunshine. Give it to us straight, London. Give us some old-time gospel. For Lord's sake."

The mirth went out of the pastor's eyes and his eyes were serious and he looked down at his deacon and then out at the trees, new-green, and the sky clear blue, and the children walking from the annex back to the church for the services. "What is the old-time gospel, Cliff?" He said it softly and touched his friend's hand as he said it.

"Christ and Him crucified," Cliff said emphatically. "The love of God Who gave us His Son. His only begotten Son that whosoever believes on Him shall not perish." Tears flooded his eyes at the mere thought of it, the Promise, the Fulfillment, and the tears slipped out of his eyes and down the sides of his nose. "That's all there is, London. That's all we need to know and everything will be all right if we know that. It'll take care of everything. Just loving the Lord."

London Wingo closed his eyes and felt the gratification that comes to some men in the beauty of a truth, the rapture conceived in the hope of brotherhood and born in the testimony of friendship. He put his arm around his friend's shoulders and held him tight. "Pray for me, brother. Pray for all of us."

They got on their knees on each side of the chair and bowed their heads, and their heads were close together. They were silent for a minute, for two minutes, and then Cliff whispered his needs. "Lord, have mercy on us and forgive our sins. Bless London, Thy servant. Empower him with a great message. Direct us, God, to feed the hungry and share with the poor and to love one another."

A few seconds passed and London took it up. "Our Father, grant us the courage to change things that need changing, serenity to accept things we cannot change, and wisdom to know the difference. Amen."

They stood and neither looked at the other and the pastor walked to the door with his deacon. "Don't worry, Cliff."

"I won't." He reached for the doorknob.

"Benton Andrews doesn't happen to be out there, does he?"

"No, London. Not old Bent. I'll see you after preaching."

The door was closed and London walked back to the table and picked up his Bible and opened it to the New Testament. He wet the tip of his finger on his tongue and quickly, surely flipped the thin pages. St. John—The Acts—Romans. Then Romans 6—7—8, and there it was: "For I am persuaded, that neither death, nor life, nor angels, nor principalities . . ."

Nothing shall separate man from the love of God.

It was so clear to him, as clear as the sweet tone of the bell that tolled the eleventh hour, the hour of worship, and rolled its call through Plymouth community, to the factory and across the woods and fields, and the river.

The choir began singing and London listened, fingering the knot of his tie and brushing the lapels and shoulders of his coat.

"Be still, my soul: the Lord is on thy side . . ."

The song swelled and again his heart leaped in rapture. It was Sibelius' "Finlandia" and he was so pleased that Sisler Mason had chosen it to open the service, never knowing that Forrest Roberts had requested it as the first song of the first day in a new church because it was her favorite.

London opened the door from his study into the church, and entered the church and walked slowly up the three steps to the rostrum and over to the big chair behind the pulpit. There he stood and joined the singing:

"Be still, my soul: the waves and winds still know . . ."

Not all the congregation knew the song, as it was a little high-falutin for the Plain People. However, those who knew it bore down hard; some because they loved it and others because it was a chance to show that they were not the Plain People at all, but the elite and therefore different from their brethren, and better.

London raised his head and surveyed the congregation and they were not aware that they were being judged. He still was singing and his eyes seemed filled with the song, but they missed nothing. He estimated the crowd at three hundred. Perhaps two hundred of them were churchgoing Baptists. The others were there out of curiosity or to hear a new voice. It was easy to identify the Methodists and Presbyterians. They were on their best behavior and stood very erect and proper while the Baptists opened hymnals for them and pointed to the song. The Episcopalians were the easiest of all to spot. They obviously were out of place and they all knew the song and sang it in reserved dignity, almost a stern dignity, which was in sharp contrast to the raucous joy of the Plain People.

Paige and Forrest were sitting over near the Upjohns, and Vance was there too. In the same row with Clark Upjohn and between

Paige and Mary. Cliff was at the back of the church, watching everything; ready to raise a window or lower one, to sooth a crying baby or pass out a hymnal. Buck Bledsoe was with him and learning fast.

The family in the eighth row right would be the Wentworths. Dr. Blythe Wentworth had a tapering beard and looked learned and medical, rather like a doctor in a cigarette ad. London found himself wondering if the doctor would be surprised to know how many Christian sects once denounced beards and had forbidden them.

The song ended and London stepped to the pulpit and rested his hands on the edge of the pulpit and closed his eyes and led them in prayer. It was short and simple, thanksgiving and petition. He waited until they sat down and the shuffling ceased, until Cliff Carter had lowered one window and Buck Bledsoe had raised another, until the men in the congregation had crossed their feet and the women had looked around at the other women and wiggled their girdled bulks into all the comfort the hard pews offered, until noses were blown and throats cleared and the children admonished to silence.

Then he opened the big Bible on the pulpit, running his hand down the black ribbon marker. "Dearly beloved——"

It was his opening and it wasn't strange at all coming from London Wingo, neither strained. Even the children were still and watched him and understood what he said.

"One day the Apostle Paul was in the city of Corinth, in Greece, and he sat down and wrote a letter to some friends in the city of Rome. It was a long letter, the longest he ever wrote, and he was worried because he was afraid he would never have a chance to preach in Rome."

He rested his arms on the edge of the pulpit, but not on the Bible, and leaned forward and seemed to be close to them. They felt that he was close and they, too, leaned forward.

"This is the letter that changed Christianity from objective ethics to subjective religion——" He caught himself. That was too high-flown for the Plain People. "From a set of rules into a matter of faith. This is the letter that stresses salvation by faith rather than by works. Hence, salvation is a matter of what we believe rather than what we do. I will read a part of this letter."

His voice came strong and clear, each word caressed, and yet no bombast or magniloquence. " 'For I reckon that the sufferings of this present time are not worthy to be compared with the glory which shall be revealed in us.' "

The way it sounded, the sweetness of the promise, the comfort thereof—it was bread and wine to the hungry in spirit.

On and on he read Paul's letter to his friends in Rome, the message of a preacher proclaiming a new substance for everlasting life; the manna of faith and not action.

" 'Who shall separate us from the love of Christ? shall tribulation, or distress, or persecution, or famine, or nakedness, or peril, or sword? As it is written,

> " 'For thy sake we are killed all the day long;
> We are accounted as sheep for the slaughter.

" 'Nay, in all these things we are more than conquerors through him that loved us. For I am persuaded, that neither death, nor life, nor angels, nor principalities, nor powers, nor things present, nor things to come, nor height, nor depth, nor any other creature, shall be able to separate us from the love of God, which is in Christ Jesus our Lord.' "

The people were as still as the spirit that worked within them and then they sang again and Cliff and Buck took up the collection. Dr. Blythe Wentworth dropped a five-dollar bill into the plate, green and crisp and new as it lay on the black velvet of the plate. Clark Upjohn contributed fifty cents and it dropped noiselessly onto the black velvet and then rolled against the edge of the plate and rattled.

London's sermon was in the same mood as Paul's letter and not once did he lift his hand in a gesture, only leaning forward to be as close to them as possible. But his eyes were bright and his words were burning brands kindled in the embers of his faith and fanned by the ardor of his conviction.

"Man's first sin was vanity and greed disguised as knowledge. In his own vanity he assumed that he was superior to all other creatures and therefore created in the image of God. Actually in his vanity man dared create his God in his own image. There lay his evil."

He hesitated and lowered his eyes and looked at the children in the front row and then raised his eyes, facing them all. "Man was in debt to God and spiritually bankrupt and God redeemed the debt through the sacrifice of His own Son, manifesting Himself to man in the image of man; eating, sleeping, troubling, loving, dying.

"The Kingdom of God is at hand when we believe this. The foundation of the Divine Plan is faith, and out of faith the good works grow: love, charity, brotherhood, tolerance, sympathy, equality, and all the things the Christian must practice if his faith is sincere."

The sermon was only a few minutes long. There were things to be said and nothing to be added, and his first service in Plymouth Baptist Church was over before noon. They were singing again—"I Love to Tell the Story"—as he stepped from the rostrum and walked up the aisle and opened the doors.

Cliff was the first man out and he grasped London's hand and said, "On the beam, brother. Right on the beam."

They all filed out and Mrs. Ramsey was clinging to Mrs. Wentworth's arm and introducing her around. Dr. Blythe Wentworth gripped London's hand. "Mighty fine sermon, Dr. Wingo. Good diet. None of this social gospel nonsense. Just meat and potatoes."

The young people gravitated into groups and Sloan Wentworth joined Paige and Mary and Vance, and the older folks loitered a few minutes in the spring sunshine and then dispersed slowly, some for the post office and the morning mail, others to the newsstands for the St. Louis papers, and all eventually to their homes for big, hot Sunday dinners.

Paige and Mary came up to London at the same time and Mary spoke first. "It was a stirring message, Brother Wingo."

Paige squeezed his arm and it said more than all the others. "You mind being left alone for the afternoon?" she asked.

"I possibly can survive. What's up?" He glanced at his daughter's saucy hat and over at Mary's drab one.

"Vance and Sloan Wentworth—you met him——"

"Uh-huh."

"Well, he and Vance asked Mary and me to drive over to St. Louis." Paige brushed a kiss against his cheek and whispered, "I'll be home early. I want to be tip-top when I see Mr. Andrews tomorrow."

Mary tugged at her coat and fluffed the edges of her hair as Paige often did. "There is a good concert in St. Louis this afternoon." She said it almost apologetically.

"Good ball game, too," said London. "And maybe a good movie."

Mary Upjohn was shocked. Or was she? Anyway, she said, "Do you go to picture shows on Sunday, Brother Wingo?"

"I never have the time," he said, avoiding the question. He had never been to a Sunday movie in his life.

Vance called to them and the two girls walked away from London and Mary said, "I'd like to go by home and change clothes. I have a prettier dress than this."

Paige said, "You look all right."

"But I'd like to fix my hair. I ought to take better care of my hair like you do. Don't you think so?"

"Your hair looks fine. It's real pretty."

They joined Vance and Sloan and got into Vance's car and drove off. London watched them and then turned and saw that Cliff was watching them, too, a frown puckering the tight skin of his high forehead. "Well." London reached for the iron handle of the big door. "We might as well close up for the day."

"At least knock off for dinner," Cliff said. "Big day, brother. Big day. I'll stand you for a feed."

"O.K. if you'll bring me back here. I want to be in my study all afternoon. I'll probably have callers."

They left London's car parked in front of the church and got in Cliff's Buick and he stepped on it hard and they spurted away, and London braced his feet against the floor board. Cliff did most of the talking.

"Uh-huh. We're off to a good start. Lots of Harry Ward's members were with us. We had more than three hundred folks."

"How was the gate?" The pastor said it facetiously.

"Aw, now, London. You shouldn't talk that-a-way. The offering was seventy-odd dollars. I think we ought to start a building fund pretty soon. New church plant. Parsonage. Playground. Recreation rooms for Boy Scouts, Girl Scouts, and all them. Big kitchen. How's about that?"

London shrugged, indicating nothing. He disliked the expression "church plant." It sounded like a factory, an assembly line. However, he really was paying scant heed to Cliff's babbling, but was thinking of Paige and Mary and of how drab Mary looked alongside his daughter.

They reached the post office and went in and Cliff opened his box, one of the big boxes, and raked his mail into his left arm. He took it over to a glass-top writing table and dumped it there and began sorting it. London was interested. More than half the letters and journals were dumped into a wastebasket without being opened and Cliff flipped through them all, discarding many and saving a few.

London was thinking: I'll preach a sermon on waste someday. The waste of time and talent. How long will God tolerate the sin of waste in America? When will we pay for our cap and bells?

Cliff held up one of the letters and ripped off the end and read the page of printed figures. "Huh. Caskets going up again. Funeral grass, too." He stuffed the letter in his inside coat pocket and turned to his pastor. "You know we spend $700,000,000 a year to bury folks?"

"Is that a lot?" London was baffled by any figure over a million.

"Lot?" Cliff scratched his fringe of hair. "It's a whole lot more than we pay for hospital care. And no kidding. It costs more to die and get in the ground than to stay well and walk on it." He dropped several more letters into the basket. "You learn a lot about folks in my business. Now take cremation. That's the cheapest and best way to do it. But only educated folks and well-off folks will let you cremate their loved ones. The poorer the family, the more they pay out for funerals. Four hundred. Six hundred. Maybe a thousand. And the kids needing milk and the old woman a coat, but you can't tell 'em nothing. You can't advise folks about their dead, London. They get mad every time."

The minister was fascinated and a theme for another sermon came to his mind: We are closer to Egypt than to Jerusalem, closer to the pyramids and the graves of the Pharaohs than to the simple grave where lay the body of Jesus.

"Yes, sir." Cliff dropped a newspaper into the trash without glancing at it. "About sixty-five or seventy medical colleges turn out doctors every year, while twenty-five or thirty mortuary colleges turn out undertakers. Sort of nip and tuck, ain't it, brother?"

London laughed and then Cliff laughed and opened another letter. "I figured it was about time."

"*Time* or *Life?*" It was too good a pun for London to miss.

"*Life,*" said Cliff, and tapped the subscription card against his thumb, then held it up to the light and the light came through the little holes in the card. The holes infuriated Cliff Carter. "I don't mind being an income-tax number, but I don't like being a hole on a magazine's list."

London was getting hungry and wished his friend would get through with his mail, but Cliff was in no hurry. "Wrote 'em another letter last week."

"What now?"

"Aw, they had a big write-up and pictures about spring in the United States, but it was just New York and New England. I wrote and told 'em that spring is sort of general all over."

"No answer?"

"Naw. And they won't print it. Those folks never been out of New York, and you know as good as me that New Yorkers are the dumbest folks in the world. You know that."

London nodded rather than argue. There was no need to try to tell Cliff that New Yorkers knew as little about Missouri as Missourians knew about New York. The national appraisal of New York, both contempt and envy, was too high a barrier even for a preacher to climb, and besides, he was hungry.

Cliff passed up the best restaurant in town, the Linden Hotel, and drove him down to the Post Office Café. "Greek woman runs it," Cliff explained. "Widow. Her husband was a Baptist."

"But can she cook?" London asked, and was slightly annoyed. He did not have a denominational stomach.

"Sure she can. Needs the business, too." Cliff opened the door and led the way to a booth. The Greek widow of the Baptist was at home, thank goodness, and London Wingo could get on with the business of eating without further delay for introductions and palaver. He said a quick silent prayer of gratitude and reached for the menu. Cliff put two coins in the juke box and "Ghost Riders in the Sky" galloped into the Post Office Café and "Mule Train" was right behind them.

The steak was fair, but the French fries were terrible and the coffee worse. However, Cliff was bubbling enthusiasm, his teeth clicking between bites and his tongue releasing a chain reaction of words.

"Going out to see Doc Wentworth this afternoon." He took a big swallow of coffee. "Need Doc in the church." He chewed vigorously on a mouthful of steak. "Aim to hit while the iron's hot. Lizzie Ramsey will take care of Mrs. Wentworth. But that's the trouble. Might take care of her too much. Might overdo it. Got a good mind to sic Forrest Roberts on Mrs. Wentworth. She'll bring her around." He stopped abruptly and glared across the table at London. "You ain't paying a bit of attention to what I'm saying."

"Oh yes, I am." London pushed his coffee cup aside. He simply could not go the bitter brew. "But I've got a million things on my mind."

Cliff apparently relished his coffee and drained the cup and sighed his comfort. Then he picked up his fork and toyed with one of the limp French fries on the edge of his plate. He did not look up at his friend, but maneuvered the potato across the platter, through the ketchup, and to the brink of the plate. "Paige will make it all right in that job. You know that."

"I was thinking about Mary Upjohn," said London.

"Oh." Cliff worked the potato back across the same route, still not looking up. "She ain't got much gumption, has she? Much get-up-and-get. A preacher's wife needs gumption, don't she?"

"That's one way to put it."

The deacon was about as subtle as a meat cleaver, a chopping block. He crossed his knife and fork and folded his napkin. "She can't shine a-tall when she's around Paige. She looks like she came out of a mail-order catalogue and Paige out of a bandbox."

"Is it money or inclination?" London asked. "Or ignorance?"

Cliff dropped a fifty-cent tip on the table and stood up. "Some of all of it. Bent sees it and he's softened a lot toward Mary in the last few days. I met him in the coffee shop just before church and he was talking about it. He was wishing Mary had a little money to fix herself up and somebody to show her how. Maybe Forrest Roberts or somebody."

London sensed the conversation was moving toward Paige, and that he would not abide, so he detoured it. "Well, it will work itself out. Now, I'll have to get back to the church."

The subject was closed, or rather shelved, and Cliff paid the check and bought two packs of gum and they drove through town and on out to Plymouth. A dog had crawled under London's car and was sleeping and four or five children were playing around the church, running and shrieking and trampling the grass and shrubbery. Neither the pastor nor the deacon called them down. Cliff took off his hat and rubbed the top of his head and sighed. "I don't know of a better place for 'em to play than around the Lord's house. Do you?"

"No. And the grass will grow back. See you later."

He went into the study and closed the door and opened a window. Then he lit his pipe and stood by the window, staring out toward the Sunday-school annex. Yes, they needed a new annex, but the church must come first. The thing to do was to buy this church, not build a new one, but buy this one and install a baptistry and build a new annex; the same kind of stone and roof and ivy. He was sort of drowsy and wished he were home to take a nap. It was after two o'clock. Paige and the others were in St. Louis by now if Vance drove anything like as fast as she did. They probably were in a restaurant and Paige was ordering with confidence and composure. No indecision at all, no fuss and bother, but the proper soup, the best salad, the choice meat. And Mary Upjohn was trying to do as she did, the right fork, the right word—trying so hard to shine; an asteroid in the shadow of a star. London put it out of his mind and sat down at the table and began reading.

His first visitor was Estes Oliphant and he bustled in, exuding good will and lots of words and rubbing his hands together in approval of his own enthusiasm. "You were cooking with gas this morning, Preacher." He slapped his hands together and rubbed them briskly. "Hitting on all eight. We're on our way."

He and Mrs. Bledsoe already had begun the religious census and here was a list of sick Baptists for the pastor to visit. "We're beating the bushes," Estes said. "Flushing 'em like rabbits. We aim to fill this church house for you."

London thanked him and walked with him to the door and sent him on his way with a back slap and an encouraging word, bragging on him.

Two of the children came in. They wanted a drink of water and to go to the bathroom, but they couldn't find it, so London showed them over to the Sunday-school annex and watered them and pointed out the toilet.

The next visitor was Sisler Mason and his blue serge suit was shiny at the knees and his black shoes were glossy and spotless. The hairs grew long out of his nostrils and he sat very erect in his chair, his feet firmly on the floor. Yes, London assured him, the singing had been fine that morning, and now what's really on your mind, Brother Mason?

The choir leader ran his long, bony fingers around his collar and shifted in his chair. "I thought I'd use Mrs. Ramsey and Mrs. Bledsoe in the choir."

"You're the doctor," London said, and slipped on his glasses and looked down at the list that Estes had prepared. He knew a cautious man like Sisler Mason had thought the thing through.

"Think it'll work?" The choir leader folded his hands and leaned back.

"You're the doctor," London repeated. "The Bible says the lion and lamb shall lie down together."

"But it don't say nothing about two lions, does it, Preacher? Or two tigers?"

"Not that I recall." London folded his hands behind his head and leaned back too.

Sisler Mason was as serious as a diplomat should be. This was important to him. Next to his soul, his church was the most important thing in the world to him. "I don't aim to let 'em lie down together, Preacher. They're both sopranos. I'll use one for a month, then the other." His wise old eyes showed a spark and the spark was gone and his expression was placid and benign. Here sat good clay into living flesh.

London knew he was in the company of a strong man, of a humble man, and he felt good. "You'll handle it all right. I'm sure of that."

"Just one thing more." Sisler Mason lifted his long leg and clasped his hands around his knee. "I want you to know that Clark Upjohn is one of the best friends I ever had. And I love Mary Upjohn like she was my own. But she ain't much pianist."

"She's the best we have," said London.

"Ain't your daughter a pianist, Brother Wingo?"

The pastor did not answer him directly, for here again was thin ice. "Mary wants an organ. Maybe she will be better when we get an organ."

"She'll be married to that Andrews boy and long gone by the time we get an organ. But right now we ought to put our best foot forward at the piano, and there ain't no use of ducking behind a bush. She ain't got no spizzerinctum."

London took off his glasses and chewed the end of the plastic earpiece, looking up at the ceiling and then at his choir leader. "Want you to do me a favor, Brother Mason."

"Shoot."

The pastor laid his glasses on the table and rubbed his eyes. "Mary is our pianist."

"O.K." Sisler nodded agreement. "If that's the ticket."

"That's the ticket," London said. "And I want you to arrange for her to play a solo during the offering. Say every other Sunday."

"Solo?" A light of understanding came into Sisler's eyes and he peered over at his pastor.

"Solo," said London Wingo.

The choir leader lifted his lanky frame out of the chair and stuck out his hand to the minister. "It might work. With all the folks looking at her, it might do it." He smiled for the first time during his visit. "If she can't see that she needs to spruce up, then maybe her folks will see it. But she ain't no soloist, Preacher."

"I don't care if she plays chopsticks," said London.

"Me neither," said Sisler Mason. "If she just gets some spizzer-inctum."

They walked together to the door and shook hands again and then London was alone and sat at the table, tapping his glasses against his teeth and thinking of Mary Upjohn and how she watched Paige, and how Vance Andrews watched Paige too.

His daughter a preacher's wife? The thought stabbed through his mind and he closed his eyes and rubbed his forehead. "Lord help us, Kathie," he mumbled. "I don't know what to do now. I just don't know."

The knock at the door interrupted his thoughts and he looked up and through the window and recognized Harry Ward. He hadn't changed much. From that distance he could tell that Harry Ward hadn't changed much; a handsome man with wavy black hair and a pin-striped suit that was tailored faultlessly. Yes, he looked much younger than Shelby.

London greeted him affably, more affably than he felt, and Harry brushed into the room, glancing at the bare floor and walls and talking all the while.

"Just dropped by to pay my respects. Sorry I missed you the other day. You're looking good. I'm mighty busy but had to take a minute to drop by and see my old friend."

It was a trained voice, the emphasis on the right words and the flow steady. London indicated a chair and Harry sat down and kept on talking.

"Had a big day today. How about you? Mighty nice of you to drop by and see Shelby. Sorry you missed the offsprings. Shelby tells me that your daughter looks like Kathie. You getting settled?"

London said he was getting settled.

Harry crossed his legs and rubbed his hands briskly, as Estes Oliphant had done. "Let me know if you need anything. I'm president of the Ministerial Alliance this year. You'll join us, of course."

London did not commit himself. He didn't have to because Harry never slowed down for an answer. "Fine bunch in the Alliance. Most of us a little bit younger than you, but a fine bunch of hustlers. Why didn't you tell me you wanted to come back to Linden? Maybe we could have arranged a swap. You come back to the old church that you and Kathie built and I could have gone to Kansas City."

London Wingo was appalled and tried not to show it. It wasn't his old church any more, not the ark that God and the Plain People had built. It was a plant and not a church at all. He reached for his pipe but didn't light it. "Harry——" He was striving to conceal his disgust. "It's never wise for a man to go back to his first church or remember his first love too long."

"Aw, I was just kidding, London. Don't take things so seriously." He smiled when he said it and the smile told nothing, but it was a perfect smile, a thing rehearsed before a mirror. London thought of all the smiles he had seen in advertisements; tooth paste and lovers content with their sweethearts' soap and deodorant, idle men safe in the glory of pensions-through-plans—and this was the most perfect smile of all, security of soul and purse.

"You going to the convention this year?" London asked, and lit his pipe. It was the stock question of one Baptist preacher to another.

"Sure. I'm on the program. Going to tell them how to raise money for educational work."

That opened the way for preacher talk and they had something in common and made the most of it. Reminiscences about other preachers and where they were and how they were doing, who was dead and who had the big churches. The denomination's retirement fund for preachers, the insurance program came in for their share of discussion. Also the Southern Baptists' enormous expansion into the West, particularly California, and the controversies within the denomination, including social justice for Negroes, federal funds for church schools and hospitals, an American representative at the Vatican, and the Baptist movement in Russia.

And they did not agree. London Wingo opposed the status quo, whatever it was, and Harry Ward wanted things to stay as they were, or move slowly. "Aw, you're just like you always were." He held up his hands in surrender. "Same Wingo. Still preaching in the wilderness. Repentance and revolution. Where's your raiment of camel's hair and your leather girdle? Your locusts and wild honey?"

London laughed and shrugged it off and Harry changed the conversation abruptly, completely reversing his field. "Shelby and I were talking about it last night—the seminary gave you your D.D., didn't it?"

"That's right," said London, and nodded. "Strictly honorary."

"Goodness knows you deserved it," Harry said. "But where did you get your LL.D.? Shelby wasn't sure."

London explained that a denominational college had awarded him the honorary degree after he had helped raise an endowment. He wasn't at all proud of it, not any more.

Harry cocked his head to one side and smiled again. "You know——" He reached over and tapped London's knee. He might have been selling bonds or vacuum cleaners. "I'm up to my neck in money raising for schools. I ought to get a doctorate out of it. Huh?"

"Probably." London looked into the bowl of his pipe and could not look up at the man.

"A letter from you wouldn't hurt."

"I'll do what I can." London wished Harry Ward would go away.

But the pastor of the First Baptist Church had more to say and lost no time in getting to the point. "Have they picked a man for your place in Kansas City?"

"Not that I know of." London was cringing inside of himself. "I understand they are in no hurry."

"They thought a lot of you up there. And I'll make no bones about it. I'd like to have that church. Good plant. I could make it hum."

London restrained his tongue and his temper. "I cut all ties when I left Kansas City. Churches usually resent any pressure from former pastors."

"Not from you," Harry insisted, and turned on his smile again. "I don't want you to do anything unethical or un-Baptist. But I'd like a chance to preach a trial sermon for them. A word from you would do it." Again he tapped London's knee. "Pray about it, will you?"

London hoped his indignation did not show in his eyes or in the flush he felt creeping over his face. "All right. I'll do what I can." It was a promise without meaning, but anything to be rid of this man.

Harry got up to leave and tugged at his coat lapels and brushed his hand over his suit. "If you help me get to Kansas City I can work it so you can get my church. Then you can work a young preacher in out here. Say Vance Andrews. This little church is not the place for a man of your reputation. Think it over. Pray it through."

"I will," said London, and walked with him to the door and bade him good-by, then closed the door and stood there, feeling wretched and almost ill. Should he have rebuffed Harry Ward? Or scorned him? Nothing could have been gained by it. Let God judge and the people choose. Harry was one of a type and the type was rather rare, thank goodness. The barking fox in the vineyard, the fat worm in the wine. He understood why such men as Benton Andrews were skeptics and cynics. They saw and heard the Harry Wards, the power preachers, the drunken priests, the thieving rabbis—and they passed judgment on all the wine and all the vineyards.

The shadows were closing around the church and the children were gone and London Wingo was forlorn and lonely. The concert in St. Louis would be ending, if they went to a concert instead of a ball game or a movie. He wished for Cliff, for Sisler Mason—for anybody to warm his heart in the beauty of the brotherhood that Harry Ward had defiled. The room was depressing, the walls crowding in, and London jerked open the door and walked out and breathed deeply of the good clean air.

Then he got in his car and rode off without destination or purpose, just riding. Out beyond the factory and over country roads and the spring air tingled his face and turned nippy at twilight; the trees smelling good and the ground good too.

There was no service at the church that night and he was free and spring was for everybody, even a preacher with a trace of gray at his temples, a man who had remembered his first love too long.

He turned the car around and drove fast back to Plymouth and to the first drugstore he saw. Then into the telephone booth, where he dialed Forrest Roberts.

"This is London Wingo," he said.

"Why, yes, Mr. Wingo." She apparently was surprised, as her voice rose almost to a question.

"You told me you had some Roger Williams material." He must have an explanation for calling, a reason.

"Reams of it," she said, and laughed. "I was just looking over my notes. I thought I'd take them over to you in a few days."

He laughed, too, and propped his elbow against the booth. "Did you know that Roger Williams had hay fever? The vapors, they called it in those days."

"Oh no." There was surety in her tone. "They called it catarrh. The vapors and melancholia were the same." Her laughter came again. "And Brother Williams had melancholia all right. He was a Baptist preacher with the blues."

"Well, here's another one," said London impulsively, and then in the same breath. "Will you have supper with me?"

"Yes," she said, and without a moment's hesitation.

"I know a tearoom——"

"Tearoom!" she interrupted. "I know a place on the Moberly road where you can get steaks this thick. You know how thick I mean?"

"Sure. This thick." He was laughing between each word. "Run by a Baptist?"

"Is Cliff going with us——"

"No."

"Then this man's no Baptist. But he cooks like an angel——"

"I'll be there in fifteen minutes, Miss Roberts."

"I'll be ready in ten minutes, Mr. Wingo."

That was the night she called him London for the first time.

Chapter 10

The Wingos moved into their new apartment on a Thursday, and that was two days before Paige was to broadcast her first program over the Voice of Linden.

Cliff came out early to help London with the heavy work and Paige wrapped a towel around her head and assumed a woman's prerogative of direction, telling what went where and denying them the right of dispute or appeal from her commands.

They didn't mind. In fact, they enjoyed it; hauling and tugging furniture from one corner to the next, then shoving it somewhere else to please her whims. There was a satisfaction in taking orders from a woman in a home, a remembrance of things as they used to be.

Oh, they grunted and grumbled and exchanged trite remarks about the strange logic of the female mind, but they enjoyed it. "You know something," Cliff confided to London. "The first squabble me and my wife ever had was over moving furniture."

London said, "Kathie and I had fusses over the same thing."

Benton Andrews joined them and the minute he appeared Paige jerked off the towel and fixed her hair and he propped against the doorway into the living room and agreed with every order Paige made and offered a few suggestions of his own.

"Straw boss," Cliff grunted.

"Management stooge," said London.

Paige and Benton began talking about her job and she called him into the music room to rehearse her program again after apologizing for the dusty piano and the crated radio. London and Cliff exchanged glances and grins and got more done with Paige out of the way.

By noon the bedrooms were ready, except for Paige's final touches, and the rug was down in the living room. Benton and Paige went out for sandwiches, but London did not want to stop to eat. "The thundering herd will stampede this afternoon," he said, and plopped a floor lamp near the end of a couch, then stood back and studied it for effect.

"He means his members," Cliff explained to Benton. "That's the way he talks about folks who pay his salary." He didn't like the couch-lamp arrangement as London had it and moved the lamp to a corner. "The folks will be dropping by pretty soon."

"Oh, good heavens," said Paige. "Looks like they'd let us get settled." She trimmed the lettuce on a stack of sandwiches and handed one to Cliff and another to Benton.

"We'd better get the pictures up," London said. "Lizzie Ramsey will come breezing in with a dozen suggestions about the pictures if they are not up."

"Or if they are up," said Cliff, "she'll want to move them."

"I'll help," Benton volunteered, and washed down his sandwich with a swig of milk. "We don't want to be caught with our pictures down when Lizzie Ramsey arrives." He entered right into the spirit of things, laughing with them.

Cliff took two empty Coca-Cola bottles to the kitchen and called to Paige. "We better get a tablecloth or something on this table in here. Maggie Bledsoe will bring a cake. You can't put Maggie Bledsoe's cake on a bare table."

Benton caught a cloth that Paige tossed to him from a drawer and helped her spread it across the table. "I've never seen a pounding party. Heard about them all my life but never saw one."

"Neither have I," said Paige, and looked up as her father entered the room. "And I don't intend to see this one."

"Oh, they really don't pound preachers any more," London explained. "They used to drop by with a pound of this and a pound of that, but now they just drop by."

"And look you over," said Paige. She smoothed the cloth and brushed some excelsior from the kitchen cabinets into a wastebasket. "It's not for me. I'm going downtown. To the studio."

"More rehearsing?" London was rather hopeful she would remain at home that afternoon and meet the folks. However, he didn't insist. He never had and now he didn't know how.

Paige put the wastebasket away and quickly surveyed the kitchen. It would do. A box of utensils still was in the pantry, but the kitchen should meet the sisters' approval. Besides, it was none of their business how their pastor's kitchen looked. "Vance is going to help me go over my program again." Paige jerked off her apron and flung it across a towel rack by the sink. "I'll be back to help with supper."

"I think I'll stick around," Benton said. "If you fellows don't mind."

"We can use you," London replied. He had the feeling that Benton wanted to stay with them because he liked them and because he was lonely.

"We sure can," said Cliff as he came in from the dining room. "Take off your coat and earn your keep."

But Benton kept his coat on until Paige was gone and then he shed it and hung it carefully in a closet and gave a hand with the work.

With no woman present, they made a campaign of the job, a program, and automatically organized themselves into a team, moving systematically from one room to the next and getting much done with a minimum effort. London supervised by common consent and hummed snatches of "The Third Man Theme" and soon Benton and Cliff were humming, too, and they worked without comment or dissension.

The last rug was down and most of the pictures hung before the Upjohns arrived, the first of the members to come a-visiting. Mary had a bouquet of flowers and she put them in a bowl on the dining-room table and there was no grace in her arrangement; just flowers in a bowl.

Clark stood in the center of the living room and looked around, his hands in his hip pockets. "Plum' snazzy," he commented in an outburst of originality and enthusiasm. "As Bob Burns used to say—plum' snazzy. Mighty fancy diggings for a Baptist preacher."

"That's the music room up there in front," said Mary. "See the piano? That's the music room. Isn't it lovely?"

"Uh-huh." Clark Upjohn looked from London to the fireplace and then went over and leaned against the mantel. "I didn't bring you nothing, Brother Wingo. But you know what I aim to do?"

"What's that?" asked London.

"Send you a load of wood. Oak wood. Oak is the best burning wood there is, huh, Mr. Andrews?"

"Hickory is mighty good too," Benton said. "Come on, let me show you the music room." He acted as though he were a part of the whole thing and led them to the front room and then showed Clark the incinerator while Mary stood in the doorway to Paige's bathroom and stared at the wallpaper and the gay yellow curtains.

The Bledsoes arrived next. Mrs. Bledsoe had two cakes, an old-fashioned pound cake and a newfangled cake with stuffed dates and cherries on top. Cliff cut himself a sliver of the pound cake. "I know'd you was coming and that you'd bake a cake. You make the best pound cake in Missouri, Sister Bledsoe. Always did."

With that, she sliced a hunk of the cake and forced it upon him.

Buck Bledsoe had a sack of presents for the preacher, a pound of nails, a hammer, a pair of pliers, and a screw driver. "Look at this screw driver," he said, and held it up. "Ain't it a pistol? Look. You unscrew the top and inside is another screw driver." He demonstrated. "Then you unscrew the top of that one and there's another one inside. Five in one. Ain't that a pistol?"

London agreed that it was.

Estes Oliphant brought a box of groceries from Kroger's and a twelve-pound ham. Cliff sniffed the ham and took out his penknife and cut off a bit and tasted it. "Boone County ham. Best in the world. Folks make a big to-do about Virginia hams and Kentucky hams, but Missouri hams are the best in the world."

Mrs. Ramsey came wearing white gloves, and soon the apartment was filled with people drifting around aimlessly or gathering in little groups. Benton sensed the confusion and called London aside. "Oughtn't we feed them?"

"Sure. We got to feed them." He wished for Paige.

"Cliff and I will go for hamburgers. Or something." Benton had put his coat back on and kept tugging at his lapels. He was nervous in the presence of so many people. "And I'll get Mary Upjohn to make coffee."

It was then that Shelby Ward came in and London sighed his relief. She moved gracefully and expertly among the guests, organizing them into conversational groups, and Benton grinned at London. "Looks like the cavalry has arrived."

"And just as we were getting scalped," said Cliff. "Mrs. Ward can take over. She's an old hand at this sort of thing."

Shelby went into the kitchen and motioned for London. "Where's Paige?"

"At the radio station. Rehearsing." He said it almost abruptly. He didn't like the way Shelby had asked the question.

"Oh, I see." She peered into the coffee can and looked around for cups and saucers. Then she called Mary Upjohn. "If you are going to marry a preacher you'd better learn how to handle these things. Now get the women into that front room——"

"The music room?" asked Mary.

"I don't know what you call it," Shelby said. "But herd them in there. Get them to talking. Church. Clothes. Anything. Then come back here and help me."

London opened the refrigerator and took out the cream. "I'm grateful that you came in, Shelby. Things were getting out of hand."

"You knew I'd be here, London Wingo. And I expect you and Paige for supper. I thought Forrest Roberts would be here. I could use Forrest."

"She's still at school, I suppose."

"Oh yes. Of course." She snatched the apron from the towel rack. "Now you get the men in the living room and don't worry about a thing." Shelby patted his arm.

Soon everything was under control and Shelby and Mary served coffee and cake, lingering in the music room long enough to switch the conversation to missionary work. Then she served the men and put out ash trays and tarried with them long enough to get them all embroiled in conversations and discussions. Buck Bledsoe told a Truman joke that they had heard only once and Benton Andrews' reserve melted completely. He ate two pieces of Mrs. Bledsoe's pound cake.

At five o'clock, straight up and down five o'clock, Shelby Ward let it be known that it was five o'clock and time for her to be home to feed her children and fix supper for her husband. The folks took the hint and then took their leave, all of them shaking hands with London and wishing him joy and happiness in his new home, and most of them saying, "Remember us in your prayers, Preacher."

Clark Upjohn went out of his way to shake hands with Benton, and Benton went out of his way to shake hands with Mary and patted her shoulder as he bade her good-by. She was flattered and happy and turned to London. "I'm sorry I missed Paige."

"So am I," London said. "She's pretty busy, you know."

"Yes, I know. I wish I could do something like that. Being on the radio. But I'd be scared to death."

Shelby remained until all the guests had gone and then she and Cliff washed the cups and plates while Benton dried them and London put them away.

"Well, that's that," Shelby said, and whipped the apron over the towel rack and dried her hands thoroughly. "I'll expect you for supper at six-thirty, London."

"I am sure Paige will be home by then," he said.

Shelby Ward put her hands on her hips and tilted her head. "You call her, London Wingo. Call her and inform her that supper will be at six-thirty."

Cliff and Benton exchanged quick glances and Shelby cut a slice from each of Mrs. Bledsoe's cakes. "My husband likes cake," she said.

The three men saw her to the door and then they sat down in the

living room and relaxed; London with his pipe, Benton with a cigarette, and Cliff with a stick of gum.

"That Harry Ward's got himself a real woman, ain't he?" Cliff
said. "She saved the day."

"And it was quite a day," Benton said. "I never saw anything like
that before. Mary Upjohn fitted in all right."

London was silent, puffing his pipe and staring at the empty fireplace, and then Cliff and Benton were silent, too, each thinking his
own thoughts. It was coming twilight and Benton said, "We better
be going, Cliff. You eat supper with me. O.K.?"

"O.K." Cliff put his hands over his head and stretched.

"Then we'll drop by the Elks Club or something," Benton said.
"Or go to a movie."

"I sure thank you fellows," London said.

"We had a big time." Benton got up and leaned against the
mantel. "I wouldn't have missed it for the world."

Cliff got up, too, and stretched again, yawning wide. "Knew
there was something I wanted to tell you all. But I forgot it in all
the excitement. I figured out a way to get even with *Life* magazine."

"For not publishing your letters?" London cut his eyes over at
Benton.

"And for pestering me with those punched-hole subscription
cards," Cliff said. He reached into his inside coat pocket and took
out one of the subscription cards and handed it to Benton. "Look
at it." He was grinning his triumph. "See anything funny about
it?"

Benton held it up to the light. There was Cliff's name and address
and the little square holes that annoyed him so. Benton shook his
head. "Looks O.K. to me." He passed it to London.

"Look at those holes," said Cliff proudly. "I added four."

London began laughing and took the card over to a lamp and put
on his glasses and examined it closely. Only then could he tell that
Cliff had cut four extra holes in the card, the exact size as the
legitimate ones and on the proper lines. "What's the idea?" he
asked, and peered over his glasses at his deacon.

Cliff just beamed.

Benton looked at the card again. "That's a dirty revenge against the machine age."

"Sure it is," Cliff said aggressively. "Those extra holes will throw their subscription machine haywire. All hell will bust loose in a claw-hammer coat."

London rubbed the back of his neck and was puzzled. At times his imagination stalled, and he was a practical man. "It won't work. The machine simply will discard this one. It's faulty."

"Faulty, huh?" Cliff chewed his gum fast and there were tight wrinkles on his tight forehead. "It ain't like all the others, so it's faulty and won't work. O.K. But that ain't the idea and I'm going to tell you something. Both of you." He ran his fingers through his fringe of hair and stood straight, his back braced against the mantel. "They'll slide my card into that machine and the machine will clatter and clank and throw it out because it ain't like all the others and don't fit exactly. Some brother will have to pick it up because the machine won't have it. He'll take it to a supervisor, and the supervisor will take it to a foreman. Then on and on and up and up until it gets to a vice-president, or something. A vice-president in charge of wrong holes. And he'll look at it and turn it over and over and wonder what's going on. Then he'll see my name—Cliff Carter, Linden, Missouri—and maybe he'll know that there's one brother in the world who don't like being a hole in a card."

Nobody laughed. Not even Cliff. London put his hand on his friend's arm and Benton was staring down at the hearth.

"You don't get it, huh?" Cliff asked.

"Yes," said London Wingo. "I get it. How about you, Bent? You get it?"

"Uh-huh. I think I do. It's a thing you either understand or you don't understand. And if you understand it, then no explanation is necessary. If you don't, then no explanation is any good."

London lifted his hand from Cliff's arm and put it around his shoulder and held him tight. "I wish I had a stamp. We could address it and fix it here and get it in the mail tonight."

Benton flipped his cigarette into the fireplace and stepped to the hall closet for his hat. "Come on, Cliff. I want in on this. I'll buy the stamp. The post office is closed, but there's a stamp machine at Eubanks Drugstore." He jerked on his hat and tugged at the brim.

"I want in on it too," said London. "Here's a nickel for the stamps."

"I'll take it." Benton rubbed the coin between his fingers and tossed it up and caught it. "I'll put it in that stamp machine and jiggle the crank and out will come four one-cent stamps. You'll put three of 'em on your letter, Cliff. But you'll have one left over. You can't throw it away. That'd be waste. So what do you do with a one-cent stamp? You put it under the sweat band in your hat and forget it."

"Or if you ever need it," London said, "it's stuck and no good."

Cliff grinned then and scraped his fingernails across his dry scalp. "They pay the postage at the other end. A nice envelope comes with the card. They think of everything."

The three men laughed. It was not merry laughter, but just laughter with no meaning at all.

Benton reached for the doorknob and turned it. "I'll keep the nickel, London. For luck. I used to carry a silver dollar. Lost it a while back. So I'll keep the nickel. Come on, Cliff. Let's go mail that damn card before you change your mind."

London held the door open and watched them walk down the corridor of Elmscourt and he knew them better, and knowing them better, he loved them more.

Gently he closed the door and stood in the hallway for a full minute perhaps, his hands deep in his pockets. Then he walked into the living room and all the furniture was in place, each thing exactly where it fitted. The room was filled with furniture and still it was empty.

Maybe he ought to build a fire. That would cheer the room and him too. But what is a fire without someone to share it?

He went on back to the kitchen and drank a glass of water that he really didn't want. There were no geraniums in the windows. Perhaps ivy would do better there. Or African violets. Then he walked back into the living room and his rubber heels sounded lightly on the hardwood floors and were noiseless on the rugs.

He looked at the pictures and they were straight. The curtains and drapes, the lamps and the divan—they all were there, but for the first time in so long Kathie wasn't there at all. He closed his eyes tight and rubbed them and went into his room and changed his shirt.

Paige was home before six-thirty. She dashed into the apartment and tossed her coat across the back of a chair and hugged her father. "It went swell, Dad." Her eyes were glowing. "Moved like clockwork. Vance is a whiz in this radio routine." She glanced around, really for the first time. "Why, everything is fixed. Did the thundering herd stampede?"

"Sort of," he said, and laid his pipe on a table, then picked it up and blew through it and put it down again. "But everything went off all right."

She looked at him quickly. "Did you need me? Maybe I should have stayed here."

"No, we didn't exactly need you. Everything moved all right. Don't let it bother you." He took off his glasses and slipped them in his coat pocket. "We are going to the Wards' for supper."

"Must we, Dad?"

"Yes, Paige. We must."

"Then I will be ready in a few minutes," she said cheerfully.

She put on a fresh dress and fixed herself as smartly for the Wards as she ever had for the studio or the Andrewses, and that pleased her father very much.

And the Wingos enjoyed their visit far more than Paige had believed possible. Harry Ward was a different man in the presence of his wife and the food was good. Shelby seated London to her right and gave him the little attentions that he had missed so long, insisting that he take two biscuits and buttering one for him herself. She kept his coffee cup filled and when he tasted his broccoli to be polite she laughed and said, "If you don't like it, don't eat it. I don't like it much myself."

Only once did Paige's radio job get into the conversation and Harry congratulated her and then Shelby worked the talk from the daughter back to the father; his youth in Oklahoma and Texas and the early days in Linden, teachers and friends in Baylor University and the seminary, and styles and music of World War I.

She made him take the most comfortable chair in the living room and had cigars ready for him and her husband, good cigars and lots of hot coffee. Harry told a preacher story and then London told one. They spoke the vernacular of their calling. "Uh-huh. That happened during protracted meeting. Twenty additions. Five by conversion and fifteen by letter. Five candidates for baptism. Good meeting——"

"Sure, I remember. Folks were pretty generous. Gave the preacher seventy-five dollars for a week's meeting and one brother gave him a new automobile tire."

They did not discuss their members at all, any more than a doctor would discuss his patients or a lawyer his clients. And the righteousness of the Church was assumed as a lawyer would assume the justice of the law, a teacher the integrity of his profession.

Paige never had seen her father in such an expansive mood nor heard him laugh as long or as loud as he did at some of Harry's stories. There was no gossip and no discussion of money, but only a broad tolerance of human frailties. They were relaxed and, safe in the confidence of their mutual calling, they were very human. Paige enjoyed every minute of it and found herself wondering how Vance Andrews would fit into such a group, and Mary Upjohn.

The Wingos were home early and Paige bathed and put up her hair. London kissed her good night and went to his own room and read Pierre van Paassen's *Why Jesus Died,* and disagreed with it. He got in his bed but couldn't sleep because the walls were strange and close about him. Then he heard Paige turn out her light and he closed his eyes and slept soundly.

It was almost eight o'clock when he woke up, and Paige had breakfast ready, a thing that seldom had happened before. The eggs were sunny-side up and the yokes intact, and the whites were firm and not runny at all. The salt and pepper were by his plate and the butter knife was clean and shiny. He glanced toward the sink and saw the eggshells and knew she had ruined several to get two just right.

"What are your plans today?" she asked.

"I am going to fix my study." His stomach was warm with coffee and his heart was warm with love. He enjoyed a good breakfast. It was his favorite meal if prepared and served right; the eggs firm and a bit of parsley on his plate, the butter knife clean and no coffee in his saucer.

"Need me?" She refilled his cup. It wasn't empty, but she refilled it nevertheless.

"No, I really don't, honey. You'll be busy, and besides, I'd rather fix my study by myself." He stacked his plates and took them to the sink. "I'll pick up a bite of lunch somewhere, but we'll meet for supper. What do you say? We'll go to the Cuckoo Tearoom for supper."

She took the dishes from his hands and began washing them. "We'll have supper here. You stop by Kroger's and make Mr. Oliphant sell you some of his best meat."

"Ground round, Miss Wingo?"

"Sirloin, Reverend."

He did not let on that he was surprised. "You drive me out to the church and you keep the car."

"No, you keep the car. I'll manage."

She followed him into the living room and helped him with his coat and brushed off his shoulders and straightened his tie. She hugged him and walked with him to the door, and he felt like a king as he stepped out of Elmscourt into the bright morning.

The day in the study was his and he fixed things just as he wanted them, and often he talked to himself as he hung the pictures and straightened his books. He didn't stop for lunch, partly because he wasn't very hungry after such a good, late breakfast, but mostly because he wanted to be very hungry for supper.

It was coming twilight when he drove down to Kroger's and asked Estes Oliphant for the best steak in the store. "Sirloin," London said.

Estes made quite a to-do over cutting the meat. He trimmed off most of the fat and put the steak on the flat of his hand and held it up for examination. "Now that's a fine piece of meat. Who's going to cook it, Preacher?"

"My daughter."

"Well, tell her to put it under a hot flame and don't spare the butter——"

"Oh, she knows," said London.

"Most women don't, you know," Estes confided. "But don't ever let on that I told you."

The apartment was prettier than any apartment London had ever seen or wanted to see. A fire was burning bright and there were life and color in his home, and shadows on the walls. A bowl of flowers was on the table in the living room, the same flowers Mary Upjohn had brought the day before, but they were no longer just flowers in a bowl, for Paige had touched them and now they bowed instead of drooped and curved instead of twisted.

She came out of the kitchen and met him and he stood in the doorway to the dining room, looking first at her and then at the table; the candles ready for the tapers and the china plates stacked at the head of the table, at the master's place. It was Kathie's china and had been used maybe three or four times since her death, and now Paige had put it there for them. And that was Kathie's silver, taken out of the chest where it had been so long, and polished for use again. The crystal glasses too. They were a wedding present.

He looked a second time at the table and saw that it was set for three persons. "Cliff?" he asked. "Benton Andrews?"

Paige shook her head and walked around the table, touching the napkins and straightening the candles just a bit.

Then it must be Vance. He was sorry she had asked him, and yet he must not show his disappointment. He had hoped all of this was for him alone.

She came close to him and put her hand on his cheek and kissed his cheek. "Forrest Roberts, Dad. I asked Forrest to supper with us."

He was startled and flushed up quickly. "Why did you do it?" An indication of reproof was in his tone, but more bewilderment. "Why did you do it, Paige?"

"Because a woman can feel things. That's why."

"But your mother's china. Her silver."

"They are for use, Dad. Not for memories."

London Wingo looked at his daughter, trying to see with his eyes what only the heart can see, striving to plumb the mystery of a woman's way, and the woman a part of him.

"I called her this morning," Paige said, and moved back to the table, avoiding his gaze.

London continued to look at her and then she raised her face and he, almost timidly, held out his arms and she flung her own arms around him and put her head on his chest and began sobbing. He stroked her hair and felt the sobs rack her body, and he let her weep until she raised her face again and then he wiped her eyes and she tried to smile and the outburst dwindled into sniffles.

"She likes her steaks medium rare," Paige said, and stepped back from him.

"Yes. I know."

"Now you go spruce up." Paige ran her fingers across the table-cloth and smoothed a wrinkle. "She will be here pretty soon."

London went to his bathroom and bathed and he spent a long time shaving, staring at himself in the mirror and really not seeing himself at all; but only the blurred image of a man who for so long had shared his heart with his daughter and a memory and now was sharing his heart between his daughter and another woman.

He shaved close under his nose, a spot he sometimes missed when he was in a hurry, and he cooled his face with shaving lotion and put on his best suit.

Forrest arrived before seven o'clock, and London helped her remove her coat and Paige commented on how nice she looked. And she did. She was wearing a black crepe dress with a rhinestone collar. Her hose were sheer and dark and her hair was parted and pulled tight into a chignon at the back of her head and over the nape of her neck.

"Now you sit right here in front of the fire with Dad," Paige said. "Dinner will be ready in a few minutes."

London poked the fire and Forrest did not volunteer to help in the kitchen and he was glad. She was there as a guest and this was Paige's night. Only once did Forrest even glance toward the dining room and, seeing the china and the silver, she looked away and then into the fire.

The candles were glowing when Paige announced dinner and she sat her father at the head of the table and Forrest on his right, still the guest. She nodded to her father and he bowed his head.

"We thank Thee, our Lord, for this, Thy bounty. Amen."

In a quick, unnoticed glance London took in the table, hoping everything was all right. The steak was sizzling, oozing butter and gravy. There were the French fries, the lettuce and tomatoes, the bread. But no butter. The butter plates were just so. Kathie's butter plates and her butter knives, but no butter.

London began talking about how beautifully the steak was cooked. He put a piece of bread on his butter plate so it would not be so empty, and at that minute no visible power could have made him comment on the absence of butter.

However, Paige saw it and without fuss or fluster got up and went to the kitchen and returned with the butter. "I hope that's my only mistake," she said. "I'm no cook, Forrest. I hope the steak is half as good as it looks."

It was. The lettuce and tomatoes, too. But the potatoes were limp and soggy and the mayonnaise was store-bought and flat.

London ate everything on his plate and so did Forrest Roberts.

They returned to the living room, where Paige served coffee, and then her father filled his pipe and they sat before the fire. Paige did not smoke. There was no reason she should not smoke, but she just didn't want to.

"Do you play canasta, Forrest?" she asked. "Three can play, you know. So can two."

"Why, yes," said Forrest. "I play."

"Dad has never learned how. But we can show him. How about it, Dad?"

London knocked his pipe against his palm. "I have no strenuous objections. But I've never played cards. Oh, rook and old maid——"

"And flinch?" asked Forrest.

He smiled at her. "And flinch. My father was quite a card man, but my mother disapproved. She called them 'spot cards' and they were the devil's tools."

Forrest did not look at Paige, but only at London. "I care nothing whatsoever about playing."

"Neither do I," said Paige quickly. "Maybe we can get something good on the radio."

"Why don't you play for us?" London asked.

"All right. But, Forrest, don't you play?"

"A little bit. By ear."

"Then you play for us." Paige led the way into the music room and opened the piano.

Forrest sat down and fingered the keys, not expertly, but good enough. "What'll it be?"

"Play some of the old songs," Paige suggested. "Dad likes the old songs."

Again London smiled at Forrest and rubbed his hand over his mouth so Paige could not see his smile, and Forrest looked down at the keys and began playing "That Naughty Waltz."

"That's a popular song," Paige said. " 'That Naughty Waltz.' That's not an old one."

London pulled his chair closer to the piano. "Right after World War I, wasn't it, Forrest?"

"Yes. And this one always went with it. Remember?" She began playing "Three O'Clock in the Morning."

London hummed it, remembering few of the words, and Paige sat apart, only watching them and saying nothing.

"You name the year," London said, "and I'll name the song."

"All right." Forrest ran her fingers across the keys and her eyes were lively. "Nineteen-twenty."

" 'Let the Rest of the World Go By,' " London said promptly. "Give or take a year or so. I know I was in Baylor when it came out."

She played it through and he sang it, remembering all the words.

"Nineteen twenty-eight," she challenged.

" 'I'll Get By.' "

"Those are not old songs." Paige got up and went over to the piano. "We still sing them."

"Then here's an old one." Forrest looked away, trying to recall the melody, and over at London. "Oh yes. Now I remember it." She began humming to refresh the tune in her memory. " 'A garland of old-fashioned roses——' "

Paige turned away, unable to look at her father. London, however, took up the lyrics and began singing them, and Forrest said, "You know all the words. I'd forgotten exactly how they went, but you know them all."

"It was one of Kathie's favorite songs," he said.

A lesser woman than Forrest Roberts might have avoided the issue, but she played the song through, evading nothing.

"It's the theme song for my radio program." It was the first time Paige had mentioned her program that evening. "I had chosen it before Dad told me it was one of my mother's favorites."

"It's a lovely song," Forrest said. It was a trite thing to say, but the proper thing.

London drove her home and drove slowly, and they sat in his car and talked, and when he got home Paige was in bed, although her light was still burning, and the china and silver were washed and put away.

He went into her room and bragged about her dinner and kissed her good night and then he lay awake for hours, staring into the darkness, while an old melody soothed his memory and a new song stirred his heart.

It seemed a long night and he was up an hour before Paige, and this time he cooked breakfast and took it to her on a tray. She glanced up at him and then at the cereal and steaming coffee and the toast browned lightly. "Did you remember the butter?" she asked, her face expressionless but her eyes twinkling.

"Uh-huh." He put the tray before her. "It's after eight."

"That late!" She reached for the coffee. "I promised to meet

Vance at the studio by eight-thirty. We're going to run through it one more time."

He went back to the kitchen and was eating alone and reading his paper when she joined him. "Are you coming down to the studio to hear the show?" She filled a glass with water and sipped it.

"Do you need me?"

"No. Not unless you just want to be there."

"Then I'll listen here, honey. I might upset you. Besides, I have a feeling Cliff will drop by."

"And I have a feeling Mr. Andrews will too," she said. "Vance gets nervous if he works around his father. I'm sure Mr. Andrews feels it. So he'll probably come out here and listen with you."

"That'll be fine."

"Do you want me to call Forrest? You all can make a little party of it."

London folded his paper and stood. "I will call her, Paige. I can handle that." There was a trickle of petulance in his tone.

She went for her hat and coat and he waited for her in the hallway and helped her into her coat and squeezed her shoulders. "Good luck." He said no more, for he was filling up.

"Now don't you worry," she reassured him. "I'll stand 'em on their ears. Vance says I'm a natural."

He opened the door for her and watched her down the corridor and then returned to the kitchen and washed the breakfast dishes. He didn't pray for her as some fathers might have, for London Wingo never asked his God for personal triumphs, never demanded to see the burning bush, never bargained his faith with his Master, but asked only the right to serve. He put the dishes in the cabinet and called Forrest Roberts.

"I'll be there," she said.

"So will Cliff, I'm pretty sure," he said. "And probably Bent. I'll call him to pick you up."

He laid a fire in the fireplace but didn't light it. The day was warm and he opened the windows in the music room and tested the radio. WLMO came in strong. They were selling soap again and he snapped it off.

Cliff arrived soon after ten, and then Forrest and Benton. They sat in the music room and talked about many things, but only a few words about the program. Benton, however, kept glancing at his watch and was as nervous as London and showed it more.

It was almost eleven when the doorbell rang and London jumped. He hurried to answer it, and Mary Upjohn was there. "I tried to call you earlier," she said apologetically, "but your line was busy. May I hear Paige's program here? Hers and Vance's? Our radio is broken. The kids broke it."

"Come right in," London said with a graciousness he did not feel, for somehow this girl made him feel guilty of something as she walked across the polished floor of his hallway, her coat drab brown while his own daughter had so much.

He showed her into the music room and they all greeted her warmly and Cliff got her a chair and pulled it close into the circle, but nevertheless she seemed apart, her hands limp in her lap as she stared at the radio.

Benton leaned forward and switched it on and a commercial faded and the bells sounded the hour. "She'll be on in a minute," he said excitedly, and twisted the volume until it was too loud. Quickly he cut it back and fidgeted with the knobs. "Here's her theme song."

That's what it was, all right. A few notes of the old song and London felt his stomach tightening. Then an unctuous voice proclaimed the tidings that now was the hour for "Paige Wingo's Scrapbook." Benton gripped the arms of his chair until his knuckles were white and London stared out of the window, daring not even look at the radio for fear he might see her and know that she was frightened.

"Hello, and how do you do today? This is Paige Wingo." Her voice was as clear as the morning outside, as calm and warm as the spring sun, and as persuasive as the breeze in the maple leaves.

"She's got it," Benton said hoarsely. "She's got it, I tell you. She's good."

London said nothing, only listening and hurting inside—the good hurt of fear relieved. They looked at him and each saw something different. Cliff saw his chin trembling and his own eyes filled. Benton saw the pride in his face. But Forrest Roberts saw his realization that his daughter did not need him any more, that she was a woman in a world he could not share, and that now he was a free man, if a father ever is free.

"She's good," Benton said over and over. "She's got everything."

There was no doubt about that. Paige's voice sparkled confidence and the program moved with perfect timing. Chatter and sentiment. Observations on the weather and advice on clothes and food. An old poem and a little music: "The Third Man Theme." Then an interview with the mayor, who, in Paige's hands, seemed to shed his stuffed shirt right there in public and once he actually chuckled.

The program was almost over before Mary Upjohn spoke a word. "Vance produced it and directed it. You don't hear much about the producer and director. Like in the movies. But Vance showed her how to do it."

Benton nodded slowly. "That's right. The boy is good. Mighty good at that sort of thing."

"Paige wasn't scared a bit." Mary's hands still were limp in her lap. "I wish I could do something like that, but I'd be scared to death. I'd just die if I had to stand up there like that."

Her words were bitter seeds in the fruit of London's pride. Cliff leaned over and patted her arm and then Benton patted her arm. But not Forrest Roberts. She stood up and was closer to London than to the others. "You don't know what you can do, Mary, until you try it. Now, come on and help me fix some coffee for these men."

"I'll help you," London said. "I know where everything is."

The program ended with the announcement: "Tune in Monday for the second page of 'Paige Wingo's Scrapbook.'"

Forrest walked into the living room and London followed her, then led the way to the kitchen. "What do you think?" he said.

"If Mary doesn't quit whining I'll scream. At times I'd like to jerk a knot in her backbone."

"I meant about Paige."

Forrest turned on the gas stove and filled the kettle with warm water and put it over the flame. "She is a bundle of talent. There never was any doubt about that, was there?"

"Not in my mind." He reached for the dripolator and put in six spoons of coffee.

Forrest backed against a cabinet and folded her arms. "Paige will get what she wants. On her own. And you listen to me, London. Don't you let Mary's self-pity take a thing from your happiness in your daughter's success."

"But she has had a better chance than Mary——"

"I'm not so sure of that."

"She is sharper than Mary——"

"Maybe. But I notice Mary was smart enough to come whining around here this morning. She could have heard that program anywhere, but she comes here. Never forget, London Wingo, that the healthy beggar may be smarter than the almsgiver who confuses pity with sympathy and indulgence with justice. Now where are the cups?"

"Right over there."

"That's your best china," she said. "The ones Paige used last night."

"Uh-huh. I know." He poured hot water into the dripolator. "We'll use them again. And I'll get the silver."

Cliff drank two cups of coffee and Mary drank none, and then they got up to go, knowing that Paige would be home soon and that her father would want to see her alone and take her out to lunch.

"Come on, Mary," Cliff said. "I'll drive you home."

Mary thanked him and turned to London. "Thank you, too, Brother Wingo for letting me hear the program here. I didn't mean to butt in."

"You didn't," he answered. "Come any time."

Cliff and Mary went on ahead and Forrest and Benton tarried by the door a minute and then they, too, went out. Neither spoke until they were in Benton's car and he had pulled out from the curb. "That girl has a great future. Paige, I mean. She's a natural." He put a cigarette between his lips and shoved in the lighter.

"Vance deserves a lot of credit too," Forrest suggested.

Benton nodded and lit his cigarette and drove perhaps half a block before he spoke again. "Do you think London sees what we all see—that Mary hasn't got a chance around Paige?"

"Of course he sees it. It's as plain as the nose on your face."

"Do you think Mary sees it? Or feels it?"

"If she doesn't, she's dumb; and Vance will be better off without her."

"But it's not fair," Benton said.

Forrest turned quickly and looked at him and her look became a gaze and then a stare. "What's unfair about it?"

"It's just not fair, that's all. Mary must fix herself up, and shine. Think I'll ask Cliff to give her a job. She can answer the phone and help out around his office." He turned off Elm Street and toward Taney Avenue.

"Why don't you give her a job?" Forrest still was looking at him.

Benton flipped away his cigarette and scowled. "That would make it worse," he said impatiently. "She'd be just a little cog right there in the studio where Paige is a big wheel. So I'm going to get Cliff to give her a job. Let her make a little money. You'll help her fix up, won't you? And sort of take her in hand."

Forrest said nothing for a second or so, only watching his face and then the street. "No, Benton. I will have nothing to do with it."

He was astounded by her calm refusal and jerked his car around a corner and onto Taney Avenue. "You won't help the girl? I thought Christians always helped one another——"

"Not in cases like this, Benton. Besides, she's no girl. She is a woman. So is Paige Wingo. You know that as well as I do."

Chapter 11

His hay fever began pestering London Wingo in August of that year, two months earlier than usual, and Paige had him and Forrest on the "Scrapbook" for an interview about spring and autumn allergies. The program was humorous and informative and the station received more than three hundred letters about it, most of them complimentary.

London got fourteen letters suggesting causes and cures, and one sister wrote from Montgomery County: "Rub warm lard on soles of feet. Put on wool socks and go to bed. Baptist myself. Husband ain't much of nothing."

The hay fever, however, was among the least of his worries and so was his church. The membership had more than doubled and there was no dissension to speak of, and no organized dissension at all. He had brought into the church those deeply spiritual qualities of faith and forgiveness and sacrifice, and the people came to hear him and to heed him, coming from all the walks of life—the rich and poor, the saints and sinners, and all of them soul-starved. London exalted none of them except as brothers and shared with them his spiritual abundance, asking nothing and giving so much and never aware that he was giving.

Sometimes Negroes attended his services, but not often, because they apparently preferred their own ways, and so the issue that

Estes Oliphant had dreaded was never an issue at all. The Negro pastor of Tabernacle Baptist Church explained it to the white pastor of Plymouth Baptist Church. "We want the right of choice, Brother Wingo. The right to seek God in your church or my church or out yonder in that oak thicket. Just the right of choice, Brother Wingo."

London gave one day each week to pastoral visits and another to the sick and aged, and in it all, in everything he did, he never compromised his calling but preached and lived the brotherhood of man and the fatherhood of God; fighting evil in all places, sternly but not stridently, and never in shouts or clashing cymbals or neon lights.

Yes, Plymouth Baptist Church was strong and growing and was no serious problem to its pastor. But Buck Bledsoe's mother had cancer and Buck was drinking too much. That was a care for the pastor. Estes Oliphant's wife was nagging because Estes wasn't getting ahead fast enough to suit her. "She don't understand me, Brother Wingo," Estes complained. "She wants me home ever' minute I ain't working and yet she wants me to get on quicker. She just don't understand."

There was a new cashier in the store. She was about twenty-four, and her cash register was near Estes' meat counter. She had a shrill laugh and a wiggle and kept her hair wavy with a Toni.

That was only a bothersome fret to the pastor, but Sisler Mason's one good eye was weakening, and that was a worry. And, too, Harry Ward was growing morose and Shelby Ward was taut and more brittle than ever.

The skin on Cliff Carter's face was tighter and he could not throw off a summer cold. Now that really troubled London; and so did Benton Andrews—for he had come to love Bent as much as he loved Cliff.

Benton was retreating deeper inside himself and was more cynical than ever and sometimes even sullen. London saw him and Cliff three or four times a week, and Benton was emotionally stagnant. He talked often of his youth. "The wasted years," he said. His only interest was his radio station, particularly Paige's program, and whereas he bragged about her to London, he told Cliff: "Vance is the meshing gear on that job. She's the voice and the personality, but my son is the brain behind it."

To Cliff it was all quite simple. Benton was struggling to live in a spiritual vacuum and it couldn't be done. "Man does not live by bread alone," Cliff said over and over, and that explained everything. "Ol' Bent's got to find God."

"God is not lost," London said ambiguously. "Man is lost, not God."

However, he was baffled. He had known Benton about six months and had known three different men: first the belligerent Andrews, next a man almost happy, and now a sullen man. He never probed Benton's emotions and never questioned him, only prayed that whatever was troubling his friend would be removed.

And so that, too, was a problem.

Then there was Vance. The boy had not mentioned the ministry to London in several months. In fact, come to think about it, he hadn't seen Vance alone in three, maybe four, months. He saw him at church every Sunday and once or twice during the week when he brought Paige home from the studio, but never alone. Was Vance avoiding him? Nonsense. The boy was busy, that's all. There was Paige's program and his office as superintendent of Sunday school. Still, the seminary would begin its fall term in a month or six weeks, and London could not help wondering about Vance's plans. No further mention had been made of his ordination or a calling, and again London Wingo did not pry, for that was a matter between God and His servant.

Vance continued to see Mary Upjohn, and there was no obvious indication of any drifting between them. He took her to Sunday school and sat by her during church, and all in all, except for work, he saw Mary more often than he saw Paige. Nonetheless, he laughed and was relaxed when he was with Paige, but was serious and moody when in Mary's company.

London presumed to ask his daughter about it in a roundabout way, not caring to know the exact truth if the truth were as he suspected. Paige answered him frankly and without guile.

"You want to know if I am in love with Vance. Is that it, Dad?"

"I didn't ask that——"

"But that's what you mean. And I don't know. Vance goes steady with Mary. He has never mentioned love to me. Do you think Mary will make a good preacher's wife?"

"No. Do you think you could?"

"I have never intended to try, Dad."

"Your mother did——"

"And it broke her heart——"

"No! Your mother's heart was never broken. Neither was her spirit. The ministry killed her, if you want it put that way. But she never broke."

"Is that why you have never married again?" Paige shifted instinctively from the defensive. "Because you could not ask another woman to go through all my mother went through?"

"We were talking about you." He said it gently. "Not about me."

She kissed him then and tweaked his chin. "When I fall in love you will know it. I'm choosy, Dad. You've set a high standard. Maybe too high."

London Wingo melted completely and believed her because he knew so little about women; so much about God, perhaps (if a man can know about God), and so little about women. Even had he understood women he still would have believed her because she was his daughter and therefore unlike any other woman. Maybe she believed it herself. Anyway, the subject was closed—with him.

Mary Upjohn had changed none at all, but she was no longer a worry to her pastor. He had done all he knew how to do, and if she did not care to help herself, then that was that. She was working for Cliff and making good money too. However, she gave her money to what she called "the Lord's cause" instead of spending it on herself. She tithed. Of course she tithed. Every Sunday ten per cent of her income was in her church envelope and each dollar was designated properly: this for home missions, that was foreign missions, and the other for support of Plymouth Baptist Church. She taught a class in the primary department of the Sunday school and bought religious books and crayons for the children.

Cliff thought she was an angel. London wasn't so sure, and Sisler Mason wished she were a soloist.

It was always the same with Mary. At eleven o'clock, on the split second, she left Vance in the pew and walked slowly down to the piano for her part in the Sunday service, her role in the drama. She played the hymns precisely as they were written. Twice a month she played a solo, and then there was a look of rapture on her face, but her hair was straight, almost stringy, and her brown dresses—always brown—were high over her shoulders and over her neck. A covered angel, she was; a drab angel.

On solo days she was the center of the opening scene of the drama, and yet the spotlight affected her not one bit. Often she played "Rock of Ages" and seemed to cling to the rock, her long fingers clinging to the piano keys as though the instrument itself were the rock, an anchor in a storm, and the keys were broken boulders. Never once did she fluff her hair or wet her lips and betray any hint of feminine vanity. The rapture in her eyes, however, lighted her pale face and she seemed all eyes, like a staring child.

Rock of Ages . . . Let me hide myself in Thee . . .

The people watched her play and some saw the rapture, but mostly they saw the lifeless hair and glanced from her to Vance and then to Paige, and they felt sorry for Mary Upjohn.

Forrest Roberts was disgusted by it all. "Martyrdom," she warned London. "Martyrdom plotted and planned."

"I'm not so sure," he said.

"That's because you know as little about women as I do about flying saucers. Can't you see through her, London?"

"Sometimes I think I do. Then I am not sure. All I can see is the rapture in her eyes and only wish that I had it."

"Tommyrot. You've got the same rapture, only you don't turn it on and off like an electric light." Forrest was emphatic and scornful. "Rehearsed sainthood. That's little Mary. Can't you feel it?"

"You could be wrong, you know."

"I'm not wrong, London Wingo." She stamped her foot impatiently. "It is the safest role a woman can play. Because you can't slap a saint. She just stares at you. You can't rob a saint, or desert one." The color was high on her cheeks and her eyes were snapping. "She has whined and raptured her way into your sympathy and has put you between Vance and Paige. What chance has Paige got against a saint? She can't brush Mary aside. If she holds out one little finger to Vance she would be robbing a saint. And Vance can't quit her. He can't walk away from a living saint, even a phony one."

"Why not?"

"Could you?" She touched his arm and repeated, "Tell me, could you?"

"No."

"And why not?"

"Because I'd never be sure." London rubbed his hands over his cheeks and looked away.

Forrest gripped his arm as though to awaken him. "Because you'd be afraid the rapture might go out of her eyes. And that you'd be responsible." She took her hand from his arm and touched her new fall hat as though needing to feel something in the world of vanity. "Vance feels the same way. It is the ancient saint-martyrdom role and it always works. I wish I knew the lines and the gesture."

"I hope you are not misjudging Mary," he said. "She is beyond me, and I never worry about her any more. If her rapture is true, then she is far, far beyond me. If it is not true, then it is a matter between her and God."

"I am not bearing false witness." Forrest's chin came up and was trembling, and then it was firm again and she was certain of herself. "The whole thing is like a bad Russian drama. Machiavellian more than Russian, perhaps. And I will say no more about it. Except this. There have been women saints. And there will be more. But not Mary Upjohn. She has a hussy heart behind a mask of martyrdom."

"You could be wrong, you know." He had said it before and he said it again.

She drew away quickly and looked up at him and down at her hands and fingernails, her nails red and freshly manicured. "Yes, I could be wrong." She wondered if she had said too much. She had dared discuss Paige's problem and that was not her right. She had presumed to share his confidence and now she was embarrassed and apprehensive of his disapproval. "Yes—I could be wrong," she repeated, and looked up at him again. "Very wrong, my dear."

London almost took her hands to tell her that he loved her and needed her, that he needed her because he loved her and because he was lonely. The words almost came. They were in his heart and on his tongue, and then he caught himself and stifled the impulse.

He was very near to saying the things he ached to say. After more than twenty years the flesh challenged the spirit and then it passed and a deep mortification was upon him in the knowledge of how close he had come to breaking the vows of all those years.

For never again must London Wingo ask any woman to share his life as Kathie had shared it; the sacrifices, the humiliations, the restrictions were more than he could ask Forrest Roberts to bear. The spirit must deny the flesh because his life was dedicated and because he loved her too deeply to ask her to share his ministry. Marriage was an honorable state for most men. That he believed, but as for himself, he accepted the council of St. Paul, spoken by permission and not of commandment, that some men should abide as he—and Paul was unmarried.

He had so written to the church in Corinth, to them who were sanctified in Christ and called to be saints. It was in the Word.

"For I would that all men were even as I myself. But every man hath his proper gift of God, one after this manner, and another after that. I say therefore to the unmarried and widows, It is good for them if they abide even as I."

And so instead of taking her hands London took her arm, and they walked to his car and drove downtown to have dinner with Cliff and Benton.

Cliff wanted to eat at the Post Office Café and Benton insisted they dine at the Linden Hotel. "I can't take grease and smoke and a juke box," Benton said. "Not today, anyhow."

"They got pot roast," Cliff protested, and smacked his gum to emphasize that he wanted no aspersions cast on the Post Office Café.

They were his friends. "Told me yesterday they'd have it today. Besides"—he looked to London and Forrest for support—"we ate at the hotel last time. Just four days ago. London, he had curried shrimp——"

"I had the shrimp," Forrest said. "London had roast beef. But I agree with Benton. I'd like a quiet dinner. What about you, London?"

"It doesn't make any difference to me." He did not feel up to a discussion of food.

Cliff gave in. "All right. O.K. Hotel, then. But during the war they served black-market stuff. Just want you to know that. And the Post Office Café didn't fudge a bit. Not a frazzling bit. Just let your conscience be your guide."

"I am," said Benton, and led the way into the hotel restaurant and ordered first for Forrest and then for his friends. He was pleasant enough during dinner but didn't have much to say and wasn't very hungry.

Forrest also was contemplative and so was London, but Cliff talked a blue streak and complained that his food was tasteless.

"It's your cold," London said. "You'd better watch that cold. Summer colds are bad."

Cliff spooned some beef gravy on his bread. "Don't you worry about my cold. You watch your hay fever. Apt to bust out in asthma. I had an aunt——"

"That would be the aunt in Moberly," Forrest said. "The one who was allergic to cats."

"Feather pillows too," said London, and grinned.

Forrest laughed and Benton smiled, somewhat wryly, but a smile nonetheless, and Cliff quickly was gay because his friends showed even a tiny measure of happiness and good humor. He began telling anecdotes about his kinfolks and himself and laid it on thick, although many of his stories were pointless.

No, nothing startling had happened recently in his business. Mary Upjohn had billed a corpse for his own burial. But nothing really exciting. Just funerals.

Yes, he had received another subscription card from *Life*. "I never heard from 'em about that trick card I sent 'em. I suppose a lot of folks do it all the time and *Life* magazine is used to it. I thought maybe it might be something new, but I suppose a lot of folks thought of it ahead of me."

And so with all of them, the young and the not-so-young, it was like a spring bubbling, the water pulsing up from down deep, but going nowhere because a wall held it. Their paths crossed daily and they met together on Sunday and praised God, all except Benton, who was aloof from the church and stood on the perimeter and watched them, loving them but scorning their ways, then looking away in his loneliness, often at Paige.

Something had to yield gradually or break violently. The spring was ceaseless and the wall was static and the first cleft in the wall came from Vance Andrews.

Paige and Benton Andrews were in St. Louis at a radio meeting of some kind and London was alone in the apartment, his Roger Williams notes on a table before him. The doorbell startled him and annoyed him, as he was in no mood for company, but when he opened the door and saw Vance his mood changed and he led the way into the music room and made the boy feel at home.

"Nice weather for a change," London said, and relaxed in an easy chair. "Been a muggy summer, though." His hay fever was easing, but his nostrils were raw and red from the strong drops he had been taking for weeks.

"Yes, sir. It's been rugged." Vance rested his hands on his knees and sat forward in his chair. "How's your hay fever?"

"Better. You got any ideas?"

"No, sir."

"Good." London lit his pipe, but it didn't taste right and he put it aside. "You are the first person I've seen who didn't have a hay-fever cure. Now, how's everything? Sunday school all right?"

Vance leaned back a bit and his hands dropped between his legs. "Everything is O.K. I suppose you'd wondered why I hadn't been around?"

"Yes." London was never one for subterfuge. "We haven't done any talking in a good while and I did wonder about it. However, I assumed you had your reasons. Busy, or something."

For a second or two Vance was silent, looking down at his hands, and then he put his hands back on his knees and leaned forward. "Tell me something, Brother Wingo——"

"Shoot. What's on your mind?"

"Is it necessary for me to be licensed by the church before I can preach?" Vance said it rapidly, as though anxious to have the words out.

London did not reply immediately but reached for his pipe again and tapped the stem against his teeth. "Why, no, it's not necessary. A licensed preacher is sort of a freshman preacher. An ordained minister is a graduate, as it were. If you are ordained, you are automatically licensed. Is that clear?" He was watching the boy closely, although not obviously.

"Yes, sir. And that's what I thought. Paige, too. She said the same thing."

London looked him full in the face then, and Vance's eyes were steady, returning the gaze. Neither spoke for an interval, a long pause, and they dropped their gaze at the same moment, Vance turning his eyes toward a window and London looking down at his pipe. "Let's get down to cases, son," said London gently. He wanted to make it as easy for the boy as possible. "You don't want to be licensed to preach here in Linden. Is that it?"

"That's about it, Brother Wingo. It would be a slap in my father's face. I should have thought about it before. It would be rubbing salt in his wounds."

"Perhaps you are right."

"If we had the service in our church he wouldn't want to attend. But if he didn't attend the people would talk. I don't want my ministry to start off on that level."

"Yes. You are exactly right, Vance."

"So I am going back to the seminary next month." Vance crossed his legs and was almost at ease. "I am going to do a lot of thinking. A lot of praying. And next spring if I feel like I feel now I will be ordained. But up there, Brother Wingo. In Rochester."

London got up from his chair and walked over and stood by a window, staring into the night at the cars passing along Elm Street and the distant glow of the city's lights. A heavy hand was on his heart, almost despair and dread. Had Paige dared intrude herself into this boy's plans for a ministry? Had she dared interfere with God's plan, a divine calling perhaps? He turned from the window and faced his young brother. "If I can be of help, let me know. Only one thing. Be sure of yourself. Don't put your hand to the plow and turn back. Don't try God's patience." He crossed the room and laid his hand on Vance's shoulder. "Now, let's go fix some coffee. Have you heard from your father or Paige? Hope they are not getting city-slicked."

"Oh, they are talking to sponsors. A couple of St. Louis houses are interested in the 'Scrapbook.'" He, too, got up and followed London to the kitchen. "I'll get the cups."

"Over in that cabinet——"

"Yes. I know. Paige and I have fixed coffee here a few times." He pushed the coffee can toward London and reached for the cups and saucers. "Come to think about it, I did hear of a cure for hay fever."

"Warm lard and woolen socks?"

"That's it," said Vance, and laughed. "Tried it?"

London put two heaping spoons of coffee in the dripolator and filled the kettle with water. "No. I don't intend to, either. Hay fever is like hiccups. Everybody who has never had it knows a cure. Like religion. Those who have none know all about it."

They took their coffee to the music room and sat there talking for maybe an hour, first about St. Francis and T. S. Eliot, until Vance changed the subject to Roger Williams to please London. And it did.

There was no immediate evidence of any rift in the wall. The water did not gush through and free itself, but only seeped through, and the spring was still bubbling.

Paige herself was responsible for the second cleft, looking back at it now. Her radio reputation was spreading, and the St. Louis *Globe-Democrat* had carried a short feature about her with a picture, and Benton was trying to interest the *Post-Dispatch* in a piece on the "Scrapbook." All the Baptist papers—and there was one in each Southern state—had made mention that the daughter of London Wingo, D.D., LL.D., was becoming a radio personality.

Therefore, London was not particularly surprised when the letter arrived at the apartment from a Baptist Youth Conference, requesting her to take over all radio programs for a two-week meeting at Ridgecrest, North Carolina.

Paige was excited and very proud. "Where's Ridgecrest? I've heard of it, but what's the gimmick, Dad?"

"Ridgecrest is in the mountains near Asheville, North Carolina." London folded the letter and handed it to her. "It's where Southern Baptists hold summer assemblies. Thousands and thousands flock there for meetings. Twenty, sometimes twenty-five thousand people——"

"Oh, sure, sure." Paige kicked off her shoes and wiggled her toes. "Now I remember. The Methodists and Presbyterians have big doings down there too."

"Uh-huh. Methodists at Lake Junaluska and Presbyterians at Montreat." Some of her enthusiasm was reaching him, and he stuck his pipe in his coat pocket without knocking out the ash.

Paige reread the letter. "They'd be honored to have me. They are looking forward to it. Well, now, what do you know about that? Let's take them up on it, Dad. Let's go down there and do it up brown."

"They didn't ask me." London felt his pipe hot in his pocket and jerked it out. "Preachers are a dime a dozen at Ridgecrest. Besides, I can't get away. But why don't you go down?"

There was no indication of her disappointment that he could not go. She long since had learned that his time was not his own or hers. So she didn't argue but accepted things as they were. "Mr. Andrews will let me off," she said. "Why shouldn't I do it?"

"No reason at all." He knew she wanted to go and only needed urging. "You can fly down from St. Louis. To Asheville, and they'll meet you." London enjoyed talking about plane schedules as much as he did about trains. "From St. Louis to Cincinnati. Then to Lexington, Kentucky, and Knoxville, and across the mountains."

"It will be good advertising for the station." She cocked her head to one side as she talked, debating with herself and convincing herself. "I can buy a new fall outfit. Suit. Hat. Pocketbook to match." She reached for her shoes and slipped them on and stood and wiggled her feet tighter into the shoes. "I am going right now and talk to Mr. Andrews."

"They want you next Monday."

"Can't make it Monday. Can make it Tuesday, though. Leave St. Louis Monday night." The more she talked about it, the more excited she was, and she perked her hat on her head and hurried downtown to talk it over with her boss.

Benton agreed wholeheartedly on the trip and volunteered to pay her plane fare and to take her to the airport. "Dad will take me," she told him. "He likes airports and railroad stations."

"I hate them," said Benton. "Now if you need any money, draw on the station. And don't worry about a thing. One of the announcers will take over the 'Scrapbook.'"

He gave her an alligator bag as a going-away present, and that night she had dinner with Vance.

Forrest was almost as excited about it all as Paige and helped her shop for a fall suit. "I'll buy your stockings," Forrest said. "That will be my present."

London bought her a blouse, and she wore the new outfit to church for the first time and Sloan Wentworth commented on how pretty she looked. Mary Upjohn admired the clothes, too, but evidenced no envy whatsoever and actually seemed proud, and surely satisfied, that her own dress was plain. She put five dollars in the collection plate that morning and her solo was "Praise Ye the Father."

Paige put in fifty cents and heard almost none of the sermon, but kept looking down at her new shoes and pocketbook and thinking about the trip.

She and London left home around ten o'clock Monday morning, and she didn't ask why such an early start. She knew why.

"We'll make a day of it," he told her, and put her two bags in the trunk compartment. "We haven't had a day to ourselves in a long time."

"Baseball, Dad?"

"If you don't mind."

"I don't mind," she said, and eased the DeSoto through town and to the open road and stepped it up to about sixty.

They had lunch at a roadside stand and then drove straight to the ball park. The Cardinals were at home. London didn't like the Cardinals as he did the Browns. They were too good. Won too often. They were almost perfection, and perfection troubled him, like machines. He didn't like the Yanks for the same reason, or the Dodgers. He preferred the White Sox and the Pirates and, above all, the Browns because so few others did.

Paige did not know the difference between the White Sox and the Red Sox, although she did know that the Browns and the Cardinals were St. Louis teams and that everybody laughed at the Browns.

London splurged and bought box seats and tried to show Paige how to score the game. "You number the players, honey. Pitcher is No. 1. Catcher No. 2. And so on. One line right here." He marked the score card with his Mikado pencil. "That means a single. A little upshoot line to the right means a single to right."

She was completely baffled by the intricacies of scoring baseball and really wasn't interested. Her main concern was her sheer stockings catching on the rough edges of the seat.

However, he enjoyed every play of the game and she pretended to, and then they filed out with the crowd and to their car. "Now what?" she asked. "It's several hours to plane time."

He stretched and lit his pipe and felt better than he had in days. "We are going to the best restaurant in town. Thick steaks and all the trimmings."

She put her hand on the switch to start the DeSoto and glanced over at him. "Let me pick the restaurant. I know a little place 'way out. Candles in bottles and tallow running down. Red and green and yellow."

"Sure. If it suits you, it suits me." He mopped his brow with his handkerchief, and his skin was tingling from the sun.

They drove first by the airport and she checked in and left her baggage, and then they headed for the restaurant. She had a little trouble finding it, but she found it all right. A doorman showed them in and the hat-check girl looked at his bare head and his empty hands and stepped back and shrugged.

London Wingo had never been in a restaurant quite like this one. The tablecloths were red and white checks and there was only candlelight, the shadows dancing on the walls. A Negro pianist was low over his keys and playing "Summertime." Suddenly London felt gay in a sense of unrestraint, like an adventurer in a strange land. He wanted to dance, to take Paige by the hand and whirl around. He had never danced in his life. Oh, a square dance or so when he was a boy, and a few reels, but never spinning and gliding as he wanted to do now.

He selected a table in a corner across the room from the piano and Paige excused herself, and while she was gone London went over and gave the pianist a dollar and asked him to play "My Foolish Heart." "When my daughter comes back," he said. "Play it when my daughter comes back."

"Is that pretty young lady your daughter?" the man asked.

"Yes, sir. She's leaving tonight. Thought I'd treat her to the best dinner in town."

"Only one you got?" The pianist ran his fingers over the keys and looked up at London and smiled.

"Only one."

"I got three."

"All girls?"

"Three girls and a son." He rested his hands on the piano and smiled again. "I'll play 'My Foolish Heart' when you've ordered. Then I'll play 'The Third Man Theme.'"

"How did you know?"

"She told me. She walked by here and told me to play it. She is a beautiful young lady. I know you are proud of her."

"Yes, sir." There was a catch in London's throat and he had an urge to sit down by the man and talk to him and tell him he was a Baptist preacher and ask him all about himself. And yet he didn't want to remember that he was a Baptist preacher. He didn't want to forget, either. Forget or remember. "She's leaving tonight. Oh, that's right. Told you that before."

"Be gone a long time?" The pianist put his hands back on the keys and felt for a tune.

"Two weeks."

"That's not long."

London returned to his table, and when Paige came back he arose gallantly and held her chair. Then he pulled his own chair close to the table and opened the menu. "What'll it be?"

"Not steaks, Dad. Not steak and potatoes. But something different."

He studied the menu carefully and saw the word and almost mumbled it. "Pompano."

"It's a fish," Paige explained. "A very fine fish."

Her father nodded slowly. "Uh-huh. I know." He didn't tell her because there was no need to tell her: that years and years before he and Kathie had visited New Orleans and had eaten pompano for the first time. He had never eaten it since, had never thought about it since until this minute. "I think I will have pompano," he said.

"So will I." Paige lit a cigarette from the candle. "And a tossed salad. And please don't ask the waiter what church he belongs to."

"I won't," said London Wingo, and motioned for the waiter. "The pompano. Do you recommend it?"

The waiter nodded. "Yes. We are proud of our pompano. Fly it up from New Orleans."

"Then pompano for the lady," said London. "And one for me. Tossed salad. Brush the bowl with garlic. No vegetable oils. Only olive oil."

"Naturally, sir."

"Coffee later," London said, and glanced from the waiter to Paige, and her eyes were wide in surprise and delight.

She did not know her father could order a pompano dinner that way, so easily and with such confidence. She had heard him order a thousand meals but never by candlelight and in such a place as this. He wasn't preachery at all, but very handsome, the candlelight dancing in his eyes and the shadows on the gray hair at his temples. She reached across the table and touched his hand, squeezing it. "It's a shame you never had your cape with a red lining and a gold-headed cane and a cummerbund."

"I've had much more," he said.

The pianist slipped into "The Third Man Theme" and London patted her hand and said nothing. Then came "My Foolish Heart" and Paige's eyes moistened. "Oh, Dad. You are so much fun."

"So are you," he said.

The pompano was perfect and they ate slowly, enjoying each minute of it and each other. London bought a cigar and even tipped the doorman, whose only service was a perfunctory "Good night."

They drove to the airport and he purchased magazines for her and a package of mints. They stood on the ramp until the flight was announced, and he kissed her and watched her walk out to the plane, and then the plane was aloft and into the night.

He waited until it was out of sight, the lights blinking until the night accepted the plane into its mystery and hid it from London Wingo. There was an emptiness within him. She had been away before. Many times. But now she seemed so far away; so fast. He felt no particular concern, only loneliness. She was in the sky and the sky was his world, for his image of God was always in the sky and never on the sea or in the forest, but always in the sky with the stars and the clouds.

It was late when he got home, and he slept late the next morning and spent the day visiting the sick. Harry and Shelby Ward asked him to dinner, but he had promised the Ramseys. They had chicken and mashed potatoes and he kept thinking of candles and the tallow red and green and yellow.

The phone was ringing when he stepped into his apartment about nine o'clock. It was Paige calling. No, nothing was wrong, she quickly assured him. Yes, the trip was fine.

"Are you sure everything's all right?" London insisted.

"Oh, sure. It's beautiful here. But the radio setup doesn't suit me. I need Vance or somebody from the station to handle production. If we are going to do it at all, we ought to do it right."

"Have you talked to Benton?"

"No. Called you first. I wanted to let you know I am all right. Now you get in touch with Vance and tell him to call me. And don't forget there's an hour difference in time. O.K.?"

"Why don't you call him, honey? If it's business, I don't want to butt in——"

"Please don't argue, Dad. I know what I'm doing. Vance will be at the Upjohns' and I don't want to call him there. If I wait until he gets home it will be awful late down here, and it's the very dickens to get calls out. But he can reach me easy."

"O.K.," London said. "I'll get in touch with him. Now you're sure everything is all right?"

"Perfect. You'd love it here. Baptists thick as bees. Nicest, friendliest folks you ever saw."

They talked on for a few minutes, and then London called Benton and relayed Paige's message. "We should have sent one of our staff down with her," Benton said. "I was afraid of a production snarl. She and Vance are a team——"

"You'll send somebody down?"

"Sure, London. Like she said, we might as well do it right. I'll send Vance if he wants to go. I'll call you the first thing in the morning."

Vance caught a plane for Asheville the next afternoon. That was Wednesday. London had supper with Cliff and Bent that night and told them all about the Cardinal game he had seen with Paige and about the dinner. He spent Thursday morning in his study and had lunch with Forrest and told her about the game and the dinner. The next day he caught up with his pastoral visits, and the telegram was stuck under his door when he got home.

It was from Paige.

"Vance and I were married this morning in South Carolina. I am very happy and love you very much."

Chapter 12

Not since Kathie's death had London been so stunned or felt so helpless and alone. He did not look at the message again, knowing it was true and not caring to see the words, but crumpled it in his pocket and stood there in the hallway, staring down at the floor and seeing nothing.

Slowly he walked into the living room, still staring about, and sat down, his head drooping and his hands listless in his lap. She had deceived him. She had promised him her confidence without being asked for the promise. And now this—a hurried marriage in a distant state. He always had assumed that he would perform the ceremony, and now he did not know exactly where she was married or when.

Many times, since she was sixteen or seventeen, he had heard her talk about "when I get married," as girls do. No plans, of course. Only dreams. "You will perform the ceremony, Dad." She had always said that. "And I want an announcement in the paper. And my picture. Lots of parties, too. A church wedding and a reception. I want to carry little white rosebuds. Tiny white roses."

And so she had deceived him.

Then instinctively he began defending her to himself. He had indicted her and now he defended her. She must have a reason. Paige would never do such a thing without a reason. He must not pass judgment until he knew all the story. Maybe she was in trouble. Maybe right this minute she was wondering how he was taking it and worrying about his reactions.

His mind was clearing and impulsively he stepped to the phone and called Ridgecrest. She wasn't there. The Youth Conference was in recess for the day and most of the young people were picnicking in the mountains or visiting the nearby towns.

London returned the receiver to the cradle and stared at the instrument. He must call Benton. Maybe Vance had wired his father or even talked to him, but if he hadn't, then London must tell him. He telephoned Benton's home and then the radio station, but Benton was not available either.

A twinge of panic came to London Wingo. He was alone and troubled and needed to reach out and touch something real, anything to sustain him and reassure him. Quickly, hopefully, he dialed his phone again and Forrest Roberts answered.

"Forrest——" There was a catch in his voice.

"What's wrong, London?" Her intuition warned her.

"It's Paige. She and Vance are married."

"Where are you?"

"Home. I just got the telegram."

"Stay right there." It was a command, a comforting command. "I'll be right over. Have you talked to Benton?"

"No. Not yet. I couldn't locate him." Already he was feeling better and the panic was gone.

"I'll take care of that." Her tone was confident and authoritative. "I'll call Cliff too——"

"What about Mary Upjohn——"

"The devil with Mary Upjohn." She was impatient. "Don't you do anything until I get there."

She hung up and for a minute, perhaps longer, he sat in the hard, straight chair by the telephone stand, tapping his foot and trying to collect his thoughts. Then he filled his pipe but didn't light it, and walked around the apartment; into Paige's room and quickly out, and back to the living room, where he slumped into a big chair and closed his eyes. "Take care of her, Lord. Please, God. Take care of her."

Although it was only a few minutes, it seemed an hour before Forrest arrived. He met her at the door and she put her hands on his arm and smiled her assurance that everything would be all right. "I couldn't find Benton, but I got Cliff. He'll get Benton."

"What did Cliff say?"

"For me to come right on over here. And that he'd get Benton. That's all he said."

They walked into the living room and sat on the divan, and London said, "Wasn't Cliff surprised?"

"Not much. May I see the telegram?"

He took it out of his pocket. It was still crumpled and he smoothed it and handed it to her. "It was under the door when I got home."

Forrest read it quickly, and then again. "South Carolina." She glanced up at him. "It is very simple to get married in South Carolina, but it's the one state where you can't get a divorce." Carefully she folded the message and handed it back to him. "Well——"

"Well what?"

"Well, it's done. That's all." A car stopped in the driveway of Elmscourt and she crossed to a window and looked out, but it wasn't Cliff or Benton. "It was as plain as day that they loved each other." She came back to the divan and sat by him. "Have you had supper? May I fix you some coffee?"

"She didn't confide in me, Forrest. I had no inkling of this."

"You should have. She's your daughter, and if you did not know her heart you were blind. No crime has been done. She's grown and she got married. That's all."

"She had a reason." He was defending her again. "There is a reason for all this."

"Of course there's a reason." Forrest loosened her jacket and slipped it back on her shoulders and crossed her legs. "She's in love. That's reason enough. And they used their heads; marrying down there."

"I'm glad to hear you say that." He lit his pipe and was almost relaxed. "I was beginning to think along the same line. If they were going to get married, maybe this was the best way."

She went back to the window and looked out. "No question

about it, London. A church wedding here and all the commotion would have been most unwise. People would have felt sorry for Mary Upjohn and would have condemned Paige. It might even have split the church."

He was grateful for the words, grateful for an explanation. "Paige thought of that. I know she did."

Forrest said, "As it is now, it's done. There will be some gab-gab. A few folks will say, 'Poor little Mary.' Then they'll forget all about it."

London said, "I can't believe that she left here with this in mind. She would have told me."

"Of course she would. No, they didn't have it in mind. I'm sure they didn't. But when they met down there—well, moonlight and mountains, and away from home and the pressure; away from all of us and everything—well, they just up and got married. It makes sense to me." She uncrossed her legs and stood up. "Now, what about some coffee?"

He walked with her to the kitchen and got down the cups. "I feel better, Forrest. But Paige never wanted to be a preacher's wife. I've heard her say it."

"She's not a preacher's wife."

"That's what bothers me." He put the cups in the saucers and peeped in the kettle. It was full. "She might try to persuade him not to be a preacher."

"You think so?"

"I'm afraid so."

"You think she can do it?"

"I don't know."

"Neither do I," said Forrest. "But I know one thing. If she can influence Vance away from the ministry, then he is not fit for the ministry."

"He might go on and try it and she might be unhappy. She's no preacher's wife. She is not cut out for the ministry."

"How do you know?" It was a soft question, and Forrest did not look at him. She, too, peeped into the kettle and saw that it was full. "She could change. And let me tell you something right now."

She looked at him then, full into his eyes. "A woman is as capable of sacrifice as a man. Her spiritual depth is just as deep and her spiritual height is just as high. The Kingdom of God is not for men only. You preach faith. Well, believe in it. God can call Paige to His service as easily as He can call Vance Andrews. And she can give as much because she loves God first, but she loves Vance too. Don't you ever forget that, London Wingo; not as long as you live."

It was what he wanted to hear and he might have asked her more, but the doorbell interrupted the talk and in came Cliff and Benton. Cliff's face was set in a fixed smile, an obvious attempt at cheerfulness, but Benton made no effort to conceal his dejection. His face was haggard, and Forrest looked at him steadily, ignoring Cliff as she watched him, and hoped that London did not see all that she saw.

Benton went straight to London and put his hand on his friend's shoulder. "Well. There it is." The words were almost a mumble.

"Have you heard from Vance?" London asked.

"A telegram was at home when I got there." Benton turned his face from London and looked at the others. "They were married in South Carolina. That's about all it said."

They compared the telegrams and they were almost identical.

Benton lit a cigarette and tried to relax and forced a smile to his lips. "There's nothing I can say, London, except it's probably the best thing my boy ever did."

"You know how I feel about it," London said, and offered his hand to Benton. "He's your son. I'm proud of that. And now I'm proud that he's my son."

Cliff's eyes filled and Forrest turned away. The kettle was boiling, and she walked back to the kitchen and poured the hot water into the dripolator and rejoined the men in the living room.

"I ain't so surprised." Cliff broke an interval of silence. "Looking back at it now, I ain't surprised a bit."

"I was," Benton said flatly.

"So was I," said London.

"And I wish we could hear from them," Benton said. "The least Vance can do is call us and let us know they are all right."

Forrest went to the divan and sat on the edge and looked from Benton to London and back at Benton, a long time. "They are all right. They just happen not to be thinking about you two right now. They wired you. What do you want them to do? Call up and bawl?"

"I tried to call Paige, but she wasn't at Ridgecrest," London said.

"Course they ain't at Ridgecrest." Cliff crossed the room and sat down by Forrest. "I bet you I can tell you what happened. They decided last night to get married." He stuck a piece of gum in his mouth and chewed thoughtfully. "So bright and early this morning they lit out for South Carolina. All it takes to get married in South Carolina is good health, a license, a J.P. fee, and a girl. They got down there about the middle of the morning. Got married and wired home. Then they headed back for Ridgecrest or somewheres in the mountains. You'll hear from 'em. Vance got any money?"

"Not much," said Benton. "Not with him."

"Then you'll hear pretty soon," Cliff said, nodding his head slowly.

London turned on the lamp by the divan and then every light in the room. He suddenly wanted light and no gloom or shadows. "What about Mary Upjohn, Cliff? Does she know?"

"Not that I know of. But I'll handle that."

The doorbell startled them all, particularly London. He didn't feel up to a visit from any of his members. The Bledsoes, for example. Or even Sisler Mason. Or the Upjohns. He started for the door and Cliff waved him aside. "I'll answer it."

Harry and Shelby Ward were at the door, and Cliff bowed them in and he and Harry faced each other. "Good evening, Brother Carter." Harry offered his hand.

Cliff grasped it in genuine good will. "Glad to see you, Dr. Ward. You all go right on in."

Shelby was the first into the living room, and she hurried to London and kissed his cheek and held out her hand to Benton. "Congratulations——"

"How did you know?" London frowned slightly as he asked it.

"Good heavens! Is it a secret?" Shelby glanced from London to Benton and over at Forrest. "And what is it? A wedding or a wake?"

London smiled then for the first time that evening. "We just heard a little while back, and I was wondering how you heard so soon."

"I told her," Forrest explained. "I called her right after you called me and told her that if I wasn't over here in fifteen minutes for her or Dr. Ward to come up and stay with you."

Harry walked over near a window and stood by Cliff. "Have you heard any more? J.P. or preacher? South Carolina is the best place in the world to get married. No rigmarole. They tie the knot and you can't get it untied in South Carolina."

Benton had nothing to say, but London tried to explain. "We were sort of expecting them to call——"

"Expecting *them* to call!" Shelby Ward put her hands on her hips and stared at him. "You go call that girl right now. They used their heads and you tell her so and tell her you are tickled to death. You, too, Benton Andrews——"

"How do you figure that?" London asked.

"Common sense." Shelby visibly was irritated. "They were going to get married. Everybody saw it but you and Benton Andrews. So they did it without any commotion or fuss and avoided any big to-do around here."

Her words brought a warm feeling to London because they were in defense of Paige. "That's what Forrest and I were thinking——" he began.

"Do you think this is the way Paige wanted it?" Shelby interrupted him and moved close to him and looked straight at him. "Like any girl, she's probably been dreaming about her wedding for years. Big church wedding and all that. Beautiful bridal gown and you performing the ceremony. But, oh no. It couldn't be that way. She's a preacher's daughter and her life wasn't her own. She had to think about the church and you and Mary Upjohn. You go call that child right this minute."

"I tried to call her at Ridgecrest, but she's not there."

Harry Ward stepped to his wife's side and put his hand on her shoulder and patted her. "They haven't had time to get back to Ridgecrest. But I can find them. I've got contacts in Ridgecrest. Raised money for one of the buildings down there. I can find them if you want me to."

"I wish you would," London said.

"All right. You all wait right here." Harry moved toward the door. "I'll use my phone. Can charge it to business and save you money. Cliff—come on, go with me."

"I'll walk along with you." Cliff ran his finger under his collar and adjusted his tie. "But can't hang around. Got a little errand to do."

"Upjohns?" Benton spoke for the first time in several minutes. His face was still drawn and he was aloof from them all.

"That's right," said Cliff, and stepped over to London and clamped his hand on his pastor's arm. "We might as well get that behind us, and I'm the one to do it."

London's eyes spoke his gratitude. What a storehouse of treasure he had, for he had so many friends.

Shelby and Forrest both nodded to Cliff, approving his plan, and Shelby lifted his hat from the table and handed it to him. "And look, Cliff——"

"Yes'm." He seemed surprised that she called him "Cliff." She had always called him "Brother Carter."

"While you're out there sort of ask around and find out what size stockings Mary wears. I'd like to get my hands on that girl and fix her up."

"So would I," Forrest said. "I wouldn't take sides before, but now it's different. This may be the best thing that ever happened to Mary. May wake her up."

Cliff and Harry left them, and Shelby stood in the doorway and watched them walking together down the corridor, and when she came back into the living room her eyes were happy-bright and her lashes were damp.

Benton pulled a chair nearer to the divan and sat down and lit another cigarette. "Never thought I'd see Cliff and Dr. Ward together again. Funny how things pull folks together."

Shelby changed the subject quickly. "Thought I smelled coffee when I came in. Did you make some coffee, Forrest?"

"Uh-huh. Probably cold by now, though. Come on, let's make some fresh."

The four of them went to the kitchen, and Forrest assumed command and filled the kettle and turned on the gas. "Get two more cups, London. And aren't there some Nabiscos or vanilla wafers or something?"

"Fig newtons. Right there in the pantry." He reached for the cups and looked at them. They were chipped. "These are sort of beat up. They are our everyday cups, and Paige and I only had two good ones." He pushed the cups away and they clattered. "Forrest, look up there in the cabinet and get our best cups. The pretty ones."

The pretty cups were Kathie's cups, and Forrest saw Benton raise his eyes and look at her, a wry smile on his lips, almost a sardonic smile. She knew that Shelby was watching her, too, and she stepped to the cabinet and reached for the china.

A sudden fear touched her and held her. What if she dropped one? Her hand trembled and then she was annoyed at herself. After all, they were cups and nothing more, and she was going to share coffee with him and with their friends. Her hand steadied and she took down the cups and saucers and handed them to London Wingo.

"They need rinsing," London said.

"Uh-huh. They sure do." Forrest turned from him and faced Benton, meeting his gaze. "Here, Benton. Make yourself useful. Rinse these cups. And be careful. It's beautiful china. They belonged to Mrs. Wingo. Isn't that right, London?"

"Yes. They were Kathie's." He said it casually and without any particular meaning. A statement of fact and nothing else.

Shelby helped Benton wash the cups, and Forrest moved about the kitchen arranging things. Her step was sure and light and her head was high, her eyes shining and the surety of triumph in her manner. But only Shelby saw it—Shelby because she was a woman.

They took their refreshments to the living room and were sipping the coffee when Harry Ward came back. He had a slip of paper in his hand and obviously was pleased with himself. "They are at a place called Cattaloochee Ranch. Back in the Great Smoky Mountains. Here's the number." He handed the paper to London.

"Thanks," London said, and put his cup and saucer on a table.

"It's not far from Ridgecrest." Harry sat down on the divan next to Shelby. "Now, how about some coffee?"

"Coming right up," she said, and walked toward the kitchen.

"Be sure and get one of the best cups," Forrest called after her. "He has earned the best."

London gave no attention to the words, even if he heard them, for his mind was on other matters. He memorized the number on the paper and stood up, facing Harry. "Did you learn anything else? It might save me asking her some questions."

"Uh-huh." Harry picked up a fig newton from Shelby's saucer and began nibbling it. "The Youth Conference was in recess today and they drove down to Greenville, South Carolina. They were married by a justice of the peace."

Not even by a minister. Not even in a church or a parsonage. Harry hated to tell it.

"I see," said London. "Anything else?"

"They drove back to North Carolina and notified Ridgecrest they'd be back there Monday morning. Then they headed for the Great Smoky Mountains. That Cattaloochee place, or how ever you pronounce it."

London brushed a crumb of fig newton from his coat and walked into the hallway and dialed long distance. "I am calling Mrs. Vance Andrews." His voice was husky and the operator did not understand the name or the number, so he cleared his throat and repeated both. "Yes, operator, it is person-to-person. No, I will not talk to anyone else."

Forrest stepped to the hallway and closed the door between them and him and tiptoed back to the divan. Benton put his cup and saucer aside and leaned back in his chair. Shelby reached over and patted her husband's hand.

The connection between Linden and North Carolina took only a minute, and then a voice at the other end was saying, "Mrs. Andrews—it's for you. Not, not you, Mr. Andrews. Your wife.

Somebody's calling from Linden, Missouri. Or something like that."

London Wingo held his breath and then he heard her voice and it was faint and a bit frightened and seemed so far away. "Hello—hello. Dad? Is that you, Dad?"

"Hello, honey." The lump was heavy in his throat and he swallowed hard. "You all right?"

"Oh, Dad! I knew you'd call." She was laughing and crying at the same time. "I knew it. Hold it. Let me close the door." She was back on the line in a second. "You there, Dad?"

"I'm still here. You all right?"

"Of course I'm all right. And I knew you'd call. I was telling Vance just a few minutes ago that I knew you'd call. You all right?"

"I'm fine." His voice was no longer husky and the lump was gone from his throat.

"You're not upset?"

"No. I'm not upset, honey. I was surprised, but everything's all right now. Everything's all right. Don't you worry about a thing——"

"I wasn't trying to put anything over, Dad. Honest to goodness. It just happened. You believe me, don't you?"

"Of course I believe you."

"When Vance stepped off that plane I knew I loved him. I couldn't tell you because you were not here. I started to call you, but I just didn't, that's all. So we went down to South Carolina this morning and got married."

"I hope he paid the preacher." London was trying to be witty and the words slipped out.

A moment of silence and he compressed his lips and wished he could recall the words. Her voice was steady and clear when it came again. "We were not married by a preacher, Dad. A justice of the peace married us. Don't blame Vance. Blame me. He wanted a preacher, but I said that if you couldn't marry us, then I didn't want a preacher. So we went to a J.P.'s house and he married us."

"What's wrong with that?" He was hiding his disappointment. "If you are happy—I'm happy. Now what are your plans? Need anything?"

"Oh, Dad—Dad. I knew you'd take it this way. I knew you wouldn't be mad. Does Mary Upjohn know?"

"I suppose so. Cliff went out to tell her."

"What about Mr. Andrews? How did he take it? Was he surprised? Is he mad at Vance?"

"He's here with me. Forrest and the Wards too. Want to speak to him?"

"Not now. I want to talk to you. Tell Forrest to look in my closet and send me that light blue dress and all my skirts and blouses. And my blue shoes and every pair of stockings I've got. My bathing suit too. It's in my bottom drawer——"

"Sounds like you plan to be away awhile."

"Uh-huh." She was laughing. "We are going back to Ridgecrest Monday and finish the conference. Then we are going to Cape Hatteras for two weeks. By then it will be time for us to go to the seminary."

To the seminary? He was sure he heard her right and his heart began pounding. "Did you say seminary? You're going to the seminary?"

"Of course." She said it with emphasis, as though he should have known it. "You don't think I'm going to let Vance go alone, do you? If I'm going to be a preacher's wife, I've got to learn the ropes."

He didn't reply immediately. He couldn't. His heart was filling his chest and his throat suddenly was dry. She was going to the seminary. She and Vance—as he and Kathie had done. The seminary, then the field; the calling.

"Dad? You there?"

"Yes, honey. I'm still here."

"Surprised?"

"Uh-huh." He closed his eyes tight and felt the tears squeezing through. "You and Vance have talked it through?"

"Yes, sir."

"And prayed it through?"

"Yes, sir."

"Then God bless you, honey." He could say no more at that moment and was silent, and she, too, was silent, and then he said, "I'm proud, Paige. I'm proud and grateful. But think about it a long time, Paige. And pray and pray."

"I have." Her voice dropped to a whisper and then broke into sobs. "I'm so happy, Dad. I'm crying because I'm so happy. I'm going to be a preacher's wife. Like my mother." The sobs dwindled into sniffles and she began laughing. "Crying on my honeymoon. Crazy, isn't it? Now, hold the line. Vance wants to talk to you."

He heard her open the door and heard her call, "Vance. Dad's on the phone, darling. He wants to talk to you." She picked up the receiver again. "Hello, Dad. He's coming. Now we'll be home in about three weeks. But just for a few days. We won't have but a few days at home."

"Let us know if you need anything."

"O.K. Good night, Dad. I love you."

Vance's voice was strained and he, too, seemed a bit frightened. "Brother Wingo? How are you? You all right?"

"I'm fine, son." London laughed in spite of himself. "How about——"

"Yes, sir. We got married this morning and came straight up here, and this is one of the prettiest places you ever saw." His words were running together. "Away back in the mountains and one of the prettiest places you ever saw and you and Dad and Mr. Carter ought to come down here sometime and rest up——"

"You need anything, Vance?" London interrupted the nervous flow of words.

"No, sir." The tension was broken and the boy's tone was almost calm. "Paige told you our plans?"

"Uh-huh."

"We are going to the seminary together. She's going with me, Brother Wingo."

"So she said. You two do the work and I'll do the praying." He was trying to be gay and was gay; well, almost gay, anyway. "Now anything I can do for you?"

"Yes, sir. Call Dad to the phone, please. I want to speak to Dad."

"I'll call him, son."

"And I'll take care of her, Brother Wingo."

"I know that, Vance. And God bless you. God bless both of you." He laid the receiver on the table and put his hand on the knob to open the door into the living room, and then he stopped and lowered his head. "Take care of them, please, God. Help them to be useful, and if this is Thy call, bless them to Thy glory. But don't let them make a mistake in this thing, God. Please, our Father."

London Wingo straightened his shoulders and opened the door and spoke to Benton Andrews. "He's on the line, Bent. He wants to speak to you."

He reached out and touched Benton's shoulder as he passed and closed the door to the hallway, and went over to the divan and sat by Harry Ward but was looking at Forrest. "Everything is all right. She's going to the seminary with him. She is going to be a preacher's wife."

"God be praised," said Harry Ward in the most reverent tone London ever had heard him use.

"I thought so all along," said Shelby. "It's her heritage."

"It's a call," London said. "God calls women as well as men. I believe that. And now she must learn to give so much and expect so little."

Forrest Roberts said nothing, only looking at him and wishing he could see her heart and know that she, too, could give all and ask nothing except the joy of sharing his life and his ministry.

They all were silent, and Benton's voice drifted through the closed door and they all began talking at the same time, but really saying nothing. Then Benton came out of the hallway and some of the misery and doubt were gone from his eyes, although his face was still drawn. They looked at him and he didn't say a word until he had lit a cigarette and broken the match into an ash tray.

"I suppose they told you they are going to the seminary together." He was speaking to London, as though the others were not there at all.

"Uh-huh. In about three weeks."

Benton remained standing, his hands in his pockets, where he nervously jingled some coins and his keys. "I suppose it's out of our hands now."

"It has never been in your hands," Forrest said.

"Maybe you are right." He pulled back his sleeve and glanced at his wrist watch. "The boy asked me to send him money. He didn't take much with him. That's a pretty good sign that this thing wasn't planned."

"I'm sure it wasn't," London said. "Paige said it wasn't."

Benton put out his hand and London got up and took it and they did not speak, although each started to say something and then apparently realized that nothing was to be said, that the handshake said it all.

Harry Ward put his hands on his knees and got up too. "It's getting late. We left the children by themselves."

London said, "I'll drive you home, Forrest. You, too, Benton. I'll drop you off wherever you say."

Harry Ward said, "I'll drive them home. You are pretty tired, London. Tomorrow is Saturday and you've probably got to get up a sermon."

"That's right. I may have to dip into my reserve for Sunday."

"I've got one if you are stuck," Harry said. "I was planning to use it in about a month, but you can have it. From Isaiah. 'They that wait upon the Lord shall renew their strength.' Remember the passage?"

"Sure. 'They shall mount up with wings as eagles——' "

" 'They shall run, and not be weary——' " Shelby Ward took it up.

" 'And they shall walk, and not faint.' " Forrest finished it.

London moved from Benton over near Harry and said, "Thanks a lot. Thanks a lot, Harry. But I'll pull one together."

"I'll be with you in a minute." Forrest also stepped closer to Harry. She began picking up the cups, Kathie's cups, and took them to the kitchen. Shelby moved to help her and Harry put his hand on her arm and stopped her; and Forrest washed the cups and put them away and they told London Wingo good night and were gone.

He slipped off his shoes and sprawled in a big chair, his feet on a footstool and his eyes closed. Strange—but he wasn't thinking of

Paige at that moment. He was thinking of what Isaiah had said: "They that wait upon the Lord shall renew their strength." And he applied it to himself. He must wait upon the Lord. He must renew his strength. Where had he failed? Or had he failed at all?

His mind came back to Paige. She was going to be a preacher's wife. Then what? Would her face be long and solemn and her merriment gone? Would she subscribe to the demands of the people and change her life to suit their whims? Or would she fight back as Kathie had done and try to live her own life, and break herself on the rock that supported her husband's pulpit?

Should a preacher ever marry at all? Can he really share his commission with a woman, or does his life belong wholly to God?

Well, anyway, it was done. And now he must move again. This apartment was too much. He would move out to the Plymouth Community, out near his church.

He rubbed his forehead and opened his eyes and went into her room, still in his sock feet, and looked around. He would send her things to her himself. No need of bothering Forrest. He got a box and put it on the bed and put her things in it. The blue dress and the blue shoes, the skirts and blouses. He folded them carefully and stuffed stockings around the corners, and the box was full. He would mail it tomorrow.

The doorbell interrupted him and he scowled and walked noiselessly to the hallway and listened. Who in the world this time of night? He had a good mind not to answer it. Let them think he was gone or asleep. But it might be somebody in trouble.

So he slipped on his shoes and opened the door, and Clark Upjohn was there, his hat in one hand and his other hand slowly rubbing the brim. "Good evening, Brother Wingo. Hope you hadn't turned in."

"I hadn't, Brother Upjohn. Come in."

Clark Upjohn sat on the edge of his chair and held his hat in his lap and ran a finger up and down the crease in the crown. It was his Sunday hat and he had on his Sunday suit. "Cliff Carter just left my place and I thought I'd drop by to see you." He didn't look up but was staring down at his hat.

"I'm glad you did," London said.

"I just want you to know——" He looked up then. "I just want you to know, Brother Wingo, that there ain't no hard feelings."

"I'm glad," said London, and lifted his tobacco pouch from a table and stirred the tobacco with his finger and then filled his pipe. "But it never occurred to me that there might be hard feelings between us. How is Mary?"

Clark tossed his hat over on the divan and got out his own pipe. "Sort of upset and yet not sort of upset neither. I think she know'd all along it was going to wind up this-a-way."

He felt for his tobacco, and London offered him the pouch and said, "Try mine."

"Thank you," said Clark. "Got my own." He filled his pipe and lit it and settled back in the chair. "Yes, sir. I say Mary felt all along this is how it would wind up. And I ain't talking against your son-in-law. Vance is a good boy, but he never was the one for Mary."

"Yes, he's a good boy," said London firmly. "And this thing surprised me, Clark. I want you to know that. They hadn't planned it this way at all."

Clark looked at him, and London met the gaze and Clark nodded slowly. "If you say it's so, then it's so. Benton Andrews never wanted his boy to marry my girl neither."

"This surprised Benton as much as it did me." London pulled an ash tray closer and laid his pipe on it.

"Naw, sir." Clark stared up at the ceiling and his pipe bowl was cupped in his hand. "Mr. Andrews was against my girl at first. And then he acted like he sort of liked her. After you folks got here he began acting like my girl was tip-top with him and maybe even good enough for his boy. I don't understand a man like Mr. Andrews."

"He has had a lot of trouble, Clark——"

"Who ain't?"

"He's a good man, Clark. Benton Andrews is all right. Little strange, maybe. But all right."

"Ain't a Christian. Heard him say so myself. In the barbershop one morning. Heard him say it plain as day."

"All men are not Christians," London said. "Some good men are not Christians."

"I hear he don't even believe in God. I don't understand a man like that."

London said nothing, only puffing his pipe.

Clark was silent, too, and thoughtful, and then he said, "Mary was more like mad than upset. She didn't cry or nothing. Not a tear. She asked me to come over here and tell you that she ain't mad at nobody, that she's going to stay right on in the church, working just like she was. Me too."

"I am glad of that," said London.

"She told me to ask you to pray for her."

"I will."

"Well——" Clark knocked the ash out of his pipe and put it back in his pocket. "If you can pray for mine, I can pray for yours." He reached over for his hat and got up. "I'll be going now."

"I am glad you came by, Brother Upjohn. I thank you for coming." He held out his hand, and Clark took it and pumped it slowly.

"Maybe a little prayer would help us now, Preacher."

"It always helps," said London Wingo, and knelt by the divan.

Clark knelt beside him and rested his arm on the divan and his face on his arm.

"You lead us, Brother Upjohn."

A few moments of silence and then Clark Upjohn prayed. "Lord, look after us and make us useful. Bless Brother Wingo here by me, and bless Paige and Vance. And Mary. Look after my daughter, Lord. Show us all how to love one another and forgive one another and help one another. Bless the church. Ever' church, Lord. And bless our country. Ever' country, please. No more hate, Lord. Just let ever'body be brothers, ever'where. And bless Mr. Andrews——"

He hesitated, as though pondering the words, perhaps seeking words, and then softly, almost a whisper, "Yes, Father. Please bless Brother Andrews. Amen."

Chapter 13

The marriage of Paige and Vance caused a quick tempest in the Plymouth Baptist Church that subsided just as quickly into a ripple and was nothing more.

There were a few suggestive smirks by the back-seat and back-alley libertines who judged all others by themselves, and scattered but spontaneous sympathy for London as an unappreciated father and for Mary Upjohn as a sweet little girl who had got a raw deal.

The chitchat came from the leisured and exhausted older folks, most of them widows who lived on insurance checks or small trust funds that had helped kill their husbands. The smirks came from the jaded canasta and conversation axis within the church, the argumentative intellectuals who considered themselves a cultural clique and bantered such names as John O'Hara and Ernest Hemingway; two or three of them actually had read Henry Miller and they all had read *Forever Amber*. (The favorite saying for a straying sister was: "She's going Amber.")

The young people, however, took it in the good humor and wisdom that youth possesses and then loses. So a boy and girl had fallen in love and got married. So what?

On the first Sunday that London faced his congregation after the event, he was quite conscious of their curiosity and aware that they hoped he would mention the marriage. This he had no intention of doing. He had planned how to handle it and was calm, even more reserved than usual, when he walked from his study to the rostrum and looked out at his people.

The first shock of the day came from Mary Upjohn. She was sitting on an aisle seat, about halfway back, and next to Sloan Wentworth, and the minute he reached his pulpit she got up and walked down to the piano.

London was arranging his notes and then he glanced up and saw her and was startled. She had on new shoes and sheer stockings and there was a swinging grace to her walk. Her dress was an old one, but freshly cleaned and swishy, and her hair was waved in a professional permanent. He almost stared at her, but quickly caught himself in the sudden realization that the people were watching her and him. A whisper ran through the church.

She sat at the piano and Sisler Mason led them into the first song and London stood at the side of his pulpit and led them in prayer, then stepped squarely behind his pulpit for the day's announcements. It was all he could do to keep from glancing down at Mary.

"I have an announcement of interest to all of us." He was almost straining for dignity. "Brother Vance Andrews and his wife, Sister Paige Andrews, will leave in about three weeks for the seminary in Rochester, New York, where Brother Andrews will complete his studies for the ministry. Inasmuch as this young couple are members of this church and go forth from this church, I am sure our prayers will go with them."

He paused, then said, "There will be a meeting of the Lottie Moon Circle of the W.M.S. at the home of Sister Leo Ramsey at three o'clock Tuesday afternoon. The Building Committee will meet with the pastor in his study at eight o'clock Thursday night."

He pushed his notes aside and opened the Bible, and rested his hands on the pulpit and looked out at them, a command that the whispering must cease—and it ceased and they looked up at him, for the Word of God was now open and there must be silence.

"Our Scripture reading for today is from the Book of Isaiah." Again he paused, and read slowly: " 'They that wait upon the Lord shall renew their strength; they shall mount up with wings as eagles; they shall run, and not be weary; and they shall walk, and not faint.' "

He closed the Book and bowed his head for a minute of silent prayer, then said, "We will now worship God in our morning offering." He nodded to Mary, the cue for her solo, as Cliff and the other deacons came forward for the offering.

The first note that Mary struck brought the church to surprised attention. It was no dreary note of doubt, no whiny note of self-pity or indecision, but a clear, strong note that rang out. Then she went right into the solo—"Lead, Kindly Light"—and her head was high and her fingers, her manicured fingers, moved surely over the keys and brought forth beauty.

Sisler Mason blinked and glanced over at London and blinked again. Buck Bledsoe was so surprised that he put a five-dollar bill in the plate and forgot to take out change. Estes Oliphant sat transfixed, his collection envelope in his hand and his mouth open. Cliff leaned over to accept Forrest's offering, and their eyes met and they smiled.

London sat in the big, stern oak chair behind his pulpit, his fingers locked on his chest and his thumbs tapping together. He stared at the base of his pulpit, listening to the music and pondering its message, then he turned his face toward Mary and saw how bright her eyes were, but her face pale and intense, and there was jubilation within him, and a wonderment.

> I was not ever thus, nor prayed that Thou
>   Shouldst lead me on;
> I loved to choose and see my path; but now
>   Lead Thou me on!

He was not thinking of Paige and how she must change or of Mary Upjohn and how she already had changed. He was thinking of his own ministry, of his own soul, of the true meaning of the song as it touched him.

> Keep Thou my feet; I do not ask to see
> The distant scene; one step enough for me.

How often had he stood on the sand and reached for the sky, and how frightened he always was when the sand crumbled, and how impatient he was to run and never to walk. He had thought about it a hundred times and had sung the song a hundred times, and now it was so clear to him. Just one step. Nothing can separate man from the love of God and then one step toward God. That was all man could ask. He felt better than he had felt in a long time and his soul was refreshed.

Mary finished the solo and went back and sat down by Sloan Wentworth, and London preached only a few minutes that morning. He put his notes aside and talked about a song and what it meant, a song written by a minister who heard the call in one church and lived to be a cardinal in another.

The congregation was singing "Lead, Kindly Light" when he walked up the aisle, singing himself, and opened the door of the church. The people followed him, some of them still singing, and they gathered around him and shook his hand and asked about Paige.

Mary asked her address. "But surely she and Vance will be home before they go to the seminary?" The light of the hour and the song was still in her eyes.

"Yes," London said. "They will be here a few days."

"Anyway, I want to write her." Her eyebrows had been plucked and the wavy hair brushed her ears. "I'll write her at Ridgecrest. Tonight. As soon as Sloan and I get back from St. Louis." She put her hand to the back of her hair and fluffed it. "He's driving me over."

London was wondering if Forrest and Shelby were responsible for Mary's appearance, and to make comment said casually, "Oh yes. I'd forgotten about the concert. There's a good ball game over there too. The Cleveland Indians are in town. Feller might pitch."

"Sloan doesn't like baseball." Mary was as casual as he. "Concerts either. We may take in a movie."

Mary Upjohn at a movie on Sunday! Here was another shock. Surely she was saying it for the purpose of shock. But he wasn't sure, and she turned and left him and walked to the curb and got in Sloan's car.

Estes Oliphant asked him to dinner and they drove away, although a few people still were lingering around the church door and talking about this and that, but mostly nothing. They wanted to talk about Mary, but Clark Upjohn was among them. However, the minute London was beyond hearing, Lizzie Ramsey spoke to the group, particularly to Maggie Bledsoe. "I thought he'd mention it. I heard a J.P. did it."

"Me too," said Sister Bledsoe. "I was dying for him to mention it."

"Why should he?" Forrest asked quickly.

Lizzie Ramsey shrugged and smiled at her. "No reason. But she's got a lot to learn, that girl. If she's going to be a preacher's wife."

Forrest glanced over at Cliff and knew he was not going to comment, so she did. "Paige will be all right." She wondered why she should take it upon herself to defend Paige, but she had to. The words were out before she weighed them or their consequences. "Paige will be a good preacher's wife."

"What makes you think so?" Sister Ramsey asked.

"Because it is not necessary for a preacher's wife to be any different from any other wife." She wished then she was not in the discussion at all and was annoyed with herself for paying any attention to what Lizzie Ramsey said.

"But they are different." Sister Ramsey still was smiling, and Maggie Bledsoe was smiling now. Cliff, however, was looking away and slowly chewing his gum. The others were watching Forrest.

"Not if people would leave them alone." Forrest felt her voice rising and her temper too. "Besides, Paige is Brother Wingo's daughter. She couldn't have lived under his roof as long as she did without some of his influence touching her. She'll be a good preacher's wife."

"Maybe you are right," Lizzie said, and leaned over close to her husband and adjusted the white handkerchief in his coat pocket. "Maybe she will be like her mother. Mrs. Wingo was quite a high stepper at first. But she changed——"

"Did you know Mrs. Wingo?" Forrest asked, purring the words.

"Oh no. I heard a lot about her, though." She smoothed her gloves and flicked a spot of dust from her pocketbook. "She made him what he is. Her kind don't come along often."

Forrest drew back from the insinuation and was cold inside. Cliff stepped instantly beside her and looked at all of them and chewed his gum slower and slower. "I knew Kathie Wingo. Knew her real good. Kathie didn't change. The people did." He slipped his arm under Forrest's arm. "Shame you two never knew each other. You and her would have hit it off mighty good."

She could have kissed him. She wanted to kiss him, and she did squeeze her arm against his. Then she turned her back to Sister Ramsey and Sister Bledsoe and spoke to Clark Upjohn. "Mary certainly played well this morning. And I never saw her look so pretty."

"Thank you, ma'am," said Clark Upjohn, and his wife beamed.

"It's getting late. Past dinnertime." Forrest spoke over her shoulder to Sister Ramsey and Sister Bledsoe. "Good-by, Lizzie. Good-by, Maggie."

Mrs. Bledsoe flushed up because she hated to be called "Maggie." Buck Bledsoe grinned, and so did Clark Upjohn.

Cliff took Forrest's arm to get her away before anything else was said. "Come on. I'll treat you to dinner."

"Post Office Café?" They were walking away, the people staring at her.

"If you don't mind," Cliff said.

"I don't mind a bit."

Harry Ward helped London find an apartment about five blocks from the church. It had four small rooms, including a dining alcove and a fireplace and was just right for a man living alone. He put most of his furniture in storage and someday he would give it to Paige. He took Kathie's china and silver with him, though, and put the china on the second shelf of the kitchen cabinet and hung up twelve little hooks for the twelve cups.

He hired an elderly woman, a Negro, to come each morning at nine to wash dishes and clean up, and because there was so little to do she insisted on looking after his clothes too. Her name was Mattie and she was a Jehovah's Witness and greeted him each morning with a verse of Scripture.

"Good morning, Brother Wingo. 'Now we see through a glass, darkly.' Corinthians."

"Good morning, Mattie. 'Let all things be done decently and in order.' Same Corinthians."

The first morning in his new home he fixed twice as much coffee as he needed. The dripolator was too big, so he bought a smaller one. Then a smaller skillet and boiler, even a smaller kettle. Everything seemed so much smaller; one egg instead of two, one towel, one washrag, and he could leave his razor on the lavatory all day.

He cooked his own breakfast and ate dinner and supper out, usually at a member's home. He had the car whenever he wanted it, and because it was there all the time he did not use it often, but walked much, his head bare to the autumn sun and his step sprightly and his shoulders square.

Everything was always just where he put it, and there was no one to tell him what to do or to share anything, even the morning paper. There were no cigarette ashes in the trays and no bobby pins on the side of the tub and no discarded Kleenex in the bathroom with smudges of lipstick.

He got up every morning at seven o'clock and shaved while the coffee was boiling, and there was no one to wake up. Then he went to the door and got his newspaper and laid it by his plate and cooked an egg and bacon and two pieces of toast. He read his newspaper while he ate and at first he often looked up over his paper, but he soon learned better and did not look up at all.

Always he took his second cup of coffee to the living room and finished his paper and then he dressed and was ready for the day's work.

"Good morning, Brother Wingo. 'The Lord called Samuel: and he answered, Here I am.' First Samuel."

"Good morning, Mattie. 'Speak, Lord; for thy servant heareth.' Same Samuel."

And he had so much time on his hands. He visited and worked from nine until eleven and from two until four. His women members didn't want to see him in the mornings. They were too busy to dress up and mustn't let the preacher see them unless they were fixed properly. So he visited hospitals in the mornings and studied.

He saw three movies the first week Paige was married and had dinner with Forrest once and with Cliff twice. The days were all right and not too bad at first, but the nights were long.

Paige and Vance were at Cape Hatteras. They had been married almost two weeks and he had had two letters from her, the first one very short and the second not much longer. He had written her twice and reported all the news and gossip and about Mattie.

"Good morning, Brother Wingo. 'The voice of the turtle is heard in our land.' Song of Solomon."

"Good morning, Mattie. 'The little foxes, that spoil the vines.' More Solomon."

"Am I putting too much starch in your shirts?"

"They are just right."

"Your blue suit needs pressing."

"Thank you, Mattie. I'll take it down today."

"Found your hat way back in the closet. Squashed. Don't you wear a hat?"

"Not any more."

"Most men your age wear a hat. Never saw a preacher before who didn't wear a hat."

"My daughter made me quit."

"But she ain't here no more."

London thought the conversation would amuse Paige, and he regaled Forrest and Cliff and Benton with stories about Mattie. But soon the stories wore thin and Mattie was no longer a character, only a friend, and the spare hours were heavy on his hands.

He had more time than church.

It was Forrest who suggested that he begin writing his book on Roger Williams, that he get something on paper. For years he had talked about the book and planned it, but somehow it never had occurred to him that someday he must sit down and write it out.

This was the time. The suggestion delighted him, not that he was ready or even capable, but it was a chance to see Forrest more, a reason for dropping by her apartment every time he felt lonely.

He began his book while Mattie was cleaning his bedroom, then moved into the bedroom while she cleaned the living room. It took him an hour to write the first page, and he thought it was pretty good and called Forrest and asked permission to show it to her and, incidentally, to take her to lunch.

They never got out to lunch. Forrest showed him why his first page was no good at all, and fixed coffee and sandwiches and they sat in her living room and worked on the beginning of the book.

"You mustn't preach sermons," she advised him. "Let Roger Williams do the preaching. And begin at the beginning."

"I don't like books that begin that So-and-so was born at such-and-such a time in such-and-such a place." London realized that she knew more about books than he did, and wasn't too happy with the fact.

Forrest felt his masculine resentment but did not give in. He must be driven and aroused, not cajoled and pampered. "Matthew and Mark were pretty good," she said. "Luke too. For a rewrite. They began at the beginning."

London was forced to grin. Like any writer, he didn't relish criticism at all, but only praise. "I am not writing a gospel," he said somewhat loftily.

"But maybe you are. A gospel simply is a doctrine of philosophy."

They got into an argument over that and looked it up in her Webster's, and she was right. "Gospel: any guiding principle for action; often, any doctrine of political or social philosophy."

The fact that he was wrong made him a bit cantankerous and stubborn. After all, it was his book.

But Forrest handled him deftly. Her suggestions became oblique and in the forms of questions, and he began the book all over again, this time at the beginning. Of course he did it himself. Of course.

They had two pages completed by three o'clock, and London got up and stretched and it was evidence of how free he felt in her presence. She put her foot into the shoe that she had slipped off and straightened her stockings.

"I'm going to the Bledsoes' for supper," he said. "So I better go home and get ready."

She walked with him to the door, and there he paused and faced her. "Paige will be home day after tomorrow."

"That's right, isn't it? That's Friday and they are due home on Friday. I wrote her the other day."

"Did you mention Mary Upjohn?"

"No. Have you?"

"No. Mary could be a touchy subject between them. So I haven't mentioned her. And I was thinking, Forrest——"

"What's that, London?"

"Maybe you'd like to drive over to the airport and meet them. With Benton and me."

"I think not," she said firmly but graciously. "I will call her Saturday, though."

He thanked her for her help, and all the way home he thought about the book and about Forrest. He must show his appreciation someway. He had planned to dedicate the book to Kathie. In fact, he had planned the dedication long before he even had begun his research years ago. "For Kathie." Simple and loving. But now he wasn't sure. He wasn't sure at all.

Chapter 14

They did another page the next day, and then it was Friday and he and Benton drove to the St. Louis airport. The plane was twenty minutes late, and he drank two cups of coffee while waiting and Benton smoked three or four cigarettes.

He saw Paige and Vance hesitate at the door of the plane and look out at the crowd, and then she waved to him and ran across the asphalt and hugged him so tight that her hat tilted. It was a new hat, and she was brown and beautiful. Vance was brown, too, and his handshake was firm, and the hand on his father's shoulder was steady and affectionate.

Paige wanted to drive home and Vance insisted that London sit by her. "I can spare her that long," he said. "Besides, I want to sit back here with Dad."

Benton lit another cigarette and got in first, and when Vance sat down Benton moved a little closer to him, possibly to hear his son better above Paige's chatter. Yes, possibly.

Paige pestered them with questions all the way home but did not bring up Mary Upjohn's name. Cliff? Forrest? "And what about the 'Scrapbook,' Mr. Benton?" She glanced up into the rear-view mirror and saw how close they were.

"The staff's been doing it. I am on the lookout for another girl."

Paige changed the subject quickly, as though she didn't want to talk about the "Scrapbook" now that she had brought it up. "And your apartment has only four rooms, Dad?"

"All I need."

"My house has ten rooms," Benton said. "Most of them empty. Why don't you two stay there until you leave? No need of going to the hotel. Unless you want to."

Paige glanced into the mirror again and caught Vance's eye, and Vance nodded. Then Paige said, "Sounds like a good idea. What about you, Vance?"

"I'm all for it."

So they drove straight to the Andrews house, and London and Benton waited downstairs while Paige and Vance changed their clothes, and then Benton took them to dinner. He even told a couple of funny stories during the meal and once he laughed out loud. Vance laughed, too, and talked more than London had ever heard him.

"If you don't mind"—Paige had finished her dessert and was speaking to her husband—"I think I'll go out now and see Dad's apartment. I'll be back early."

It would give him a chance to see his father and her a chance to see hers.

"O.K.," Vance said. "But I'll go out and pick you up. No need of Brother Wingo driving all the way back to town. What time?"

"Oh, about nine or nine-thirty."

Benton and London did not comment but glanced at each other in approval of their own, of the way they were handling things and taking things into their own hands. Benton left a lavish tip for the waiter and bought cigars for London and for himself, the best cigars in the house.

Vance and his father stopped at the door to the apartment house, and Vance slipped his arm around Paige. "I'll see the apartment when I come back. I know you and Brother Wingo have a lot to talk about." He kissed her, and London felt funny inside. He never had seen a man kiss her before, and it was something of a shock. Benton turned his head and puffed his cigar.

There was a tug at Paige's heart when she stepped inside her father's home. How small it was; how neat and orderly and lifeless. He was watching her, and she looked around at the walls and the tables and the books, giving herself a minute for the pangs to melt from her heart. "Why, Dad," she said when she was sure of herself, "it's nice. Real nice. I see you have your pictures just like you like them."

"Lamps, too." He pointed to the lamps. "I know you never liked them bunched around a chair like that."

She patted his cheek and screwed up her nose at him. "You can have things just like you want them now. Nobody to boss you. How's the kitchen?"

He led the way, and she stood in the center of the kitchen and looked about: the little two-eye gas stove and the little two-cup dripolator, and one cup and one saucer and one plate on the drainboard of the sink. The tug was back in her heart, and she glanced at the cabinet and the china there. "They are dusty," she said. "Doesn't Mattie wash them?"

"I told her not to touch them," he said. "She might break one. But let's wash them. It won't take a minute."

So she took her mother's cups from the little hooks and handed them to her father, and then the saucers and plates, and they washed them and put them back again and returned to the living room. He sat on the divan, and she sat in his big chair and opened her purse and looked inside and closed it again.

"There are cigarettes in that box on the table," he said. "But they may be sort of stale."

"I was looking for a mint," she said. "You know I quit smoking."

"Oh? I didn't know that."

"I thought I wrote you. I don't think a preacher's wife should smoke, do you?"

"That's up to her, honey."

"It's not that it's important, but it's a symbol. So I quit." She crossed her legs and turned off one of the lamps by the chair. She did not slip off her shoes as was her custom, but sat quite properly and was almost like a stranger sitting there.

London was flustered and didn't know what to say. She was not his any more at all, and he just looked at her and, in a way, was proud and yet, in another way, was very sad. She began talking about Ridgecrest and the work there, and he was not interested in Ridgecrest, but only in her plans. And, too, he wanted to talk about himself, to tell her about his book and how Forrest was helping him.

However, he restrained himself and let her talk. This conference and that group. Youth study plans. Youth for Christ. Her enthusiasm was genuine, but he feigned his, for he had been through all of this before, he and Kathie; the glowing sunrise of the ministry with the clouds so quickly to come, then the hot, stirring noontime, and then the long twilight.

"Vance made several talks at country churches around Ridgecrest," she said. "They loved him. They asked him to come back and talk again at a little church named Lystra Baptist Church."

"Good experience," London said. It sounded pedantic and he didn't mean it that way. Was he jealous of Vance and the beginning of a new ministry? Absurd, and yet London Wingo was troubled.

If Paige noticed anything, she gave no indication of it. "The people down there are the sweetest things you ever saw——"

(London had preached a hundred times in the mountains.)

"They are the same way around Cape Hatteras——"

(London had preached a hundred times near the sea.)

"Of course they are rather primitive, but they have a deep spiritual quality. The Plain People, Dad. That's what they are. And we ought to help them."

He began grinning. He had been smiling and now he grinned. "If they have a deep spiritual quality, maybe they should help us."

"Oh, you know what I mean." She crossed over to the divan and sat by him. "They need a lot of things that we have."

He quit grinning and was serious and reached over and lifted her hand and held it, stroking it. "Uh-huh. I know. We want them to wear shoes like we wear and clothes like we wear. Read the books that we read. To smirk and be clever instead of laugh and be wise. To speak as we speak so they can understand us because we really don't care if we understand them or not——"

"Now, Dad——"

"I've got something to say, Paige. Christianity is not new shoes, even though they be the gift of a brother. Or new clothes. Christianity is a barefoot faith, or at best a sandal faith. And it is a naked faith, or at best it is sackcloth."

"I know that, Dad." She rested her head on his shoulder. "So does Vance."

"Of course you do." He was grinning again. "I just had to preach a little bit. You know"—he lifted her hand and looked at the wedding ring really closely for the first time, a plain gold ring, and on the other hand was the little emerald he had given her on her eighteenth birthday—"I wonder if I'm a little jealous of Vance. Taking you away from me and beginning his ministry."

She moved away from him so she could see him better and looked straight at him. "Dad. I'm going to tell you something and don't you ever forget it. If Vance is half the preacher you are, or half the husband you were, or half the father you have always been, then I'll be the happiest woman in the world."

"Don't ever tell him that." London said it quickly so he wouldn't choke up. "Steer clear of it if you can, but if it ever comes up, then he's the greatest preacher who ever lived."

"I know." She wrinkled her nose at him again. "Now tell me about Mary. We've ducked it long enough. How did she take it?"

"In stride, Paige. Changed almost overnight. Began fixing herself up and quit whining."

"Well, there was room for improvement. Oh, I shouldn't have said that. A preacher's wife shouldn't talk that way." However, she didn't seem very sorry.

"A preacher's wife is a woman," he said, and reached over to a table and got his pipe. "Uh-huh. Mary has changed. She and Sloan Wentworth are courting hot and heavy."

"That's fine. I think that's just fine. Now, tell me. How did Mr. Andrews take it?"

"He didn't say much, honey. But what could he say? Naturally, he's proud that Vance got you. On the other hand, I don't think he's too happy over Vance preaching and all this seminary thing. But what can he do about it?"

"Nothing, I suppose. And let's not talk about it any more. Now tell me about Forrest."

London began talking about the book and still was talking about it when Vance and Benton arrived. They stayed only a few minutes, and Paige went away with them. The apartment was quiet, and London took off his coat and shirt and lit his pipe. He was of a mind to call Forrest, but he had nothing to say, or so he thought. He just wanted to tell her good night. It was late, though, and she surely was in bed, and it would be foolish to wake her up only to tell her good night. So he took a warm bath and drank a glass of warm milk. He was very tired.

He slept past his usual getting-up time the next morning, and Mattie woke him around nine o'clock. She had his breakfast on a tray; coffee and toast and oatmeal. "Good morning, Brother Wingo. 'That our sons may be as plants grown up in their youth; that our daughters may be as corner stones.' Psalms."

London could not think of a reply at once. "Did you look that one up, Mattie? Or just happen to think of it?" He put cream and sugar on his oatmeal.

"Looked it up. Did she get home all right?"

"Uh-huh."

"Thought maybe they might stay here last night."

"No room. They stayed at Mr. Andrews' house."

"Well, that's how it is." Mattie turned toward the door. "Raise 'em up and next thing you know they leave you."

London shaved and put on his gray flannel suit and a blue tie. A bit of dust was on his brown shoes, and he rubbed them down the legs of his trousers, grinning as he did it. Kathie used to kid him about it and then Paige, but now he could do it without comment from anybody.

He drove by town and bought Paige a bottle of perfume and Vance a traveling kit and then on over to Benton's house. Forrest and Cliff were there. They, too, had brought presents, and Forrest was helping Paige with her packing while the men stood around and offered advice. They all were laughing and talking, and Benton greeted London with an elaborate bow.

"Good morning, Brother Wingo. 'A continual dropping in a very rainy day and a contentious woman are alike.' Proverbs by Solomon." Benton was a source of constant amazement to London and, like so many agnostics, knew the Scriptures better than many preachers.

"Good morning, Brother Andrews. 'A nagging woman and a smoking fireplace.' Lamentations by Wingo."

The men laughed, Vance the loudest of all, and Forrest and Paige exchanged long-suffering glances and shrugged. Forrest sat on the trunk and it wouldn't close and she bounced on it, and London stepped forward to help her. His gray suit brought out the gray in his hair and his blue tie matched his eyes. She noticed that and remarked how nice he looked.

Paige had always watched his clothes and colors critically, but now she gave them no attention at all and was concerned only that Vance did not pack his shoes next to his white shirts.

Harry and Shelby Ward dropped by and brought gifts. Then the Bledsoes and Sisler Mason. Cliff met all the visitors at the door and shook hands and took over, and he and Benton and London stood close while Paige opened the presents.

"Folks will be coming by all day," Cliff said. "Weddings and funerals. Folks always drop by. Sorry Mary couldn't make it," he called over to Paige. "I let her off today, and she and Sloan went to some sort of church doings out in the country."

The Oliphants arrived about noon, in time for sandwiches, and next the Ramseys, and Lizzie Ramsey looked closely at Paige and over at Maggie Bledsoe, then back at Paige. She was as trim as a sapling and, conscious of the gaze, stood straight and deliberately pulled her slacks up tight around her stomach. All the women saw the gesture and none of the men.

Lizzie Ramsey turned away, and Paige whispered to Forrest, "She's surprised. The old biddy."

"And maybe disappointed," Forrest whispered.

Vance and Paige excused themselves and went upstairs and dressed, and by midafternoon people were pouring in. The staff of WLMO brought a silver-plated coffee service. The Sunday school

sent luggage, and the Wentworths brought candlesticks. Clark Upjohn and his wife arrived properly at four o'clock and were dressed
in their best, he in his blue suit and she had new white gloves. And
they, who could afford it least, brought the most expensive present
of all—a silver platter with frilly designs around the edges. Paige
went out of her way to be gracious to them, but cringed at the frilly
work on the beautiful platter, and Cliff took them in hand and gave
them punch and showed them all the presents.

By nightfall London was exhausted, although very proud of his
people. Paige was gay and chattery, and they all went to the Wards'
for dinner, even Cliff. London sat next to Forrest and Paige sat
between Benton and Vance, and once she leaned over and patted
Benton's arm, agreeing with something he had said, and his whole
face softened and his eyes were misty for a second and then clear
and bright. Forrest glanced up, then back at her plate. She was
wearing a dinner dress with a low neckline and her hair in a
chignon.

Paige and Vance went home early to finish their packing, as they
were leaving the next day, but the others sat around until almost
ten o'clock, and London took Forrest home, driving rather slowly
in the September night.

"We ought to get back on the book Monday," he said.

"My school starts Monday. I'll be home around four, though."
She touched her hair and wondered if he had noticed it.

He had, and he told her so and told her how pretty it was, and
she preened in the pleasure of the compliment, which was one of
the few he had ever given her. Then he changed the subject reluctantly, as though he did not trust himself with any suggestion
of intimacy.

Cars were parked in front of her house and he stopped about half
a block away and they walked across the lawn, and when they
reached the door he wiped his shoes across the legs of his trousers.
Forrest laughed, and he was surprised because he was not aware of
anything humorous.

"That's the funniest habit I ever saw," she said. "Using your
trousers for a shoe rag. You do it all the time."

"Oh, that." He laughed too. "Started it back in my brush-arbor preaching days when my pulpit was the woods and dust got on my shoes."

"It is the first thing I heard about you, London. Shelby Ward told me about it. And Cliff." She began teasing him.

For a few minutes he enjoyed the frivolity and exchanged banter with her and then he caught himself up short. There was something personal about that habit. It was a joke between him and Kathie, then between him and Paige, and now Forrest was taking it up. Again he changed the subject, this time without reluctance, and began talking about the book.

She touched his arm, the soft flannel coat sleeve, and bade him good night and hurried into her apartment. London drove faster going home and sat up another hour, reading a history of Rhode Island in search of Roger Williams material. The words didn't make any sense and he went to bed, thinking about rustling silk and soft hair and the smell of Blue Grass and not about Roger Williams at all.

And then it was Sunday.

He was in his study, waiting for the church hour, when Paige and Vance came in. They were dressed to within an inch of their lives, and he knew why they were there and didn't comment.

However, Paige explained: "We didn't want to sit out there in the church with people staring at us."

"Of course not," London said. "That would spoil your entrance." He grinned at them, and Paige laughed and fiddled with the white handkerchief in Vance's coat pocket, getting it just so.

"Now don't preach long, Dad," she said. "Our train leaves at three-twenty."

"You'll be on it, honey. I don't know enough to preach that long." He leaned forward in his chair toward Vance. "I thought maybe your father might come with you today."

"He didn't say anything about it, Brother Wingo. So we didn't either."

"That's the best way, son. Christianity is not a pressure faith, although some zealots try it." He glanced at his watch and straightened his own white handkerchief. "I'll start in five minutes. That will give you time to walk around to the front and make your entrance. Take it slow and easy. Let them get an eyeful and then we'll get on with the Lord's business."

He stepped to the door and looked out. "The way's clear. Take it slow and easy, now. I won't start until you are seated and things quiet down."

"Thanks, Dad." She was nervous and so was Vance.

London watched them up the sidewalk to the corner of the church and stepped to the other door, the one between his study and the auditorium, and cracked it an inch or so and peeped through.

The church was filled, and all the people were watching the main doorway except Forrest, and she was watching the door to his study and was the only one who saw him there. She winked at him and he pretended not to see her. She shouldn't do that in church.

A quick buzz through the congregation and Paige and Vance were in the vestibule and then walking down the aisle, slow and easy, as though oblivious of the stares. The buzz and whispers increased, and the minute they sat down London stepped from his study and to the rostrum. He opened the Bible and bowed his head for prayer and the church was hushed.

He prayed briefly (her train left at three-twenty) and lifted his head and looked at his people. Paige and Vance were about half-way down the center aisle, and Mary Upjohn was four rows behind them. Her hat was as perky as Paige's and she had on a new dress, a dark green one that made her hair seem softer and her face pale.

Sisler Mason nodded to his choir and they opened their song-books, and Mary Upjohn got up and stepped out to the aisle, then down the aisle to the piano, walking as slowly as Paige had walked and as gracefully.

London was watching his daughter and saw her eyes widen in surprise, saw her glance at Vance and then fasten her stare on Mary.

The music sounded, the peal of hallelujah, and the people sang out, but not Paige. She looked from Mary to her father as though expecting him to reveal an explanation, to tell her by gesture or nod what had happened.

Mary did not return to her seat but remained at the piano through the Scripture reading, and when the offertory was announced she began her solo, caressing the keys in the rapture of her service. Again it was "Lead, Kindly Light" and again London Wingo experienced a soaring exaltation in his soul.

> . . . I do not ask to see
> The distant scene . . .

All the faithful were stilled, even the children, and he saw that Cliff was weeping as he received the offerings and that Forrest's head was bowed, that Vance's face was uplifted in a strange wonderment and Paige's chin was trembling.

> . . . one step enough for me.

The music ended and Mary sat at the piano, looking up at the stained-glass window and the light melting through, and then she arose and walked back to her seat.

He preached the wisdom of Amos that morning. It came to him under the spell of the minute. "Seek the Lord, and ye shall live." Not once did he raise his voice or his hand, and the people feasted on the promise and were full; inspired by their pastor, who himself was inspired by a song and the girl who had played it.

London walked up the aisle to greet the congregation as they filed out, and the older people crowded around him and thanked him, but the younger people hurried to Paige and Vance and congratulated them, the girls hugging Paige and the boys shaking Vance's hand or pounding him on the back.

Mary was among the first. Her face still was radiant and she put her arms around Paige and kissed her cheek and then kissed Vance's cheek, and they stood there exchanging pleasantries and good wishes. Sloan Wentworth walked on out to his car, and soon Mary joined him and the crowd thinned, leaving only a handful in the vestibule and on the steps of the church.

"I'm going to ride with Dad." Paige spoke to Vance. "We'll be there by the time you are."

"O.K. I've got to stop off for ice cream. Forrest and Cliff are coming to dinner."

She and London walked to the driveway by the study where his car was parked and she did not get under the wheel as was her custom, but sat back and watched him start the DeSoto and turn it around. Then she spoke, a whisper, although they were alone. "What is it, Dad? What happened to her?"

"I don't know." He did not look at her, and his answer was a whisper too.

"Something changed her. What was it?" There was a hint of awe in her voice.

London lowered the window by his side and let the autumn wind against his face. "Maybe it was you. Maybe you changed her."

She turned to him quickly. "What do you mean?" It was almost a demand.

He gripped the wheel and shifted into a more comfortable position. "Perhaps she realized she was not getting anywhere as she was and changed. That's all." He still did not look at her.

"That's a strange thing to say after that sermon. It was a great sermon, by the way. Made me all tingly inside."

"Paige"—he swept wide around a corner—"Forrest always thought Mary was something of a phony. That she affected that sanctimonious way to get Vance's sympathy and maybe mine too. That it was a weapon she used against you."

"I always thought so too, Dad."

"But Cliff has always thought that Mary—well, that she walks close to God."

Neither spoke again until they reached the edge of Linden, and then Paige said, "Some reason, somehow I think I was wrong and that Cliff is right. He walks close to God, too, doesn't he?"

London nodded.

"Did you see her eyes?" The awe was back in her voice. "Burning bright. And yet radiant. Like she was seeing something the rest of us couldn't see at all."

"Maybe she is in love," he said.

"Sloan Wentworth?"

He nodded again, this time slowly.

"That won't do it." Paige laid her pocketbook beside her and moved closer to her father. "I am in love, and I tell you that won't do it. Not that way."

They turned into Boone Street and passed the First Baptist Church, where Harry Ward's congregation was filing out. The organ music floated through the doorway and into the sunshine and the Sabbath. The maples had turned yellow and the earth was snuggling down for its long winter sleep. "Maybe——" She hesitated and then she said it. "Maybe we are seeing a miracle right under our eyes. A divine calling, Dad. The divine touch."

"Miracles don't wear nylon stockings, honey." He was ashamed the instant he said it and wondered why he who preached yesterday's miracles should doubt miracles today.

"Maybe it is the flesh fighting the spirit." Her faith at that minute was greater than his. "Anyway"—again she whispered it—"I am going to write her to pray for me."

He reached out his hand and touched her arm. "And you pray for me. For one step at a time, Paige, and for more faith."

The folks were loitering outside the post office and around the newsstand, but they didn't see them. London threaded his way through traffic and then they were on the street that led to Benton's house, and the autumn leaves were banked in the curbs.

They were deep in their own thoughts, riding along without words, and after several minutes London shook his head as though to arouse himself and looked over at her. "Mighty quiet."

"Thinking," she said.

"Secret?"

"No. Want to guess?"

"Clue?" He raised the window a trifle to hear her better.

"From Job. After God spoke—'Who is this that darkeneth counsel by words without knowledge?' "

He lifted his foot from the accelerator and pushed in the clutch, and the car began coasting. They were almost to Benton's house. " 'Where wast thou when I laid the foundations of the earth?' Is that the one?"

"Yes. And what were you thinking?"

"Psalms. The Forty-sixth."

"Oh, I know." She knew the words because she knew him so well and had heard him say them so often, and now she was learning their meaning. The car eased to a stop, crunching the leaves, and she rested her head on his shoulder and closed her eyes. " 'Be still, and know that I am God.' Is that it?"

"Uh-huh." He felt closer to her than he had ever felt before and was no longer troubled about the adjustments she must make for her husband's calling. "And we'd better go in now. They'll be waiting."

The leaves, the yellow and red ones together, were on the sidewalk, too, and Benton came out to the front steps and greeted them. Paige took his arm and her father's arm and walked into the house with them. A fire was burning in the living room and Benton pointed toward the poker and spoke to his friend. "Poke. Poke any time you want to, London."

Cliff beamed his joy of the good will in this house, and the firelight danced in Forrest's eyes. Paige went to the kitchen to see about things and then announced dinner and sat them all properly, Benton at the head of the table and her father next to Forrest. In deference to his friends, Benton bowed his head and said, "London, will you say the blessing?"

He could have asked Vance and they all were hoping he would, that the son and his calling would receive some recognition in his father's house, and Paige felt under the table for his hand and squeezed it.

If he noticed the slight at all, Vance ignored it and was the first in joviality. He avoided any mention of the seminary or his ministry, but told a funny story about a radio announcer who forgot he was on the air. London told a Mattie joke and Forrest related an amusing incident about one of her students.

They had second helpings of roast beef and potatoes and went to the living room for coffee. It was Vance who glanced at the big clock in the hall and said, "Well, we better be going."

Cliff backed his big Buick into the driveway, and they all rode down to the Wabash station in one car. The trunk compartment was full of luggage, and London held Paige's overnight bag in his lap. Several people at the station smiled at them and others came up and spoke, and Cliff bought chewing gum for himself and some candy and magazines for the travelers.

They stood on the platform and watched the block signals change, and then the train was in. Paige kissed them all, her father last and longest, and Vance put his arm around his father. Cliff went aboard to help with the luggage and they all waved, and then the train was gone.

London wanted to hang around the depot a few minutes and watch them move the baggage and mail because he liked depots and the things that went on there. But not Benton. He was impatient to be away. So Forrest solved it. "I need a little exercise after that big dinner. London and I will walk back uptown. You two forget about us."

Cliff and Benton got into the Buick and Forrest and London stayed there and watched the baggagemen work and peeped into the crates and commented on the stacks of mail. He explained the block signals to her and the switch tracks, and they walked over to the main street and across the tracks, window gazing as they walked along.

He stopped in front of a hardware window and she waited patiently while he looked at all the tools, and she stopped in front of a dress shop and he waited while she looked at all the dresses. Then they came to a haberdasher's, the window displaying hats, and she touched his arm and looked up at him. "I like that pearl-gray one there in front."

He didn't answer immediately but looked from her to the hats and knew that Paige was out of his life and that he was a middle-aged man with his own life before him. "I like the brown one over yonder in the corner. The one with the little feather."

"The gray one will look nice with your gray suit. But why not buy both of them?"

"A man only buys one hat at a time, Forrest."

"Then buy the brown one. Brown goes well with anything."

"I'll buy it tomorrow," said London Wingo. "The first thing in the morning."

Chapter 15

The change in Mary Upjohn was the subject of more comment and conjecture than anything that had happened in the church, far more than the marriage of Paige and Vance, and most of the members had different explanations of its meaning. London, however, was passive and reflective, watching the drama from his pulpit and in his daily work, and wondering.

Estes Oliphant called it a transformation, and Sisler Mason, proud of a few big words, called it a metamorphosis. Buck Bledsoe said she was acting like a sleepwalking saint in a beauty contest, and none knew what her mother and father were saying, only God in their frequent prayers for revelation and guidance.

Lizzie Ramsey said, "She's the prettiest girl in town and she's set her cap for Sloan Wentworth. He's wild about her."

Maggie Bledsoe said, "Wish I had a daughter her age. He's got everything—looks, money; everything."

If Mary was aware of the talk at all, she apparently gave it no thought whatsoever. Five days a week from nine until five, she worked for Cliff and divided the remainder of her time between Sloan and the church.

She reorganized the Sunday school and got Sloan elected to the office of superintendent that Vance had vacated. She gave up her solos and formed a children's choir and worked so hard on the church music that Brother Mason began deferring to her judgment.

"She's got spizzerinctum," the old man said. "I mean she's got it."

Singlehanded, but with London's encouragement, she started the Pipe Organ Fund, and Sloan drove her about the community and she solicited money and put on a Thanksgiving pageant and raised more money.

The Sunbeam Nursery was her idea, and it enabled the mothers to leave their babies in the annex while they attended preaching. The Girl Scouts took over the nursery, and if the children got out of hand the girls always sent for Mary, and she merely walked among the children and talked to them, and they were quiet and clung to her.

So did the old folks. She conducted prayer meetings on Wednesday nights, and the aged left their hearths and their easy chairs and came to hear her, the light of another world in their eyes as they nodded approval of the things she said.

"A word fitly spoken is like apples of gold in pictures of silver," said old Sister Turner, who was Estes Oliphant's mother-in-law and down in the back with rheumatism.

Cliff was so proud of Mary that he talked about her all the time and was talking about her that raw December day when he and London drove out in the country to bury old man Townsend, who after seventy years of carousing had punied up and died and didn't leave a bit of insurance.

"I tell you, London," Cliff said, and kept his car on sixty as he whipped around the country road, "she's walking mighty close to God."

"You think so?" His feet were braced against the floor board and he was wondering how much farther they must go.

"Yes, sir, brother. She's hearing angels, that girl is. The Voice of the Whirlwind, like old Job." Cliff realized that his pastor was nervous and slowed down.

London relaxed in the seat and tugged his brown hat down on the left side. He still wasn't used to it. "Where does Sloan Wentworth fit in?"

"Aw, he's crazy about her. You know that as good as me. He'd marry her tomorrow if she'd say the word." He bit a stick of gum in half and chewed fast, then put the other half in his mouth. "How far this side of saintliness can a human being go? Now tell me that."

"It's not for me to say." London took off the hat and ran his hand around the sweatband to stretch it and put it back on. "My acquaintance with saints has been somewhat limited."

"I'm serious," Cliff insisted. "Ever see anything like this before?"

"Not exactly. Sort of, though. I was too young to know what was going on, but I heard about it."

"What happened?" Cliff quit chewing and slowed his car to thirty miles an hour.

"Look, Cliff." London obviously didn't want to talk about it. "There is only a fine line between neurosis and what some call sanctification. That is, between frustration and fruition——"

"I know all that." Cliff was impatient and frowned. "And I know that ever' time somebody don't understand some'n they yell neurosis. Bent's like that. Now tell me what happened."

London peered ahead and squinted. He hoped they were nearing the Townsend place, but no houses were in sight. Well, he must not treat Cliff like a child even though he had childlike faith. "It was back in Oklahoma." He hadn't thought of the episode in many years. "This girl had a birthmark that covered all one side of her face. She was a little older than Mary and had a strange look in her eyes."

"Like Mary?"

"No. I can't say that. Mary's eyes are soft and radiant. This girl had a sort of staring look, a bulging look. People came from miles around to hear her talk. Then she began talking in unknown tongues. It was pretty bad, Cliff."

"They said she was crazy, I suppose."

"Uh-huh. She died in the insane asylum."

Cliff grunted and began chewing fast again. "When folks don't understand other folks they say they are crazy. What right did they have to do her that way? Did she hurt anybody?"

"No. I don't think so. She had an illegitimate child——"

"Oh. I see."

"Uh-huh." London ran his fingers over his eyes and looked out at the bare woods. "I used to play with that boy. Hunt and fish and all that. He was the best whistler I ever saw. He could hear any bird and then whistle just like him."

"What happened to him? Called him crazy, too, I reckon, because he whistled like birds."

"No. They sent him to the penitentiary, Cliff. He assaulted an old woman. She had a wart on her chin and a birthmark on her forehead. His name was Lowell and we called him Toby. Don't know why. We just called him Toby. I wonder whatever happened to him."

Cliff stepped his Buick back up to fifty and they drove a mile or so without a word between them, and then Cliff said, "You ain't worried about Mary, are you?"

"No. But don't expect me to understand such things simply because I am a preacher. The ways of God are as mysterious to me as they are to you. Perhaps more." The macadam road was playing out and they turned onto a gravel road. "I asked Mary to pray for me."

Cliff, from long experience, handled the car so well that there scarcely was a jolt. "Me too. I asked her to remember me. We are both on her prayer list."

"I didn't know she had a prayer list," London said.

"Well, she has. Saw it just the other day." Cliff hesitated in the words and cut the car around the inside of a curve and scattered gravel. "She got a letter from Paige, and I saw her take it out and write down Paige's name. I wasn't prying. Just couldn't help seeing it. Me and you are both on it."

"That's a comfort." London meant it.

"It's a long list." Again Cliff hesitated, as though choosing his words. "Bent's on it too. Ol' Bent's right up at the top."

London came up with a start and jerked his head around toward his deacon. "Did he ask her?"

"I don't know." Cliff was thoughtful and then shook his head slowly. "I doubt it, but anyhow his name's on it."

They both felt as though they were intruding upon something sacred and began talking about other things. London said, "Much farther?"

"Three miles, more or less." Cliff was back to sixty without realizing he was driving so fast. "What do you hear from Paige?"

London was bracing himself again. "Everything's fine. She's taking a few courses in the seminary and Vance is having trouble with his Greek."

"How come he's taking Greek? Ain't the Bible good enough as it is?" He reached down and cut off the heater because the car was getting stuffy. "Give me the good old King James version ever' time. If it was good enough for Paul and all the rest, then it's good enough for Cliff Carter."

The pastor turned his head to hide his smile, and the deacon kept right on talking. "Don't see as much of you as I used to. How's that book coming?"

"All right, I think." London was glad to be off the subject of Mary and Paige. "We have almost three chapters. But I hate to take up so much of Forrest's time——"

"From where I'm sitting I don't think she minds you taking her time." Cliff was watching the road and grinning.

London tried to shift the conversation to plans for the Townsend funeral, but Cliff would have none of it. "You know something, brother? There are folks who think a consecrated Christian can serve the Lord better if he ain't married. Or she ain't married. That's one thing that's eating on Mary. She wrestling with the spirit, trying to decide between God and Sloan. But I don't see it that way."

"No?" The cold air was sifting through a crack at the top of the window, and London raised the window as tight as it would go.

"No, sir." Cliff slapped his hand against the steering wheel. "Now I'll admit that maybe Paul was sort of lukewarm about marriage. I'll even go along that he was dead set against it, so far as he was concerned. But let's look at Jesus. He was for it. Went to the marriage feast, didn't He? Bound to have been for it."

"Wait a minute, Cliff." London turned the heater back on. "Men have been debating that question for a thousand years. I think it's up to the individual. Now how much farther?"

"Right around the bend," said Cliff, and then they were around the bend and into the lane to the Townsend place. The house, weathered and gray, was on a knoll in a clearing. A small group of mourners were huddled on the steps, obviously waiting for the preacher, but most of the people were in the parlor by the fire, and the firelight glowed through the windows. Cliff stopped the car and took off his loud four-in-hand tie and reached into the glove compartment for his black bow tie and snapped it on. Then he nodded toward the house. "Now, there's a picture for you. Good enough for *Life* magazine. Sort of sad, though. Smoke curling out of the chimney and the trees sleeping and old man Townsend gone. He wasn't worth a shucks, though."

London didn't reply and was thinking of the funeral procedure he would follow. The service should be short. It would be cold at the grave.

"What can you say over a fellow like old man Townsend?" Cliff started the car and they moved up the lane. "Drunk more whisky than anybody in the county. Always trying to mess with the sisters, too, and him with one foot in the grave. Good Democrat, though, but crazy as a betsy bug. What can you say over a man like that?"

"Oh, I don't know," said London. "Maybe I will just say that when folks don't understand other folks they say they are crazy."

The deacon broke into laughter, and his pastor joined him.

London and Forrest bundled up good the day before Christmas Eve and went into the woods for a Christmas tree but couldn't find one. So they came back to town and bought a tree and Cliff helped them put it up in the church, to the side of the pulpit and near the rostrum.

Mary dropped by and helped them trim it and didn't have much to say at first and then began talking fast about her plans for the holidays. "I have a whole new outfit, and Sloan is going to take me to St. Louis every day. We are going to see all the shows, and he may even take me dancing, and I've never been dancing. And look" —she pulled back her sleeve—"look what he gave me."

The watch had a jeweled case, tiny diamonds that caught the lights in the church and sparkled. They all admired it, and Mary, being the youngest, climbed the stepladder and fastened the star on the tree. They all stood back and looked at it, and Mary's face was bright.

"Well, I'd better be going now," she said. "Unless you need me."

"I'll drive you home," Cliff said. "Pretty cold outside."

"Never mind, Mr. Carter. It's not far, and I like to walk. The wind feels good on my face."

She left them and the church seemed almost empty without her. They cleaned up around the tree and tried the lights again and then they all went home, London to his little apartment where he wrapped a few gifts and kept thinking about Mary, the light in her eyes as she fastened the star and the light in the diamonds.

He stayed close to his own fire on Christmas Eve and there was a service at the church on Christmas Day, not because it was Christmas, as Baptists traditionally do not celebrate feast days, but because Christmas came on Sunday that year. The service was simple and mostly musical, and he and Forrest and Cliff went from the church to Benton's house.

Each had a present for the other, and they opened all their gifts, standing around the fireplace and near Benton's little tree which did not have a star at all but an ornamental spike where the star should be. London had a pipe from Vance and a scarf from Paige. It was a heavy brown scarf, and he held it up for them to see and then opened his gift from Forrest.

It, too, was a scarf, but a colorful silken scarf, and she had embroidered his initials on it; so he put Paige's gift back in the box for a colder day and drooped Forrest's scarf around his neck and wore it all the time they were opening presents.

Benton had each one's favorite dish for dinner, and then they sat around the fire and nibbled fruit and candy and enjoyed themselves far more than youth believes possible for people of their ages. It was the first Christmas London had away from Paige, and he did not miss her nearly as much as he had dreaded he would. Forrest had changed her hair, and it was in a single roll at the back of her neck. They talked about other Christmas Days and had more fun remembering their childhood than childhood ever has.

It rained all Christmas week and then began snowing. London

didn't see Mary during the holidays, but Cliff told him that he let her off every day at noon and that Sloan met her and they took off for St. Louis. They didn't return until late each night.

"I gave her a raincoat for Christmas," Cliff said. "Forrest and Shelby helped me pick it out, and it's a beaut."

London wished he had given her a present, but he mustn't single out any one of his young people for special attention. He wrote Paige about the good time Mary was having and then put Christmas behind him and began preparing a service on the visit of the Magi, called Epiphany in many denominations, although Baptists, as a rule, do not celebrate it.

However, next to Easter and the Resurrection, it was London's favorite day, the manifestation of Christ to the Gentiles, and he always read the story from Matthew and preached on the Star of the East.

He went to his study early that Sunday and studied his notes, and as the bell was ringing the hour of worship he listened to the feet of the people as they filed into the auditorium, some of them whispering and others talking loud, a thing he wished they would not do in church.

Then the whispering stopped abruptly and London glanced at his watch. It was several minutes before the service was to start, and yet the whispering had ceased. He stepped to the door and peeped into the auditorium, and Mary was walking down the aisle; alone. For the first time in months Sloan was not with her and she was wearing an orchid and the people were staring at her and were hushed.

The orchid, an exotic, alien thing, was too lush and much too large and yet it told its own story. He had given it to her and now she was wearing it for them all to see, for them to know that she, Mary Upjohn, had an orchid.

London was indignant and closed the door. Such ostentation in the house of God, such vanity and pride, and on the day he was to preach on the coming of the Wise Men and their humility and their adoration of a new King.

He waited until the flush had left his face and his cheeks were no

longer burning and then he stepped quickly into the auditorium.
Forrest was waiting for his appearance, but the others did not see
him at all. They continued to stare at Mary until his footsteps
sounded on the rostrum and then they turned and faced him. The
choir stood and Sisler Mason conducted them into the opening song
and London did not look at Mary, but busied himself with his
notes.

The hymn swept to its end in a crescendo of hosannas.

"... Praise ye the Lord!"

London waited until the choir was seated and still, and then
opened the Bible and read slowly:

" 'Behold, there came wise men from the east to Jerusalem, saying, Where is he that is born King of the Jews? for we have seen
his star in the east, and are come to worship him.' "

He read it all, and as he read the people forgot about the orchid
and the girl who wore it and came again to the fountain and, drinking, were lifted up from that place and were with the pilgrims in a
far land, the star bright, and the Wise Men seeking the Lord to lay
their possessions at His feet and dedicate themselves to His service,
and to His commands.

Once London glanced up and saw that Mary's eyes were wide,
not bulging wide but wide in wonderment as they looked at him
and then beyond him; and he was disconcerted and almost lost the
place. He paused and took a deep breath and read on until the story
was told and then he stepped back to his big oaken chair.

The children's choir arose to sing the offertory, and Cliff and
Estes came forward for the collection plates and passed them among
the people that they, too, might give of their possessions, in whole
or in part.

London tried to concentrate on the sermon he must preach in a
few minutes and looked up at the ceiling and at the windows, anything to avoid Mary's stare. He could not keep his eyes or his mind
away from her, however, and they came back to her and he saw that
her face was pale and wan and her hands trembling.

Cliff stopped in the aisle near her and leaned over and passed the plate down the row, and Mary looked at the plate and then un-pinned the orchid from her shoulder and dropped it there.

A gasp went up in the church, and London's knuckles were white as he gripped the arms of his chair. This was exhibitionism in the Lord's house and therefore blasphemy.

The hot surge of his anger was in his throat, and a wave of whis-pered portent swept his church. The choir hushed its song, a few notes trailing off, and London wasn't sure of himself at that minute and did not know what to say or what to do. Then he saw Cliff, the tears streaming down his face and the plate trembling in his hands.

"The choir will please resume the offertory." London found his voice. "And the service will continue."

But Cliff did not hear the instructions, or if he heard them he ignored them. He stood there, looking at the orchid and the money, only metal and paper, and, to him, so unworthy in the presence of her offering. Slowly he tilted the plate and the money fell out, some on the pew and some on the floor, and her gift was all that was there.

Mary bowed her head and Cliff, the tears gone and his own eyes bright, held up the plate for all to see the orchid on the velvet, and walked down the aisle and laid the offering at the foot of the pulpit.

Again a gasp of surprise and the people leaned forward to stare at it and back at Mary, and London moved to pick up the plate and put it away and be on with the morning worship, the routine of prayer and sermon and song.

Then Mary was speaking, her hands on the pew in front of her, and she spoke to him and, through him, to the church. London Wingo did not touch the offering, but left it there and listened.

"I am sorry I did that." Her voice scarcely was a whisper, yet they all heard. "It was vanity and pride and they are sinful. I should have come in sackcloth and humility."

She bit her lips and moistened them. "Last night——" She raised her face higher and her voice, too, so they could hear her better. "I learned last night, in the deep still of the night, that I must dedi-cate myself to Christ and my service to this church. I must forsake all else and do as I have been commanded. I must go to the far places of the earth, to the sick and the destitute, and tell them the only thing I know and the only thing I need to know: that nothing can separate us from the love of God through Christ Jesus."

London felt it then; the surging pulse of revival. He opened his mouth to calm his people and no words came. There was a cry of ecstatic joy from the second pew to the right, and Mary's mother was on her feet, her arms flung high and her hands wide in supplication. "I know that my Redeemer liveth! Blessed be the name of the Lord!"

He looked quickly at Cliff and at Forrest, but Cliff's eyes were closed and Forrest was looking to the pulpit for guidance.

"Walk while ye have the light, lest darkness come upon you." It came from Estes Oliphant, almost a shout, a command.

Sisler Mason, usually so stalwart and impassive, stood before them and waved his hand as though brushing the battlements of heaven and broke into song.

> "Hallelujah! Thine the glory,
> Revive us again——"

For a second London was ashamed of the emotional tempest and was glad neither Paige nor Benton was there to witness this primitivism, this pentecostal outpouring, and then he was caught up in the surge and was singing with his brethren.

> "Hallelujah! Thine the glory,
> Hallelujah! Amen!"

This was not Dr. London Wingo of dry Greek cant and theological morass. This was London Wingo, who himself had found his Lord in an Oklahoma camp meeting and might have lost Him in the labyrinth of his meager knowledge. This was old man Wingo's boy, a big man striding into Texas, the hot wind on his face, as he preached repentance and revelations to the brush-arbor folks and along the dry runs. There was gray in his hair now, but he was home again with his own kind.

> "Hallelujah! Amen!"

He forgot his sermon and stepped down from the rostrum and mingled with the people, and they gathered around him and gathered around Mary and she put her head on her father's chest and wept.

Even Buck Bledsoe was weeping his joy, and when the singing subsided he stood up at the back of the church. "I want to testify for my Lord and Savior. I've been a sinner all my life and I want you to pray for me."

Then Leo Ramsey was on his feet. "Pray for me too," he said.

"And for me. And me."

It came from a dozen throats, from Sister Ramsey and Sister Bledsoe and Brother Upjohn, and Sister Ramsey walked down by the pulpit and to Forrest and hugged her, then to her pastor. "Brother Wingo, pray for me."

Sisler Mason led them into "The Old-Time Religion," and London motioned for Forrest and Cliff to join him in the study. He closed the door, and the singing came through the door, and the happy voices.

"It's out of my hands," he said.

Forrest nodded and stood close to him, and now that she had seen this side of him she knew him better, and the knowledge warmed her.

"It's in God's hands now." Cliff put his arm around London and held him tight. "He sent us a revival. I been waiting a long time for this and prayed I'd be spared to see just one more. We got a love feast, brother. Blessed be the name of the Lord."

Chapter 16

Like a spark in dry leaves, the revival caught fire in the little congregation, and like the leaves before the wind, it spread through
Plymouth, and London was caught between the pentecostal zeal
and his fears of emotional excesses. There were services every night
in the church and prayer meetings in the homes.

Mary announced her plans to attend a missionary training school
and Cliff immediately put up the money. The people tried to shower
her with gifts, but she refused them and gave away most of her
possessions and returned the watch to Sloan Wentworth. At first he
was bitter and scoffed at it all and then, at his own family's request,
he attended a service and heard her talk and went away rejoicing.

He took over the Pipe Organ Fund and named it the Mary Upjohn Campaign, and a room in the Sunday-school annex was dedicated to her, and Sloan was among those who went to the station to
see her off. Her eyes were not so bright but were softer, and some of
the wave was out of her hair and she was wearing brown again.

Her parting words to London were, "Keep the revival going,
Brother Wingo, as long as God wills it."

Cliff and some of the other deacons wanted to build a tabernacle
and invite an evangelist to launch a Crusade for Christ in Linden.
London, however, squelched the idea and called his deacons together and put his foot down firmly.

"I will have nothing to do with such a campaign." He minced no words. "This revival is a spontaneous outburst. It is one of those religious phenomena that can be touched off by an incident and can do a lot of good. But if we fan it into a frenzied emotional spree, the hangover will be inevitable. No, sir, brethren. We will not use our church and our people as whippers-in for a spiritual fox hunt."

Cliff's feelings were a little hurt, but his enthusiasm was not. He organized noontime prayer meetings at the shoe factory and a 10 A.M. prayer meeting in Linden's Bijou Theater. He turned his fleet of funeral cars over to the church and hauled people to every service and greeted all newcomers with his revival motto: "Throw out the life line, brother." He smacked his gum and laughed his joy, exuding good will as he went to the byways and gave his money and time to round up the folks and invite them to the feast of abundance.

London preached every night and always the same message. "Repent and put your faith in the Lord and nothing can separate you from the love of God through Christ Jesus."

And the people swarmed to hear him, packing the church to the walls and spilling out into the January nights which were not cold at all, but almost warm under a new moon and a south breeze. The first week brought sixty conversions, and Cliff went down to a tar-paper shack near the freight yard and took hot soup and a clean shirt to old Branch Overton, the village sot, who was palsied and crippled from Prohibition whisky. He bathed and shaved his brother and walked with him through the doorway of the church and sat by him. Branch was bewildered and his body shook his ague until the promise of the words came to him, and he was still and the haunting misery went out of his face. He got up slowly and braced himself against the pew and walked straight and steady down to the pulpit and gave London his right hand in fellowship and brotherhood.

"It's a miracle," said Cliff when the service was over, although the people lingered in little groups and talked about the wonders they had seen.

"I'd go easy on that word," London said.

"How come?" Cliff's faith was such that life itself was miraculous. "That's what it is, ain't it?" He looked straight at his pastor, into his eyes and perhaps into his soul. "What's wrong with miracles in a Baptist church? Answer me that, brother. What's wrong with miracles in a Baptist church?"

London Wingo could not answer him, and that very night Estes' mother-in-law walked without a cane for the first time in fifteen years and Sisler Mason swore he could see dim images in the eye that had been useless so long.

A few ministers in Linden began making snide remarks about the revival and openly expressed surprise that a man of Wingo's education would tolerate such "primitive demonstrations." Two members of the school board criticized Forrest for participating in the services, and she ignored them and attended every meeting.

The Roger Williams book was put aside and she stayed as close to London as her work and propriety would allow and saw to it that he ate at least one hot meal a day and relaxed after each sermon. He wrote Paige a brief report of events, and Forrest wrote her a detailed report and also kept Mary Upjohn informed.

The Linden *Morning Ledger* assigned a reporter to the revival and his first articles featured the emotional extravagances, but soon they were sympathetic, as though he himself were under the spell, and he asked to be relieved of the assignment and went on a three-day drunk in St. Louis.

A local radio wag, not on WLMO, made a joke about "Throw out the life line, brother," and the station got more than a hundred letters of protests. The owner apologized publicly and fired the man, although he previously had approved the script. Without ado or fanfare London and Cliff visited the owner and pleaded that the employee be reinstated.

"It was a pretty good joke," Cliff said. "Throw out the life line, brother."

The radio executive was flabbergasted and in a burst of generosity offered to broadcast London's sermons, and was flabbergasted even more when London refused. However, at Cliff's behest, he was allowed to broadcast the Bijou Theater prayer meeting, and overnight the program was more popular than the "Scrapbook" on WLMO. A hospital savings association volunteered to sponsor the program and was amazed when London vetoed the offer. The association sent its promoter to see the preacher.

"It will be dignified," the promoter said. "A little soft music and a spot announcement. Then the prayer meeting. It's a civic deal, Dr. Wingo. We'll contribute three hundred dollars to your revival, or to you personally."

London jerked open the door of his study and bade the man good day.

It was then that Harry Ward took it upon himself to call on London and talk things over. "How does it look?" he asked. "How long do you think it'll take to run its course?"

"I don't know." London was very patient.

Harry stuck his thumbs in his vest pockets and folded his hands across his chest. "Some of the fellows in the Ministerial Alliance are afraid it might be getting out of hand."

"So?" London tried to conceal his annoyance.

"Let's not beat around the bush." Harry got up from his chair and sat on the edge of London's desk. "We both are Baptists. Enough folks laugh at Baptists as it is without us giving them a side show."

All the color drained from London's face and he reached for his pipe, anything for a moment to compose himself. "Harry"—his voice was soft but firm—"this is not a side show. And as for people laughing—well, let me tell you something, brother. I have an idea some people laughed at the ragged multitude that went up on the mount. And I'll bet they laughed at John the Baptist, standing waist-deep in Jordan and baptizing sinners and preaching repentance."

"You know what I mean." Harry was apologetic, sincerely so. "There is no squabble between us. But, thank the Lord, Baptists are getting away from the old camp-meeting heritage——"

"Maybe too far away," London interrupted him, and refused to light his pipe and broke the wooden match between his fingers. "This thing caught me cold. And, Harry"—he pointed his pipe at his colleague—"I haven't announced a single service. The people just gather at the church. I've preached the same sermon over and over, and still they come. You explain it."

Harry Ward shrugged and picked up a paperweight and balanced it in his hand. "A neurotic girl sets it off and spiritually immature people take it up. They are bewildered and confused by world events, and they are always looking for a sign."

"Uh-huh. I read that book too." London walked over to a window and stood there looking out. The warm spell still was on the land and buds were swelling on a shrub by the Sunday-school annex. "You know something, Harry?" He turned and faced his visitor. "This age has no copyright on confusion. Man has always been confused because he is both good and evil. And have you ever thought about it, that when mankind thinks it has reached the end of the rope it turns either to the Golden Calf or to the Cross——"

"It's still sign-seeking." This time Harry interrupted.

"Have it your way." London came back to his desk and sat down in his swivel chair. "But we preachers are always talking about a spiritual renaissance. Would we recognize one if we met it in the middle of the road? We are waiting for it to come by edict or fiat." He stuck his pipe between his teeth and clamped down on the stem. "It's not coming that way. It's got to begin in the hearts of men. And it can start on a Russian farm or in a Chinese village, or in the heart of a girl like Mary Upjohn or a man like Cliff Carter."

Again Harry shrugged and laid the paperweight on the desk. "When you talk that way I am disarmed and can't argue. Do you need me?"

"No. But be happy to have you come worship with us."

"We'll be around. Shelby and I." He got up from the desk and reached for his hat. "And what do you want me to tell the Ministerial Alliance? That you said go whistle up a stump?"

"Put it in preacher talk, Harry. But that's the general idea." London put on his hat, too, and walked out to the car with his colleague and then went into the church, where Forrest and Sister Ramsey were supervising a window-washing job and an over-all cleaning.

He borrowed a rag and some wax and began polishing the top of his pulpit and Forrest moved quickly to relieve him of the chore, but Lizzie Ramsey stopped her and whispered, "Let him do it. It's good for a man to help out like that around a place. Remember that, honey. It's good for 'em."

The three of them went down to the Plymouth Cafeteria for supper, and Leo joined them, and when they got back to the church it was filling fast; and Harry Ward was there—he and Shelby sitting about midway of the auditorium with Cliff at Harry's side and Sister Bledsoe next to Shelby.

The choir sang "Jesus, Lover of My Soul," and again London preached only repentance and faith. "If we are weary and heavy-laden, it is our sins that burden us. Repent. For if the soul of man is sick, then repentance is the first step toward serenity and salvation. God give us the courage to change things that need changing, serenity to accept things we cannot change, and wisdom to know the difference."

Expertly Harry Ward sized up the crowd and wondered why no offering was taken. He gave London polite attention, but his mind was wandering, for, after all, he had preached the same sermon himself many times. He glanced at Shelby and saw her rapt intentness and the faces of all the people lifted to drink in the solace.

"We brought nothing into this world, and it is certain we can carry nothing out. For here we have no continuing city, but we seek one to come."

The echo of the words came to Harry, and then the words themselves, and he stared at London and was puzzled, then saw the window beyond the preacher, the moonlight on the colors, and felt the stillness of the room. He reached over and touched Shelby's fingers, and she gripped his hand and felt his hand cold and trembling, and then warm.

Sister Mason led the people into the Benediction, and London called upon Harry to dismiss them with prayer; and Harry Ward, usually so glib, reached for the thought and it was not there, and for the words and could not find them. He looked from Shelby to Cliff and up at London, and bowed his head and whispered, "Lord have mercy on us."

He said nothing to London that night, but held his hand in a good-night clasp, and the next day he took over the Bijou Theater prayer meeting and helped Cliff organize the Flying Squadron, a cavalcade of automobiles that toured the county and held services in the farmhouses and country churches.

It was Dr. Wentworth who first cautioned Cliff to take it easy. "You are going day and night," he said. "And that ticker of yours is pumping like an old Model T. Better slow down."

At first Cliff was indignant and then amused. "Who you kidding, Doc? I just started going good. Gave out twenty-seven Bibles yesterday and marked John 3:16 in every one of 'em. Know what I did?" He smacked his gum and ran the back of his hand across his watery eyes. "Went over to the Sunday school and snitched some of them little gold stars and stuck 'em alongside John 3:16 in every one of those Bibles. Throw out the life line, brother."

London also asked Cliff to slow down—in fact, he insisted—and for the first time in his life his deacon rebuked him. "I'll have to be the judge of that. 'To every thing there is a season, and a time to every purpose under the heaven.' We will say no more about it, London."

It was in the third week of the revival that Benton's curiosity, or loneliness, pressed him to go out to Plymouth and see what was going on. He parked his car in front of the church and didn't go in, but heard the choir singing and saw Cliff greeting people at the door, and he drove away.

He dropped by the Elks Club and accepted a hand of bridge and excused himself and tried a movie, and walked out on that too. He drove by London's apartment and it was dark, and he kept driving around Plymouth until there was a light in London's kitchen, and he went in.

London was alone, eating a sandwich, and greeted him warmly. "Hello, Bent. Pull up a chair."

"Hello, stranger." Benton leaned against the doorway. "Just thought I'd drop by. Never see you much any more."

London sensed a reason for the visit and, because he was tired and keyed up, he hoped Benton was not in a contentious mood. "Pour yourself a cup of coffee. And what's on your mind?"

Benton pulled a chair close to the kitchen table and sat down. "I haven't seen you at all since that carnival started. And Cliff only a few times. How much longer is that hoop-de-do going to last?"

The quick surge in London's throat was anger and he swallowed it. "I don't know." He was infinitely patient, but prayed that Benton would not push him too far.

"Of course it's none of my business."

"That's right," said London, and Benton looked at him and saw the flush on his cheeks and felt the tension. "I'm out of cream." London set a can of Pet milk in front of him. "This is the best I can offer."

Benton tilted the can and stirred his coffee slowly. "I want to talk to you about Cliff——"

"What's wrong with Cliff?" London broke in.

"He's running around in circles." Benton's spoon clattered on the saucer. "Neglecting his business and making a damn fool out of himself."

"Why don't you take it up with Cliff?"

"Because he wouldn't listen to me. The only way to calm him down is for you to close out your show and go back to your regular pitch."

London pushed aside the sandwich plate and suddenly was thinking of Paige and Vance, but now his anger was stronger than his tolerance. "We will have no more of that, Benton. Not another word. You don't come into my house and talk to me that way. You or no other man."

"You needn't get so upset." Benton doused his cigarette in his coffee cup. "Maybe I was a little sarcastic——"

"Sarcastic!" London felt the flush higher on his face. "Sarcasm is a weapon that only the very wise can use. Yours is not even honest sarcasm. It is smirking superiority, and I, for one, am sick of it."

"Wait a minute," Benton protested.

But the floodgate was down and London forgot his Lord's admonition to good will and brotherhood. "You've needled and needled, and I have had enough. Most agnostics I've known are intellectual zombies. Too proud to believe in God and too scared to deny Him——"

"Wait a minute, London." Benton held up his hand to stem the torrent.

It was no use. The anger of London's Oklahoma boyhood had seized him, and again he was a creature of fists and brawn. "And your atheists are a bunch of narrow zealots who'd put any backwoods preacher in the shade. I've never ridiculed your smug little anthill, and don't you ridicule my mountain. I'm not responsible for your misery!"

His own tirade was pitifully smug, and the minute the words were out he was ashamed, for he was responsible for his brother's misery. All men are. That is what he preached and that is what he believed. Benton slouched back in his chair as though he had been slapped, and he, as proud and as sensitive as London Wingo, held his tongue.

Something between them was broken, something that neither could mend because the one who preached the turning of the cheek had not turned his and now he was humbled, partly by the hurt look in his friend's eyes and the loneliness, but mostly by the whiplash of his own conscience. He picked up the spoon from the saucer and turned it between his fingers. "I'm sorry, Bent."

"Forget it. I was out of line myself."

There was a long pause and London said, "Funny weather for January, isn't it? Almost like spring."

"Uh-huh. Bad for colds, though. For the farmers too."

"What do you hear from the young folks?"

"I wrote them a couple of days ago"—Benton lit a cigarette—"but haven't heard from them in a week or so. The boy is still having trouble with his Greek."

"Cliff says he doesn't see any sense in a preacher studying Greek. That if the King James version was good enough for the Apostles it should be good enough for anybody."

It wasn't funny then. It wasn't funny at all.

"Well, I better be going." Benton got up, and London walked out to the car with him and they talked some more about Paige and Vance.

Nothing much, though. Then Benton drove off and London

went back into his apartment and tried to sleep, and slept only fit-
fully.

It was raining the next morning, a cold drizzle, and Mattie was
bundled in an old shawl and had the sniffles. "Good morning,
Brother Wingo. 'A thousand years in thy sight are but as yesterday
when it is past, and as a watch in the night.' Psalms."

"Good morning, Mattie. 'We spend our years as a tale that is
told.' Still Psalms."

He told nobody about the quarrel, not even Forrest, and that night
the church-bell rope broke while Cliff was ringing the tidings of
meeting time. It had been frayed for months, but they all figured it
would last through the revival. Cliff got a stepladder and tied a
knot in the rope. It was a big ugly knot, and everybody who came in
noticed it and commented on it.

Then the furnace went on the blink, and water got in the radi-
ators and they pounded and hissed. It was chilly in the auditorium
and Buck Bledsoe closed all the windows tight, and it was too stuffy.
He opened four of them a few inches, and the rain drifted in.

Estes Oliphant brought word that Branch Overton was drunk
again and Forrest had a touch of hay fever. The warm weather had
brought it back.

And there was no spirit in London's sermon. He kept feeling for
the words and for the people and could not bring them together, and
the people were restless, wondering about their own furnaces and if
water was seeping into their basements, thinking of their own com-
forts.

London remained in his church after everybody was gone, even
Forrest and Cliff, and he turned out all the lights except one in his
study. He sat at his desk, his eyes closed and a tug of mortification in
his heart, and then he walked softly out to his pulpit and knelt there
and prayed. There was no light through the stained-glass window;
only the rain beating against it, and the fire in the furnace died
down and the church was cold.

It was past midnight when he finally crawled into bed, and it
seemed he had been asleep only an hour or two and the phone woke
him up. He cracked one eye and it still was raining, and he reached

over to his night table and looked at his watch. Nine o'clock. Well, let Mattie answer the phone. Then he remembered it was Saturday and she was taking the morning off.

So he slipped out of bed and into his dressing gown and slippers and padded out to the living room, yawning and tousling his hair. "All right. All right," he muttered impatiently to the ringing phone, and lifted the receiver.

Paige was calling him from Rochester, and instantly London's senses were alert and he was frightened.

But nothing was wrong. She assured him of that first. "Just wanted to talk to you," she said. "You all right? Sound sleepy."

"Just got up." He pulled a chair close to the phone. "Your time is ahead of ours, remember. Sure nothing's wrong?"

She reassured him. Vance was in New York studying mission problems among derelicts and she was alone and decided to call him, that's all. "I don't know why he went," she said, and her pique was obvious. "He's behind with his Greek and yet he goes trailing off down there to work with drunks and bums."

"Aw, now, honey." London was slightly amused. "That's part of a preacher's life——"

"At least he might have taken me." Her pique was passing into temper.

"Now—now." A dreaded thought that they had been quarreling came to him. "Maybe it didn't suit to take you. And you might as well get used to being a pulpit widow. You've got a lot of it ahead of you."

"I suppose so." Her voice, usually so buoyant, was flat. "Now tell me the truth about Mary and Sloan. How did he take it? Nobody wrote me about that." She did not ask about the revival, only about a romance that Plymouth already had forgotten.

"He took it all right, I guess." London hoped his disappointment was not evident. "He didn't run off and join the Foreign Legion or anything. In fact, he's helping with our meeting." Surely she would mention it now.

But she didn't. "Maybe he turned her down. Have any of you all thought about that?"

This was warmed-over gossip, tainted with malice, and London was deeply troubled about his daughter again. However, he was firm, much firmer than usual. "Paige—whatever happened between Mary and Sloan is their affair. I wrote you all I know."

"And did she really drop an orchid in the collection plate?"

"That's right."

"And did the people get all worked up like Mr. Andrews wrote?"

He didn't reply immediately, looking down at the grain in the wood of the telephone stand. "Yes. If you want to call it that." He was ready to tell her that her father, too, had been touched by a deep religious experience and had been infused with new zeal for his calling.

However, she interrupted his thoughts. "Well, I'm glad I wasn't there. You know how those emotional demonstrations do me."

"I didn't know you had ever seen one, honey. Have they had one in Rochester?"

"Oh, now, Dad. Not up here. In fact, one of our professors asked me about such things and I was embarrassed to death. Then he lectured on the phenomenon of protracted meetings in primitive cults and Vance stood right up in class and argued with him. I could have gone through the floor."

"I see." It came slowly, and his shoulders drooped.

"When are you going to close it out? I bet you are worn to a frazzle. Mr. Andrews wrote that you and Cliff had turned into the Sawdust Trail Twins." She thought it was humorous and laughed.

"I see." It came more slowly, and then his shoulders straightened. "No, I'm not tired at all, Paige. And the meeting will continue as long as the people come. Cliff thinks it is a miracle, and you don't close the door on miracles——"

"A miracle!" The word itself seemed to amuse her and then to shock her, as though it were sacrilegious. "A miracle in Plymouth?"

He reacted instinctively and defensively. The sneers from Benton had been bad enough, but the gibes from his own daughter were unfair and cut deep. "What's wrong with a miracle in Plymouth?" he demanded. "What's wrong with a miracle in a Baptist church?"

The severity of his attitude astonished her, and she was quick to sense a change in him and knew she was on dangerous ground. "Why, Dad!" There was no pretense in her surprise, and she retreated into the hurt of her sensitive temperament. "I didn't mean to step on your toes. I didn't realize you were so touchy."

Touchy? Him touchy? What about her and Benton and all the others who pointed fingers and yet wailed intolerance if fingers were pointed at them? Live and let live, they cried, only live our way. Jeer your brother, but if he jeers you he is a bigot. Hide your inadequacies under a skein of sensitiveness. A flurry of reflections quickened his brain and at that minute London Wingo was as near to maturity as his talents could permit. A sow's ear was purse to one man and poem to another, an abomination to that man and a feast for his neighbor. A saint yonder was a crackpot here; a miracle in one place was the fakir's art in another.

"Well, I am a little touchy," he told her. "And let's not argue about it. I'll write you a long letter tonight. You need anything?"

"No, sir." All the animation was out of her voice. "How's Forrest?"

"She's fine."

"Well, I just wanted to talk to you, Dad. Just wanted to hear your voice. Don't wear yourself out now, Dad. And I love you."

"I love you too."

They exchanged a few more words and hung up, and London sat there by the phone and ran his hand across the back of his neck and across his cheeks. He needed a haircut and his whiskers bristled.

He had forgotten to get coffee cream and had to use canned milk again, and then he bathed and dressed and stood by a window and watched the rain swishing down. He tried to work on a sermon, but the place was too dreary and he was too lonely, and he tugged the brim of his hat low over his forehead and ran out to his car and drove over to see Forrest.

She had plenty of coffee cream and toasted some cheese sandwiches. He liked his cheese soft and bubbling hot and she remembered. He was determined not to tell her about Paige or Benton, and then he was telling her and she showed no surprise whatsoever.

"Don't worry about it too much." She filled his coffee cup again and buttered a hot slice of brown bread for him. "She and Vance probably had their first spat and she was upset."

"I don't like to think of them squabbling," he said. "And she was downright sarcastic about our revival."

"Now, wait a minute, London." She was wearing a blue wool dress and her hair was in a casual knot. "Paige was brought up to think for herself and to say what she thinks. You are the one person to whom she could say whatever was on her mind. And I'll bet that you yourself have made jokes about protracted meetings and sawdust trails." She reached up and pressed the knot in her hair and tightened it. "My experience has been that a mirror reflects all images, and Paige has been with you most of her life; a mirror to your moods and ideas."

He hadn't thought of it that way and nodded understanding.

"And she and Vance are going to have quarrels." Forrest stepped to a window and raised the Venetian blind to admit all the light that the gloomy skies afforded. "Just because she's your daughter doesn't make her different from any other woman. One day she can ask Mary to pray for her, and mean it, and the next day she'll want to pull her hair out, wondering if Mary knows something about Vance that she doesn't know."

Forrest glanced at the fire and it was burning bright, and she sat down and felt the coffeepot. It was still warm. "But now Benton is a different matter." She pressed her finger against a crumb of the brown bread and put it in her mouth. "He's a bitter man."

"He needn't take it out on me, and the church." London leaned back in his chair and tapped tobacco into his pipe.

"London"—she rubbed her hand across her forehead—"you are a reservoir to people. That's what makes you a good preacher. And let's look at Benton's side of it. He married into a strong Baptist family; b-i-g Baptist leaders. I'll bet his wife yapped and yapped at him about her church and her brand of Christianity. A weaker man might have compromised and joined her church to shut her up. And then what happened?" Forrest opened out her hands in a gesture of resignation. "She was the one who broke faith. She turned to an-

other man. She even tried to take his son away from him. B-i-g
Baptist and always yapping about her religion. Then his son turned
to the Baptist ministry. I wish Benton were not so bitter and I think
he is wrong, and yet, in a way, I can't blame him. And, London"—
she reached over and put her hand on his and her hand was warm
—"if you are the reservoir we think you are, you must have faith
enough for all of us. For Paige and Benton, and for me too. And,
yes, even for Cliff. Because the faith of Cliff Carter today is the echo
of things you taught him twenty years ago." She moved her hand.
"Now, what about more coffee?"

He was silent, looking at her and feeling the glow of her presence
and the depth of her humanity. "No, thank you." He spoke at last.
"I've had enough coffee. And you are right, Forrest. You usually
are."

One of the logs sputtered and he got up and poked it, and she
joined him on the hearth and straightened the big mirror over the
fireplace. "Forget about the revival for a while," she said. "There is
a book in the library you ought to look over. J. D. Knowles's *Roger
Williams*."

"That's a good idea. I'll go down there right now."

"And maybe we can get together for dinner before the service."
She stood back and studied the mirror and moved the right corner up
a fraction of an inch.

"That's another good idea. Cliff is out in the country, but he'll
be back by six. We'll get Bent and eat at the hotel." He picked up
his hat from the hallway table and thanked her again and walked
out into the rain.

The parking lot was behind the library, and he scratched a fender
backing in. He got mud on his shoes running from his car to the
entrance and almost wiped them on his trousers and then remembered, and grinned. He was the only visitor in the library and yet he
whispered his wants to the librarian and took the books into the reading room. Knowles's *Roger Williams* and a rather rare old volume
entitled *The Story of the Baptists* by a man named Cook, although
nowhere in the edition did his first name or initials appear.

He laid the Williams biography aside and began thumbing through Cook's book and was fascinated, particularly by a list of "truths practiced and defended by Baptists."

London wrote them down exactly as the author had written them:

1. The Christian church is designed to be composed of regenerate persons, who have professed faith in Christ and have been baptized.

2. The entire separation of church and state.

3. The Bible alone the only rule, or standard, of religious belief and practice.

4. The immersion of believers, the only baptism of the New Testament.

5. The Lord's Supper, an ordinance committed to the care of the church, to be administered to baptized believers only.

6. That civil and religious liberty is an inalienable right.

He smiled as he underlined the sixth one, remembering his denomination's great schism over slavery and how so many of his brethren had accepted the latter-day Ku-Klux Klan with open arms. Well—a sow's ear is one man's purse and another man's poem.

The afternoon slipped by and it was coming dark fast and he was engrossed in his books and notes when the librarian touched his shoulder. "Telephone, Dr. Wingo."

Harry Ward was calling and his voice was trembly. "London——"

"Yes. Yes, Harry."

There was a pause, a sharp silence, and the premonition came to him then.

"I've got bad news, London. It's Cliff. He's had a stroke——"

"Oh lord, no. No! Where is he?"

"Memorial Hospital. I happened to be here when they brought him in."

"Be right over. Tell him I'll be right over."

Another pause, a sharper silence, and then, "It's beyond us now, London. It's all over."

London moved the receiver from his ear and his arm drooped and he looked at the librarian, and then put the phone in its cradle. "Cliff Carter is dead." He said it calmly, as a dazed man will.

"Brother Carter is gone." He reached for his hat and turned and walked slowly toward the door, tiptoeing down the hall.

The librarian came from behind her desk and caught up with him. "I'm so sorry, Dr. Wingo. He was such a good man. Mr. Carter was such a good man. Heart trouble?"

"A stroke." The door seemed a long way down the hall and he wanted to run and yet he didn't want to go at all.

"Is there anything I can do?"

"No. I suppose not." He opened the door and was out in the rain and darkness and began walking faster. The automobile lights glistened on the wet pavement. Then he remembered his car. He started to go back for it, but he might have trouble parking at the hospital. It was always so full. So he walked on and the people he passed were only blurred images, their heads lowered against the rain.

Harry Ward met him in the corridor of the hospital and put his arm around his shoulder and walked with him to the door of Cliff's room. "Benton is in there. He got here in time. I tried to get you."

"I was at the library."

"Uh-huh. Forrest told me." Harry was steady, much steadier than London. "I'll be around if you need me. And I told Forrest there'd be no services tonight. That's right, isn't it?"

"Yes. You did right."

He opened the door slowly and a shaded light was burning on the dresser and Benton was in a chair by the bed, staring up at London, waiting for him. His eyes were dry and the shadow of the light was across his face, softening it and erasing the hard lines at the corners of his mouth.

London rested his hands on the foot of the bed and looked down at Cliff, dreading the mask and suddenly remembering how Kathie had looked; her skin tight and the agony of the last breath on her face. But Cliff's face was serene, as though he were sleeping and soon would wake up and be about all the things he did so well. Throw out the life line, brother.

"I got here in time," Benton whispered, and sat forward in the chair. The light was on his face, and his face was still soft. "He grabbed hold of my hand, London. He was holding my hand."

"I know he was glad that you were here. I wish I could have been." It, too, was a whisper.

"I thought he was going to talk to me about my soul. About things like that, and I didn't want him to. He knew I'd promise him anything. But all he did was hold my hand and thank me for being his friend. That's all he did, London. Just held my hand and thanked me." Benton bowed his head and sobbed like a child, his whole body racking in misery.

London put his hand on his friend's arm. "Let's go out and walk around a little bit, Bent." He wanted solace himself and still he must give solace, although he had none to spare.

"You mean leave him?" Benton asked. "Go out and leave him alone? No. I won't do that. You'll look after things, won't you? You're a preacher and know about such things. But I won't leave him here in the dark."

"All right, Bent." There was immeasurable gentleness in his voice and he looked once more at Cliff's face, and he, London Wingo, was sustained by a conviction and in the faith that he would see Cliff again, and know him.

Then he turned the lamp until the light was on the ceiling and the room was brighter, for he, too, hated the darkness. He glanced over at Benton and saw that he was composed, and opened the door and stepped back into the corridor.

Harry Ward hurried to him, and Dr. Wentworth and Sisler Mason were with him. London spoke to Wentworth. "Keep your eye on Benton. He's pretty upset."

"Yes, I know." His stethoscope was around his neck, the badge of his trade, and he took it off and held it in his hand. "They'll be over for Cliff in a little bit and I'll go back to the undertaker's with them."

Harry said, "I sent wires to the children, but there are others to notify and I don't know the addresses."

It was all so efficient, the rituals for the dead; the instructions in whispers and awe, but the machinery moving smoothly. And London, for a reason he didn't analyze, was thinking of a book called

The Loved Ones and then quickly pulled his mind back to the problems at hand. "I'll call in the telegrams from home. Harry, will you come with me?"

They paused on the steps of the hospital, and he tugged down the brim of his hat and pulled up his overcoat collar. "Mind walking around a little bit? Mind the rain?"

"No." Harry rammed his hands deep in his overcoat pockets and hunched his shoulders against the weather. "Anything you say."

London swung down the sidewalk, and the rain pelted his hat and dribbled off the brim. The cold air awakened his brain, and he slowed down because his steps were longer than Harry's. They walked several blocks toward the railroad and into the warehouse district. "Kathie died on a night like this." They were London's first words since leaving the hospital. "Rainy and cold."

Harry did not reply.

They walked on and London asked, "Did he suffer?"

"No. I think not. Anyway, he didn't say anything about it. He was unconscious most of the time and then he came to for a few minutes, and Benton and I were there, and then he was gone."

"You getting cold?"

"Sort of."

They walked back to the library, and London got his car and they drove out to his place. He lit the fire to take the chill from the room and got a sheet of paper and wrote down the names of the people to be notified, including Paige and Vance—and Mary Upjohn.

Harry called in the telegrams while London fixed coffee, and they sat in front of the fire, staring at the blaze and hearing the wind and rain against the windows.

"What about the revival, London?"

"The revival is over." He pulled his chair closer to the fire and held out his hands for warmth. "Tomorrow is Sunday, and I'll announce that the revival is closed."

"It did a lot of good, brother."

"I wonder."

Harry held out his hands, too, and rubbed them. "It did me a lot of good. Cliff and I saw a lot of each other during the last few weeks." He stood up and turned his back to the blaze and rubbed the seat of his trousers. "He and I had a little spat a couple of years ago. That's when he pulled out of my church."

"Uh-huh. So he told me."

"Well——" He rocked on the balls of his feet. "There was more to it than he seemed to realize, but we won't go into that now."

London leaned over and picked up the poker and held it near the fire, and then he paused and looked up at Harry and handed it to him. "Go ahead. You poke."

Harry nudged the logs and the sparks flew and he tapped the top log for luck, and London smiled.

The room was warming up and they moved back, and London glanced at his watch. They surely had moved Cliff, and soon he must go to the undertaker's parlor and see about Bent, and sit with the dead. He felt the coffeepot and refilled the cups, but Harry left his on the table and moved over to the hearth and stood there with one arm on the mantel and stared down into the fire.

"What am I going to do, London?" It was a plea for help, and he murmured it. "I've been wanting to talk to you for a week or two and I can't wait any longer. What am I going to do?"

"What do you want to do?"

"I am a preacher." Harry looked up from the fire, and the light that London had seen so often in Cliff's eyes was in the eyes of this man. "The revival taught me that. But I can't go on like I am. A man cannot serve two masters, can he? Not God and Mammon."

"I couldn't. That is, I don't think I could. How bad is it?"

Harry put his hands at the small of his back and stretched. "Pretty bad. I've made more money than one man needs and I'm up to my neck right now in business deals." He pushed a chair to the edge of the hearth and sat down and crossed his legs. "I got in it by accident. It could have happened to you. Or to any preacher. I was trying to help."

London nodded but said nothing.

"When I first came here I preached a social gospel." Harry's words came fast, as though he wanted to be rid of them. "I tried to arouse the people, and nothing happened. And then I tried to show them how to do it. I left my pulpit for the countinghouse. And I was caught. Everything I tried was successful; everything except my ministry. And now what can I do?"

The fire licked the bark of one of the logs and blazed bright and flicked shadows across the room, and London walked over to a window and looked out toward his own church and could not see it in the rain and darkness. "I wonder——" He did not turn around. "I wonder if it was raining the night that Nicodemus came?"

"Is that the only way, London?"

"It's the only way that I know." He turned then and faced the man. "There's a Bible on the mantel. It's in John."

"Yes, I know." Harry picked up the book and opened it.

"Read it out loud," said London. "I need help too."

So Harry read and the firelight touched the words:

" 'There was a man of the Pharisees, named Nicodemus, a ruler of the Jews: The same came to Jesus by night, and said unto him, Rabbi, we know that thou art a teacher come from God: for no man can do these miracles that thou dost, except God be with him.

" 'Jesus answered and said unto him, Verily, verily, I say unto thee, Except a man be born again, he cannot see the kingdom of God.' "

Harry closed the Book and held it in his hand. "I know it. I just wish I could have told Cliff that I know it." He returned the Bible to the mantel and lifted the poker and began toying with the fire. "You'll help me put it where it can do the most good, won't you? I want to give it to the poor."

"All of it?"

"All of it."

"What about Shelby and the children?"

Harry placed the poker back in the stand and stood straight, rocking on the balls of his feet again. "I will educate my children on the earnings of my calling and I will support my wife the same way. She's wanted it like that for a long time."

They knelt by the divan, and the firelight was on them and against the windows, touching the night with its cheer.

London was the first to his feet and then Harry, and Harry said, "I'll be going now. I want to talk to Shelby."

"Take my car," London said. "And call up the funeral parlor and tell them to send for me in about an hour."

He helped Harry with his overcoat and walked with him to the steps and came back to his apartment and took the coffee things to the kitchen. Then he put in a call to the chairman of the Board of Deacons of Kansas City's Immanuel Baptist Church. His name was Travis Wiley.

It took only a few minutes for the call to get through. "London? Well, now, this is a pleasant surprise." Travis Wiley had a deep bass voice and sang bass in the choir. "How you doing?"

"I'm all right, Travis. But I had a blow today. Lost one of my deacons. My best friend——"

"Not Cliff Carter?"

"Uh-huh."

"Oh, good lord, London. Heart trouble?"

"No. He had a stroke. But that's not what I called you about. You folks never have filled your pulpit yet, have you?"

"Not yet. Been looking a long time. You got any ideas?"

"I've got the man you need. And the man who needs you. Harry Ward."

The dead silence at the other end told its own story, and then Travis Wiley was speaking again. "Harry Ward? Did you say Harry Ward?"

"That's right."

"Well, now, London——" The hesitation spoke for itself. "You know the situation up here. You'll be a hard man to follow."

"And now I know Harry Ward." There was no hesitation in London's words. "He just left here. He came by night, Travis."

"I see." There was a rising inflection in his tone, and instantly the doubt was gone.

"He's your man, Travis. There's no doubt about it."

"All right." The snap in the voice indicated confidence. "I'll put his name before the Pulpit Committee next week. I can say you recommended him?"

"All out," said London Wingo. "All down the line."

They talked a few more minutes, but not about Harry at all, only about Cliff, and then London hung up and put the screen in front of the fireplace and changed his clothes. The car was waiting for him, and he rode down to the funeral home and walked through the little knot of whispering people in the hall and on into the reception room.

Forrest was with Bent, and Shelby and Harry were there, and Shelby came over and kissed his cheek and Bent motioned for him to follow, and they stepped across the hall to Cliff's office.

"Have you seen the new *Life?*" Benton asked.

"No."

"I got it out of the post office a few minutes ago. Cliff hadn't got his mail all day." He pushed some papers aside and picked up the magazine and opened it and folded it back and handed it to London.

It was the second letter in the Letters to the Editor column.

SIRS:

Re: Your article on the revival meeting at Wheaton College in Illinois. That's the town where Red Grange, the great football player, is from.

CLIFF CARTER
Linden, Missouri

P.S. We are having a revival in our town too.

London removed his glasses and took out his handkerchief and wiped his eyes.

Benton said, "He wrote that one himself. I wrote all the others for him. The ones they didn't print. But he wrote that one himself."

Chapter 17

Cliff's family, the grown sons and the host of kin, requested a simple funeral service, but even then it was the biggest thing of its kind ever held in Linden.

The local newspapers published editorials in praise of Cliff, the *Morning Ledger* quoting Matthew's "Well done, thou good and faithful servant," and the *Evening Record* quoting Paul's "I have fought a good fight, I have finished my course, I have kept the faith."

The papers estimated that five hundred people jam-packed the church and that two thousand more were at the cemetery. However, Lizzie Ramsey's report was more accurate. She counted exactly four hundred and eighty-six persons in the church and thirty-five in the vestibule and scribbled her tally on the flyleaf of a songbook while the other mourners bowed their heads in prayer. Sister Ramsey knew the funeral would be discussed in weeks to come, particularly at missionary society meetings, and she wanted facts and figures.

London forbade any ostentatious display of flowers in the church, and only one rose, a white one, was on Cliff's casket, but Sister Ramsey counted every wreath at the funeral parlor. There were six hundred and forty-two. The most elaborate was from Cliff's fellow undertakers. It was a five-foot cross of tuberoses flown in from south Texas.

Mrs. Bledsoe also jotted down a few figures, but her interest was diverted when Benton entered the church with the other honorary pallbearers. He was shy and ill at ease, and Mrs. Bledsoe whispered to her husband, "First time he's set foot in a church since his wife left him. He looks tuckered out. Wonder why he ain't an active pall-bearer?"

The reason was quite simple, for Cliff's casket was bronze with silver handles, known in his trade as the Everlasting. It was selected by a committee of his business associates, and a man of his standing must have the best. The family wanted it that way too. Therefore, it was not in London to protest, and Cliff Carter, who hated pomp and pretension and who believed in sackcloth, lay at rest on satin. The casket was so heavy that it could not be trusted to novices like Benton Andrews and Clark Upjohn. The active pallbearers were undertakers themselves.

London did not preach a funeral sermon. He read the Twenty-third Psalm and Harry Ward spoke a few words and the choir sang "In the Garden," and then the procession moved from the church to the cemetery.

There, with a handful of soggy dirt, London committed the body of his friend to the earth whence it came. The rain had quit and a cold wave was nipping in, flapping the canopy over the grave and browning the flowers. The frail tuberoses died first.

A final prayer, and the crowd dispersed, moving slowly away from the grave and then rapidly toward the gate to the cemetery. Sister Ramsey wrote down the number of cars and the makes of all the big ones. Nine Cadillacs. Twelve Buicks. Six Lincolns . . .

She did not list the Plymouths, Chevrolets, and Fords.

London and Forrest rode back to town with Benton and they were silent, but in the other cars some of the mourners were wondering about Cliff's money—how much and who would get it.

"Bet he'll fix that preacher for life," somebody said. "He sure loved him."

"That church, too," said another. "They'll have silver communion things now and a memorial window as big as they come."

London had no idea of Cliff's financial affairs and neither did

Forrest or Benton. They knew he had made a lot of money and had given a lot away, but they were too depressed even to think about such matters until that night when, at Benton's suggestion, they ate at the Post Office Café.

Dr. Wentworth saw them there and came over and sat in the booth next to Benton. He reached over for a sliver of celery. "They are going to read his will tomorrow," he said. "Then probate it. Have you heard?"

"No," London said. "I've heard nothing about it."

"Well, you will. Cliff was mighty well off, and you know he'll remember you."

Forrest felt for London's hand on the seat beside her and gripped it, cautioning him to silence. Benton, however, threw his napkin on the table. "Good God, Doc. You too? They bury a man like Cliff in a cold metal monstrosity. Parade him to his grave in a Roman triumph. And now you talk about his money. Why not build a pyramid over him? Or carve out a Sphinx?"

Wentworth was flustered. "I didn't mean anything——"

"Of course you didn't," London said. "We are all sort of edgy."

"Edgy!" Benton stood and looked down at all of them. "You worship a God of poverty and humility. He was born in a stable and buried in a cave. But what do you do to a man like Cliff? A fellow who believed it all and lived it. You bury him in silver and satin. My God! Why didn't you hire a band to play 'Pomp and Circumstance'?" He squeezed past Wentworth and stepped out of the booth. "I hope you folks won't mind a heathen going out and enjoying a little fresh air." He jerked his hat from the rack by the booth and left them.

Wentworth began toying with a fork, and London and Forrest did not comment because, down deep, they agreed with Benton. They finished their coffee and excused themselves and headed for Forrest's apartment, but stopped off first by the post office.

A letter from Paige was in London's box, and he read it and handed it to Forrest. It was a warming letter, condolence for his loss and her genuine regrets that she and Vance could not be home with him and Mr. Andrews. She specifically sent her love to Forrest and promised to write more often.

They went on around to Forrest's place, and London built a fire and she opened a can of peanut brittle and they sat by the hearth and played phonograph records until almost nine o'clock, neither saying much, just listening to the music and watching the fire.

The sky was clear and the stars were cold and far away when London walked out to his car for the drive home, and he glanced back at her apartment and saw her moving about the living room, and the fire's warm glow on the frosty windows. An impulse, an urge, to go back and tell her good night again came to him and he was surprised at himself, and then, really for the first time, he honestly admitted to himself that he didn't want to leave her at all, or, better still, he wanted her to come with him and share everything.

It was a selfish, worldly impulse, he thought, and he forced his mind to banish the yearning, and instead of going home immediately he drove by Benton's house, but the place was dark and he drove out to the cemetery, and there was Benton's car parked by the gate.

London got out of his automobile and walked over to Benton's. "Pretty cold out here," he said as he opened the door and got in.

"Clean, though." Benton flipped his cigarette away. "How long will they keep that tent over him? And all those flowers?"

"Oh, I don't know, Bent." London lit his pipe and lowered the window and threw out the match. "That's up to the family and the funeral home."

"Why did you let them do Cliff that way?" Benton demanded. "A circus parade!"

"It was out of my hands," said London patiently. "We kept the church services simple, but the rest of it was out of my hands."

"You could have put up a howl."

"That would have made matters worse." London removed his glasses and wiped away the frosty moisture. "The body of the dead belongs to the living. Particularly the family——"

"Nonsense." Benton was even more irascible than usual.

London was as edgy and testy as his friend, but never again must he lose his patience or temper with Benton Andrews. "Well, that's only my opinion, Bent. Funerals have become profitable promotions. Cliff used to talk about it a lot. I don't recall ever hearing any church advocate bronze caskets and Cadillac funeral cars. But I've heard your radio station do it."

Benton scowled quickly and bristled. "Now you're trying to start an argument."

"Then let's not talk about it any more," London suggested.

"I know how much you thought of Cliff." Benton was persistent and naggy. "But you are taking this thing in stride. I suppose you have something to sustain you that I haven't got."

London held his pipe tight in his fist, and the ash glowed red. "Now *you* are trying to start an argument." He remembered the letter from Paige and, thinking it might cheer Benton, felt in his pocket for it. "Just got it." He slipped the letter from the envelope and passed it over.

Benton turned on the dash light and leaned forward and read it. "She says exactly the right things." He switched off the light and tapped the letter against the steering wheel. "She always does. I thought I would hear from Vance. Or that he'd send flowers."

"You'll hear from him. And I don't know about him, but Paige would never send flowers. She belongs to your school; that flowers are inadequate testimony at such a time as this. Now, come on, Bent. Let's not stay here. Come on by my place."

He went back to his own car and started for Plymouth, driving faster than Benton, and had his apartment as cheerful as possible by the time his friend arrived. Benton dropped his overcoat on the divan and stepped to the fireplace and kicked back one of the logs and warmed his hands.

"How about some coffee?" London asked.

"No, thanks. I'm up to my neck in coffee." Benton pulled a chair near the hearth and held out his long hands to the blaze and was silent, then glanced over at London. "What happened to Harry Ward? He started unloading his property this morning."

"Why don't you ask Harry?" London moved the overcoat and stretched out on the divan.

"I did. He told me to read the third chapter of John." Benton pushed back his chair and folded his hands behind his head. "Good God! I cut my teeth on it. In fact, it was my wife's favorite chapter, and she quoted it coming and going." He dropped his hands to his sides and turned his face toward London. "All my life I've heard hypocrites spout Scripture on Sunday and break it on Monday. How do you stand it?"

"Well——" London closed his eyes and sighed. He never remembered being closer to exhaustion than he was right then. "I worry about it as much as you do, Bent. And then I try to keep in mind that as far as I am concerned I must not confuse spiritual values and human behavior." He sat up and rubbed his eyes, shoving his glasses to his forehead as he did so. "Why don't you spend the night here? No need of going back to that big empty house."

Benton got up slowly and stretched. "No. Much obliged."

"You can have my room," London said. "I'll sleep here on the divan. Mattie will bring your breakfast to you, and you can rest as long as you want."

"No. I'll be going along." Benton simply would not allow himself the luxury of relaxation or of close companionship with London Wingo; as though he dreaded it, as though he were afraid of it.

However, he insisted that London not walk out into the cold with him. It was a consideration he never had shown before, and London thought about it after he got into bed. Not for long, though. And neither did he think about Cliff, but only about Forrest and, as tired as he was, he could not go to sleep immediately for thinking about her.

Mattie was puttering around the kitchen and London was lining up his work for the day when Cliff's lawyer telephoned and asked him, as a friend of the family, to attend a conference at the Farmers & Merchants Bank. Only then did the possibilities impress themselves on him. Suppose Cliff had left him a lot of money.

He thanked the lawyer and went to his bedroom for his coat and then sat on the bed and rubbed his forehead thoughtfully. It would be nice to have money. He could do all the things he often had wanted to do. But hold on. Money would impair his ministry, and he could only give it away as Harry was doing. But why? He had given the ministry his youth and most of his life. He had planned to retire someday, and his ministry and service were the only barriers between him and Forrest. If he were a retired preacher with a steady income they could be married and live in Florida. He could preach every now and then, say once a month, and his life would be his own. He began smiling and actually laughed. How silly. How utterly ridiculous.

He was embarrassed, and didn't know why, when he joined the conference and was surprised at the size of Cliff's fortune, the business interests, the insurance, the stocks and the bonds. There was insurance money for the family, including several aunts and cousins, and the undertaking business was left to his associates and workers.

"Mr. Carter's will——" The lawyer was not pompous at all and glanced up after he read the first few provisions of the document. "At Mr. Carter's request I drew up this will a few days before he died. He wanted to include some personal bequests." Then slowly he read them.

An Irish linen table service to Shelby and Harry Ward.

A cherry drop-leaf table to Forrest.

His pearl handle pocketknife to Benton.

His watch to London Wingo, and nothing else.

The bulk of his fortune went to the missionary training school where Mary Upjohn was studying, and not a dime was left to the Plymouth Baptist Church.

Even Cliff's family was surprised, but not London, for he knew his friend's feelings about such matters; that a church should support itself and that the Kingdom of God is built on tithes and sacrifices and not on trust funds.

As for himself, he was ashamed for ever thinking that Cliff might leave him money.

The will set many tongues to wagging, and some of the Methodist brethren chided their Baptist neighbors and some of the Baptists grumbled that Cliff easily could have endowed the church. London ignored the gossip until the following Sunday and then preached on stewardship and apportioned Cliff's work among the people.

He explained that Cliff's contributions must be raised from other sources, and the people responded without stint, particularly the new members who had come in during the revival.

Then came the news that Harry Ward had been called to Kansas City's Immanuel Church, and the people had something fresh to talk about and squeezed the subject dry. The First Church approached London on the possibility of his accepting Harry's old pulpit, but he was not interested, and they began casting around for a new pastor while London reorganized his own work out at Plymouth.

The revival had swelled the membership, and he increased the Board of Deacons and began pressing for his building program. He kept Paige and Vance posted on all the church and community news and maneuvered Forrest onto the committee to select a pipe organ, not quite trusting the judgment of Sister Ramsey and Sloan Wentworth.

The Carter family wanted to install a memorial window to Cliff and tactfully London persuaded them to donate a baptistry instead, and the little church inhaled new breath and, strengthened by the revival, was firm in its evangelical mission.

He gave two nights a week to Roger Williams, partly because the book was important to him, but mostly because it gave him an excuse to see Forrest. And thus he stayed busy, working harder than he ever had worked before. He saw Benton often and Forrest more often, and the winter slipped by, the days filled with accomplishments, and only the nights were long and empty.

The clover was greening up and the shrubs were swelling when a letter arrived from Paige that she was coming home for a few days and that Vance would not be with her. "He is in the middle of exams," she explained.

London immediately called the news to Forrest and Benton and they offered him rooms, Benton almost insisting that they stay at his house during her visit. "I got room to spare," he said. "No need of crowding up out there in that little cracker box of yours."

The offer was declined, however, as London wanted her to himself. They would eat with Benton and Forrest and he wanted Benton and Forrest to eat with them, but the evenings must be their own as they had been for so long. Benton said he understood, and perhaps he did.

Mattie was instructed to scour the kitchen from top to bottom and to buy two red geraniums for the kitchen window. London himself rearranged his room to suit her taste, as he remembered her taste. He emptied his closet and dumped his things in the hall closet and tacked new shelf paper in the bathroom. He put an embroidered runner on the night stand and took out all of his books and that pile of old magazines and Sunday supplements from the corner. He bought a potted azalea and fussed and fumed over whether to put it on the night stand by her bed or on the dresser.

The living room was rearranged completely, and he moved the divan over by the windows. He would sleep there and be up early enough each morning to remove the sheets and things before Paige got up.

Forrest came over to help him and shared his happy enthusiasm, although he paid no attention whatsoever to her suggestions. Mattie, so wise in so many ways, offered no suggestions and kept shaking her head in amusement at all the to-do.

At Forrest's direction Mattie helped her straighten out the hall closet, and they brushed his suits and overcoat and hung them up. London was in the kitchen, and Forrest herself brushed his hat and unconsciously assumed a proprietary air about the matter that caused Mattie to glance at her and grin as though they, being women, shared a secret.

London made another round of the apartment and said that it would do and sat down in the living room and lit his pipe. His shirt was open at his throat. Forrest poured two Cokes for them and joined him, and London leaned back and stretched out his legs in the way of a man who has done a job.

"And now that's that," he said. "You and Bent will have dinner with us the first night. Right here. Let's see——" He pursed his lips in deep thought. "We'll have shrimp cocktail to begin with. Then rare roast beef and potatoes. Little asparagus, too. And lettuce and tomatoes. How does that sound?"

"Very good," Forrest said. "Original, too."

London looked quickly at her and wasn't sure if she were teasing or not, but her face revealed nothing. "Will you bake a cake?" he asked.

"A Lady Baltimore." She folded her handkerchief on the freshly waxed table and put her glass on the handkerchief. "I'll come over and help Mattie while you are gone to the airport."

"Now that's just fine. The next day we'll eat with you——"

"I suggest the next day with Bent," she said.

"You're right. The second day with Bent and then with you——"

And on and on, planning every day of Paige's visit.

He had the DeSoto washed and polished and drove over early to the airport, although her plane wasn't due until 2 P.M. It was twenty minutes late, and he fidgeted at the delay and complained to the bored agent and vehemently criticized the whole American transportation system.

The plane came in while he was drinking his third cup of coffee, and he hurried to the gate, jostling and being jostled, and began worrying when she was not among the first passengers to disembark. Then he saw her speak to the stewardess and step to the door and look around.

She had changed. From that distance he could tell that she had changed. She was thinner and her hat was not perky, but a simple hat, almost stern, and a nose veil. She walked slowly down from the plane, all poise and dignity, and no excited exuberance or bubbling joy.

He nudged his way through the gate, and she saw him and smiled and lifted her hand in a little wave. She did not run to him and fling out her arms, but she did walk faster and her kiss on his cheek was affectionate and comforting.

She scarcely glanced at his hat and did not comment, but noticed the gray hairs encroaching higher on his temples, and then she looked into his face, his eyes misty and blinking. "You all right, Dad?" She squeezed his arm and patted it.

"Sure. I'm fine, honey. Let me have your baggage checks."

She opened her bag and took them out. "I'll look after it." She asked no assistance. She expected none. It was a thing he had always done—looking after her luggage—and now she did it for herself without realizing that he was there to help.

Paige moved away from her father, and he watched her go and knew then that she had her life and that he had his, and that the cord between them was broken; the silver cord was loosed, the golden bowl was broken, the pitcher broken at the fountain and the wheel broken at the cistern.

For a second, and for a second only, there was a longing hurt within him and a vast emptiness, and then it went away. For as a Christian, London Wingo was something of a Stoic and submissive to things he could not change.

His daughter was a woman, that's all; the wife of a man like himself, as good, as evil. Nothing about her belonged to him any more, only memories that already were faint—a few tears and tantrums and laughter. Time had robbed him of Paige, but time was a strange thief, for in taking one thing it always gave another, and now there were his church and Forrest, and Benton and all the others.

They were walking toward the parking space and he said, "Want to drive, I suppose."

"If you want me to." She slipped under the wheel, not with the gay carelessness of only a year ago, but sedately, and she drove very cautiously, as though not quite sure of herself.

They talked for a minute about Vance, mostly about his health, and she changed the subject to Linden, particularly the Harry Wards. London thought nothing about it and answered all of her questions and then got back to Vance.

"You say he's making that Greek all right?" St. Louis was behind them and the Missouri River was to their left, spring-muddied and sprawling.

"He's getting by." She had the car on fifty, which was a slow speed for her. "It's been a headache, but he'll graduate next month. Then his ordination."

"I'll be there." London tilted his hat to the side of his head and opened his coat. "I'll be there with bells on." He glanced over at her and grinned. "Any sign of a church yet? I don't suppose he has been called to Dr. Fosdick's pulpit, or Dr. Poling's?"

Paige did not reply immediately. They were making a sweeping curve, and she hugged the inside and leveled off. "He has been sounded out about a teaching job at a Baptist school in North Carolina."

"Wake Forest?"

"Uh-huh. Yes, sir."

"Pretty good school. And going to be better. Pretty liberal school for a Southern Baptist college."

"But he's not interested, Dad." Her veil blew down over her eyes and she brushed it back and tightened it over her hat. "A church down there also has written him."

"So?" London perked up.

Paige looked out at the fields, fresh green and the furrows turned. "It's that little church where he talked while we were at Ridgecrest. Lystra Baptist Church." There was no enthusiasm in her voice, no pride.

However, London's eagerness was enough for both of them and, in his own zeal, he was not aware of her dejection. "Well, now, that's something." He locked his hands on the lapels of his coat and beamed his pleasure.

"It's just a little church," she said. "They want him only half time."

London slapped his right knee emphatically and then rubbed his knee and slapped it again. "That doesn't make any difference, honey. For a country church to reach way up to Rochester for a pastor is a tribute to Vance. Those folks are hard to please."

"They only pay twelve hundred a year." She shoved down the accelerator for the first time and whipped the car around a bend. "Vance thinks he can fill in with other country churches and that we can live in some little town near Asheville and make out until he gets going."

"He's right." The flat assumption was too emphatic for a man who did not know all the details, but, like most fathers, London was anxious for Vance to seize a job and start wrestling with it. He came from the root-hog-or-die school, and it was difficult for him to realize that things had changed. "Vance can line up enough country churches to stay busy. And he has no financial worries. There's always his mother's money."

"There's not as much there as most people think." It came quickly, impulsively. "Besides, Vance has some silly notion that now that he's about through school he shouldn't use that money. That the ministry should support us."

London jerked his head around and stared at her.

She gave him no chance to speak but kept right on talking. "Dr. Ward's behavior upset Vance a lot. He's been mulling it over. I think you ought to talk to him. And I'm going to talk to Mr. Andrews about it."

"Don't do it, Paige." He spoke his admonition firmly. "That's a matter between you and Vance and God. It doesn't concern Benton Andrews or me or anybody else."

"But our situation is different from Dr. Ward's. Vance's mother left that money for his education and for him to get started on. I don't think we have started yet."

London was inclined to agree with her but did not say so. After all, that was Harry Ward and this was his daughter and that made things different. "Just don't dive headfirst into anything," he said. "You and Vance talk it through and pray it through, but don't enlist your father-in-law against your husband."

She made no promise and switched the conversation completely. "Good-looking hat you're wearing." The mischievous twinkle was back in her eyes for the first time in so long.

"I was wondering if you were going to notice it."

"Mr. Andrews wrote us that you were a backslider and had gone back to hats." She glanced at him and feigned severity. "I assume Forrest approves."

Everything was all right now. The fun was back in her eyes and she was teasing him again. "I suppose she does." He took off the hat and brushed the brim with his fingers. "She picked it out."

Paige slowed the DeSoto and reached out her hand and patted

his arm. "I get lots of letters from Linden," she said. "Forrest writes often, but she never mentioned any hat. And we heard quite a bit from Mr. Carter and several others. Tell me something. Am I going to be the daughter of a groom?" She asked it frankly.

He put his hat back on, tilting it at a jaunty angle and flipping the brim in a quick gesture. "Well, now——" His face was straight ahead, but his eyes cut over her way. "It strikes me that as a preacher's wife your job is souls. Not hearts."

"Well, now——" She imitated him perfectly. "It strikes me that I should be consulted about such things."

"I wasn't."

"Strike one!" She lowered her head over the wheel and laughed. "Then all right. But tell me just one thing." She was determined on one more effort to prime him into conversation about Forrest. "Do you still think Paul was against marriage?"

London looked out at the low hills and stroked his chin. "You know something? The older I get, the more I realize that I am not Paul."

Paige felt that further questions would be intrusions and she dropped it there and began asking about the book. That started him on Roger Williams and led to Forrest, and he talked about her most all the way to Linden.

Benton and Forrest met them at the door, and after an exchange of greetings and a quick report on Vance, Paige went into her father's room and London headed for the kitchen. Only then did he miss Mattie.

"She's not here," Forrest explained.

"What!"

"Now keep your shirt on," Benton said. "She called us right after you left that she was sick. But Forrest and I came on over and everything is under control."

London was disappointed. "I promised to pay her extra. John Brown it! Just when I needed her, too."

Paige heard the discussion and joined them. She had taken off her hat and veil and had changed shoes, and Forrest looked at her trim figure and was conscious of her self-possession and mature composure. "Don't let it bother you, Dad," Paige said. "I can fix supper."

"It's just about ready," Forrest said, and nodded toward the dining alcove, then spoke to London. "I supposed you wanted your best silver and linen."

"Of course," London said. "But I didn't expect you to do it. You and Bent are our guests."

The table already was set. Kathie's damask cloth was smooth and snowy and Kathie's silver was polished and shining. A flower arrangement was between Kathie's candlesticks.

Paige glanced at the table and turned slowly to Forrest, and the older woman felt the gaze and was flustered momentarily and quickly was annoyed that this girl—no, this woman, this wife—could upset her. However, Paige's gaze was a question and the look in her eyes was an answer, and Forrest felt that Paige was seeing right into her, that her emotions were being disrobed, one garment at a time, before the eyes of the daughter of the man she loved. At that moment she didn't like Paige Wingo or Paige Andrews. She almost hated her.

She stepped back into the living room and gave Paige a chance to take over, to let her be the woman of the house and the mistress of the occasion. But Paige made no move to assume authority, and Forrest, fearing the men might sense what the women knew, took the situation into her own hands without another second's hesitation.

"You sit here with your father and Benton." She indicated a chair to Paige. "I will go see about the roast. It's just about ready."

"I will help you," Paige said, and followed her into the kitchen, the swinging door closing behind them.

Forrest opened the oven and examined the roast, then pushed the door up quickly before the heat ruined her make-up. "London"— she said it deliberately because it was more familiar than "your father"—"London chose the menu. Roast beef and potatoes."

Paige smiled knowingly. "And a vegetable and lettuce and tomatoes. Now what can I do? Fix the coffee?"

"If you don't mind." Forrest glanced in the calendar mirror on the pantry door. Her chignon still was perfect. Her make-up too.

"Which cups shall we use?" Paige was deferring to her, leaving to her the decision on the revered Kathie cups.

Forrest wondered if there was any malice in the words and detected none, but again she felt Paige watching her and was tense. "I'm sure London wants his best china," she said, and was struggling to retain her composure and conceal her nervousness.

"So am I." Paige picked up the kettle. "You get the cups and I will fix the coffee."

For an instant Forrest debated in her mind whether to direct Paige to take down the cups herself and put them on the table. But it seemed silly, an issue over such simple things as tableware. She must not notice it. So she stepped to the cabinet and opened the glass doors and reached for the first of the Kathie cups.

Then she knew it was going to happen. That nothing could stop it. Her hand trembled and there was no strength in her fingers, and she stared helplessly at the cup and watched it slip free and shatter on the floor.

Her face flushed hot in mortification, but she was cold inside and wished she could melt away or that a vast hole would open up and let her hide. She dared not look at Paige, but stood there staring down at the broken pieces, and then she stooped and picked up the handle. It was so dainty and fragile.

"I broke one of your mother's cups," she said, and it seemed to take forever to say it, and all of her courage.

"I never knew my mother, Forrest." Paige bent over and brushed the pieces into her hand. "I never knew my mother at all. And I'm glad one of the cups is broken." There was infinite tenderness and understanding in her voice.

"But they were so beautiful." Forrest whispered it and still was trembling. "And your father loved them so much." She said "your father" then.

Paige walked over to the sink and brushed the pieces into a little pile. "I can't speak for Dad. But as for me—well, I'm glad you broke one of the damn things."

It was such a strange thing to say and yet Forrest understood, and suddenly a warm glow heartened her and her hands were steady. "I will go tell London I broke it."

"Not right yet," said Paige, and walked back across the room and stood beside her and was as tall as she. "Maybe what I said doesn't make sense."

"Maybe it does," Forrest said, and longed to put her arms around his daughter and find comfort for herself and to give comfort.

"All my life"—Paige leaned against the cabinet and folded her arms—"as long as I can remember, those twelve cups have hung on twelve little hooks. Useless. Fragile. And beyond my reach." She unfolded her arms and rested her hands on the cabinet, and Forrest did not interrupt, feeling her yearning and really knowing her for the first time.

"I know my mother was a great woman. Everybody told me so. Not Dad as much as the others. But over and over they told me that I was her daughter and must be like her. Yet nothing to guide me except twelve cups on twelve little hooks. I used to want to take them down and play tea party." She smiled at the recollection and shook her head slowly. "But I dared not ask permission to play with them and, worse still, I dared not slip them. She was watching me. She was watching everything I did and knew everything I thought. Oh, Dad would have let me play with them, but I couldn't ask him because they were Mother's, and he was Mother's, and I was Mother's.

"And I tell you something else——" The words flowed as though she wanted to have them out and be done with them forever. "When I was a little girl I prayed that Dad would marry again and give me a mother I could see. One of my own kind to stand between me and my mother in heaven, who was watching me, and eternally waiting. Also, I didn't like for the other kids to have something I didn't have. I used to play like Dad brought me a mother. But, Forrest, I am glad he didn't. Now that I know you I am glad he waited."

She was smiling and then tears gushed to her eyes and streaked her cheeks, and Forrest opened her arms and they hugged each other and wept their joy as only happy women can.

"And now," said Forrest, "I will go tell London about the cup."

"I will go with you."

They fixed their faces and went together to the living room, and Forrest said, "London, I'm sorry, but I broke one of your best cups."

She saw Benton glance quickly at her and then at Paige. However, London's expression didn't change. He took his pipe from his mouth and said, "Which one, Forrest?"

"The one on this end. The first one."

"Oh, that one." He tapped his pipe bowl against an ash tray. "It was already cracked. I cracked it myself when I moved in here. They lasted a long time, didn't they?" His smile was warmer than she had ever seen it, and very tender. "You two need any help with that roast? Bent and I are starving."

Chapter 18

London prided himself on his carving and, after the blessing, he pared thin slices from the roast and passed the plates to Forrest, who served the potatoes and asparagus, chatting all the while in obvious exhilaration.

She talked with Paige about some plays she had read and that Paige had seen in New York, and to Benton about the virtues and evils of television. The St. Louis Browns and the American State Department; her conversation flowed from one topic to another, and she expounded wittily and wisely and never too long on any subject.

London also was expansive but was only an accompanist to her stimulating overtures, and Paige and Benton might just as well have been stage hands. She served coffee in the living room, and when London turned on the radio she began singing and he turned it off quickly and she kept singing, first some modern songs and then the old ones that were coming back—"Oh, Frenchy" and "Little White Lies" and "Harbor Lights."

At Benton's request she mimicked Bette Davis and Katharine Hepburn and Mrs. Roosevelt and then, with a big wink at London, showed Paige how jelly beans and flappers used to dance the camel walk. Benton joined her in a soft-shoe routine and London laughed at the capers, but Paige sat in silent surprise at such uninhibited merriment.

It was after midnight when Benton took Forrest home, and Paige sprawled in a chair and her arms drooped over the sides. "Well, now!" She ran her fingers through her hair and shook her head. "I never knew all that about her."

"Neither did I," London said. "It was like touching a spring and out pops a jack-in-the-box."

"She's quite a talker." Paige slipped off her shoes and wiggled her toes in sensuous delight.

"But when she says something, she says something." London emptied an ash tray into a wastebasket.

Paige stood and stretched. "Yes, sir." Her eyes lit up in that impish sparkle. "But I don't know about a preacher's wife who shags around like that and cuts a rug."

Her father did not take the bait. He undid his collar and yawned big. "Well, we'd better get to bed. Got a big day tomorrow. We go to Bent's. Good night, honey."

"Good night, Dad."

She picked up her shoes and was walking toward the bedroom when he spoke again. "And, Paige. I'm mighty glad you didn't mention that money situation to Benton."

"I wouldn't have tonight, anyway," she said, and turned at the bedroom doorway. "Not with Forrest here. And I don't think I will mention it at all. It'll work itself out."

"Of course it will. Just have confidence in Vance and in your prayers."

She stooped and scooted her shoes across the floor and to the edge of the bed. "I wonder if Forrest will teach me that old camel-walk dance. I know a few students at the seminary I'd like to shock."

"I'm sure she will."

"Maybe I could learn a lot from Forrest." She was reluctant to close the subject.

"I wouldn't be surprised," said London, and got sheets and a blanket from the hall closet and spread them on the divan.

Paige closed the door, and London undressed and hung his clothes on a chair and was in bed ready to turn out the light when she reappeared in the doorway. "By the way"—it was a casual opening, as though she had just happened to think about it—"what do you hear from the Wards?"

"They are fine." He yawned again.

"Well, Dr. Ward certainly should be grateful to you."

"For what?" He slipped his arms under his pillow and relaxed.

Paige was in her negligee and was removing bobby pins from her hair and holding them between her lips. "You got him that call, didn't you? He wanted Immanuel Church and you got it for him."

"Oh no! No, honey!" He was emphatic. "I simply was God's instrument that brought a preacher and a church together. And Harry is going to be one of the best preachers in the country. You just watch."

She took the bobby pins out of her mouth and massaged her scalp briskly. "Well, anyway, you got him that pulpit. Everybody knows that."

London propped on his elbow and fluffed his pillow. "Have it your way." He was too tired to argue. "However, I'm not running an employment agency for the Lord. A good church needed a good pastor and I had an opportunity to bring them together. That's all there was to it. Now, good night, honey. I'm a tired man."

She closed the door and he turned out his light.

Mattie did not show up for work the next morning and Paige fixed breakfast, and he noticed that she still did not know how to cook bacon crisp and dry, but the eggs and toast were just right. So was the coffee, and he drank two cups, although Paige took only a few sips of hers. She had no appetite whatsoever.

"All right." London leaned back in the chair and rubbed his hands together. He was full of warm food and good humor. "What's the ticket? What do you want to do?"

"Let's walk down to the church," she suggested. "I want to see it first. Then let's ride over to Elmscourt and see a few of our old neighbors."

That pleased him, of course, and he got up from the table and helped her wash the dishes. "I'll be ready as soon as I shave."

Paige spread out the dish towels and washed the sink. "And

speaking of Elmscourt"—again it was casual—"did Dr. Ward sell that out too?"

"Uh-huh."

"Vance and I wrote them our congratulations on his new church. But I still say you should get the credit."

London frowned slightly. "God's work is not a matter of debits and credits, Paige."

"Just the same, Dr. Ward asked you to help him get that church and you did." She was persistent in the matter.

He pushed the chairs closer to the breakfast table and put away the jam and butter. "That's true, and yet it's not exactly the truth. Dr. H. Harrington Ward who came to me last year about that church was not the Brother Ward who came by night a few months ago. Dr. Ward was Ward's man. Brother Ward was the Lord's man. Now, I'll be with you in just a minute. Think I'll wear my gray suit."

She put on a light blue spring suit and they went down to the church and he showed her where the pipe organ and baptistry would be, and then they got in the car and drove around Linden.

Paige was at the wheel, and to get to Elmscourt she cut over two blocks and rode by the First Baptist Church. The door was closed tight and the shrubs needed tending. "I hope the next pastor gets rid of that neon sign. It's terrible."

"I think so too," he said.

"They haven't called a preacher yet, have they?" The car was throttled down to about fifteen miles an hour.

"No-o-o. Not yet." London wasn't looking at the church at all, but at the trees along Boone Avenue where he and Kathie were living when Paige was born.

"They shouldn't have any trouble." She speeded up to make the next green light. "They pay about forty-two hundred dollars, don't they?"

He glanced over at her and then away. "Exactly forty-two hundred dollars, honey. And they've sounded out two or three men, but the Lord hasn't seen fit to bless this field yet. He will if the people heed Him. He always does."

The subject was dropped and they went on out to Elmscourt and then to the Cuckoo Clock Tearoom for lunch. Paige called on Forrest that afternoon and London took a nap, and they both dressed semi-formally for Benton's party. It was a lavish dinner, prepared and served by Linden's only caterer, and several of Paige's friends from WLMO were there.

Forrest was more subdued than on the night before. In fact, she was on her sedate behavior. Not prim by any means, but all dignity and decorum. She kept Paige in the center of things and gave the younger woman a chance to shine, and she did.

At her own dinner the next day, Forrest served only Mexican food, and she and Paige dressed in costumes Forrest had purchased on a visit to Mexico; lots of spangles and bracelets, and each wore a mantilla and a high comb.

Benton, not to be outdone, sang a Spanish song in a flat monotone, and London, to the utter amazement of his daughter, danced a fandango with Forrest and tried to slip in a few of the fancy steps he had learned as a young man in Texas. It wasn't too successful, but that didn't matter, for the evening belonged to him and Forrest.

Then it was Friday, the day Paige was to leave, and she asked Forrest over for lunch. At first Forrest declined. She had classes that afternoon and, besides, she thought that father and daughter should have the last day to themselves. However, Paige insisted so strongly that finally Forrest agreed and got a substitute teacher and arrived at the apartment shortly after noon.

The luggage was packed and in the living room and Paige's hat with the veil was on a chair by the door, and already the place was beginning to feel empty again. Forrest's flower arrangement, slightly faded, was still on the table, and it was a good lunch of fresh spring vegetables, and London strained to make the occasion as happy as possible; and then the blow fell.

Paige waited until he had finished his second cup of coffee and deliberately reopened the conversation about the Wards. London parried her questions and Forrest, sensing tension, suddenly was embarrassed.

She began talking about the church, and that was exactly what

Paige wanted her to do. Forrest was the one who first mentioned the church. It was she who opened Pandora's box.

Paige folded her napkin and put it beside her plate. "Dad, I've been thinking——"

He knew what was coming and his nerves constricted instantly. She had brought Forrest there perhaps as an ally, and surely as a buffer.

"You can get the First Church to call Vance. If you will." She said it as easily as though she were shopping for a trifle or bargaining for a trinket.

Forrest's nerves also were taut and she was of a mind to get up and leave, but that would only make matters worse. She sat motionless, her eyes downcast, and she felt sorry for London and very sorry for Paige.

"Well, now, honey——" He challenged all of his patience and knew it was not enough. "I doubt if Vance would want me to do that."

"He needn't know. If they would call him I could persuade him to accept and he'd never suspect that you had anything to do with it."

Forrest turned and stared at her, and London drew back as though he had been slapped. He felt his anger slowly rising and strove to conceal it, but his face was pale and his voice was strained. "I hope I am not the kind of man to deceive my son, and I know I am not a man to bargain with my God."

"You did as much for the Wards." She dared provoke him even more, for never in her life had she really felt the righteous anger of her father or suffered his chastisement.

London pushed his plate aside and dropped his napkin on the table. "We have discussed that before, Paige, and unless you have something new to add—the subject is closed. Once and for all."

But she would not hush. "Why should Vance and I take some little church down South and struggle for years unless it is necessary?" Her voice was as sharp as his and her chin as firm. "I'm thinking of my husband and our future. This is his home town and that church would be lucky to get him. I could go back to my radio job." Then she played her trump card, turning to Forrest for sup-

port. "You see my side, don't you, Forrest? And don't you think
I'm right?"

A lesser woman than Forrest Roberts would have evaded the
issue, this clash between the man she loved and the daughter he
loved so much. "I knew nothing about this when I came over here."
She wanted that clearly understood.

"But don't you think I'm right?" Paige pressed for an answer.

"No!" She did not quibble. If Paige could turn London against
her—well, that was the candle to be burned, for there comes a time
in every life when evil trumpets its muster or the little foxes bark
their threats, and then the valiant must step forth and be counted
as one worthy of creation in the image of God.

Paige's chin began trembling. "You both are against me." She
said it bitterly, and the words were steeped in resentment.

"Enough!" London slapped the table with his open hand and
stood up. "I've had enough, Paige. It is not hard for a daughter to
fool her father——"

She started to interrupt, and he slapped the table again. "Silence,
woman! I've had enough, I tell you." His eyes blazed his indignation, and Paige recoiled from him and put her hands over her mouth
and stared at him, and was afraid; for the first time in her life she
was afraid of her father. Forrest hurt for her and yearned to touch
her and comfort her, but she, too, suddenly was afraid of London
Wingo.

He bit his lower lip and took a deep breath and brought his temper under control, but when he spoke his words were cold. "You
have schemed this for days. Perhaps that's why you came home——"

"That's not true, Dad." She would be heard.

"Just the same, you have tried to finagle a church for your husband. As though the highest calling that comes to man is just another job to be schemed for a bagatelle." He snapped his fingers,
then clinched his fist and struck the table. "For money and prestige.
For bread and roof. A barter with God, and your own father as the
broker. Is this the fruit of the hope a father has for his daughter?"

"London!" Forrest tried to halt him, at least to soften his anger.

He did not hear her. He did not even glance her way but looked down at Paige, and his face was drawn in the stress of his misery. "You fret and fear about money his mother left your husband. A tittle and a mite. She never earned a dime of it and neither did he. And if Vance is called of God and that money stands in his way, then it must go. But that is for him to decide. And I hope he never knows that his wife came a thousand miles to plot and scheme for his commission in the army of Christ. He volunteered, Paige. And you followed him. Now go to your camp. To your tents, O Israel!"

London turned from the table and walked out of the dining room and through the living room and out the door, bareheaded, his hair tousling over his forehead. They heard his steps echo down the hall, and Forrest put her hands over her eyes and squeezed back the tears.

"I thought you'd help me." Paige still was awed and afraid.

Forrest did not reply.

"I was only trying to help the man I love." Her attempt at defiance was weak, for her face was a mask of humiliation and submission.

"So was I," said Forrest.

Paige got up and went to Forrest and put her arms around her. "I'm sorry. I hurt him. And I hurt you too. I was looking for the easy way."

"Not for yourself." Forrest patted her cheek and smiled. "You were looking for an easy way for your husband. I understand that, but men never do. They never learn the weapons that women will use for their men."

"Where has he gone?"

"To his church, I suppose. Or maybe he's just walking around."

"I'm going to him." Paige kissed her on the temple and hugged her. "I'll find him. You wait here. I'll bring him back. Then I'm going to my husband and leave my father in your care."

She hurried out of the apartment and almost ran down to the church and swung open the heavy door. The bell rope in the vestibule was new, and she peeped into the auditorium. He was not there, but there in the cool shadow stood his pulpit as testament to the covenant, and the light was drifting through the stained-glass window. She tiptoed down the aisle and to the door of his study and opened it.

London was at his desk, his head lowered on his arms.

"Dad?" She called softly.

He raised his head. "Come in, honey."

Paige ran to him and threw her arms around him and buried her face in his shoulder. "I don't know why I did it. You'll forgive me, won't you?"

"It is not for me to forgive." He put his hands on her arms and held her and looked at her. "I ask your forgiveness, Paige. I humiliated my own daughter for a thing I tried to do when I was younger. I tried to bargain with God."

She backed away from him, not to be away from him, but to see him better. "You?" It was as though the ark had trembled or a rock had melted away.

"Yes. I tried to bargain with God for your mother's life. And when she died I reviled Him."

The little room was not a room at all any more, but a confessional for a father to his daughter. It was the bitter well of Beersheba and the sweet pool of Siloam. She felt for a chair and sat down, and was limp.

"God did not choose me for His ministry, Paige." He began his contrition. "I chose this work as a man might choose the law or medicine or any other profession. I put my hands to the plow and was afraid to turn back. I reached out and touched the Cross and then could not wipe away the stains. I bargained with God that if He would spare your mother I would continue to preach. Your mother died."

He bowed his head and was silent. They both were silent, so still that he heard the ticking of the watch Cliff had left him.

Then he raised his face. "Next I bargained with God that if He would let you grow into a great woman—well, I'd keep on preaching. Like God needed me instead of me needing Him."

She clenched her hands until they were white, and her voice was low in her throat. "And I failed you."

"No." A spark lit his eyes and he sort of smiled. "No, honey.

That's the miracle. You are a creature of God, and that itself is a miracle. Someday you will mother a child, and that is a greater miracle. And you are a Christian, and that is the greatest miracle of all. So you are a great woman and—well, I'll keep on preaching. I will keep my bargain."

"I am your daughter," she said. "All my life I've been told I am like my mother. But I am like you."

"Yes." He nodded slowly. "The same doubts. The same fears. The same yearning to race up the mountain and plant our banner for all to see." He shook his head in humble resignation. "It has taken me a long time to learn one thing I wish I had known when I was your age. I must not ask to see the distant scene, honey. One step enough for me."

They were silent again, each thoughtful, and then Paige came close to him and patted his shoulder and his cheek. "Vance and I will be at that little church in North Carolina pretty soon. I am sure of it. Maybe he can see the distant scene, but I'm like you—one step enough for me." She stood very straight and smiled her vow. "And it will never matter where I am because every step I take I will take with you. Now—to your tents, O Israel!"

She held out her hand and he took it, and they stood together. "Let's go out through the church," he said. "You lead the way."

"No, Dad. One step. Remember? And together." She opened the door and they walked into the auditorium, and she glanced high at the light through the window and he glanced at his pulpit, and then she took his arm and they walked out together.

Forrest had cleared the table when they got back and had thrown away the jaded flowers. London began apologizing for his outburst, and Forrest dismissed the whole thing as though it had never happened. She glanced at her watch and turned to Paige. "I hate to be a timekeeper. But you haven't too long for your plane."

"You are going over with us, aren't you?" Paige asked hopefully.

"If you want me." She looked from Paige to London and saw the plea in his eyes, and her heart skipped. "I'll have to go by my place for a coat. It will be night when we get back."

Paige reached for her hat. "I want to tell Mr. Andrews good-by.

You all drop me off and then get Forrest's coat and pick me up at his office. I'll be waiting on the corner."

London picked up his own hat and curled the brim in that flippant gesture of his and took the luggage to the car. They let Paige out downtown in Linden and drove on to Forrest's place, and maybe she was not sitting closer to him, maybe she just seemed closer.

All the way over to the St. Louis airport Paige talked a blue streak: the things she and Vance were going to do. "We can live in Hendersonville, North Carolina. It's not so far from that church that wants us. He will be ordained the last week in May, and I am going to make him buy a new suit. A blue one. Not too preachy, but a nice blue suit with a little pin stripe. You'll be there, won't you, Dad?"

"I'll be there."

"And what about you, Forrest?" There was a sly suggestion in the question.

"My school is not out until June." Forrest skirted the web and did not change expression.

They had only a few minutes at the airport, as the flight was being announced when they arrived. London hurried to the ticket counter and Paige kissed Forrest good-by. "You'll take care of him?"

"If he will let me."

London joined them on the walkway to the plane and Paige kissed him, clinging to him tight, and whispered in his ear, "One step enough for us, Brother Wingo. Together."

He squeezed her arm, and she left them and did not look back, but up the steps and into the plane; then away.

They watched it soar into the horizon and vanish in the twilight, and they walked slowly to his car and he threaded through traffic, and they were on the road home again. It was coming dark and he switched on the lights and neither had much to say, and Forrest was hoping he wouldn't talk about Paige. She didn't want to talk about Paige or the church or any divine calling, but only the calling in her heart.

The spring things were out, a firefly here and there and the water insects peep-peeping around the bridges they crossed. And he did talk about Paige. He had to. "She's going to be all right," he said.

"Of course she's going to be all right." Forrest hoped her pique was disguised and yet, in a way, she didn't care.

"But she's got a hard row ahead of her. A preacher's wife has a hard life."

That was too much. "What's hard about it?" She sat up straight, and her eyes, usually so calm, flashed her own impulsive temperament. "If a preacher's wife is different, it's because she wants to be different."

His foot slipped off the accelerator and he stared over at her, seeing the fire in her eyes and sensing the storm in her heart.

"A preacher's wife is just like any other wife." The words tumbled out, and she looked straight at him, throwing the words in his face. "Just as good and just as bad. Like I am. She can hate like any other woman. And fight as hard——" She hesitated, and then it came without shame or guile: "Or love as much!"

The car eased to a stop, and he put his arm around her and pulled her near him.

"Don't interrupt me, London Wingo." She didn't move away, however. "I have something else to say. The only preacher wives I know who have a hard time ask for it—beg for it. And they'd whine if they were married to the best man on earth." She felt his hand warm on her shoulder and instinctively relaxed and swayed closer. "I don't understand the high calling of God to man, but I know the call of man to woman. And now kiss me. Like you mean it."

He did, and they didn't see the automobile approaching until the lights were full upon them, and she pulled away quickly. London laughed. "They don't know who we are."

"That's right." She snuggled back into his arms. "I'd like to see their faces if they knew us. A preacher and a schoolteacher." She laughed too. "But we'd better move along or dim your lights. I think love-making on a main highway is against the law, or something."

"Bad law," he said, and eased the car to the side of the road and dimmed his lights.

The stars bloomed out and the moon joined them and many

automobiles came by, blinking their lights or sounding their horns, but they sat there whispering and saying all the things that each had waited so long to say.

Finally Forrest, reluctantly but in good judgment, slipped his arm from around her waist and straightened her hair as best she could. "We'd better be going, darling."

"I suppose you're right," he said, and started the DeSoto. "I want to drop by the church for my notebook. Tomorrow is Saturday and I'll never be able to prepare a sermon. I'll have to take one off ice."

"Let's go by my house first." Already she was making decisions. "I'll fix a snack and then we'll go to the church, and I'll wait for you."

"Let's call Bent as soon as we get home." He had the car up to sixty, a reckless speed for him, and was taking the curves in steady confidence. "I want him to be best man. And we'll get Harry Ward to perform the ceremony."

"In the church?"

"That's up to you."

"In the church," she said. "There's never been a wedding in our church."

"We'll launch it, my love. With flowers and music. The pipe organ will be in by then."

They made a hundred plans and knew they would change them a hundred times, and then the lights of Linden were down the hill. The shoe factory over in Plymouth was working the night shift, and the Wabash's luxury train was pulling out for Moberly, its whistle echoing down the valley.

London tossed his hat on a table in Forrest's living room and they went to the kitchen. "Uh-oh." She clasped her hand to her forehead and groaned. "No coffee. I intended to buy some this morning and forgot it."

"We don't need coffee." He took some cheese from the refrigerator and some radishes and celery.

She got peanut butter and homemade bread and they feasted, enjoying the cozy familiarity of sandwiches in the kitchen.

"Now, let's go call Bent." London rinsed his hands in the sink and dried them on one of her dish towels.

"Don't you want to wait until tomorrow?" Somehow she wanted their secret to be theirs for a while longer.

"Aw, we ought to tell Bent. He'll keep still until we are ready to announce it."

"All right," she demurred. "If that's your wish."

She went to her bedroom and fixed her hair while London called Benton and located him at the Elks Club. "I'm at Forrest's," London said. "Come on over."

"Anything wrong?"

"I hope not." London laughed.

"Paige get off all right?"

"Sure. And come on over. We got something to tell you."

Within ten minutes they heard him walking up the hall and they moved quickly from the divan, London crossing the room to the hearth and Forrest hurrying to the door.

Benton took one look at her and leaned forward and kissed her cheek, then saluted London. "Congratulations."

"How did you know?" London was surprised and Forrest was laughing.

"Who you kidding?" Benton met him halfway across the room and took his hand. "It's written on your faces in neon lights."

"Want you to be best man." London shoved his hands in his back pockets and rocked on his feet, from heel to toe. "We'll announce it in a few days and be married in the church."

"The church?" Benton scowled and was not conscious at all that he was scowling.

"Yes, the church," said Forrest emphatically, and sat down on the divan and tucked her feet under her. "I want to be married in my church."

"You'll come to the church for that, won't you, Bent?" London asked earnestly.

Benton did not hesitate. "Of course I will." The scowl lessened into a frown, but it was so natural for him to frown that London and

Forrest thought nothing about it. He stepped to the divan and sat by Forrest.

London walked over to a window and looked out, for no reason except that he was too excited to sit down. He began telling Benton their plans, and Forrest interjected frequent comments and explanations.

Benton listened politely. Not attentively, though, and the frown deepened. The haunting loneliness was back in his eyes and he struggled to conceal his forlorn misery. Cliff was gone. And Vance. And now London and Forrest were to have each other and he was to be alone.

He heard all the plans, some of them several times, and finally he asked, "What about Paige? Does she know?"

"Not yet," London said. "I'll write her and Vance tomorrow."

"Well, you might as well know——" Benton ground out his cigarette. "I was sort of hurt because you didn't ask me to go over to the airport with you. But I guess it's just as well. I might have been in the way." There was a trace of self-pity in his tone.

London and Forrest looked at each other in surprise, and London was ashamed. "I didn't know, Bent. Why didn't you say something about it? I didn't know you wanted to go."

"Oh, it's not important." His contentious streak immediately was evident, and Forrest tightened inside, and so did London. Benton felt in his pack for another cigarette, but the pack was empty and he crushed it and dropped it in the ash tray. He found a new package in his coat and ripped it open. "Paige came by. She told me that she and Vance are going to some two-bit church down South. I tried to talk her out of it."

Forrest was incensed that this should come up now, but she held her tongue, and London was hurt deeply. But not angry. Never again must his patience forsake him in the presence of his friend or his daughter. "They are going to accept a little church in the mountains——"

"Down with a bunch of shouting hillbillies, huh?"

"That's right," said London. He was humble but never meek. "Down where Andrew Jackson and Andrew Johnson came from."

"But why?" Benton almost snarled it. "Why should they go down there and waste their time on a bunch of primitive ignoramuses?"

London refused to be plagued into an argument. "Vance's ministry is taking him there," he said mildly.

"Well, if he's got to preach, why don't you get him here? Why not line him up with Harry Ward's church?"

"Because his ministry has not called him here." The color was draining from London's face and all the light was out of his eyes, but his voice still was calm.

"Ministry?" Benton laughed derisively. "How can he get anywhere unless somebody helps him? And what has the ministry done for you? It killed your wife and confused your daughter——"

Forrest could stand it no longer. She jumped up from the divan and put her hand on London's. "I must have some coffee. A store around the corner will be open. Will you go for me, dear?"

London smiled at her, but Benton said, "I don't want any coffee. You needn't get any for me. Thanks just the same."

"It just happens that I want some," said Forrest coldly. "Perhaps London does too. Besides, I'll need some for breakfast." She picked up London's hat and handed it to him and walked with him to the door, her hand on his shoulder.

He was glad to go. He wanted to feel the cool night air and soothe the anger he was striving so hard to subdue. He had been commanded to walk the first mile. Well, he must walk two miles. But one step at a time; one step enough for him.

London scarcely was out of the apartment before Forrest turned on Benton, and he anticipated her reprimand and spoke first. "I suppose I was out of line again. I'm sorry I sounded off——"

"You were not out of line, Benton." Each word oozed contempt. "You were exactly in character. But I want you to know that I, for one, am sick and tired of your moody tantrums and your petty needling. I defended you once, but never again."

"You defended me?"

"Yes. To London Wingo."

He looked at her sharply. "Did I need a woman to defend me against London Wingo?"

She ignored the question but stepped closer to him and stood straight and proud before him. "And I will tell you something else. Never again will you insult him about his calling or about his daughter. For if he will not fight back—I will."

Benton got quickly to his feet. "That sounds like a threat, Forrest."

"It is a dare, Benton. And I dare you twice. I dare you to tell him the truth."

"What are you getting at?" Again he looked sharply at her, and a flicker of dread was in his eyes.

"That you were in love with Paige."

His mouth trembled and his face turned an ashy gray. "Good God, woman! Are you crazy?"

"I am neither crazy nor blind." She was merciless. This man had dropped his gauntlet at London's feet and London had left it there, but she must pick it up. Gideon carried a sword and Aaron carried a rod and Christ Himself once lifted a whip. She would never walk the second mile with those who tormented London Wingo. She would never turn the other cheek to the little foxes that gnawed in the vineyard. "I saw it coming and I saw it happen. I am sorry for you, Benton. But I warn you."

His cloak of pretense dropped from his shoulders and there was no armor underneath. No shield. No buckler. He felt for the divan and sat down, staring at her in helpless appeal. "My God! My God, Forrest. Does Paige know? Did she ever suspect such a thing?"

"Of course not. I doubt if it ever crossed her mind." She was almost sorry for what she had done. It was tragic to see a strong man so helpless.

"It is true." He buried his face in his hands and sobbed his abject humiliation. "You are the only one who knows. Thank God you are the only one who knows."

She sat beside him and put her hand on his arm. "It is safe," she promised. "You did nothing wrong."

"The girl who was to marry my son. The daughter of a friend. And I wanted her. But I couldn't help it." This, too, was a confession, a man who thought he had lost so much to a woman who knew she had found all she wanted. "It shamed me to bitterness, Forrest. Now what can I do? Where can I turn?"

"Where?" She repeated it to be sure of herself, to be sure of his plea. "You ask me where?"

"I ask you where."

Without another word she went to the little table by her bed and brought him her Bible. "The Forty-sixth Psalm. That's where I always turn."

"I know that one," he said. "I know them all."

"Then read it to me, please, Benton. I need it always."

And so he read, softly and in honest search for sanctuary:

" 'The Lord of hosts is with us; the God of Jacob is our refuge. Come, behold the works of the Lord, what desolations he hath made in the earth. He maketh wars to cease unto the end of the earth; he breaketh the bow, and cutteth the spear in sunder; he burneth the chariot in the fire.

" 'Be still, and know that I am God.' "

He closed the Book and held it in his hands, and a measure of peace was in his eyes, only a tiny portion, but there it was.

Then they heard London coming back, and Forrest returned the Bible to its place and met him at the door and kissed him. He was flustered because Benton saw it, and handed her the can of coffee and stepped into the living room.

The appeal in Benton's eyes, the fleeting intimation of decision and serenity, caught London's attention and held it, and then Benton got up and stood by him and spoke his heart. "How much forgiveness can one man spare and another man expect?"

"All a friend needs, Bent. And more for a brother."

"That's what I wanted to hear. That's what I was waiting to hear. And now I'll be going." He gripped London's arm and turned to Forrest. "May I call a cab? My car is in the shop."

"We are going in just a minute," she said. "We are going out to the church."

"Will I be in the way?" Benton asked. "May I go along?"

London Wingo's cup suddenly was full and running over. "To the church, Bent? Out to the church?"

"A little later—maybe. But first let me off at home. I want to get a few lines off to my boy."